COWBOY

Bob Holt

Outskirts Press, Inc.
http://www.outskirtspress.com

Paperback ISBN: 978-1-4787-9871-2
Hardback ISBN: 978-1-4787-9873-6

Library of Congress Control Number: 2018904264

Cover Photo © 2018 thinkstockphotos.com. All rights reserved - used with permission.

Outskirts Press and the "OP" logo are trademarks belonging to Outskirts Press, Inc.

PRINTED IN THE UNITED STATES OF AMERICA

For Butchie and Robyn – my loves, my life, my reason.

PART ONE

CHAPTER 1

S tars were filling the evening sky when the lean fourteen-year-old got to the house empty handed. Jimmy stood his bolt-action .22 rifle in the corner of the porch and nodded to his mother as he passed through the kitchen. "No luck, today. Missed that jack rabbit you saw in the garden."

"Your daddy's waiting at the barn." She didn't look up from her cooking. "Baines said to come out as soon as you got back. Your brother's with him."

"Something smells good." The aroma of fresh baked cornbread filled the room.

"He said y'all won't eat till that young cow drops her calf."

Jimmy paused a moment to watch Cronkite and the evening news on the TV in the den. A young senator and his attractive wife stepped off a sail boat at the family compound on Cape Cod.

"Go on. They're waiting!"

"I'm going. I'm going." He glanced back at the TV. A Lucky Strike Cigarette box with shapely legs was doing a high kick. He pushed open the back door and stepped into the cool night air. He tugged the brim of his beat-up cowboy hat low steeling himself against his old man's demands and his big brother's first-born arrogance.

A bare lightbulb in the tack room lit the corral, and a full moon hovered over the horizon. Looking bored, his brother, John Henry, perched on the top rail of the stall, his hands stuffed in his jacket pockets. Their father leaned against the ranch truck, scraping mud off his boots with a screw driver. Jimmy was in no hurry. It had been a long day with school and chores and was sure to go into a good part of the night. He slapped at an insect on his neck and saw movement at the barn.

"Hey, Dad!" John Henry had leaped to the ground. "Need some help, here! This little heifer's in bad trouble. Oh, God! There's a lot of blood! She's down on her knees breathing real hard. Her stupid calf's coming out butt first. Dang. It's—"

"Keep it calm, son." His father climbed through the rails. "Just stay still. She's got help now." He knelt beside the trembling animal and rubbed her heaving side. After a minute, he shook his head. "Get me some rope." He looked up. "Jimmy, get us some rope—and bring my pistol."

A week later, Jimmy sat at the desk in his bedroom after school struggling with a freshman English paper. He stared at the yellowed Roy Rogers shade on the desk lamp and thought of the dead cow and her calf. He wondered if pulling the trigger had bothered his father. There had been no sign, no evidence of it. The phone rang in the house, and he heard his mother pick it up in the kitchen.

"He did? He quit varsity?" After a few moments of silence, she said, "Any son of mine that doesn't play football, won't eat at my table."

Jimmy looked back at his paper and wondered which of his brother's friends quit the team—a rare event in Morrison, Texas.

A Buddy Holly song played on the radio between his and John Henry's beds. He started to pencil another paragraph when the bedroom door crashed back against the wall. His father filled the doorway. His khakis were smeared with calf slobber, but Jimmy's eyes locked on the rolled up object in his hand.

"Where'd you get this?" Baine's voice nearly broke, "And don't lie to me. Where'd you get nasty thing?"

Jimmy pushed his chair back and stood beside his desk. He

stared down at his white-socked feet. School boots stood paired at the foot of the bed. "What—?"

"You know damn well." His father flung the magazine at him. It crashed on his bed with pages splayed open.

A lump crowded Jimmy's throat. His brother had pulled the "Sun N Fun" nudist magazine out from under his pillow last night after everyone had gone to bed and waved it in his face. Said he'd bought it from Stump Bosworth who got it from a cousin home on leave from the navy.

Jimmy had watched him thumb through the pages of naked men and women playing volleyball with all their hairy parts showing and things flopping. He'd worried the old man would come in and catch them. John Henry hadn't seemed bothered about it.

"I'll ask one more time." Baines glared at him. "Where'd you get this? And tell me the truth. Mama found it under your mattress this morning."

He didn't know what to say.

His father lifted his Stetson and ran a callused hand through graying hair. He shook his head. "And don't think you're too big to get my belt across your backside!" Another moment passed before he jammed the hat back on his head. "So, till I say different, you will stay in your room except for school and chores. You got that, mister? And I'll say when you can come out!"

Baines grabbed the magazine off the bedspread and with spittle flying, ripped it to pieces. Red faced, he fisted the remnants in front of him. "And don't bring this crap around ever again. Understand me? Your brother would never bring this shit into my house."

Jimmy blinked. He wanted to yell that the magazine wasn't his. That his brother had more of 'em stashed around. But he didn't.

"If you're as smart as you think you are, you'll get on your knees and beg the good Lord for forgiveness."

Jimmy's gaze returned to the floor.

His father paused like he wanted to say more, then spun and slammed the bedroom door behind him.

Jimmy listened to heavy boots pound down the hallway. When

the sound drifted away, he dropped back into his chair and stared at the unfinished paper. He read and reread the first sentence, but the words failed to register. He put his head down on his arm and rubbed his face across his sleeve. Both fists slammed down on the desk. *God damn him! God damn him! God damn him!*

He stared at the bedroom door. *It always works this way. John Henry turns them against me.*

After several deep breaths, he closed his eyes. "Forgive me, Jesus, for. . .for. . .well, forgive me for my sins. Also, forgive the old man for not knowing, and forgive John Henry for—for being stupid. Amen."

CHAPTER 2

Jimmy picked a seat several rows behind the driver on the afternoon bus and set his books beside him as they departed school. The ranch was only ten miles from town, but the route home took over an hour. A month had passed since the discovery of his brother's contraband. Two days of confinement and nothing more had been said about it.

"Hey Jimbo." The driver's voice sounded far away. "Your stop, son"

He lifted his head and blinked to jump-start his brain. After the bus rumbled away, he crossed the cattle-guard and headed up the dirt road toward his family's red brick ranch house. Two walnut trees provided shade in the front yard, their trunks encircled with old tractor tires painted white and filled with his mother's flowers. A metal lawn chair lay on its side in the yard, a victim of the north winds that blew across the High Plains this time of year. Beyond the barn, the waning sun looked like an orange ball teed up on the windmill.

His boots kicked up dust as he hiked the quarter mile. He'd never owned a regular pair of shoes. Cowboy boots and football cleats were all he'd ever worn on his feet, and his boots, like most everything else he had, first belonged to John Henry.

The screen door banged behind him. The house was dark, and the familiar odor of pine-oil hung in the air. He picked up a note on the kitchen table.

Jimmy,

Gone to town to watch John Henry's football practice.

Will be back by supper. Baines says feed the steers in the barn and bring the milk cows up from the canyon. Cornbread and milk are in the icebox. Don't leave a mess.

Love, Mother

He crumpled the paper and tossed it in the direction of the trash bag next to the refrigerator. After pouring a glass of sweet milk, he carried it down the hall to the bedroom. He pulled off his red western shirt with white pearl snaps, lifted it to his nose and sniffed. Not bad, he thought and hung it in the closet crowded with John Henry's things.

He pulled on denim work clothes and a pair of scuffed boots with broken down tops. In the kitchen, he spooned mayonnaise between two slices of white bread and stepped out the back door to do his chores. Passing the barn, he decided against saddling a horse. *Too much time to tack up and groom out after.*

As he crossed the wire fence between the pasture and field crops, he thought of his mother's note. *The old man never watched me practice. Even the summer I made the Little League All Star Team that Billy Thompson's dad coached.*

He kicked a loose stone off the track that led to the canyon. At least Coach Thompson doesn't blame Billy for things he didn't do.

The cow path snaked a quarter mile through pasture to a deep canyon gouged out eons ago by fast-moving water. The sun sat on the horizon. He finished his sandwich and picked up his pace. He stalled the two cows in the barn each night, so John Henry could milk them before the bus came in the morning. Baines divided their chores this way because of football practice.

Standing on a rock ledge, he scanned the canyon floor a hundred feet below. The setting sun cast shadows and light shafts across the scarred landscape. Yellow streaks of limestone were brushed in grand strokes through the cliffs, and green clusters of cedar and cactus dotted the landscape. He felt at home here, having played in this canyon nearly every day of his life dueling rattlesnakes with pointed sticks, trapping scorpions in his mother's Mason jars, and spying on litters of coyote pups. A polecat once sprayed him in the face.

He found the two Jersey cows in an arroyo with several beef cattle. A couple of well-thrown stones got them separated and headed up the path. Halfway to the barn, he wondered who'd bring the cows up next year when he would be a sophomore and had varsity football practice.

It was dark when his two charges clopped through the opening in the board fence and into the stall. He slipped the iron bolt through the hole, securing the gate, and went to tend the steers he and John Henry raised for their 4-H project. They made their spending money each year selling them at auction. Baines thought allowances were only for city kids.

Walking from the barn to the house, Jimmy saw the television flickering in the den. His mother had convinced Baines to buy a TV, so the family could sit in their own home and watch Billy Graham's "Worldwide Crusade for Christ" televised from places like Korea and South America where the reverend converted the masses in soccer stadiums. When he entered the kitchen, his mother was setting the dining room table for dinner, and Baines stood in the hallway in his stocking feet talking on the phone. Neither said anything to him as he passed through the house to his room. Hank Williams played on the radio.

"Damn, I'm sore." John Henry lay on his bed, groaning. "Coach had bull-in-the-ring this afternoon and I got hit a hundred times. I kept yelling at that fat bastard, 'Keep 'em coming, you shit-for-brains.'" John Henry held a pillow against his ribs and laughed and moaned at the same time.

Even though two years younger, Jimmy stood a few inches taller than his brother, and his sandy hair matched their father's, while John Henry's stocky frame and black curls favored their mother's side of the family.

John Henry rolled onto his side. "Hey! Wanna see my new girlie magazines? Stump came through with two more. I'd show 'em to you, but you'd let Mom find 'em—just like you did my last one."

Jimmy pulled off a boot and dropped it on the floor. "I didn't touch it. Just keep 'em on your side of the room." He tugged off his other boot. "Next time, I'll tell Dad the truth."

Even so, he knew his folks didn't want to hear bad things about their star fullback. The Morrison High School football field belonged to John Henry on Friday nights, and the hometown fans cheered every time he touched the ball. Friday night games were as important to their mother as Sunday morning church services. She never missed a game and yelled herself hoarse in the stands.

John Henry arched his back on the bed and expelled a loud fart. "Ah man." He laughed. "By the way, you see Sweeeet Aneeeta today?"

Jimmy ignored him and began changing clothes for supper.

"Well, Miss Prissy Pants was at the practice field this afternoon with some of her friends watching us scrimmage," John Henry went on. "When I left, she was by her mother's Cadillac talking to Ronnie Jinkins."

Jimmy shot him a go-to-hell look.

"Just ask Mother."

"So, what?" Jimmy pulled his jeans off over his bare feet.

"So, what? So, what? I'll tell you 'what.' We all see ol' Ronnie in the locker room every day." His brother grinned. "And he's sure got a lot more to offer Sweeet Aneeeta than you do."

"Oh yeah?" Jimmy glared at his brother who clutched a pillow to his ribs trying hard not to laugh. "And you can go to hell!"

CHAPTER 3

Jimmy stared out the bus window while mesquite trees passed by in a blur. Surely his brother had been busting his balls last night about Anita liking Ronnie Jinkins. *No way she's interested in that dick-for-brains.*

Anita Beth Brown had been his date to the junior high football banquet when they were both in the seventh grade. His first date. Back then she was too beautiful to talk to, and he too shy to try. The day before the deadline for ordering corsages for the banquet, he left a note on her desk, asking her to the annual event. The next morning, he shut his locker and turned to go to his first class when she startled him by putting her hand on his arm.

"That was a very sweet letter you gave me." She spoke so softly he almost couldn't hear her. "I'd be proud to go with you to the banquet."

He stared at her small hand clutching him. For a moment, he forgot to breathe. "Gee, thanks. I. . . ."

"Last Sunday in church," she continued, "I prayed that you'd ask me." She glanced away. "I wanted to tell you that."

She looked up into his eyes, and a dazzling smile broke across her face. "Oh, and Mother said to order a yellow flower to go with my dress."

She tossed her blonde hair, blinded him with her smile, and went off to class. After that, he wasn't so shy around girls anymore. The prettiest, richest girl in town had prayed in church to be his girlfriend.

Anita was milk and honey, Easter and Christmas, all rolled up in a perfumed doll. After the football banquet, she'd stepped up to him at her front door, closed her eyes and presented her lips for the goodnight kiss. He'd been anticipating this all night. Would she, or wouldn't she?

He closed his eyes and leaned in, managing to catch her bottom lip and a lot of her chin, when the outside lights came on.

"Oh! Hi, Daddy." Anita giggled when the front door opened. "See the beautiful corsage Jimmy bought me? It was the biggest yellow one at the banquet." Her father nodded to Jimmy and turned away, leaving the door open. Frank Brown was known in Morrison as a very successful rancher. Jimmy's mother had said once that he was one of the up-and-coming young men in the state, and there was talk of him running for Congress.

Jimmy looked down at his boots. "Uh, thanks for being my date tonight and—"

Anita clasped her white-gloved hands together in front of her. "Oh, thank you for asking me, even though we know God made it happen. I mean. . .you wrote me that beautiful letter and all, but God's words were in your heart."

"Yeah, I guess." He started backing toward the walkway. "You sure were pretty this evening."

"So were you." She giggled and waved at him.

That had been two years ago.

All day at school, he wanted to ask her about Ronnie Jinkins, but didn't. He was pretty sure John Henry made it up just to get his goat. At the JV game that evening against a team from Spur, Texas, he sneaked glances at her with the freshman cheerleaders on the sideline. After a close win, she met him at mid-field and walked him to the clubhouse holding onto his arm.

"Oh Jimmy." Her eyes sparkled in the stadium lights. "We won tonight because of you." She held his arm against her sweatered breast. "I'm so proud to be your girlfriend."

He leaned down to kiss her cheek. *Yep, John Henry's full of horseshit.*

During the Christmas break, he and Anita discussed marriage for the first time and agreed to put it off until they graduated high school. Anita wanted him to ranch with her father after they were married. Jimmy thought that'd be okay. He didn't have a better idea.

In January, the calendar changed over to 1960, and for his birthday his mother baked his favorite chocolate cake with chocolate icing. After placing it on the supper table with fifteen lighted candles, she and John Henry sang "Happy Birthday." Baines worked his teeth with a toothpick and watched him blow out the candles. His father started to speak, and everyone turned to look at him, but he just grunted something that sounded critical and reached for his glass of iced tea.

Now that he was older and in high school, Jimmy wondered if he spent too much time thinking about sex. It wasn't all the time but seemed like it. He especially liked the calendars on the wall at the machine shop in town where Baines took his tractors to be serviced. Every month there was a different naked girl showing off her perky breasts.

Masturbation was a common subject in junior high and especially in the locker room but didn't mean much to him until his big brother demonstrated the act once when their parents were away. Soon afterwards, he was alone in the tack room when he looked up in a daze and saw his father watching him. Baines had left without saying anything. Jimmy shuddered whenever he thought of that moment. Still, the act took the edge off daily life. He just wondered how much was too much.

When spring came, he and Anita took Driver's Ed together at school and got their licenses. Farm and ranch kids in Texas could drive at fifteen if they completed the class. Anita's father surprised her just before the summer with a brand new 1960 pink Chevrolet Impala, sporting a white leather interior. The dealer mounted a brass plate on the glove compartment inscribed:

This Car Was Specially Made For
Anita Beth Brown
by the General Motors Corporation

Jimmy and his brother were allowed to drive the ranch pickup, but the family Oldsmobile was off limits. John Henry didn't date so it didn't matter. He preferred going with friends to the drive-in on Saturday nights or hunting jackrabbits with spotlights and shotguns. Jimmy wasn't keen on taking Anita out in the pickup, but he also didn't like driving *her* new car on all their dates.

One Saturday evening in early June they were at the drive-in after John Henry had used the pickup to haul manure loads to their mother's garden.

"Hey!" Someone yelled from the next car over. "What's that stink? Is that you Davis? It's enough to gag a maggot."

Anita turned up the sound on the window speaker and kissed him on the cheek. It was still better than being seen in her new Impala all the time.

CHAPTER 4

The last Saturday in June, John Henry shifted the pickup into gear and headed south out of town. "If we drive hard all day, we'll be at the border before midnight." He glanced past Jimmy at his buddy, Jake Tannihill, riding shotgun. "We'll spend the rest of tonight and tomorrow gettin' laid and scoot home on Monday. I paid Stump Bosworth a few bucks to handle our chores till we get back. Nobody'll know we was gone."

"And a good time will be had by all." Jake laughed, rubbing the front of his jeans.

Baines and Helen had departed the day before for Central Texas to attend a funeral and weren't due back until Tuesday. The two older boys had decided while drinking coffee at the highway truck stop the previous night, that this was the perfect time for their senior trip to the whorehouses of Via Acuña. After a lot of argument, Jimmy convinced them to let him come along. John Henry said it was better to have him as a co-conspirator than a snitch.

A pre-dawn rain had left puddles on the road. The summer storm had moved on to Oklahoma, and the morning sun was drying out the blacktop. Just before the city limits sign, they turned into the Conoco Station and braked to a stop by the gas pumps.

Artie Norton, the station's owner, approached wiping his hands on a rag. "I can tell you little pig fuckers are up to no good."

"Maybe." John Henry pushed his cowboy hat back on his head. He threw open the driver's door and stepped out onto the hot concrete. "We're goin' over to Lubbock to run errands for my old man."

Jimmy slumped down in the middle seat and pulled his hat over his face. Next to him, Jake giggled like a girl.

"Don't bullshit me, John Henry Davis." Artie chuckled as the pump dinged out the gallons. "The whole town knows you delinquents are headed to Cuña to stick your little peters in anything you can get a rope on."

Jake's snorting in the front seat gave them away.

"If Baines finds out, he'll cut yer balls off with a number two pencil." Artie grinned a gappy grin while John Henry counted out five one-dollar bills for the gas.

After paying for three packets of peanuts and three Dr Peppers from the cold box, John Henry jumped into the pickup. "You laughing hyenas nearly blew it just then," he said through clenched teeth. "Better hope that dumb butt doesn't tell the old man." He ground the pickup into first gear and peeled out, leaving a black rubber mark on Artie Norton's driveway.

Jimmy felt more than a little anxious about this trip to the border. It would be his first time with a girl, and he tried acting like it was no big deal, but every kid in in elementary school heard the stories about Via Acuña. By the time graduation came around, each boy on the varsity had his own personal tale of crossing the Rio Grande at Del Rio and returning as a man of experience.

His best friend, Billy Thompson, would be pissed when he discovered he'd gone without him. He also hoped Anita wouldn't be too mad. They had talked about "doing it," but a few feels and chapped lips were as far as they had gone. Once, in the back seat on a double-date, she had whispered in his ear that when the time came, she wanted him to lead. Hell, he thought as they sped toward Mexico, how can I lead if I haven't been there?

The map in the glove compartment showed it was five hundred miles to the border—a twelve-hour trip given the condition of the old pickup. A metal cooler sat on the floor underneath Jake's legs. Jake had raided his dad's beer supply. The first one foamed over Jimmy's tongue and down his throat. He winced at the bitterness but sucked at the amber bottle until it was empty. Baines preached that alcohol was the fastest road to hell. Jimmy wondered if he'd spend eternity in hell for drinking beer and going to Via Acuña.

Another bottle emptied, and then another, before he relaxed and began enjoying Jake's lurid descriptions of the whores who'd be sore for a week after experiencing their cannons. The banter about what awaited them in Mexico made Jimmy feel even more concerned about his lack of experience. He didn't want to make a fool of himself. He also hoped Baines never found out they had gone to Mexico in his pickup specifically to sin.

The beer made its way to his brain, and the dirty talk caused him to grow hard in his jeans. He thought maybe he just needed to piss. He laid his head on the back of the seat and closed his eyes. Visions of naked, perky-breasted, Mexican women filled his thoughts. A few minutes later his leg muscles clinched, and he felt a wetness along his leg. He removed his hat and placed it over his lap. The wind blowing through the open windows soon dried his jeans stiff.

The Cristobal Bar looked like every other saloon in the bustling border town. It was dark inside and inadequately lit by strands of colored Christmas lights that blinked on and off in a disconcerting pattern. Booths with red vinyl seats lined the walls, while yellow Formica tables were clustered in the middle of the smoke-filled room. A wounded air conditioner circulated a blend of cool air, stale beer, and bleach that inflamed the nostrils.

It was past one in the morning and the place looked packed. It had taken fourteen hours to drive down, including all the piss stops and the times John Henry pulled over so Jake could throw up. Inside the bar, perfumed señoritas moved among the crowd talking dirty and soliciting business. One lit like a flea on John Henry's lap. She looked older, but it was difficult to tell in the bad light. Her teeth looked like dominoes. His big brother was too drunk to care.

John Henry put his arm around her thick waist and groped a loose breast. She pushed his cowboy hat onto the back of his head, pressed her flat nose into the side of his face, and said in his ear, "Ju wan mee?"

John Henry laughed and grabbed her other tit while she flicked her wet tongue in his ear.

"Les go upstairs, beeg boy. I geef bueno time for tree do-lar."

Jimmy saw her hand snake down beneath his brother's belt.

"How about two dollars, honey?" John Henry winked at Jake.

"Two do-lar, feefty," she countered.

John Henry moved her off his lap and stood up. He chugged the last of his beer and looked down at Jimmy. "Be at the pickup by eight o'clock Monday morning if you don't want to get left behind."

Jimmy watched them make their way through the crowded dance floor and up the stairs. John Henry pinched her butt and the woman gave out a loud laugh.

A few minutes later, Jake went up the stairway with a short, feisty girl who led his skinny, long-legged body by the end of his belt. He stopped at the top of the stairs and let out a piercing holler. The crowd in the bar whooped and shouted in response.

Alone at the table, Jimmy sipped his beer and watched the action. Across the room he caught the eye of a pretty girl on the lap of a fat cowboy who was moving his hands over her body and bellowing obscene remarks to his friends. The girl let out a litany of profanities in Spanish that made the oaf and his friends laugh louder. Jimmy watched her squirm off the cowboy's lap and make her way toward him. She didn't sit on his lap as seemed to be the custom but slipped into the chair across the table from him. She studied his face for a moment and smiled. He looked away, lifting his beer for another swig. *God, I hate this stuff.*

"'Ow old are ju?"

Jimmy looked at her. For the first time, he wondered if it made a difference that he was only fifteen. She smiled. He forgot the question. Her teeth were straight and flashed white against her caramel skin. Her long dark hair was parted in the middle and held away from her face with tortoise shell combs.

"'Ow old are ju?" she asked again.

"Old enough," he mumbled.

She leaned forward. *"Para que*, for what?"

He didn't answer. He didn't know what to say.

"Old enuff for what?" she baited.

"Just old enough."

Moments of awkward silence passed between them. She reached across the table and traced the back of his hand with a red fingernail. His hand went numb.

"Ju like mee?"

"How much?" Jimmy asked, catching his voice before it broke.

"Ten do-lar." She batted her brown eyes.

"Okay," he squeaked. He finished off his beer and they both stood up. *She's the same height as Anita.*

She led him up the stairs and down a narrow hallway lined on both sides with closed doors. Muffled sounds emanated from several of the rooms. He wondered which room John Henry was in—and what he was doing—and how he was doing it. At the end of the hall, an old woman wearing a white apron and heavy black shoes sat on a stool dispensing a pitcher of water, a bar of soap, and a towel to each girl before she entered her room with a customer.

When the door closed behind them, Jimmy sat on the bed and surveyed the sparse room. The girl placed the water pitcher on a table that held a full ashtray along with a framed photograph of a boy wearing the uniform of the Mexican Army. His gaze locked on a wooden crucifix hanging on the wall over the bed. Its presence was disconcerting but forgotten when the girl's dress dropped from her shoulders and puddled at her feet. His throat went dry.

Their eyes met and held while she knelt before him and unbuttoned his shirt. Pointy nipples capped her pear-shaped breasts. She eased his shirt off and leaned forward to kiss each bare shoulder, her lips warm on his skin. She sat back on her heels to unbuckle his belt. Deft fingers moved down the brass buttons on his jeans. He felt himself growing hard. She smiled up at him.

He rose to his feet, and she tugged down his jeans along with his white briefs. She studied him for a moment then looked up. Her brown eyes locked on his. She clasped his butt cheeks with her hands and dragged her nails down the back of his legs. Jimmy's eyes closed, and his body jerked like an electrical current was passing through him.

"Jur boots," she whispered.

He heard but didn't understand.

"Boots," she said, tapping them with the flat of her hand.

"Oh, sorry." He sat down on the mattress and pulled off his boots and socks, then finished removing his jeans.

Some hours later he'd mastered all she had to teach. When dawn broke, he fell exhausted beside her. Her name was Sarita Sanchez. She had come to the border to make money before moving on to Mexico City. In halting English, she talked as she trailed her fingers across his bare chest.

Pounding on the door interrupted the quiet peace.

"Sarita, Sarita?" was all he understood of the shrill voice outside in the hall. Sarita hurled back an angry reply in Spanish, and all grew quiet.

"Ju mus go," she said, sitting up and taking a robe from a hook beside the bed. "Ow much do-lar ju got?"

"Oh, uh. . . ." he stammered. "How much you need?"

"*Veinticinco*. Twenty-fife for all night."

Jim reached to the floor for his jeans, found his billfold and pulled out a twenty plus five singles. That left him two bucks and some change. Sarita counted the bills, kissed him on the forehead, and scrambled from the bed. Wrapping the robe around herself, she went out into the hall. After the door closed he swung his legs over the edge of the bed and picked up his clothes. A cockroach dropped from his shirt, skittered across the floor and disappeared under the baseboard. *Jeeezus.*

When he finished dressing, he stepped out into the empty hallway and looked back at the room. Morning light illuminated the crucifix over the bed. Holy eyes had watched his fornicating. A shiver ran up his spine. He closed the door and made his way along the corridor.

Downstairs, sunlight from the open front door revealed the grime camouflaged at night by the bar's winking Christmas lights. A few stragglers sat at cluttered tables. John Henry and Jake were not among them. Out on the street, he squinted in the brightness of day. The border town looked different. When they drove in the night before, the place had been lit up like a carnival. This morning, only a couple of cars moved about.

Three blocks away, uniformed border officials checked automobiles back and forth across the Rio Grande. The stores along the main street were already doing a thriving business from gringo tourists. He crossed the street not far from the Cristobal Bar and came to a tree-shaded plaza, a good place to wait for his brother. He found a bench under a large tree and sat to watch people.

Jim felt a tap on his arm and turned to see a small boy, no more than seven, lugging a wooden box filled with cans of shoe polish and brushes.

"Shine, *señor*?" The dark-eyed boy pointed at Jim's boots.

"No thanks," he said, remembering he had only two dollars left.

"Maybe, thees?" The boy fumbled with a smudged envelope.

Black and white photographs were laid out on the ground, and Jim leaned down for a closer look. There were postcard size prints of couples engaged in every sex act imaginable and some he hadn't thought about. The raw pictures made him think of Sarita.

"No thanks, amigo," he said, watching the boy put everything back into the envelope. He tried to remember his own thoughts about sex when he was seven but drew a blank. As the boy packed, Jim saw the defeated look in his eyes. "How much for a shine?"

The boy's face lit up. "Feefty ceents. Bueno shine."

"Let's do it." Jim sat back on the bench and watched the boy dig through his box for a rag and polish.

After paying the boy and assuring him it was "the best shine these old boots ever had," he left the plaza and walked the streets for an hour looking in store windows. He spent his last money on a burrito and a soda. Broke and with nothing else to do, he went to find the pickup and take a snooze. He figured John Henry and Jake would be with their whores until tomorrow morning at least. As he approached the rear of the pickup, he found Jake snoring on horse blankets in the back and John Henry's boots sticking out through the window on the passenger's side of the cab. Jim shooed flies off his brother's face and dug through his pockets for the keys. The cab reeked of whisky. When they reached the border, the uniformed officers saw John Henry asleep on the seat and Jake sprawled in the back and waved them through.

The long drive home gave Jim time to reflect. Like Adam in the garden, he'd tasted forbidden fruit and now possessed the knowledge. It was what men did. It was what men knew. Something important had changed. He felt different. Like a great valve had opened and a keen tension eased.

As the hours and miles passed, his thoughts turned to Anita. He wished she were there beside him, her head on his shoulder, her fingers caressing the back of his neck. He wondered what he'd tell her when she asked him about this day. He smiled as he thought about her freckled nose, her blue eyes, and her little-girl giggle. He loved her as much as any boy could love any girl, and he would love her forever. "Sweet Anita," he said aloud.

A glance at the dashboard clock told him it was nearing midnight. Cool wind blew through the cab's open window. John Henry jerked in his sleep, scuffing a boot against Jim's leg. In the rearview mirror, he saw Jake leaning against the cab wrapped in a horse blanket. As they drove through the night, he hoped their parents hadn't returned home early.

The fuel tank was nearing empty. He scanned the horizon for the next town and wondered if his father had ever gone to Mexico to drink beer and get laid. *Surely, not ol' Baines Austin Davis. Not never wrong, always right, don't question me, just do what I say, Baines Austin Davis. Not ol' B.A. Davis, ol' Bad Ass Davis.* He laughed out loud and pounded his open palm on the steering wheel.

The lights of a town straddling the highway appeared in the distance, and he recognized the neon sign of a 24-hour truck stop. A tank of gas and a chicken fried steak platter could be had thanks to the twenty-dollar bill he found in John Henry's pocket while searching for the keys.

As they entered the town Jim thought about the struggle to win his father's approval. If asked, he couldn't explain it, but Baines' approval had become the prize. At some point along the way he had determined to earn it on his own terms, and that seemed to cause most of their problems. *He don't care about me. I doubt the bastard'd even piss on me if I was on fire.*

CHAPTER 5

Three weeks after returning from Mexico, Jim stopped the pickup in town to let his brother out at the barbershop and then parked in front of the post office. His mother wanted him to see if the post office had a package for her. Curtains ordered from Sears were overdue. He hoped to grab a burger at the Dixie Dog Stand before heading back to the ranch. It was Saturday morning and their dad wanted new wire strung on the canyon fence before day's end. He hadn't said anything about the extra miles on the pickup's odometer. Artie Norton had surprised them all by keeping mum.

Jim read the FBI bulletins in the glass case in the post office lobby while waiting for two women at the counter to finish their business. They were sisters who lived in the Victorian house over by the high school. He didn't know them personally, but his mother had said you never saw one without the other. A ceiling fan stirred warm air in the fluorescent-lit lobby.

Betty Mae Jackson, a thin woman with gray hair pulled back into a tight bun and red frame glasses perched on the end of her nose, had been Morrison's postmistress for thirty years. Her liver-spotted hands moved lightning fast, slapping labels on packages while she chatted with the sisters. "Isn't that a shame about Frank Brown?" She flicked coins from the drawer and counted change into an open hand.

"Goes to show that you can never know another person's problems until you walk in their shoes. Who would've thought he would do something like that? Pastor Stillwell was in here and said it must've been financial problems. He said a smart man like Frank

Brown doesn't go kill himself unless the bank is about to kick him off his land."

Jim watched the scene unfold in slow motion. *Anita's dad?*

"I think the preacher's got something there," Betty Mae continued. "I don't go to his church, but I agree with him on this one. I—"

"What about Frank?" Jim stepped up to the counter. "What about Anita's father?"

"Oh my." Betty Mae looked pained. "Jimmy, I didn't see you come in. Hasn't anyone told you? They just brought his body to the funeral home. One of his hired hands found him in his office this morning out at the ranch. He'd killed himself with his shotgun."

Jim started backing away toward the door, his heart pounding in his ears.

"It's a good thing his wife and little girl weren't home," she continued, picking up a rubber stamp. "The way the world's going now days, I'm not surprised by anything, anymore."

Outside on the street, Jim ran toward the Rexall Pharmacy to find a phone. Betty Mae had mixed up her gossip before, and this didn't make sense.

The white-coated pharmacist nodded permission to use the phone behind the soda fountain. Jim dialed Anita's number. The line beeped busy. He called home.

"Yes," his mother replied, her tone weary, "I heard. No, Anita hasn't called here. Jimmy, are you all right?"

"Don't know," he said. "I've got to find her." He hung up before hearing her response.

Leaving his brother in the barber's chair, he jumped in the pickup and headed out of town toward the Brown ranch. He drove fast, his mind a jumble of questions and emotions. Eight miles later he turned off the pavement, passed through iron arches marking the entrance to the ranch, and gunned it up the tree-lined drive. The whitewashed adobe house looked like a cathedral crowning the hill. Anita's mother had modeled it after an old Spanish mission she had seen in Santa Fe. Frank had built it using bricks made with mud and straw from his own land. At the top of the hill, he saw cars crowding the drive around the house. Frank's El Camino sat parked over by the stables. Anita's Impala was in the garage next to her mother's Cadillac.

Lucille Appleby, Beth Brown's best friend, opened the front door, threw her fleshy arms around Jim's neck, and sobbed against his chest. "It's the worst thing," she wailed. "So young and so god-damn good. Why's it always the good ones? I told my husband he'd better not make me a widow while cleaning his stupid guns or I'd shoot him myself."

Jim's nose burned from her brandied breath. "Where's Anita? I came to see Anita."

"Oh Jimmy, I'm sorry. I'm so sorry." Lucille pushed her heavy mass away from him. "She's in her bedroom with the doctor. We called Doc Samuelson out to help. It's just too sad." She covered her face with her hands and sobbed.

Jim made his way toward the bedroom wing of the house, past family and friends talking among themselves and several people he'd never seen before. The doctor was just coming out of Anita's room.

"How's Anita? Can I see her?"

The doctor stepped back and eyed him. "Well, now. I just gave her something to help her sleep. Her mother's sedated and resting in her own room. They took it awful hard, poor souls. I remember when my own wife passed some years back. I—"

Jim opened the door to Anita's room and stepped inside. Closing it behind him, he paused a moment. Her curtains had been drawn tight. A small lamp next to the bed gave off a soft light. Her room was all pinks and whites. An army of stuffed animals guarded her as she lay in the middle of a white-canopied bed.

"Oh Jimmy," she whispered, reaching a hand out for him. "My daddy's dead."

He sat on the edge of the bed and cradled her hand. He didn't know what to say. Everything that came to mind seemed stupid.

"I'm glad you're here," she said. "I wanted you to come. I hurt so much, and I just wanted. . . ." She rested her head on his leg and closed her eyes.

He brushed her hair away from her face and stroked her cheek. "It's okay, I'm here now." He swallowed hard. "You sleep. We'll talk later."

He caressed the back of her hand. Cool air, from a vent above her bed, cycled the familiar scent of her Jungle Gardenia perfume. He didn't get to say any of the things he wanted to say, had practiced saying all the way out from town. There would be time for talk later. His heart ached seeing her so sad, so broken. He would make it better, make her happy again. But right now, he held her hand. *Her perfect little hand.*

At midnight the doctor came to check on her. Knowing she wouldn't wake until morning, Jim reluctantly left her side and drove home. The house was dark when he parked in front. As he made his way down the hall, no sound came from his parents' room. His brother snored while Jim undressed and lay on his back in the dark. Staring up at the ceiling he thought about how he might help Anita and her mother. Being the only man in their family carried a responsibility he was prepared to shoulder. It was almost dawn before he said a prayer and fell asleep.

The next morning, it worried him that Anita hadn't phoned. He thought about going over there again but figured her house was full of relatives. He attended Sunday morning church services with his mother and stayed in his room all afternoon making lists of things to review with Anita. He'd thought it all out. They would need help running the ranch. Why not him? *We can wait a couple of years to get married. It'll pass quickly.* He turned sixteen in a few months.

He was staring at the list on his desk when John Henry entered their room to change clothes for evening services. He had gone swimming that afternoon with his buddies over at Roaring Springs State Park. Neither spoke, and he was relieved that John Henry didn't say anything about being left stranded at the barbershop.

The day of Frank Brown's funeral, the main sanctuary of Morrison's First Baptist Church overflowed. A crowd outside on the grass stood in groups chatting about the hot August weather and the high school football team that would soon start two-a-day workouts. Inside the sanctuary, Jim sat between his parents in the row just behind the bereaved family. Beth Brown had seen to it that they were included in the section reserved for close friends.

Jim felt his father shift beside him and wondered what he thought about Frank killing himself. Baines once referred to Frank Brown as a "windshield rancher," someone who directed their hired hands through the open window of their pickup and never dirtied their boots. Jim knew a few windshield ranchers in town who had inherited their land, but Frank Brown wasn't one of them. Frank once told him that sweat alone didn't make a successful rancher; that many of his neighbors toiled from sunup to sundown six days a week, spent Sunday in church for insurance, and still barely scratched out a living. He said that hard work was important but so was *smart* work. Jim figured his future father-in-law knew what he was talking about. Twice, he'd been named the state's "Outstanding Rancher of the Year."

Jim stared at the closed casket in front of the altar. *God this is weird.* He'd never seen a dead person before. This was his first funeral, and he wasn't sure how one was supposed to act. He'd spent an hour that morning polishing his boots and squeezed into his one suit that had first been John Henry's. His mother had helped straighten his clip-on tie. It wasn't that he didn't know how to dress up, he just didn't have the clothes for it. He also figured that everyone was watching him and probably expected certain things—him being Anita's boyfriend. He feared he wasn't representing her well.

During the service, suicide wasn't mentioned. Instead, the preacher spoke of the "terrible accident."

"It's the living that matters now," his mother said in the car going to the cemetery. "Anita and her mother must be protected."

Anita didn't acknowledge his presence at the church or later at the town cemetery. He figured she was distracted by grief or medication. Later that night, he lay awake in bed worrying about her until the wee hours. After breakfast the next morning he picked up the phone and called the Brown ranch.

"I'm sorry," some woman spoke crisply, "Anita and her mother are not taking calls. The doctor has already seen them this morning. Maybe tomorrow. Why don't you call tomorrow?"

"Yes ma'am. Tell her I called and—"

"I'll do that," the voice said, and hung up.

He waited until the next afternoon before phoning again. The man answering didn't identify himself. "She's not here. Can I have her call you when she returns?"

"Yes, please," Jim said. He wanted to ask where she had gone but decided it improper. "Tell her Jim Davis called. She has the number."

Two long days later, he answered the phone on the first ring.

"Hi, it's me."

"I. . .I've been waiting to hear from you. After the service, I called but. . .I didn't want to be a bother."

"That's okay." Her tone sounded flat. "Thanks for coming to the funeral. Tell your parents that Mom and I appreciated their flowers."

"I. . .you're welcome." *God, this isn't sounding right.* "Uh, when can I see you? We need to talk. I've got some ideas to go over with you and your mom, and—"

"Oh, Jimmy," she interrupted him. "Mother and I are going to Houston with Granddaddy tomorrow morning."

A long silence passed. His lungs felt like they were full of ice water. "Oh, uh. . .when are you coming back?"

There was another pause. "That's what I'm trying to tell you." Her voice dropped to a whisper. "Mother's selling the ranch and we're moving to Houston."

"But what about us?" The words tumbled out before he could think about how they sounded. "I mean, how can we go together? How can I help you and your mom when y'all are in Houston? I mean. . .I don't want you to leave." He was drowning and grasping for anything afloat.

"I knew you'd feel this way. You're so sweet, but Mother's right.

She says we need to go start our lives over. We have to keep on living, you know. That's what Daddy would want."

He felt empty. A deepening silence ensued. Each waited for the other.

"Jimmy?"

"Yeah?"

"You know I loved you."

"I know. Me, too."

A low hum in the phone was all he heard. He held the receiver to his ear a few moments more just in case.

He bolted out the back door and sprinted to the barn. There, he kicked at the dirt floor, scuffing his polished boots till dust clouds boiled up in the shafts of sunlight streaming in through the barn windows. He screamed curses in the solitude of the manger while hot tears streaked his face. "It's over. My life's over. I've lost the only one I ever loved, will ever love."

He climbed into the hayloft and curled up on a pile of straw. *Oh God—What have I done that you would punish me so? We were so good, so right together. I was going to marry her and make her happy for the rest of her life. Frank Brown understood that. He wanted it that way.* "Why, God?" A flock of sparrows exploded from the eaves. "Why? Why? Oh God, why?"

At dinner that evening, the family ate in silence while Jim stared at his empty plate.

Baines ladled out more salad and passed the bowl to Helen. "The Stalcup brothers told me they've got some interest in Frank Brown's place if it can be bought at a good price." He glanced at Jim then turned his attention back to Helen. "I told them Beth would probably take any reasonable offer. Her rich daddy doesn't want that big spread left unattended for long."

An awkward silence settled over the table. Baines coughed and took a few gulps of iced tea. He swallowed another bite of food and wiped his mouth on his napkin. "I'd consider bidding for it myself if Frank hadn't put that big house of his right in the middle of the best grazing acreage. That was the dumbest thing I ever saw. I bet the Stalcups dynamite that pile of adobe and return that hilltop to good grassland. That's what I'd—"

Jim pushed away from the table and raced down the hall to his room, slamming the door behind him. He leaned back against it and let out a long groan to ease the pressure in his chest. He didn't expect anything different from Baines, but his mother should've known better. He fell onto his bed and fisted the covers. "Damn him," he hissed into the pillow. "I wish he died instead of Frank Brown!"

CHAPTER 6

After dinner, Baines took his hat from the peg behind the door and stepped out on the front porch for some air. The events of the last few days had unnerved him. Frank was young enough to be his own son. *A man shouldn't die that young unless he's fighting for his country or something like that.*

He hadn't known Frank Brown that well, which he thought was wrong since they went to the same church and their kids were close. He knew it was his fault. He hadn't made the effort.

The noise of a television game show leaked out onto the porch. He crossed the yard to the pickup and drove across the back pasture to the canyon rim. He pushed open the door and sat with a .22 rifle across his lap, waiting for a jackrabbit or some other target to show up. He removed his hat and set it on the seat. A glance in the rearview mirror revealed a full moon rising over the plains. A coyote howled from across the canyon, and the memory of another moonlit night pushed all other thoughts aside.

⸻

It happened almost fifty years ago—on his sixteenth birthday. He had spent the day stumbling along in a cloud of dust behind two draft mules dragging a furrow plow over the bottomland of the family farm in Central Texas. Things had been good that year. Most of the boys from Byrus Creek had returned home from the Great War in Europe, and cattle and horse prices hadn't tumbled like was predicted. A bumper cotton crop had provided cash money to buy new dresses for the girls and a used truck for Papa. It was a year they'd always remember.

Baines finished plowing the field, and he half dozed in the wagon as it neared the house. The Model T truck parked in the yard caused him to sit up and pull back on the reins. The mules pawed the ground while he studied the truck. *They shouldn't be home now. They ain't due back till after dark.*

Baines unhitched and led the team inside the barn. After dumping two buckets of oats into a trough, he hung the halters on wood pegs in the harness room and headed out across bare dirt toward the house. The day had been a scorcher and the inside of his overalls felt swampy. Sweat ran from under his floppy field hat and streaked his face. He wiped away the grime with the back of his hand and studied the truck. His father and brothers had left at dawn to gather hay over at the Smith place. Papa told him to stay home and ready the lower field for planting. Today was his birthday, and Papa knew he hated hauling hay.

At the back porch, Baines ladled a drink from the well bucket. He gulped another and poured one over his head. A basket of ripe peaches by the porch reminded him of the covered-dish supper last Saturday night at the Baptist Church in town. Winnie Hamlin had made a peach pie just for him.

He lifted another drink to his lips when his father's voice boomed through the screen door. "Don't say that, daughter. Don't ever say that in this house. Your little sisters look up to you, and then you. . .you bring shame on this family!"

"No Papa. No!" He recognized his oldest sister. "He loves me."

Another sound caused him to drop the tin cup, spilling water over his boots. He'd never known his mother to cry before. Baines picked up the cup and hung it on a bent nail by the bucket. He stepped off the porch and slumped against a hackberry tree in the yard. Last night he'd teased Sassy about plumping up. Now he felt bad about it.

It's that Josh Culver, Baines thought. Everyone in Byrus Creek knew he'd set his eye on Sassy when he came home from the war.

Papa wasn't keen on it. He spat on the ground and drove it into the dirt with his boot heel. The sun was a tight red ball slipping off the horizon. Insects gathered awaiting the night. The screen door slammed, and he watched his father move past him with long strides toward the barn.

The family ate supper in silence. Mama's face looked puffy and Sassy's chair remained empty. Out of the corner of his eye, Baines watched Papa clean the last bit of pork drippings on his plate with a wad of bread. Papa swallowed and stared at the floor. The only sound in the room was metal ware scraping pottery plates. Papa's chair screeched backward, and all eating stopped. Everyone watched him rise, towering over the table. He wiped his napkin across his mouth and dropped it beside his plate. His voice sounded tired. "When you boys are finished, come see me on the porch."

Baines finished his dinner and followed his brothers outside. Crickets chirped in the night. A June bug, attracted to the kerosene light in the parlor, crashed against a window screen. Papa rocked in his rocker and rolled a cigarette. The fire from the match illuminated his face. Baines saw a steely glint in his eyes.

His oldest brother, Thomas, leaned against a porch post staring into the yard. At twenty-one, he and Josh Culver were the same age. Carter Allen, the next oldest at nineteen, sat on the front steps picking sticker burrs out of his socks. Ten-year-old Bobby toyed with a wounded bug near the screen door.

"Thomas!" Papa's voice rang out like a rifle shot. "That Culver boy. You know he was pesterin' Sassy?"

"No sir." Thomas faced Papa from across the porch. "Never knew nothin'."

Papa stopped rocking and leaned forward in his chair. "How 'bout the rest of you?" His tone held them all responsible.

Baines dug his hands into his pockets and stared down at his boots. No one answered.

"That son of a bitch seeded your sister." Papa's eyes raked each one of them. "He claims it ain't his, and he ain't marryin' her." Papa leaned back in the rocker and flicked ash off his smoke. He took another drag. Baines watched the end glow red against the dark.

"A wrong against your sister is a wrong against this family," Papa's voice rose. "No one's gonna make it right. No one, cept'n ourselves." He flicked an ash and continued rocking back and forth. Acrid smoke fouled the night air.

"What can we do?" Thomas broke the silence.

Baines watched his father take another drag from his cigarette then crush the fire out between calloused fingers.

"We'll go talk to him," Papa said. "His daddy's no good, but we might reason with the boy. Our Sassy's a prize. Any real man in this state would marry her given the chance."

"What if he don't?" Carter Allen blurted out then stared down at his shoes.

Papa looked at him a moment before answering, "Then he ain't a real man."

Papa stood up and his chair kept rocking behind him. "Let's go see him. No use waitin'. Thomas, you come with me. The rest, git in the truck."

The screen door opened, and Papa disappeared into the parlor. Carter Allen crossed the yard and climbed into the truck bed. He sat back against the cab and Bobby crawled up beside him. Baines held the passenger door open waiting for his father and Thomas to return. A few moments later he saw them step off the porch, each with a double-barreled shotgun hooked under their arm.

Papa got in behind the steering wheel while Thomas carried the crank around front. A couple of turns, and the motor sputtered to life. Thomas stepped into the cab, and Baines followed. As the truck clattered out of the yard into darkness, Baines saw his mother and sisters silhouetted in the windows of the house.

Clouds in the night sky shielded the earth from the full moon. The truck lights illuminated the road only a few yards in front of the wheels. Baines held his hand out the open window catching wind in his fingers.

Near the Culver place, Thomas leaned forward to peer through the windshield. The clouds parted for a moment, setting the moon free. "There," he pointed. "On the road, Papa! Watch out, goddammit!"

Papa swerved.

"Shit asses!" A voice hollered out as they hurtled past. "Look where ya goin'! Ya dumb shit heads!"

Papa worked the hand brake, stopping the truck. The clouds thinned, and gray light flooded the countryside.

Baines exited the cab and watched Josh Culver weaving toward them in the middle of the road. Tall oaks cast shadows across his path. Papa and Thomas came around the truck and stood beside him. The figure disappeared near a large tree. A gust of wind rattled the leaves.

Stones crunching under boots signaled Josh's reappearance on the road. "Whats'a matter? Can't you drive that fuckin' machine? Damn near kilt me back there. I ought'a bust someone's fuckin' head."

Baines saw the short tree limb in Josh's hand and his back stiffened. Papa shifted his shotgun; the barrel still pointed toward the ground.

"Joshua Culver?" Papa's voice pierced the night.

The figure on the road stopped. It rocked from one foot to the other, then leaned toward them like it was squinting, attempting recognition.

"He's so drunk he don't even know who we are." Thomas spoke loudly.

The figure straightened. "Tommy Davis? That you? Why, you ol' shit."

"I'm Thomas' Pa," Papa said. "Want to talk to you, Joshua Culver. Want to talk about my daughter, Cassandra."

The figure remained motionless a moment then began rocking again, left foot to right, right to left, back and forth. "So what y'all want with me?"

Papa and Thomas moved toward Josh Culver, and Baines joined the others at the rear of the truck. He watched the three confer in the shadows, then move ghost-like into the adjoining field. Another slow-moving cloud blocked the moon. Alarm crept into Baines' throat. *Why'd they leave the road? Makes no sense.* He started across the ditch.

"Where you going?" Carter Allen called in a hushed voice. "Papa don't want us out there."

Baines picked his way across plowed ground. His breath came and went so fast his lungs felt like they'd burst. He heard voices and stopped.

"Sassy claims you're the one, Joshua Culver." Papa spoke clear and steady. "Says you're the only one."

"I'm. . .That li'l. . .Your girl said that? Hell, ask Tommy. Every cock in Byrus Creek knows she'll open her skinny legs to any man carrying a big enough carrot. Oh, no, no, no. She's not snaring me in her snatch trap. Nope, this ol' boy ain't gonna—"

Both shotguns lifted. With four deadly barrels pointed at him, Josh Culver blinked once, again, and began to laugh. It sounded like Satan himself in that high-pitched cackle. Baines wanted to run back to the truck, but his feet were rooted to the ground. He saw a pained look on Papa's face. His eyes glinted like cut diamonds.

"Fact is. . ." Josh wiped his cheek with the back of his hand. "Your sweet Cassandra could teach some tricks to the Frenchies we had in Paris for no more'n a dollar."

Flame and thunder ripped the night.

Josh Culver took three steps back before a leg buckled. Baines watched the hands and feet jiggle until they stilled. He turned and saw his father looking at him; the empty shotgun lay in the crook of his arm.

"Git yer brothers and bury him," Papa spoke softly. "Thomas and me'll be in the truck."

Baines turned and dashed across the field, staring up at the white moon, arms pumping, fear rising, thoughts racing. He leaped the ditch and came out on the road.

Carter Allen ran to him, "A gun fired. Who shot? Did Papa shoot that fucker?"

"Get the shovels. Come on." Baines pushed past him. "Bobby, grab a shovel. Let's go, now."

In gray light, in a field ready for planting, their shovels bit into the loose dirt. No one spoke as the shovels jabbed, dumped, and jabbed again. Four feet down they hit hardpan.

"Push him in," Carter Allen said. "I ain't touchin' him."

Baines knelt and rolled the body into the hole. A cloud moved, and moonlight flooded the shallow pit. A low groan escaped Baines throat. The body had fallen onto its side. . .knees bent and neck twisted. . .eyes staring. . .mouth open. . .accusing.

———❦———

Baines sensed movement and saw a cow nosing around the rear of the pickup. "Got no feed for you tonight," he said. The sound of his voice made her scramble away toward the herd. He shifted the rifle to the seat beside him and stepped out of the cab. The moon was overhead—so close he could almost reach up and touch it. He wondered why the man upstairs let him live such a long life; sire sons, live into old age, when others like Josh Culver and Frank Brown were dealt lesser hands. He shuddered to think his sons might ever find out he'd helped kill a man.

Baines started the pickup and backed away from the canyon. As his headlights passed over the herd clustered around the windmill tank, he wondered if Papa had made it to heaven; if Thomas or Carter Allen did after they died, and if Frank Brown could get there after killing himself? The scriptures were against them. . .and him.

CHAPTER 7

Jim's sophomore year and John Henry's final year at Morrison High started the first week of September. Anita's moving away had left a painful void that Jim filled with football. After grueling two-a-day practices in the August heat, he was the only sophomore to make varsity. Their mother was doubly excited about the new season since both her sons played on the team.

During the fall, Jim endured practice as a second-string halfback and got to play more than he expected on Friday nights. By the end of the last game in November, John Henry had earned all-state honors, but the team finished one win short of the district championship. Everyone in town said, "Wait till next year." But with his brother graduating, Jim wasn't so sure.

Anita's occasional letters stopped arriving after the Christmas holidays. He continued to write her, detailing his feelings and ending each correspondence with a plea for her to come back to Morrison. Rereading his letters, his words embarrassed him, and a stack of un-mailed envelopes piled up in his dresser drawer. In April he attended the school all-sports banquet by himself.

"Mama?" John Henry's voice carried down the hall. Jim lay on his bed reading a comic book. It was the last Saturday in April, and he had spent the morning putting fresh straw in the calf pens.

"Mom. I got a letter from A&M."

"Oh?" Jim heard Helen's voice. "Is it about your scholarship?"

There was silence and then something slammed against the wall.

"Shit!"

Jim closed the comic book and sat up.

"Don't talk like that in this house." His mother's voice grew louder. "You keep that language out in the barnyard where it belongs. Now let me see that letter."

The back door opened and banged shut. He could hear John Henry hollering outside at the top of his lungs. "Shit! Shit! Damn! Damn! Shit!"

The noise stopped, and the house grew quiet.

"Oh, my." His mother's voice came from the kitchen. "Oh shit."

Two days later, Jim found the crumpled letter on the floor of their closet.

Dear Mr. Davis:

After a review of your game films, the coaching staff has decided to not offer you a scholarship to play football for Texas A&M. The requirements to play football in the Southwest Conference are considerable. Unfortunately, your stats are below our minimum standards.

Thank you for considering the Aggies, and good luck in your future athletic endeavors.

Sincerely,
D.D. Abernathy
Assistant Football Coach

By the time graduation came around in June, John Henry had announced he would still attend A&M, which made their mother very happy.

The Stalcup brothers purchased Beth Brown's ranch as Baines predicted and bulldozed the adobe house. John Henry worked for the brothers, planting a pecan orchard on the hill where the house had been. Jim was also offered a job but declined. Baines had him drive a tractor in their fields, which gave him plenty of time to feel sorry for himself. At summer's end, any sign that Frank Brown's family ever lived on the land had disappeared. Even the steel arch marking the entrance to the ranch had been dismantled and sold to a scrap iron dealer in Lubbock.

CHAPTER 8

Jim's junior year of high school started in the middle of August with spleen-splattering, gut-puking, two-a-day football work-outs. "GO MATADORS - WIN DISTRICT" was painted in white letters on all the store windows on Main Street. Jim was named one of the starting halfbacks which thrilled his mother. He wrote to tell Anita about it and offered his letter jacket to wear at her school in Houston. She sent back a congratulatory card but didn't mention the jacket.

During the first two weeks of practice, he had a recurring dream. It always began with him and Anita walking together off a lighted field after a football game. She clutched his arm and smiled up at him, her golden hair radiant in the stadium lights.

At the sideline, she let go of his hand and walked away without looking back.

"Anita? Anita!" he called out as she disappeared into a crowd.

"Bless his heart," a lady said, her voice sounded familiar.

It was always then that he opened his eyes and found himself alone in his room, facing another day without Anita, another football practice.

At Thanksgiving, the family drove to College Station to visit John Henry and attend the big annual game between A&M and the University of Texas. The afternoon of their arrival, his big brother, spiffy looking in his Aggie Corps uniform, showed them around campus. At dinner, Helen kept him primed with questions while he prattled on about college life. Jim noticed Baines seemed uncomfortable with the conversation.

Before the game the next day, they met at the Reveille Cafe near the stadium for an early Thanksgiving lunch. Aggie alumni filled the restaurant, devouring turkey and dressing and boasting about how their team would *whomp* the hated "Tea-Sippers" from Austin.

"And when the two guys came back to the dorm," John Henry continued his story after the waiter delivered their order, "they tried to push the door open. The darn thing barely moved cause we'd stuffed their room clear up to the ceiling with wadded up newspapers."

Baines cleared his throat and scowled. Helen took a sip of her coffee. "Did they find out who did it?"

"Didn't take long," John Henry said. "We had so much ink on us, we looked like we'd been wrestling in a coal pile." He laughed and punched Jim on the arm. "How's it going, li'l bud?"

Jim looked up from his plate where he had been rolling a French fry around in his gravy.

"Too bad about the football team this season." John Henry took a bite of turkey. "But wait till next year. Y'all should have a good team since most of you starters are coming back. Tell Coach I said not to go soft and turn y'all into a bunch of sissies. By the way, what do you hear from ol' Sweet Aneeeta?"

Jim shrugged and continued making patterns through the gravy with the broken French fry.

"Look here, Mom." John Henry turned his attention back to his mother. "This is how we freshmen eat in the dining hall. They make us sit at attention."

"But what if you drop food on your uniform?" Helen laughed.

Baines started to say something but was stopped by a withering glare from Helen.

Jim didn't like thinking about why he hadn't heard from Anita. It hurt too much.

CHAPTER 9

O n the last Monday in April, Linda Sue Wilson stepped out of the car in front of Morrison High School and waved to her father as he drove away. It was a bright spring morning, and yellow forsythia bloomed in yards all over town. Linda Sue pushed the wrinkles out of her skirt and swung around to face the day. Her shoulder-length hair was curled under at the edges and held behind her ears by a pink ribbon that matched her sweater. Freshly applied makeup made her eyes look bigger and bluer, and her pretty smile, now free of dental scaffolding, bright and vivacious. *Okay, Jimmy Davis. Here I come.*

Jim sat on the trunk of Billy Thompson's Ford waiting for Billy to finish a smoke. Jim nudged his friend in the ribs and nodded in the direction of two girls walking together across the grass. "Isn't that Linda Sue over there with Charlotte?"

Billy laughed. "Nope, not ugly enough. Someone said he took her out in the country after a basketball game to get a feel and couldn't even kiss her cause of her braces. Said it was like she had a mouthful of razor blades."

The bell rang, and Billy flipped his cigarette to the ground. They both slid off the car and headed toward the school door. "She's a strange one," Billy continued. "We haven't said five words in the years we've been in school together."

Before first class, Jim stood at his locker. He turned to ask Billy for a ride home after school and saw Linda Sue hovering nearby like she was waiting for him.

"Hi." She smiled. Her teeth were white and ruler straight.

Two Saturdays later, they sat in his mother's Oldsmobile at the drive-in watching Kim Novak in *Bell, Book, and Candle*. It was their first date, and he wasn't sure who had asked whom out. It just happened. Linda Sue sat close to him, close enough that he could feel her heat. She had undone the top buttons of her sleeveless blouse, and a gold barrette held her hair back, exposing one ear. Jim kept stealing glances at her, and each time she smiled at him.

She moved closer, pulling his arm around her shoulder. She turned her face to him and leaned her head back. He waited a moment, then with two fingers lifted her chin and looked into her eyes. Her braces were forgotten.

Their lips touched. Her tongue found his open mouth, his ear, and his mouth again. He slid down into the seat, pulling her with him. His hand found her breasts packaged in nylon armor. She tugged his shirt out of his jeans and he felt her hands roaming over the smooth plain of his chest. At one point she sucked on his tongue like it was a baby bottle. Just as the taut wire in his lower belly was about to snap, she pushed back against him.

"No, no more tonight," she said breathlessly into his neck. "I can't do this right now. Let's watch the movie."

"You okay?" He sat up and watched her straighten her clothes. "I didn't mean—"

"Shhh." She smiled at him in the glow of the movie screen. "I'm fine. Just wasn't sure I could stop you—or myself."

She wrapped herself in his arms and leaned back against him. "We better watch the show or we might do something we shouldn't."

He paid scant attention to the movie while she toyed with the hair on his arm. Everything was moving so fast. A few weeks ago, he only knew her as one of the girls in class. Tonight, their friends thought they made a cute couple. *Is this right? Is this what Anita wants me to do?* Two years had passed since Frank Brown died.

Underneath the porch light at Linda Sue's house after the movie, she stood on tiptoe with her arms around his neck and licked at his face while he attempted to catch her darting tongue with his teeth.

"Did you have fun tonight?" she asked.

"Yeah."

"Me too," she whispered in his ear. "Let's do it again."

"How about tomorrow evening," he said, sucking air when her tongue found a sensitive spot on his neck. "Let's go to the drive-in after church."

"But it's the same show we saw tonight," she said, looking up at him.

"I know." He grinned. "We won't have to watch it again."

On his way home, he tuned the radio dial to KOMA in Oklahoma City. It was almost midnight, and a warm breeze blew through the open window. Hank Williams' "I Can't Help It If I'm Still In Love With You" started to play, and a sad feeling washed over him. He blamed it on the song, but also knew it was because he'd been unfaithful to Anita.

It was warm in his bedroom when he took off his clothes and lay naked on top of the quilt. All was quiet except for the house's familiar settling noises. He closed his eyes while the fingertips of one hand traced across his chest, and his other hand moved lower. His toes curled and his back arched. His imagined partner was neither Anita nor Linda Sue, but little Sarita Sanchez of Via Acuña.

The next day, he took Linda Sue to Sunday evening services. Afterward, they drove out toward the drive-in.

"I couldn't wait for church to be over," she said, slipping out of her sandals and curling her legs up under her on the seat beside him. She wore a gathered cotton skirt and a white eyelet peasant blouse that bared her shoulders. "The preacher gets so excited on Sunday nights, talking about sin and all, like he knows everyone's going out afterwards to do something they shouldn't." She nuzzled his neck with her lips and traced circles on his leg with her fingernail.

On the radio, George Jones sang "The Race is On" and Jim felt Linda Sue's hand slide between the buttons of his shirt and caress his bare skin. He passed the drive-in without slowing and drove toward the state park at Roaring Springs. Underneath the trees on the riverbank, he killed the engine. The stars were reflected in the slow-moving water. He turned and smiled. "You scared being out here alone with me?"

"Not particularly." She raised an eyebrow. "Maybe you should be scared being out here alone with me." She pulled him down on the seat and kissed him long and hard. Her strong little tongue wrestled with his, each seeking the advantage. Every now and then she pulled away to catch her breath. He lifted her blouse and unhooked her bra. She didn't stop him when his hand inched down to her panties. He was alert for a signal, any sign that he had gone too far. That he should stop.

Their first effort was cumbersome as they were still clothed. They undressed, and he kicked open the pickup doors for more room. Linda Sue's sharp gasps and the traces of blood on his hands proved it was her first time. He cursed himself for not bringing a rubber and pulled out just in time. He hoped.

Linda Sue felt Jim's weight shift on top of her. She closed her eyes and held him tight, feeling his chest crushing her breasts. Being Jim Davis' girl and all that meant in Morrison filled her thoughts. He had been Anita Brown's boyfriend. She felt him stir and tightened her legs around him. This was the most important moment in her life, and she wanted it to last forever.

His fingers toyed with a swollen nipple and a warm feeling threaded its way from her breast down to the sore place between her legs. She traced the muscles in his bare back and imagined holding onto him as they left the football field together after next fall's games, her armored champion. The whole town would know she was Jim Davis' girl.

Jim stared at the radio dial glowing green on the dashboard. The disc jockey said something about the temperature outside and then Elvis sang "Love Me Tender." He closed his eyes and imagined it was Anita's breath in his ear. He felt warm lips on his bare shoulder.

"Jimmy, I love you," Linda Sue whispered.

He opened his eyes.

CHAPTER 10

Two weeks later, they sat in the pickup at the Dixie Dog Stand. It was Saturday, the first day of summer vacation. She wore denim shorts and a white blouse. Bobby socks and penny loafers were crossed at her ankles. She sipped a cherry coke.

"John Henry and I walked fences all morning," he said, pointing at his muddy boots. "That rain last night slopped things up good." His straw cowboy hat rested on the seat between them. His sun-streaked hair needed a trim.

"Linda Sue," he continued, "I. . . ."

She looked at him without expression.

"I don't know how to do this," he went on. "I've never. . . ." He closed his eyes and took a deep breath. "We just can't date anymore. I mean, it's not fair to you or. . .I've tried, I've tried hard these past weeks, but. . .it's Anita. I think about her all the time. I—"

"You don't love me?" Linda Sue made it more a statement than a question.

"Oh, I like you a lot," he continued stumbling through it. "I don't think I can love anybody right now. Except, maybe. . .I'm sorry."

"You don't love me." Linda Sue turned toward the side window. Her eyes brimmed with tears. "Why don't you love me?"

Jim started the pickup and backed away from the Dixie Dog Stand. Neither spoke as he drove through town toward her house.

The next Saturday, he accompanied his brother and Jake Tannehill to the Cowboy Reunion and Rodeo over at Stamford. John Henry and Jake went to drink beer and hustle married women at the dance after the rodeo. Jim went along because he didn't want to stay in Morrison and run into Linda Sue. After the rodeo, everyone congregated at the dance hall to two-step to western music provided by two guitars and a fiddle player who made every song sound like "The Orange Blossom Special."

The beers snuck up on Jim. He started to laugh at a story Jake was telling and couldn't stop. Two hours later, his big brother found him on all fours beside the pickup. It was his first time to get drunk, and he worried that Coach would kick him off the football team. John Henry said he'd whip anyone that told.

The next night, just before the Sunday evening church service began, Jim looked up to see John Henry and Linda Sue enter the sanctuary together. They slid in the pew next to Baines and Helen. His brother's oiled hair indicated he was on a date. He hadn't said anything about it. During the closing prayer, Jim peeked and saw Linda Sue watching him. At the drive-in with his friends after church, he spotted his brother's pickup parked in a remote spot.

When John Henry returned home that night, Jim pretended to be asleep. At breakfast the next morning, nothing was said about it. For the next several weeks, he didn't ask, and his brother didn't share the particulars of their dates. His brother's poaching bothered him. Every time John Henry referred to her as "my girl," pangs of jealousy needled him. He wondered if his big brother had discovered she'd already given him her virginity. He hoped so.

After Labor Day, John Henry readied his return to A&M for his second year, and Jim started his final year of high school. He had decided to attend Texas Tech in Lubbock after graduation instead of A&M. His parents seemed satisfied with the decision.

The night before John Henry left for College Station, Jim watched him beat up Jake Tannehill at the Conoco station. After several beers, Jake had teased John Henry about *doing it* with Linda Sue. Jake lay bloody on the ground and John Henry stood over him with clenched fists. "She ain't no Cuña whore, you cocksucker."

At Easter break John Henry came home to see Linda Sue and was taking her out to the drive-in. "I know you'll love the apartments," he said, as he turned onto the highway. She sat beside him staring down into her coke.

"I don't know if a bug just flew in, or flew out," she said looking up at him.

"The married students' apartments on campus are small," John Henry continued, "but we don't have a lot of stuff. Dad said when I graduate in two years we can buy one of them trailer houses and put it on a piece of land down the road from their house." He shook his head. "I had my doubts about it financially and everything, but Dad said I could have the earnings from his wheat crop each year till I graduate. What do you think?" He glanced at her beside him. "When should we tell your parents the news?"

Linda Sue looked at him. He had sneaked into her motel room in Austin at Thanksgiving when the family was there for the football game, and they had gone all the way. He had concluded that marriage was the natural result and first broached it at Christmas. She hadn't thought him serious.

The sun was about to dip below the horizon, and she felt him gun the car. She'd grown fond of him but hadn't forgotten the real reason she had arranged herself in his life. It was his brother she wanted. On the other hand, this might be just the thing to bring Jim Davis to his senses she thought. She leaned over and kissed him on the cheek. "Let's tell my folks tonight. When can we tell your family?"

He put his arm around her. "Let's go out to the ranch tonight and surprise them. My little brother will just shit."

CHAPTER 11

June 1st, 1963, was a wet, windy day in Morrison. Not a great day for a high school graduation or a wedding. It rained most of the week, which pleased the ranchers in the community. Next to forgiveness of sin, rain was the most often request made of the Almighty in Motley County. It rained all morning, causing the high school commencement to be moved into the gymnasium.

During the wedding ceremony at the church that afternoon, Jim thought his brother looked handsome in the summer khaki uniform of the Aggie Corps. While they exchanged vows at the altar, he detected a hint of sadness in Linda Sue's eyes. He had noticed it earlier at the gym where she'd been surrounded by friends congratulating her on her double good fortune of graduating high school and getting married on the same day. Twice he saw her wipe her eyes.

At the wedding reception, he stood off in a corner of the church basement watching the bride and groom cut the cake. The fellowship hall had been decorated in the bride's chosen colors. Green and yellow crepe paper crisscrossed the ceiling in the hall like on prom night. The serving table, covered with a yellow cloth, held a stack of green napkins in one corner surrounded by clear-glass punch cups. On the other end was the tiered wedding cake studded with yellow sugar flowers and green leaves. The center of the table was crowned with a bouquet of yellow mums served by a court of cake plates and stainless forks. Jim thought it impressive, but like funerals, he hadn't been to many weddings.

His brother and Jake were laughing about something with a couple of guys also wearing the A&M cadet uniform. It impressed him that his brother's college friends came all the way to Morrison for his wedding.

Linda Sue appeared at his side carrying a plate with a slice of wedding cake. Folds of white lace framed her face. "I thought you might want some."

"Sure, uh, thanks." He took the plate and noticed a tremor in her hand.

She grasped his wrist before he pulled away. "I thought you might want to kiss the bride," she whispered. "Everyone has but you."

He studied her face a moment and saw the pleading look in her eyes. "Uh, okay, I'd like that."

"Not here," she said. "Is there some place we can go? I have to tell you something."

"The nursery." He nodded to an open door across the room. "Let's go in there." *Oh shit, John Henry knows.* He set the plate back on the serving table and followed her into the room lined with cribs. An odor of soured milk hung in the air. He closed the door, and for the first time in a long time found himself alone with her.

She turned away from the rain-streaked window and looked at him. Tears trailed down her face and her bottom lip quivered. She moved to him, put her arms around his neck and laid her head against his chest. When her sobs subsided, she pulled away and looked at him through red swollen eyes. "Jimmy Davis, I love you so much." Her voice was barely audible. "I've always loved you. After we broke up last year, I thought if I could make your brother love me, then you'd want me back. But it didn't work that way." She started to cry, again. "Now, I've cheated all these people—you, me, and poor John. All this happened because I love you so much."

Jim opened his mouth to say something, but no sound came out.

She wiped her eyes on the lace sleeve of her wedding dress. "I've made my bed, so now I'll sleep in it. Don't worry. I'll be a good wife to John Henry. I know he loves me. I don't even know why I'm telling you all this. I'm sure I'll regret it later, but I had to say something, or I'd burst. I'm sorry Jimmy. Sorry for both of us." She went up on her toes and gave him a long kiss that was anything but sister-in-law sweet. He watched in a daze as she backed toward the door and left him with the lingering feel of her lips on his own. He knew something important had just happened, but the ramifications were too dangerous and too uncomfortable to think about.

CHAPTER 12

November 1965

The phone in his dorm room at Texas Tech rang again before Jim grabbed it. "Yeah, what?"

"Son, is that you?"

He recognized Baines' voice. "Uh. . .Yes sir. I. . .I was studying."

"That's good. You coming home this weekend?"

Jim paused a moment before responding. "Uh, I wasn't, at least not till the Christmas break in a few weeks. I've got exams and—"

"Something's come up," his father interrupted. "We need to talk."

"Okay. Yes sir. I'll drive home Saturday morning."

There was another long pause, and Jim heard the line click. His dad had hung up. No "Drive safely, see you Saturday." *Nothing personal intended, none taken.*

On Saturday, he grabbed breakfast in the cafeteria before making the sixty-five mile trip to Morrison. It was a cold blustery morning. He parked in front of the house next to his father's pickup, cleaned the sole of his boots on the mat and opened the front door. His mother was just finishing the breakfast dishes.

"Well, look who's here." She smiled and wiped her hands on her apron.

Jim sensed her evaluating him to see if he were eating right and representing her well in public. He poured himself a cup of coffee. "What's dad want to talk about that's so important it can't wait a few weeks?"

"I think he wants to tell you himself. So, how're you doing for money?" She always asked him that.

"There's enough in the bank from those calves I sold last summer to last the rest of the year. Where is he? I saw his pickup outside."

"At the barn," she said, and went back to washing dishes.

Jim watched her brush a lock of hair away from her face with a hand gloved in ivory bubbles. "How's John Henry and Linda Sue getting along?"

Helen shrugged. "Like any old married couple, I guess. You should stop over and see them in their new trailer house. She keeps it fixed up real nice."

Jim put his empty cup in the soapy water and kissed her offered cheek. The screen slammed behind him as he stepped out the back door. He found his father breaking hay bales for a pen of feeder calves.

"Good looking bunch of calves."

Baines glanced at him and removed a straw from his mouth. "They're going over to Muleshoe to that new feedlot. Got a good price for 'em. They want all we can deliver this spring."

They both remained silent a moment, watching the calves go at the hay.

Jim started to say something when his father spoke. "Son, what do you think 'bout this thing in Vietnam?"

Jim wasn't sure he'd heard right. On the drive to the ranch that morning, he had tried to prepare for all the eventualities of this meeting—how he might respond if his father said he was selling out, giving the ranch to John Henry, or even had a terminal illness. He thought he'd covered all the possibilities. He hadn't.

"Gosh." His mind shifted into overdrive. "Haven't really thought about it. I'm guessing it'll be over before I get out of college. I've got two more years left of my student deferment and. . . ."

Baines put the straw back in his mouth.

Jim sensed his answer wasn't acceptable. "But I know the president says we should do it, and he's got a lot more information about it than the rest of us. And, they attacked our ships in that Gulf of Tonkin thing."

Baines looked at him. "Glad to hear you say that. I sometimes worry about what they're teaching over at the college."

He spat on the ground and paused a moment before continuing. "Last summer I was asked to serve on the draft board in the county. Thought it was my civic duty. We've just been told to conscript a lot of boys in the next few months. The army needs more men until this Vietnam thing is over." He looked at Jim again. "I saw the list here in the county who's eligible to be drafted and your name weren't on it."

"But. . .it's. . .my deferment." Jim responded. "Like I said, I'm exempt until after I graduate."

"That's what concerns me," Baines said. "On that list were names of your friends, sons of my neighbors, and I'm responsible for sending them to war. You're not on that list 'cause I can afford for you to go to college. 'We then order up another boy to go instead. Now tell me how that's fair. How can I look people in the eye at church or anywhere else in this county?"

Jim locked his thumbs through his belt loops and began busting mud clods with his boot heel.

Baines pulled off his gloves and stuck them in his back pocket. "Son, as I see it, you should volunteer for that first group being drafted. You'd go in January, right after the new year."

Jim's back stiffened. "What about John Henry? He's already finished college. He's—"

"Your brother's a married man." Baines interrupted. "He's got responsibilities, a wife at home depending on him. We're not drafting family men yet and won't if I can help it."

"But, I've got a deferment to attend college. Every guy I know at Tech has a deferment. I have at least two years before—"

Baines scowled. "It's settled!" He took the straw from his mouth and threw it on the ground. "And I'll hear nothing more about this from you or your mother. As the Bible says, 'When in Abraham's house, ye will do as Abraham says.'"

Neither spoke for several moments. Jim jabbed his boot heel into the ground, turning clods to mush. He wanted no part of this.

It wasn't on the horizon of possibilities when he woke this morning. Three semesters of college separated him from his degree. *And he wants me to drop out to go in the army?*

Jim wanted to say "no" but also knew he had no more choice in the matter than he did as a kid about going to church on Sundays. After a few moments passed, he looked at his father. Their eyes met. "Okay," Jim said. "Whatever you say."

Baines turned back to the calves in the pen. He pulled his work gloves out of his pocket. "You done right, son," he said. "We raised you that way.

CHAPTER 13

The evening before Jim left home for the army, Baines complained of nausea and had no appetite at supper. Helen scolded him about picking at his food and helped him into bed. When she shook him awake sometime after midnight, he was lathered in sweat and mumbling about someone named Josh.

The next morning after breakfast, Jim was alone in his room packing a bag. Barry Sadler's "Ballad of the Green Berets" played on the old Philco radio by his bed. John Henry had just left after stopping by to wish him well. Jim looked up to see his father at the door.

"Son. . ." Baines began, dark rings under his eyes. "You'll be far from home. . .far from your mother, for the next couple of years. We. . .I expect you to return safely. I'll pray for that. But I also expect you to honor yourself and your family. Dishonor yourself, and you dishonor your mother. Dishonor yourself, and it's your town and family that you shame."

A lump crowded Jim's throat. "Yes sir."

PART TWO

CHAPTER 14

Sunlight streamed through the porthole and danced around the hot stuffy cabin. Jim rolled toward the bulkhead and attempted to stretch his legs out in the cramped bunk. No air stirred in the room and his skivvies felt plastered to his loins. A ball of greasy matter served for lunch in the officers' mess rolled around in his stomach. He pushed up on one elbow and flipped his pillow. Afternoon naps onboard the ammunition ship provided the only escape from the boredom at sea, but today he couldn't sleep. He blamed the heat.

He and his team had boarded the freighter three weeks before in North Carolina on special orders from the Pentagon. It was hard to believe that two years had already passed since he graduated from Officer Candidate School. That had not been on his list of things to do when he entered basic training at Fort Bliss after being drafted, but his test scores were high, and the company commander convinced him to apply to OCS even though it added two more years to his enlistment. He thought becoming an officer would impress his father. Two years later, he still didn't know the answer to that.

As the ammunition ship's escort officer, he had been assigned the hospital room as his quarters while the enlisted men with him were provided bunks on the fantail with the ship's crew. He assumed he'd been given an officer's special consideration until discovering the hospital room sat directly above the ship's engine room where heat from the pounding diesels turned the small cabin into an oven. The captain had directed him to voice his complaint to the ship's engineer. The engineer said he'd get used to it.

The heavily loaded freighter heeled as it rode over an ocean swell. Jim rolled onto his back and stared at the rivet pattern in the ceiling above his bunk. The last thirty days had flown by. It had been the first of February and a cold day in Washington when he was summoned to the Pentagon.

Colonel Dawson had stood alone at the window gazing out across the river at the Washington Monument. "Come in, Lieutenant." The colonel turned. "Have a seat. I trust you're up for something more challenging than courier duty? Must be pretty boring for an Infantry OCS fella."

"Yes sir," Jim said. Everyone in the department knew he'd welcome something other than transporting diplomatic pouches to embassies and consulates. "What do you have in mind, sir?"

Dawson passed him a large manila envelope, returned to the window and clasped his hands behind his back. His bushy eyebrows joined together as he squinted through the icy rain raking the glass. "Lieutenant Davis, those orders state that within the next ten days you are to assemble and train an explosive demolition team to escort classified ordnance by ship to the U.S. Army Terminal at Sattahip, Thailand."

Jim placed the unopened packet on the colonel's desk and sat back to listen.

Sounding like one of his memos, the colonel continued, "The cargo will be off-loaded at the port under your supervision and convoyed up-country to one of our airbases on the Laotian border. On arrival at the airbase, you will transfer responsibility for the cargo to the commanding officer and return with your team to Washington. We will want a full report."

Dawson moved away from the window and sat behind a gray metal desk. He leaned back in his chair, raised his legs, and dropped his spit-polished size twelves in the middle of the cluttered work area. "Lieutenant, you need to know this ordnance is an experimental anti-personnel mine. The President and Secretary of Defense asked the army to impede the North Vietnamese movement of troops and supplies into the South. These nasty little mines will be disbursed by aircraft over the DMZ and along troop trails coming down through the jungles from the North."

Jim nodded.

"Here's a mockup for your team to study." The colonel tossed him a small canvas bag. "Looks like a kid's bean bag. But it's a mean-ass bean bag with a hand grenade in it. Three hundred of those are packed like sardines into a plastic canister the size of a five-gallon petrol can. Fighter aircraft carry the canisters under their wings and drop them over the target areas. At five hundred feet, the canisters blow apart, and the mines scatter like seed corn along the trails and underbrush. They'll lie there and wait to make life uncomfortable for some NVN soldier or supply carrier that steps on it."

He paused a moment and looked over at the rain streaked window. "If this works as the Joint Chiefs hope," he said, turning back, "we can keep the NVN at bay long enough to train the South Vietnamese to fight for themselves. That has to happen before we can bring our boys home. Maybe then those bastards in Congress will stop whining."

Colonel Dawson took his feet off the desk and lowered his voice, "Lieutenant, I can't over emphasize the importance of this project. The highest levels of government are interested in its success. You should also know that the general picked you for this assignment."

"Thank you, sir. I—"

"Just don't fuck it up." The colonel smiled. "Everyone's watching."

Jim left Dawson's office with the packet under his arm, his heels clicking cadence down the tiled Pentagon corridor. He smiled. *It's not slugging through jungle with a rifle and a fifty-pound pack, but this stuff should blow hell out of a lot of bad guys in black pajamas.* He nodded to a passing admiral and hoped Baines someday learned that a general had personally selected him for such an important assignment.

It had been almost two years since he and his father had spoken.

He called home often enough and spoke with his mother and his brother, but he never asked about Baines. He knew that hurt his mother. He heard it in her voice.

In the days following his meeting with Colonel Dawson, Jim selected six good men from the Explosive Ordnance Demolition Unit at Aberdeen Proving Grounds in Maryland and then spent eighteen-hour days with them in training. In less than two weeks, they were to meet their ship at the Military Ocean Terminal in North Carolina where its cargo holds were being loaded to the brim with crates containing the new mines. The Jacob Anderson, an old merchant marine vessel on its way to being mothballed had been selected instead of a regular navy ammunition ship.

When Jim and the team arrived in North Carolina, Colonel Dawson informed him his mission had been upgraded to a Joint Chiefs of Staff 1-A1 Priority. Next to a Presidential Order, it was the highest designation any military operation could receive. An hour before the Jacob Anderson threw off its docking lines and moved out to sea, Colonel Dawson had pulled him aside. "Lieutenant, I just received a call from Washington. The White House wants regular reports."

CHAPTER 15

J im turned in the bunk once more trying to find a cool spot and the elusive sleep that provided relief from the oppressive heat. He'd finished reading all the good books in the freighter's limited library. After passing through the Panama Canal and now a week into the Pacific, he was midway through the bad ones. His men stayed engaged in marathon poker games with the ship's crew in their own effort to fight the tedium. So far, they'd had nothing to do aboard but eat, sleep, and wait. The Jacob Anderson, as all Victory Ships, had been built for transporting supplies to the allies in Europe during World War II. Constructed in a few weeks, each ship had been built with the expectation of completing one trip across the Atlantic before taking a torpedo.

"Twenty-five years and two wars later, and they're getting another trip out of this rust bucket," Captain Daniel Garth, the ship's master, said to him their first day out. Jim asked why the navy didn't select one of their ammunition ships for the assignment. The captain had ignored the question.

Jim wiped beaded sweat from his brow, and his thoughts drifted to the streets of Washington in April. Cool, crisp, sunny days, and his girlfriend's warm hand in his as they strolled along the Potomac, enjoying the cherry blossoms.

His face began to feel heavy and sweet sleep finally arrived on a cool breeze blowing off the river. The thud, thud, thud of the ship's engines faded into the sounds of a distant storm. The throbbing diesels, or was it his heartbeat, evolved into a high-pitched wail, sounding close, then far away. A shrill alarm blared throughout the ship. Jim sat upright, banging his head on a towel bar.

"Damn it." He rubbed his forehead. The noise continued. "Shit!"

He jumped down from the bunk and grabbed fresh fatigues off the back of a chair.

Pulling his pants on, he heard banging on the cabin door. «Lieutenant, you in there, sir?"

Jim opened the door with one hand while buttoning his trousers with the other. Sergeant Lewis, his team leader, stood in the doorway clad in denim cutoffs. The sergeant, like himself, was twenty-four. Jim noticed Lewis was barefoot.

"Sir, the captain sent me to get you. We have a live one."

"What hold is it in?" Jim plunged his arm through a starched fatigue shirt sleeve. The ship had four cargo holds, each the size of a school gymnasium and each crammed to the ceiling with wooden crates full of mine canisters.

"Don't know, sir." The sergeant tried to catch his breath. "We need to move fast. The captain's worried the crew wants to abandon ship."

Jim bloused his trousers into combat boots. Ever since they left North Carolina, rumors had run rampant among the crew about the danger of their cargo. Okay, he thought as he tucked in his shirttail and buckled his belt. This is the main event, the reason we're on board. He grabbed his fatigue cap with its silver bar and curled the brim. "Where's the team?"

"Moving equipment on deck, sir."

Jim stepped out of his room followed by the sergeant. "Get our tools ready while I see the captain. Break the alarm cables till you find the hold with the problem canister. I'll meet you on deck. Any questions?"

"Yes sir! No sir!" The sergeant turned and double-timed down the stairs.

Jim took the steps two-at-a-time up to the bridge. Pushing through the door, he saw the ship's officers gathered around their chain-smoking leader. Captain Garth had been a ship's master for over thirty years. Due to retire soon, he had told everyone on board that this was his last trip.

All eyes were on Jim as he approached the captain. He was glad he'd put on a fresh uniform. The alarm blared throughout the bridge.

"What are the sea conditions, Captain?" The tone of command in his voice surprised even him.

Captain Garth blew a cloud of smoke above his head. "Calm and flat."

"How long can we expect these conditions to last, sir?"

"At least a week while we pass through these southern climes, Lieutenant." The captain took a long drag from his cigarette then stubbed it out in an ashtray on the table beside him.

"Good," Jim said. "We ought to get this little problem solved by then." The captain showed a nervous smile and took out another cigarette. The chief engineer chuckled and the tension on the bridge visibly eased.

"Captain," Jim spoke loud enough for everyone to hear. "A mine canister in one of the cargo holds needs attention. It's probably a false alarm, an electric short in the monitoring system, but I need to go down and check. We'll first locate the hold the alarm is coming from, then enter with our equipment, identify the canister, and if necessary disarm and remove it. No reason to be too concerned. The Pentagon put my team aboard just for this purpose. They're well trained and can perform this operation in their sleep." He grinned. "I'll do the surgery myself."

After a long pause the captain spoke. "How can we assist?" He struck a match on his pant leg and lit his cigarette.

"We need an empty oil drum, at least two bags of cement and enough scrap iron to sink the drum to the bottom of the ocean. We'll need it on the stern ready to go when the canister is brought up on deck. Also, if you'll keep the ship steady at minimum speed, it'll be easier for us to move around in the cargo hold."

The captain nodded at the chief engineer. The engineer picked up the phone and called down to the shop to order the supplies while the helmsman set the throttle. "Two knots slow enough, Lieutenant?" the captain asked. "We need some momentum to control the helm."

"Two knots is good, Captain." Jim's face hid the fact that his stomach had turned on end. "Okay, let's go find the little son of a bitch." He turned and exited the bridge.

Sergeant Lewis and the team had located the hold and had boxes of tools stacked beside the open door. The alarm continued to scream over the deck from a speaker high on a pole by the bridge.

"Turn that damn thing off," Jim hissed through clenched teeth.

The noise ceased, and Jim watched his team go about their work. Each man knew his job and equipment. While they strung wire and installed batteries for the portable lights, he thumbed through notes he took during training. Studying the canister schematic, he remembered his conversation with the chief chemist at the arsenal in New Jersey where the mines were manufactured.

"As you can see, Lieutenant," the chemist had said, pointing to a chart on the wall, "the canister is packed with mines, then filled with liquid Freon, the same Freon used in household refrigerators. Freon lubricates the igniter gravel inside each canvass bag, preventing friction, which detonates the explosive. After it's dropped from an aircraft, the canister breaks apart and the mines fall to earth saturated in Freon. The liquid Freon boils away after a few minutes leaving the little bags on the ground, dry and deadly.

"A leak is the main risk during shipment. A small leak will boil away the Freon in seconds leaving the mines dry and armed. A single mine can detonate a canister, and an exploding canister can blow the entire cargo, basically vaporizing your ship."

The head scientist on the project could not answer his question about the stability of a dry canister. "We don't have enough data, Lieutenant. That's why you and your team are accompanying this first shipment. The device is too new. Unfortunately, the army didn't have time to run many tests. If I were you, I'd take all possible precautions."

Jim watched his crew assembling equipment and thought of the sign behind the bar at the officer's club at Fort Myer in Washington.

IF YOU CAN KEEP YOUR HEAD
WHILE EVERYONE AROUND YOU IS LOSING THEIRS,
THEN YOU PROBABLY DON'T UNDERSTAND THE SITUATION.

CHAPTER 16

Sergeant Lewis appeared at his side. "Everything's in position, sir. I'm ready to go below."

"You handle things here on top. I'll take Jamison and go down. Ready, Corporal?"

"Uh, yes, sir." Corporal Jamison looked surprised. He was the youngest member of the team, just barely nineteen.

Jim climbed down the ladder first. In his tool bag, he carried a spotlight and a strange little electrical box with one red bulb and two rows of five yellow lights recessed in the top. Jamison followed bringing a toolbox and a can of diesel oil with an attached hand pump. At the bottom rung, Jim directed the beam of a spotlight around the hold. Wooden crates crowded the cavernous room and the heat, combined with the darkness, made it oppressive. No air circulated in the space, and Jim's shirt was soon plastered to his back.

The spotlight revealed row after row of wood boxes, stacked one crate wide and three crates high. Each canister in the crate could be accessed by removing a sideboard. Two-by-four braces crisscrossed the hold like a spider's web, holding the heavy crates in place when the ship pitched and tossed on rough seas. The hundreds of braces slowed their progress through the hold as they crawled over, under, and between them. Jim stopped to rest and wait for the corporal to catch up. *It all looks so peaceful*, he thought. *Just a lot of sweet smelling pine boxes.*

As they moved along the rows, he connected the small electrical box to a socket on the side of each crate and watched for the red bulb to glow. An hour had passed when midway through the hold, on a top box, the red light flashed.

"Bingo," Jim said.

"Found it!" the corporal called toward the shaft of light coming from the open door on deck.

Sergeant Lewis turned to the captain. "They found it, sir."

Down in the dark hold, Jim wiped sweat from his face and plugged the electrical box into the second socket. An amber light indicated the number-eight canister. "Hand me the crowbar, Jamison."

Jim pried away the access board, exposing five brown plastic canisters sitting side-by-side. "The number eight canister's right here," he whispered, and plugged the box into the canister's socket. The yellow bulb flashed confirmation.

The corporal assembled a hand drill and passed it to Jim. Before drilling the first hole in the canister, he visualized the cutaway schematic they had practiced with in training. The mines were layered to within four inches of the top. That thought burned into Jim's mind as he prepared to drill. One dry bag would explode in his face if he hit it with the drill bit.

He measured two inches down from the top, placed the drill bit on the mark, and turned the handle. The steel bit cut through the plastic, dropping drill dust to a growing pile on the lip of the crate. The bit slipped forward into the void.

"It's through," he whispered to Jamison who stood behind him holding the light. Jim reversed the drill's rotation and pulled the bit out of the hole. He leaned close and sniffed. The odor of Freon would indicate a false alarm. No odor, no Freon. Bile rose in his throat. The canister was bone dry. With clammy hands he took a threaded pressure gauge from the toolbox and screwed it into the hole. His legs cramped as he half stooped, half-squatted, on a wood brace. Until this moment, there had been a good chance that it was a false alarm. Now he knew they were working with hot mines.

Jim measured two inches down from the top for the second hole. Aligning the bit on the mark, he turned the handle. An eternity passed before the bit finally eased through. Handing the drill to Corporal Jamison, he felt sweat trickle down his back and into his trousers. A wave of nausea rolled over him as he waited for Jamison to prepare the oil pump.

"How's it going, Lieutenant?"

Jim turned at the unexpected sound of the captain's voice. *How long has he been watching?* "Okay so far." Jim whispered into the darkness, as if the words themselves could set off an explosion. "She's a live one, totally dry. We're lucky the seas have been calm."

The captain said nothing.

Jim selected a brass valve from the equipment box, screwed it into the second hole, and tightened it a few turns with a wrench. He placed the tools back in their box and sat back on his heels. His mouth felt cottony, like he had been chewing sawdust. He wiped perspiration from his face with his sleeve, cleared his throat and swallowed what saliva he could accumulate.

"The next step is to connect the diesel can to this valve and pump the canister full of oil," he said, watching the captain's face. "We'll keep it under pressure for an hour until the oil soaks all the gravel." Jim felt himself gulping air and paused a moment to calm his breathing. He wiped more sweat out of his eyes with his fingers. "The canister will then be safe to move. Pumping the oil is a tricky step because if it goes in too fast, it could jostle the bags.

"This gauge here will tell us when we have fifty pounds per square inch," he continued. "It'll take an hour under that pressure to saturate the mines. Then we'll remove the canister from the crate, carry it up on deck, and dump it overboard." Jim pointed the spotlight directly at the captain. "You follow all that, sir?"

Captain Garth looked into the light without expression. "You're the expert, Lieutenant. Let's get on with it."

Jim attached the hose to the brass valve and said a brief prayer. When he lifted the handle and started to pump, the captain and Jamison took a step backward. As the oil coursed through the hose, the captain unexpectedly coughed. Jim ceased pumping. When his heart slowed, and he could breathe again, he resumed with long smooth strokes. Ten more minutes of steady pumping and the pressure gauge registered 50 PSI.

Jim stopped. His legs were cramping again. For a moment he thought he might pass out. He shifted his weight on the wooden braces and wiped his face on his sleeve.

The captain moved back into the light. "How're we doing?"

"So far, so good. Have to wait an hour for the oil to soak the gravel before we move the canister. The hard stuff's done."

The lines in the captain's face eased. "I'll tell the crew, Lieutenant. I'll also see that the supplies you want are standing by on the stern."

Jim watched the captain move away toward the ladder. He and Jamison waited in the heat for the hour to pass. There wasn't enough air to stir a cobweb.

"How're we doing, sir?" Sergeant Lewis stepped into the light. He was dressed in fatigues and combat boots.

"She's stable. A little longer for the diesel to work, then we'll move her." Jim leaned back against a wood brace and closed his eyes. "How's the team?"

"Enjoying the excitement." The sergeant laughed. "They were pretty bored after riding this old tub for three weeks."

Jim opened his eyes and took several deep breaths. The ship had started to roll again.

Sergeant Lewis flicked sawdust off his fatigue shirt. "They're pretty proud of themselves right now. The crew's been giving us a hard time, saying we're a bunch of lazy asses along for a cruise. Now they're grateful we saved their butts."

Jim smiled. His eyes refocused and the buzzing in his ears abated. He directed the light onto his watch. "Time's up. Let's feed it to the fish. We're lucky it's a top crate."

An oil drum and other requested supplies were waiting on the fantail. The canister slid into the barrel, and the chief engineer supervised the adding of cement and placement of scrap metal for more weight. When the cement began to set, the drum was ready to go overboard.

The chain gate was opened, and the barrel scooted to the edge. At Jim's signal, Sergeant Lewis and Corporal Jamison pushed it off the stern where it tumbled end-over-end, splashing into the blue

Pacific followed by a loud cheer from the crew. Jim watched it bob a moment then disappear beneath the surface in a circle of white foam.

"Increase to fourteen knots," Captain Garth instructed the first mate. He turned to Jim who was watching the spot on the water. "Lieutenant, I'd like you and your men to join me in my quarters for dinner this evening. I dine at six bells which is nineteen hundred hours to you."

Jim looked at his team. "It'd be our pleasure, sir."

"Good. I think you'll like the wine. I've been saving it for a special occasion on my retirement voyage and this certainly qualifies." The captain started up the stairs. "By the way," he turned back to Jim, "you and your men did a great job today."

At dinner that evening, white-coated Filipino stewards carried in a steady stream of food from the galley while the captain entertained them with his thirty-year collection of sea stories. The more wine consumed, the longer and more eloquent the captain's toasts to the team.

"Hell, we were just doing our job," Sergeant Lewis said after the third toast.

The stewards cleaned the table and passed around a humidor of cigars while a projector was set up.

"I think you boys will enjoy these home movies I made during my trip around the world last year on a tanker for Hess Oil," the captain said. He lifted a reel of film out of a silver can and threaded the projector.

After half an hour of seeing the captain in the same pair of yellow Bermuda shorts, tee off in Korea, sink a putt in Cairo, and sip a cocktail overlooking the eighteenth green in Athens, Jim wondered how much of the world the captain actually experienced. The manicured greens at the Crown Colony Country Club in Hong Kong and at the Royal Golf and Tennis Club in Bangkok provided no hint of the mysteries of the East, or the exotic wonders that dazzled Marco Polo. After an hour of the captain's home movies, Jim excused himself. Before the door closed behind him, he heard the sound of someone snoring.

The moon bathed the ocean in silvery light. As Jim made his way forward on the ship, out of the corner of his eye he glimpsed a shooting star sparking across the sky. At the bow he leaned against the rail and looked out over the dark ocean. He raised his arms over his head and stretched muscles still sore from stooping that afternoon in the cargo hold. *Colonel Dawson will be proud of the team. I'll call him when we dock in Thailand*. He also wanted his mother to know he was alright. She was concerned when he told her he'd be out of the country on a secret government project. She'd probably told everyone at church.

Jim looked up at the vast array of stars in the night sky and thought about the decision he'd been struggling with for some time. He was due to be discharged in five months and Colonel Dawson wanted to know his intentions. Everyone he knew in Washington assumed he was a career man. He had thought so too but had delayed submitting his papers to extend. He hoped to have the issue finalized before returning to Washington. So far, each evening had ended with him going to bed more confused than ever. Tonight, he felt different.

He wasn't sure about a lot of things right now and a career in the army topped that list. It hadn't always been that way. The idea of silver stars on his shoulders someday appealed to him, but the freedom of being a civilian intrigued him. Should he leave the army he would finish college, maybe some place different than Texas, somewhere new. His savings and the GI Bill were enough to pay for it. He wouldn't have to ask Baines for permission, or his money.

Another important question followed the first, and that was what to do about his fiancée, Michelle Redding, the beautiful, spoiled, and only child of General Winston Redding, Commanding General of the Army Materiel Command (AMC) at the Pentagon and Jim's benefactor. Michelle counted on him being a career officer, "a general like Daddy." Their engagement the previous Christmas in Washington occurred because everyone had been expecting it. The general and Michelle's mother were very pleased.

They had been together now for two years. He couldn't remember the exact moment he'd asked her to be Mrs. Jim Davis but must've proposed at some point. The ring had been purchased and she now wore it.

He had experienced real love only once, and that was a long time ago with Anita Beth Brown. For the past two years, Michelle Redding, known as "the general's daughter," occupied the top spot in his life. All their friends said she'd be a great asset to his military career. *But what if I don't stay in the army?*

They met during his last weeks of Officer Candidate School in 1967 at Fort Benning, Georgia, where her father had commanded the Infantry School. The orders assigning him to the Pentagon after graduation from OCS had come directly from Michelle. "Oh, Jim, you're going to love Washington," she gushed as they strolled in the woods behind her parent's quarters. "Daddy will get his fourth star next month, and we'll stay in Washington until he retires. Mom is so happy about it. She just hates the Georgia summers and was afraid Daddy would go back to Vietnam again before he retired. We'll all be together in DC. Isn't it exciting?"

"I don't know where I'll be assigned," he replied. "They haven't told us if we'll get any time off before reporting to Saigon. With the shortage of junior officers over there, the guys think we'll be on a plane within the month."

"You silly, sexy, lieutenant." She slid her arms around his neck. "I wouldn't let Daddy take me to Washington without you." Looking up into his eyes, she undulated herself against him.

While receiving his orders as a new commissioned officer that night in the Georgia woods, at least one part of him stood stiffly at attention.

CHAPTER 17

He leaned on the ship's rail watching the moon slide down toward the ocean and wondered what Potts Potter, his best friend and housemate, was up to. *Probably in the sack with some deb's legs around his waist and her tongue in his ear.* Jim smiled to himself. They had reported to Fort Myer on the same day. After checking in at the admin building, they drove together to the officers' club for a beer.

"Have you found a place to live in this Gawd-awful town?" Potts asked after the waiter took their order.

"I might stay at the Bachelor Officers Quarters for a while," Jim said. "My girlfriend's parents live here. I figure they'll help me find a permanent place."

"You 'figure.'" Potts laughed. "You must be from Texas. I've heard only one other person say, 'I figure,' and he, too, was a spawn of the Lone Star State."

"Yep, you got me." Jim grinned. "And you?"

"I don't want to unduly influence you about where you should live," Potts said, ignoring the question, "but have you seen the BOQs? They're overflowing with guys on temp assignment at the Pentagon. Two and three to a room some nights. No privacy if you know what I mean."

The waiter set two beers in front of them.

Jim studied his new friend as they raised their mugs to each other.

"I have an idea," Potts continued, setting his glass on the table. "I met a fellow at breakfast with two housemates shipping out this week. He's looking for replacements. What do you say? Shall we check it out?"

They saw the house in Arlington that afternoon and moved in the next. The two-story brick home on a quiet street was roomy, clean, and affordable. More importantly, Michelle approved of his bedroom with its own bathroom.

"I love it," she had said as they drove away. She scooted next to him on the seat and nuzzled his neck. "Besides, we can't fuck in the BOQ. You make too much noise."

John Witt Potter, III, called "Jack" by his father and "Potts" by everyone else, was the scion of a prominent Connecticut family and a photo negative of Jim Davis. Where Jim was fair, Potts was dark with wavy, black hair. He claimed it was the genetic endowment from a wild Gypsy that an ancestor had tamed in a townhouse on Boston's Beacon Hill. Potts had attended all the proper schools, including Dartmouth for two years before being asked to leave because of late night parties and sleeping all day. His father had agreed with the dean and convinced Potts that a stint in the army might sharpen his interest in his studies. Like Jim, Potts drew a two-year assignment at the Pentagon after completing OCS.

While it was common knowledge around Fort Myer that Jim was the property of the general's daughter, Potts dated every available and oftentimes unavailable female in Washington. Most of the girls he went out with were office secretaries in the federal buildings clustered around the city, or daughters of Washington society matrons. He claimed he had no desire to become involved with anyone while in the army and could give only half a commitment, his best half, the half below his belt.

Jim took in a deep breath of ocean air and gazed out over the water. He felt the steady vibration of the ship's engines while pondering his future. His path to date had been decided by others, and he'd always gone along with what was expected. An army career meant thirty years of more of the same. General Redding was fond of saying "You've got to play the game, son. A good officer knows which side his bread is jammed. You learn that and it's an easy road to the top. You've got a good start under your belt."

Much had changed since he left home. The war protests troubled him. When the communists seized power in the North, millions of Vietnamese had fled to the South and now depended on America for their freedom. Just like Korea. The protestors' long hair, and revolutionary language had seemed odd, but curiosities seen only at a distance. He'd never met one in person.

He, Potts, and the other young officers in Washington were cut from the same cloth. Their families and communities had taught them the Golden Rule, the virtues of hard work, winning versus losing, and respect for authority. They'd passed competitive selection processes to earn their commissions and were now leaders of men. A proud, cocksure lot, who believed when told by their commanders that they were the crème de la crème. But now, to a growing segment of their peers, they were baby killers.

As the ship steamed through the night, he thought of the antiwar march in Washington before he left on this assignment. The crowd had crossed the Potomac and moved toward the Pentagon where a line of troops awaited them. From his third-floor office, he watched two pretty girls approach the GIs guarding the building. They looked about his age and were demonstrating against the war, against America, and against him. He didn't understand.

They had flowers in their hair, and their bare feet were blackened after the march from the ellipse. They moved down the line of soldiers placing flowers into rifle barrels held at the ready. The officer-in-charge glared. Jim had smiled when they tip-toed up to kiss the captain on his cheek and then skipped away. Jim wanted to talk with them, to understand why they were out there and he was inside. *What do they know that I don't? Am I being left behind?*

He ran his tongue across his lips and tasted salt. That afternoon in the dark hold of the ship, his life could've ended in a split second. There would've been no more tomorrows. If he stayed in the military, he'd never know the two girls he saw at the Pentagon. If he left the army on his separation date, he could return to college in August for the fall semester and perhaps catch up with his generation.

He looked down at the ship's bow cutting through black water. A flying fish sailed from the silvery crest and skipped like a flat rock across the water before splashing back into darkness. He watched a minute longer and decided to turn in.

As he made his way across the deck to his room, he spotted another shooting star hurtling through the night sky. For the first time in weeks he felt at peace. August was only five months away. Not much time to submit his papers and apply to college for the fall term. He paused at the top of the stairs and arched his back to stretch his sore muscles. *How will I tell Michelle? And the general? And Baines?*

CHAPTER 18

Jim's plane landed at Andrews Air Force Base outside of Washington just at noon. He stopped by the house in Arlington to drop off his bags and change out of uniform to jeans and boots. Potts' note on the hall table said to meet him at the officers' club annex.

The sky over Washington threatened rain. A Mamas and Papas song played on his car radio as he turned the station wagon he had bought when he graduated from OCS into the gates at Fort Meyer. It was early afternoon when he entered the club. The lunch crowd had already gone back to work. The grill looked empty. Next to the bar, a major with a black MP armband was dinging bells on the pinball machine. Jim chose a table to wait for Potts. He felt anxious about seeing Michelle later that evening and was still unsure how he was going to tell her he had decided to leave the army. He hoped Potts had some ideas.

"Hey! Hey! Hey! Welcome home." Potts dropped his hat on an empty chair at the table and shook Jim's hand. He wore his dress greens. The brass needed polishing, as usual.

"Tell me every detail about your trip," Potts said, turning his chair around backwards and straddling it. "After your long ocean adventure, you must be ready to go sail the seven seas."

"Not quite." Jim laughed.

The elderly waiter took their drink order and shuffled away, mumbling to himself.

After a couple of beers and a lot of laughs, he stretched his legs out and crossed his boots at the ankle. "I tell ya, Potts," he said, shaking his head. "When that damn alarm went off on the ship, I thought we were dead. The crew just knew the freighter was going to blow right out from under us."

"But the army had super lieutenant there to handle it," Potts teased. "I told the general, your future father-in-law, just the other day that they should send you to Vietnam to kick butt with your pointy-toed shoes," he nodded toward Jim's boots. "Our troops could be home by Christmas." Laughter danced in his eyes before the grin reached his lips.

"Screw you, bean breath." Jim laughed.

"Welcome home." Potts lifted his beer in the air. "Your mates missed you."

The cold beer tasted good.

"Have you called Michelle?" Potts slid his glass on to the table.

"Yeah." Jim narrowed his brow. "Phoned her during our stop-over in London to say I'd be in today. We're going out tonight."

"So, tell me," Potts said, slipping into his fake Gestapo accent. "An vat are you plannink vit Herr General's dotter?"

Jim toyed with his beer glass, watching the bubbles rise to the top. "I'm telling her I'm getting out." He looked up at his friend. "I'm leaving the army in August."

Potts slammed his fist down on the table. "My God, I don't believe it, Cowboy. That's great. That's just fucking great."

The old waiter looked over at them from behind the bar.

Potts poked Jim on his arm. "So, you've finally come to your senses, have you roomy ol' pal? Seen the light, been to the mountaintop and had the blinders removed from your eyes. You'll now join the rest of us citizens in having a real life. All I can say is she must have been one special piece of ass, Cowboy. Who was she, some Siamese goddess in Bangkok?"

"Potts, I'm serious."

"So am I." Potts drained his beer. He set the empty glass back on the table and studied Jim a moment. "So, spill the beans here. What are your plans, and what about Michelle?"

"Unfortunately, I think those two subjects are mutually exclusive. I'll go somewhere to finish college. I have a year and a half left to graduate. Maybe attend a university in the Northeast. But I don't know about Michelle. Her heart's set on being a general's wife. She'll probably break it all off."

Neither spoke while the waiter delivered fresh drinks and cleared the table of empty glasses.

"You okay with that?" Potts asked after the waiter left.

Jim stared into his beer, turning the glass around and around with his fingers. He was thinking about what he'd say to her that evening.

CHAPTER 19

"And you made this decision without first talking to me about it?" Michelle looked at him with her back against the passenger door of his car. They had stopped at a red light on Wisconsin Avenue. He had picked her up at the general's quarters on Fort Myer and was driving to dinner at a trendy restaurant in Georgetown. Potts had suggested it, saying he could use neutral territory.

"I don't believe you're doing this to me." Streaks of mascara marred her cheeks. "What will Daddy think? He won't support it at all. The army will give you a scholarship if you want to finish college. Daddy said there was a program for young officers, and he would look into it. They'll even pay your salary while you attend. Enough of this silly talk." She fumbled in her purse for a tissue.

"Let's go see Daddy after dinner about that scholarship," she said wiping her face while checking it out in the mirror of her compact. She closed her purse and scooted over to him on the seat. He felt her hand moving up his leg.

"It's more than that," Jim said. The traffic light turned green and he followed a line of cars down Wisconsin Avenue. "I don't want to spend the next twenty years in uniform. There's too many things to experience. The army's been good for me, and I've been good for the army, but now I have this desire to see what else is out there."

Michelle moved back against the car door. "Then you will damn well go without me, Jim Davis. This is very selfish of you. This is not like the man I fell in love with. You're thinking only of yourself." She paused to wipe her eyes. "And what about my feelings? The army was good enough for my mother, and it's what I want. I thought you wanted it, too. I thought you were more like Daddy. My dream is to have two children, a boy and a girl, that I can watch play from the verandah of our quarters on some manicured army post, and a smart handsome husband who becomes a general just like Daddy. That's not too much to ask for, Jim Davis. I want it. I deserve it. And I'll have it."

Jim parked in front of the restaurant and turned off the headlights. Neither spoke.

"Take me home," she said, breaking the silence.

He restarted the car and pulled back into traffic. They were on the Key Bridge crossing the Potomac when Michelle said what they were both thinking, "I guess you don't love me, do you?"

Jim looked at her. Passing car lights showed puffy eyes and fresh mascara streaks. "I don't know," he said. "I thought I did."

The next morning, Jim notified the army in writing of his intention to leave active duty on his separation date in August. When he called home to tell his folks, it didn't go any better.

"You're making a mistake, son," Baines said. "Thought you had all this figured out. There's nothing here in Morrison for you. We can't buy more land, and John Henry and I barely make a living outta this place the way prices are now. Ranching ain't what it used to be. You can't even plant what you want on your own land without some idiot in Washington saying you can. It's getting worse than Russia. You ought to stay there in the army where you got a good job. They don't grow on trees."

Three days later he received a note in the mail from his mother that made him feel bad the rest of the day.

Jimmy,

I know you believe that what you are doing is right. I just hope you have thought it through. You had such a fine career ahead of you, and Michelle sounds like such a nice girl.

I was looking forward to meeting her and her parents.

Love, Mother

CHAPTER 20

Wanting to attend college in the Northeast, he decided to apply only to state universities. He'd liked the energy and variety of activities at a large state school like Texas Tech. Not to mention he couldn't afford the tuition of a private college.

"Why not reach a little?" Potts said, looking up from the brochure in his hand. They were at their house in Arlington, studying college catalogues that came in the day's mail. Empty beer bottles littered the living room coffee table along with a stack of old "Playboy" magazines.

"My father thinks the next best thing to going to Yale is being turned down by the old blue noses," Potts said. "Every male in the Potter family has been rejected at least once by the Eli. I was afraid they'd screw up and accept my application. Fortunately, I was able to maintain the family tradition of getting kicked out of Dartmouth."

"Can't afford Yale," Jim said, dropping another catalogue onto the pile. "Even if they accepted me, my savings and the GI Bill wouldn't provide enough for the first semester's tuition much less living expenses."

"But there's financial aid." Potts looked serious. "Getting *into* a school like Yale is the hard part. Covering tuition at rich endowed universities like Yale and Harvard is easy. A lot of wealthy old farts have graduated over the years and soothed their robber baron conscience by leaving a pile of bread to their school. Believe me when I say there's plenty of money at Yale to pay the way of an All-American cowboy like you."

Jim's rejection letter from Yale followed the university's receipt of his application within days. At the same time, he'd mailed his papers off to Yale, he had also sent an application to Connecticut's state university system as a fall back option. The rejection from Yale disappointed but didn't surprise him. The rejection letter from the University of Connecticut at Storrs caught him off guard.

"Hell, it's just a damn state university!" Potts stormed through the house slamming doors. "How can they turn down any honest taxpayer, much less an upstanding American in uniform? A gawd damn officer and war veteran at that."

Jim sat at the kitchen table with the letter in front of him.

Dear Lt. Davis:

Due to the inordinate number of applications we received this year from residents of this state, we are unable to accept your application to enter the fall term at the University of Connecticut. Thank you for your interest in our University, and please feel free to apply again for a later term.

Stephen Anthony Bova
Dean of Admissions

Potts grabbed the letter from the table. "Who the hell is this Bova guy?"

Jim flopped down on the couch in the living room with his hands behind his head and stared at the ceiling. He had no back-up plan to his back-up plan.

"I'll tell you what it is." Potts fell into a ratty stuffed chair that smelled of spilt beer. "It's all those sissies trying to stay out of the army. Look at what it says, 'inordinate number of applications.' Hell man, every dick is in college to stay out of Vietnam. I'm calling Pop. He's got friends in Hartford who can kick this Bova guy in his fat bureaucratic ass."

Jim didn't hear Potts' rant. He was thinking about his brother's rejection letter from the A&M coaching staff.

In early June, he was on the patio at the house in Northern Virginia reading the morning paper. Insects buzzed in the garden and the sun warmed his bare shoulders. He had finalized plans to return to Texas Tech for the fall semester. It wasn't his first choice, but application deadlines had long passed.

Potts stepped out on the patio and dropped the day's mail into his lap. Jim picked up a letter bearing the seal of The University of Connecticut. It was addressed to First Lieutenant James Baxter Davis.

"Open it, Cowboy," Potts said. His khakis were bloused into paratrooper boots, and a black enameled cadre helmet sat over aviator sunglasses. "Let's see what the good folks in Connecticut have to say."

Jim tore open the envelope.

Dear Lieutenant Davis:

We are happy to accept your recent application for admission to the fall term at the Storrs' campus of the University of Connecticut. Registration will begin on September 8, 1969. We look forward to seeing you on campus at that time.

Stephen Anthony Bova
Dean of Admissions

"I don't believe it!" Jim paced about the patio in bare feet. "I can't believe it. Did you really call your old man or something? I thought you were just blowing off. They accepted me." Jim sat down in his chair and reread the letter.

"Anything for a friend, Cowboy." Potts laughed. "Hell, my father must have called the damn governor."

CHAPTER 21

While he waited for his separation day during his final weeks in the army, there were no further assignments. He signed in at the office each morning and then immediately signed out leaving a number where he could be reached. Otherwise, he was free to come and go.

There were several Bon Voyage parties at friends' places, a formal dinner at the officers' club, and a weekend long party in late July that the Potters gave for him and Potts at their Connecticut estate. Since Potts was getting out of the army just before Christmas, and their holiday social calendar was already full, the Potters threw a party for them both. Potts joked it would be Jim's debut, "a cowboy coming-out."

The weekend of the affair arrived sunny and full of promise. On Friday morning, he rode with Potts up to Connecticut in Potts' Corvette. The raw power of the sports car added to the excitement as they sped up the turnpike. When they passed through the leafy town of Ridgefield, Connecticut, Jim was amazed at the miles of stone walls separating manicured horse farms. It was late afternoon when they arrived at Oak Lawn, the Potter's sprawling country home.

Potts geared the Corvette down to a rumble and turned off the blacktop on to a gravel drive. The entrance to the estate was inconspicuous and the house and grounds lay hidden behind a mown grass hill. As the car passed over the rise, the magnificence of Oak Lawn lay before them. The house was an imposing three-story, yellow-brick colonial, with white columns in front, and a verandah along one side. Tall windows were framed by black shutters, and brick chimneys sprouted from the high-pitched slate roof. To the right of the mansion and down the hill, a stone carriage house served as a garage and guest quarters. Further to the rear of the property, Jim saw a barn adjacent to fenced paddocks. Horses grazed in the fields, and formal gardens displayed brilliant colors in geometric patterns. Between the carriage house and stables, a turquoise swimming pool shimmered in the sun.

This was a different world for Jim, the stuff of movies and romance novels. There was nothing like it back home. Oh, there were people in Morrison with money, big ranches and nice homes, but nothing like Oak Lawn. The estate radiated class and history, tradition and lineage. His mother would be impressed if she knew her son's friend lived on an estate like Oak Lawn. She'd definitely tell everyone at church.

In the grand foyer of the house, ceramic urns held enormous bouquets of flowers. He and Potts deposited their bags on the Oriental carpet in the center of the entry hall and looked up to see Eleanor Potter descending the curved marble staircase. Her high heels matched her expensive slacks and silk blouse.

"I thought I heard your car, Potts darling." She smiled. "And Jim, so nice to see you. We've been expecting you boys all afternoon. You must be exhausted."

Potts took the stairs two at a time, grabbed his mother around the waist and lifted her into the air. "Mum, you look great. Doesn't she look great, Cowboy? I bet you're the prettiest girl at the party this weekend."

"Oh my, I hope not." She laughed, maintaining her poise even though she was two feet off the stairs. "Now put me down, dear. And if what you say is true, I did you both a terrible disservice when I made up the guest list. However," she continued after Potts kissed her and set her back down, "I think you will be quite happy with the young ladies here this weekend."

"Knew we could count on you, Mumsie," Potts said, bounding up the stairs and calling for Jim to follow.

Jim stood before the matriarch of Oak Lawn. "Mrs. Potter, I

don't know how to thank you. I'm sure this party was a lot of trouble and—"

"My dear Jim," She slipped a hand through his arm and walked him into the parlor just off the center hall, "Giving a party at Oak Lawn is no trouble. And in our boring little lives we are too often unable to find a proper reason to have one. I can't think of a better purpose than to welcome home our only son and his best friend, gallant young officers and heroes, both of you." They stopped in front of tall French doors open to the gardens and the lush back lawns. Several young people in swim suits played volleyball down by the pool.

"As you see," she continued, "guests have been arriving since this morning. Most are family and school chums. I do hope you enjoy yourself." She turned to face him and held both of his hands. "John and I are so happy that you're here. We know Potts values your friendship. This little party is our way to show our gratitude."

"Well, hello there. I thought you two would've been here long before now."

Jim turned to see an attractive blonde a few years younger than himself breeze into the sitting room dressed in riding boots, jodhpurs, and a blue cotton shirt. Candace Potter, Sis, to friends and family, had just finished her second year at Smith. A mid-summer tan gave her a healthy outdoorsy look. Her long hair was bunched at the nape with a rubber band. Wispy sun-streaked strands framed her face.

"How was your ride, dear?" Mrs. Potter asked, obviously pleased to see her only daughter.

"Oh fun, Mother. I was putting Orion back in his stall when I saw Potts' car on the drive. And how have you been, James?" She smiled. "It's been a long time since we last saw you down in Washington." She touched his arm and presented her cheek.

"Hi, Sis." He kissed her forehead.

"Mother," she steadied herself on Jim's arm while flicking barn mud off a boot, "I called Doctor Bradley this afternoon. Orion didn't seem happy in the ring, and he still has that little cough. He was so stubborn about doing his lead changes today. I think he's ill or depressed or something." More dirt dropped from her boots onto the parquet floor.

"Oh Sis, please don't do that in here?" Eleanor Potter excused herself and went off to find someone to clean up the mess.

"I see you're still riding your sissy horses in those funny clothes." Jim grinned.

"My, my, Lieutenant Davis," she countered, batting her eyelashes at him, "Did you bring your overalls? I'm sure we can roust up an old mule so you can ride the trails with us this weekend. Or, perhaps you would rather walk behind the mule and pull a plow. I'm not exactly sure how that works." Sis took both of Jim's hands and leaned forward for a real kiss.

He smiled down at her. "If your eyes were any bigger, your little nose would disappear."

"And congratulations, Lieutenant, on your upcoming discharge." Sis changed the subject. "Potts says you're going to UConn. You know Storrs is only two hours away from us here in Ridgefield? It would be nice if you visited us here at Oak Lawn more often."

"I'd like that," Jim said.

"Me, too." Sis smiled. "But I must go change." She took his hand and started walking with him toward the door. "Maybe I'll see you at the pool?"

"I need to find Potts," Jim said. "He probably thinks I'm lost." Jim followed Sis into the main hall and watched her take the circular stairs two at a time, her riding boots leaving mud prints on the beige carpet.

"So there you are, Cowboy. Give me a hand here."

Jim turned to see Potts coming out of the dining room with a tray of triangular sandwiches. He reached for the tray.

Potts pulled the tray away and stuffed a crabmeat sandwich into Jim's mouth, "Hey! I just need help eating them."

Guests continued arriving throughout the night and into the next morning. Saturday began soft and breezy. Jim rose early, donned a pair of cutoff jeans, and selected a lounge chair by the pool and a large orange juice and vodka. Insects buzzed about the gardens, and dragonflies hovered in tandem over the pool. Tables laden with fruit, pastries, and fresh brewed coffee lined the fence. From behind his sunglasses, Jim watched a parade of catering trucks coming and going up the long drive. Potts slept late. It was nearly lunchtime when he joined the party at the pool.

"Potts, old man, how goes the war?" A tall slender boy wearing a matching swimsuit and shirt approached them. "I hear the other side is winning."

"Don't believe everything you hear, Todd." Potts rose to greet his cousin. "The Viet Cong are on the run, so the army deemed it safe enough for Jim and me to return to college."

"The hockey coach at Dartmouth will be happy to know that," Todd replied.

"As will the Viet Cong," Another boy interjected. They all laughed.

As the day progressed, new arrivals stopped by to say hello and introduce themselves to Jim. Most of the activities were at the pool and down at the stables where Sis took care of all who wanted to ride.

"Sorry, I don't have one of those heavy western saddles for you," she said, cinching the girth to the English saddle on the chestnut gelding she'd selected for him. He'd accepted her invitation for a jaunt across the fields. "I'm not sure my thoroughbreds would know how to carry one of those," she continued. "They might worry I was about to yoke them to a plow."

Jim laughed. "I always thought these little English saddles were for children."

Out on the trails they cantered along wooded paths and galloped at full speed across grassy fields. Sis led most of the time while he chased after her.

"You ride way too fast for me," Jim said after they stopped to let their horses drink from a stream.

"I can tell you've ridden before," she said. "Oscar, there, is not an easy horse to ride. He's a little willful. I watched to see if he'd get you in trouble, and you've handled him with a lot of confidence."

Jim stood in the stirrups to give his rear a rest. His jeans had rubbed the inside of his knees raw. He looked back across the field at the barn. "Race you to the stable. Last one back has to do anything the winner wants."

Sis frowned, "Well, I. . .I. . .See you at the barn, sucker!" She spun her horse away and spurred it to a fast gallop.

Jim dug his heels into the gelding and raced after her. He eased the reins and let Oscar have his head. Just before they reached the barn, he sped past her and reined up beside the gate. She approached on Orion at a walk. The big gray had his head down near the ground and was breathing hard.

"Anything?" she said.

"That was the deal."

"Well, what, then?"

"Don't know." He turned Oscar to ride beside her. "I'll think about it. How about rubbing my big. . .my big horse down for me?"

"You sure that's all you want rubbed?" Sis removed her riding hat and shook out her long hair. She leaned forward in the saddle and patted Orion on his neck.

"I could make a list," Jim said, "but Potts would take a baseball bat to my knees."

"What Potts doesn't know won't hurt you, will it?" She arched an eyebrow.

"Yeah, it would," he said. "It would."

Jim helped brush the two horses and turn them out into the paddock. Sis went to freshen up, and he found Potts at the pool surrounded by girls. As the afternoon progressed, the party became a kaleidoscope of bikinis, comely coeds, bawdy jokes, loud music, foaming beer cups, and laughter.

Most of the Potters' friends attended the same schools and all answered to names that Jim would give baby bunnies like Cricket, Bingo, Wheeler, and Minty. Every now and then the boys ganged up to toss a squealing girl into the pool. Around four-thirty in the afternoon, Potts organized a game at the pool. He positioned Jim at the shallow end to throw a football while the guys, each in turn, ran off the board and attempted to catch the ball in mid-air before falling into the water. The girls stood on the side cheering them on.

"Geronimo!" Potts yelled, leaping high off the board. Jim spiraled the ball into his hands. When Potts went under, water splashed over the edge of the pool and all the girls applauded. Jim felt like he was performing. His upper body flexed each time he cocked his arm and spiraled the ball. The beer made him swagger a little, not too much, a measured amount. He noticed the girls were watching him and whispering to each other.

"Check out the hard bod," one called to another. The attention made him pump his pecs and clench his buttocks each time he threw the ball. His wet cutoffs also revealed in detail what the girls were whispering about.

At six-thirty, two vans drove onto the lawn.

"Band's here." someone yelled.

Potts led a group to help unload equipment, and Jim carried the football through the garden and into the house. He padded up the back stairs to Potts' bedroom, removed his wet shorts and wrapped a towel around his waist. He stretched out on the bed to rest before the evening's dinner and dance. When the bedroom door opened, his hands were clasped behind his head and his eyes were closed.

Through slitted eyes, he watched Sis approach. She knelt on the floor, studied him a moment, and leaned forward to place a kiss on his bare stomach. When her deft fingers opened the towel, his erection grazed his navel, betraying any pretension of sleep. She lifted it in both hands and traced the large vein with the tip of her tongue. His back arched, and he fisted the covers. His toes curled, and he heard himself groan. When he opened his eyes, she was gone. At the party that evening, he looked but didn't see her.

"Hey, Margaret!" Potts called to a cute girl with dark hair. Jim noticed she wasn't wearing a bra under her sleeveless blouse. "Margaret Donaldson, this is a real Texas cowboy. He needs to dance."

The band broke into a loud version of "Proud Mary." Margaret took his hand and pulled him into the crowd. After dancing two songs, she excused herself. He refilled his beer cup, then danced with twin sisters from Scarsdale. Three songs and three cups of beer later, he saw Potts headed into the night with a tall slender girl in tow.

The tables of food, kegs of beer, the loud music, the dancing, and flirting all rolled together into a Bloody Mary Sunday morning. He woke in Potts' room and found Margaret Donaldson, sleeping alone in Potts' bed. He put on a fresh pair of shorts and went down to the pool. Someone said they saw Sis at the barn. Her absence the previous evening troubled him. Her signals were inconsistent.

By noon on Sunday, gallons of coffee were consumed along with much tomato juice and vodka in an effort to rid the fuzz from their brains. At four o'clock, Potts and Jim were standing beside Potts' Corvette to say their goodbyes when Sis appeared. She hugged her brother then approached Jim and slid her arms around his neck. "I've got to hug "the bod" here before he leaves."

"Thanks for everything," Jim whispered in her ear and kissed her cheek. "Where did you disappear to last night?"

She bussed him on his lips then stepped back beside her parents.

Jim embraced Eleanor Potter and shook Mr. Potter's hand. "Thank you both for everything. I'll never forget this weekend."

"Get in, Cowboy," Potts called from the driver's seat. "We've got six hours of hard driving ahead of us."

During his last two weeks in the army he didn't go to the office at the Pentagon since he had no remaining duties. Also, his hair had grown longer. Potts said he looked like a hippie and threatened to gather some friends and shave his head. Jim locked the door to his room before going to bed just to be safe.

Two days before his discharge, he stopped by Colonel Dawson's office to say good-bye. The Special Assignments Group was on the third floor of the Pentagon. Across the river, the white marble monuments reflected afternoon sunlight.

"Good to see you, Lieutenant." The colonel offered him a chair and then a cigar. "It looks like I'll be leaving Washington myself in a few months. I'm getting a combat brigade in the First Infantry Division. After my time here at the Pentagon, I don't care if I never have an inside job again."

Jim took the cigar and put it in his pocket for Potts. "I know Mrs. Dawson was hoping the war would be over before you came up for reassignment."

"She's not happy about it." The colonel licked his cigar and stuck it unlit between his teeth. "But I won't get that first star until I have a combat command under my belt. By the way, we got the report on those mines you delivered to the war zone." He paused a moment to light his cigar. "The results were far short of our expectations." He tossed the match into the ashtray on his desk. "The president and secretary were very disappointed."

"Why?" Jim moved to the edge of his chair. "Not reliable?" He remembered the close call on the ship.

"Oh, they were reliable, just not very discriminating." The colonel paused a moment. "We didn't reckon on the brutality of the North Vietnamese. After they took a few casualties, they rounded up old men, women, even children in the villages and marched them at gun point over the trails where we'd seeded the mines. We were blowing up too many innocent people and not slowing their goddamn supplies. The president couldn't take the heat and canceled the program."

Neither spoke for a moment. The colonel fingered his cigar. "Yeah, too damn bad," he sighed. "We're playing with different rules."

Jim's last day in the army started early even though he'd stayed up late packing his car. A new housemate was scheduled to move in that afternoon. Before departing for Fort Myer to process out, he shared a pot of coffee with Potts in the kitchen. His friend had been somewhat silent the past twenty-four hours.

"Okay, I'm damn jealous you're leaving," Potts said when Jim pressed him on it. "And I've got to stay here for four more months."

"It'll pass before you know it." Jim stirred his coffee. "You won't miss me, but I'll miss all this." He gestured to the dishes piled in the sink and the overflowing garbage can in the corner.

"We gotta get someone to clean this place like the hooch girls do in Saigon." Potts said. "Maybe we can get a good-hearted, big-breasted American girl that'll scrub this place for sexual favors. I'll call Michelle. One out of two's not bad."

"Ha! I know you're rich but after being with me for two years Michelle won't think your wallet's big enough."

"I can always write a check," Potts retorted, and they both laughed until their sides ached.

After carrying the last suitcase out to his car, Jim saw Potts standing beside his Corvette on the driveway.

"Jimbo, I promised Mum and Sis that you'd spend Thanksgiving with us in Ridgefield. Hope you can make it."

"I'll try."

"Great." Potts nodded. "Good luck, Cowboy. Call me when you're situated in Connecticut."

"I will," Jim said, "and thanks. . .thanks for everything."

They exchanged salutes and Jim swallowed the lump in his throat as he watched Potts get into his car. Smoke billowed from squealing tires as Potts gunned his Corvette down the residential street.

At headquarters, Jim turned in his army issued equipment to the Post G-4 and watched the Military Police Sergeant scrape the blue officer's sticker from his car bumper. At the Post G-2 Office, he surrendered his I.D. Card and received his security debriefing.

Four years after entering the army, Jim walked out of the head-quarters building at Fort Myer, Virginia, wearing the same boots and Levis he had worn the day he processed in. His uniforms were packed away in the station wagon. Getting into his car, he felt na-ked, a knight without his armor.

The line of cars exiting the post, passed slowly through the East Gate while the military policeman checked for gold braid on the occupant, or an officer's blue sticker on the car bumper. Seeing one or the other, the corporal cracked a precision salute. When Jim's car approached, the MP, seeing neither, signaled him through with a perfunctory wave of the hand.

PART THREE

CHAPTER 22

Twenty minutes past Hartford, his car headlights illuminated the exit sign for Storrs and the University of Connecticut. The dashboard clock showed it was ten o'clock.

The town looked asleep. A few cars sat in front of a twenty-four-hour Cumberland Farms store, but the adjacent businesses were all in shadows. Every now and then, headlights passed going in the opposite direction. Before realizing it, Jim had driven through the town. Looking for a place to turn around, he spotted a motel and turned onto the gravel driveway. A pink neon sign in the office window buzzed *V_ _ancy*.

He stepped out and slammed the car door. What he wanted most now was a bed and a good night's sleep. The light of a television flickered in the office. A sign on the door read "Ring for Service." He leaned on the button once, then again and slapped at a mosquito on the back of his neck. A shadow moved. A key rustled in the lock. The door opened, and a huge shape filled the void.

"Twelve dollars a night," boomed a husky voice.

"Uh, okay. I need a room. . .just for a few days." He wasn't sure whether to address the figure as "Sir" or "Ma'am." The silhouette in the doorway provided no clue.

An arm, like a boom on a crane, extended out and dropped a key into his hand. "Room seven. Come by in the morning and sign the register." The door shut. The odor of an unwashed body lingered in the warm night air.

He parked in front of a red door with the number 7 stenciled in white. Taking a bag from the car, he entered the room. It smelled of mildew. He switched on the television to find a black and white picture but no sound. He fiddled with the controls on the air conditioner, and the unit hummed. An odor reminiscent of that emanating from the shape at the office filled the room. After removing his shirt and dropping onto the bed, he framed the television between his boots. He closed his eyes. *What the hell am I doing here? I should be in Washington*. The hum of the air conditioner was the last thing he heard before morning.

Sunlight filled the room. He still wore his jeans and boots. The bedding had been pushed into a ball at the foot of the bed. He rolled onto his back, rubbed his eyes and surveyed the room. The linoleum had peeled, and cigarette burns marred the top of the dresser. A photo of John Kennedy hung on the wall. Jim showered and put on fresh jeans and a white t-shirt.

Outside, the sun beat down on the gravel drive indicating the day was going to be a hot one. The *V_ _ancy* sign still buzzed in the office window and the door had been propped open. An elderly woman sat behind the desk. "Good morning, young man, you must be the fella in room seven. I hope you found everything all right."

"Yes, ma'am, the. . .uh. . .person in the office last night said I should stop by this morning to register."

"And how many nights will you be staying?"

"A week, maybe. I'm enrolling at the college and looking for a place to live."

"We also rent rooms by the school year."

"Uh, thanks." The dingy office depressed him as much as his room. "I'm hoping to get a place to share with some guys. But thanks anyway."

"If you don't find what you're looking for, come back and I'm sure we can make an acceptable arrangement."

"Yes, ma'am. I'll do that." Jim signed the register and stepped back out into the bright sunshine.

At the main entrance to the campus, he parked in the visitor's lot and asked for directions to the Student Center. Red brick buildings were cloaked in ivy and shaded by stately trees. The campus sat nestled in a valley with dorms clustered on the surrounding hillsides. In the center, a small lake, populated by a pair of white swans, sparkled like a blue sapphire in a jade setting. Maintenance crews mowed while a few summer students sat on the grass enjoying the day. A professorial-looking man with a gray beard, removed his shirt and shoes and lay bare-chested in the sun. Jim stopped at a bench under a tree and took in the scene. The campus looked like it had been planned down to the dandelions that sprouted here and there on the lush green carpet.

The two swans glided across the lake, and a pair of black labs followed a couple strolling along the edge of the water. The unleashed dogs looked like they wanted to romp but remained obediently behind their master. The boy picked up a stick and the dogs grew alert. Before it splashed in the lake, both labs were swimming. Jim watched their heads bobbing on the surface, tongues lolling as they raced toward their target. The first dog clamped the stick in his teeth and swam back to shore. The other lab turned and followed. Their master and his companion continued around the lake, paying no attention when the two labs exited the water.

The dogs' efforts reminded Jim of his own desire to please. But today's a new beginning, he thought. *A new chapter.* Checking his watch, he saw it was already mid-morning. He headed toward the Student Center hoping to find information about off-campus housing.

The lounge area looked empty. The receptionist behind the information counter was reading a paperback book.

"Pardon me," Jim said, leaning on the counter. "Know where I can find out about off-campus housing? I'm looking to share a place this fall; an apartment or house—"

"Over there." She nodded toward a cluttered bulletin board. "People put up notices." She went back to her book.

Jim scanned the assortment of typed and hand written 3x5 cards tacked to the corkboard. Many were current, and others were left over from the previous semester. Some were personal messages:

Urgent! Urgent! Will buy as many tickets as you can spare to the Woodstock Music Festival. Also, a ride if you have room for me, my old lady and my dog. See the hostess at Guido's Restaurant. She's my sister...
—Mickey

Strawberry, call the Big Banana at home. Your absence has created too much sadness in Bridgeport.

Lost a live-in girlfriend! Anyone seeing a red-haired Scorpio on I-95 to Richmond, during Spring Break - call Dusty in West Hartford. (203) 555-5850

Then there were the organizational notices:

The UConn SDS chapter will hold a joint solidarity meeting with the Connecticut Student Non-Violent Coordinating Committee on August 18, at 8:00 P.M., in the basement of the Home Economics building. Everyone is invited to attend this very important meeting.

The Committee for Alternative Education in Amerika will meet the first Monday of each month during the summer to plan the fall campaign for free tuition, open classes, and no grades.

The Black Political Union will conduct a rally at the Quadrangle, on September 5, to protest the administration's racist decision to drop one of the new black history classes scheduled for this fall. Plan to attend. POWER TO THE PEOPLE!

He had heard about the SDS but knew little about them. The Black Political Union and the other organizations sounded like they were from another planet. Very different from the Rodeo Association, Saddle Tramps, and Baptist Student Center notices for pot luck dinners and hayrides that were posted at Texas Tech's Student Union.

Among the notices for club meetings, were also ads offering baby cribs, used textbooks, pianos, and pets for sale. Several notices were students seeking rides to New York or Boston. There were a few ads for roommates - two designated female only. The third notice looked promising. He hoped he wasn't too late.

House on a lake, four bedrooms, two bathrooms, three guys, looking for a fourth. Private room. Call Joel. 555-3122

A bank of phone booths ran the length of the wall at the back of the student lounge. Jim dug a dime out and dialed the number. After ten rings he started to hang up when the phone clicked. A sleepy voice answered, "Hello."

"I'm calling about your ad for a housemate," Jim said. "I hope it's not too late."

"I don't know. See, uh. . .Joel isn't here, and he manages the house. I'll have him call you when he gets back."

"He can't. I'm in a phone booth on campus," Jim said. "When do you expect him?"

There was a pause with muffled sounds, like someone's hand covered the phone, then another voice came on the line. "Hi. I'm Joel. You're looking for a place to live?"

"Yeah," Jim replied, "Saw your ad and—"

"Meet me for a beer and we'll discuss it."

"Great. Name the place and time."

"In an hour at the Huskie Bar and Grill on Route 175. Easy to find."

"I'll be there. By the way, I'm Jim Davis."

Jim whistled a George Jones tune as he walked back across campus toward the parking lot. Things are looking up, he thought as he passed the lake. The professor lying on the grass had covered his face with his shirt. When Jim reached his car, he stood with the door open to let out the heat. Hopefully, no more stinky nights at the B.O. Motel, he thought as he slid behind the wheel and cranked the engine.

The Huskie Bar and Grill smelled of stale beer and burnt pizza crust. UConn pennants hung from the ceiling, and sports trophies lined the shelf behind the bar. Photographs of Huskie sporting moments covered the walls. Jim picked a table and ordered a beer and sandwich from the cute waitress. Several men at the bar wore Huskie baseball caps and t-shirts. From the whistle lanyards around their necks, Jim figured they were coaches from the college. His food arrived, and he watched the waitress sashay back to the bar. Her mini-skirt just grazed the top of her long legs.

"Jim Davis?"

He looked up to see who had spoken his name.

"I'm Joel Zippen."

Jim rose and took the outstretched hand of the longhaired, bearded fellow standing next to his table.

"Hey. Good to meet you. Have a seat." Jim pointed to an empty chair. "What kind of beer do you drink? Pardon my not waiting, but I didn't have breakfast this morning."

"I'll have a Bud," Joel said.

Jim motioned the waitress over and ordered Joel's beer. He saw Joel eying her as she walked back to the bar. "Great legs," he said.

"Great ass." Joel stroked his beard and winked at him.

Jim took a bite of sandwich while they watched the waitress deliver platters of food to the coaches at the bar.

"Well," Joel said, turning back to him. "I suppose we need to know more about each other before deciding if we can live in the same house for a year. I'll show you mine, if you show me yours." Joel moved his eyebrows up and down like Groucho Marx.

Jim swigged down the remainder of his beer and leaned forward with his elbows on the table. "It all started twenty-four years ago in a small town in West Texas. . . .

"That's a long way from there to here," Joel said when he finished.

Jim grinned. "And you're the first guy I ever met whose hair is longer than my mom's."

"Hope that doesn't bother you." Joel laughed. "It's part of the costume. Syracuse University awarded me an M.S. in Psychology a year ago, and I'm in the second year of a doctoral program here at UConn. Grew up in Albany. Parents still live there. My father is Commissioner of Health for the State of New York. I'm Jewish and will pause here to see if that's a problem."

Jim shrugged. "What do you mean?"

"Let's just say there are some necks with a reddish tint that have a problem with us Jews."

"Never thought about it," Jim said. "There weren't any that I knew of back in Morrison, Texas. Lots of Methodists, many Baptists, some Church of Christ. I read a book once about Jews. It was *"Exodus"* by Leon Uris. I rode a freighter to Asia some months ago, and it was the thickest book in the ship's library. It was about Jews in Europe and the founding of modern day Israel."

"Yeah," Joel nodded. "That's my people's history. Like cowboys and Indians, there are Jews and Germans, Jews and Arabs, Jews and Gentiles. As a kid, I always played the Jew."

"Okay," Jim said, laughing. "You're a Jew and I'm a Baptist. I don't have a problem with that if you don't. What's next?"

Joel took a swig of his beer. "I admit I had a biased impression when I heard your howdy-do accent on the phone. I thought, oh no, he's a Klansman and wants to move in. Now I see only a pinkish tinge to your neck and thank God you don't chew that disgusting tobacco. So, Jim Davis, Baptist of Morrison, Texas, we'd be delighted for you to join our band of merry men and come live with us in Sherwood Forest." Joel extended his hand to seal the deal.

After paying the check, Jim exchanged smiles with the pretty waitress and followed Joel out of the bar into the parking lot.

"There's a few other things we ought to cover," Joel said. "We have two other interesting housemates. Steve Jankowski answered the phone this morning when you called. He's a good guy but also a strange bird. He got out of the army a few months ago and is starting his freshman year. He thought about the Jesuits after high school but joined the army instead and spent the last year as an infantry grunt in Vietnam. He's quiet and something of a loner. He moved into the house in June, but we rarely see him."

"Sounded a little spacey on the phone this morning," Jim said, hooking his thumbs in his jeans pockets. "Drugs?"

"Don't think so. I haven't figured him out yet. His parents live in Bridgeport and he goes home most weekends. Not real sociable but pays the rent and cleans up after himself. The army trains you guys well in that regard."

"I knew a few quiet fellows like that in the army," Jim said. "They either won the Medal of Honor or fragged their officers."

"If he had a Medal of Honor, I think I'd know it," Joel said, "So. . . ."

"Right." Jim laughed. "I'll watch my back."

"I think you'll like Belton Jones," Joel continued. "Or Ali Jabar, as he prefers to be called. He refers to himself as our token Negro. He's the leader of a black activist group on campus and is always away at meetings. I like him. You'll see he's a good guy. Real funny. We rib each other around the house, however, he doesn't like us jiving with him when he's with his black friends. Probably concerned he'll lose their respect or something. We should apply for some kind of diversity grant. We have our Catholic Son of Poland, our Jewish doctoral student, our black radical, and now a WASP from Texas."

They both laughed as Jim pulled out his car keys.

"Oh, and one more thing," Joel said. "The rent's two hundred a month split four ways, utilities included. We divide up the phone bill at the end of each month. The phone's in my name, so we break it down to the penny."

Jim nodded. "When can I move in?"

"When do you want to?"

"How about this afternoon?"

Joel shrugged. "We can use your share of this month's rent. Follow me, and I'll show you how to get to the house. It can be tricky on the roads around Andover Lake."

The white clapboard cottage was ten miles from campus and

sat on a hillside on the north end of a lake. A blacktop driveway wound up the hill from the lake road to the house. When he pulled up in front, a blue Firebird was parked in the drive.

"The cottage was the summer home of a rich family from Hartford," Joel said as they went up the stairs to the deck. "It got lost in the settling and resettling of estates. For the past twenty years, the executors have rented it to UConn students."

Joel nodded toward the car in the driveway.

"That's Steve's wheels. He's probably in his room." He jiggled the door knob. "Don't know why he's got the front door locked." He pulled out his house key. "Let's go in, and I'll show you your room."

Jim could hear the distant sound of a radio, but it was hard to tell if it was in the house or coming from one of the nearby cottages. Passing through the kitchen, he saw the garbage can overflowing in the corner and a half-eaten pizza on the table. Just like the house he left in Arlington. The living room was furnished with a pair of unmatched sofas and two stuffed chairs. Other than the kitchen, the house was tidy but not spotless, which was okay with him.

"Steve and I have the two bedrooms upstairs, and you and Ali have the two downstairs," Joel said, leading him into a narrow hallway. "There are two bathrooms, one up and one down. Your room is your own. Everyone shares the rest of the house and the responsibility for maintaining it. If you want to keep your food separate in the fridge, label it and no one will bother it. Unlabeled food belongs to everyone. The system works as long as you replace what you use. We try to minimize the hassles."

Jim liked the old lake house. It was bright and airy with large windows facing out over the water. The property was surrounded by a low stone wall dating back to the time when New England farmers cleared their land and believed, like Robert Frost, that good fences made good neighbors. Most of the homes, including the cottage, pumped water direct from the lake.

Jim stood in the living room admiring the view. "It's beautiful."

"Yeah." Joel came up beside him. "But wait till fall in a couple of months when the leaves are in full color. Some mornings when the sun is just coming up, you'd think a forest fire was raging on the hills around the lake. During the winter, the residents place torches in the snow at night and skate on the ice. That's pretty neat too, but the winters are hard. Summer makes us forget about the ice and snow and then come December, winter sits on us like a sumo wrestler."

"Why do you say it's so bad?" Jim asked, watching a rainbow-colored sail glide across the lake.

"The steep driveway is impossible to get up when iced over." Joel wiped a cobweb off the window with his hand. "We park down on the road a lot of days and walk up the hill. Come February, you'll curse this house like the rest of us."

Jim watched the sailboat jibe back across the lake. He looked at the green hills and contrasted it with the brown dryness of the ranch during August. Nothing like this at home, he thought. This is going to be just fine.

CHAPTER 23

It was four in the afternoon when he returned from gathering his things at the motel. Approaching the cottage, he saw the Firebird parked in the drive, but no one seemed to be around. He let himself in and carried boxes from his station wagon to his bedroom. He walked outside for another load and almost collided with the biggest black guy with the largest afro and broadest grin he'd ever seen.

"Hey, bro," the big man said. He looked Jim up and down, the grin not subsiding. "Joel said we have a new boarder. That better be you or I'll have to kick your white butt around the lake for breaking into my house."

"And you must be the ebony messiah Joel told me about." Jim shook hands with the black giant. "How about a beer when I'm done unloading? I picked up a cold six pack at the store."

"I'll drink your beer, brother. My name's Ali, Ali Jabar. Call me Ali. . .like the Great One that floats like a butterfly and stings like a bee." He held the door open while Jim carried a box of clothes into the house.

Three days passed before Jim met their elusive housemate that owned the Firebird. Steve Jankowski had come and gone from his room unseen. When they bumped into each other one morning in the kitchen, Steve seemed embarrassed about being caught. His conversation, while eating a bowl of cereal, consisted of a few grunts. Never once did he make eye contact.

"I don't know whether he's just shy or was being rude," Jim said to Joel that afternoon. They were outside on the deck enjoying the cool breeze off the lake.

Joel took a swig of his beer and nodded. "Been studying him for two months now. It's not that complicated. He's a shy kid who doesn't play well with others. Could be his experience in Nam. He never talks about it. A lot of guys are coming back pretty fucked up."

"Yeah, I hear that," Jim said, "But I know a lot of guys, good average boys like you and me, who went over there, did their duty and came home without being screwed up. I know some are suffering from it, but I also think some are using Vietnam as a crutch. The newspapers eat it up. If you didn't know better, you'd think every soldier is returning a drugged-up psycho. Most aren't, and some would've been fucked up if they'd gone to Disneyland." A long silence passed as they nursed their Heinekens. Jim found it difficult to read Joel behind his beard.

"Did you go to Vietnam?" Joel asked. "You know, I mean in combat, shooting gooks, counting bodies, trying to decide if an arm and a leg constituted one or two dead VC?"

"I served," Jim said, not sure if Joel was mocking him. "I was in country several times a year escorting munitions and other materials for the army. I didn't fight in the jungle. I was assigned to the Pentagon after commissioning, not an infantry company."

"Ever think about what you would've done if you'd encountered a Viet Cong?" Joel asked. "Could you have killed him?"

Jim took a swig of beer. "Yeah," he said. "If it were him or me, I would've made damn sure it was him. Patton once said, 'Heroes don't die for their country. They make the other poor bastard die for his country.'"

Joel laughed, and Jim got up to fetch another beer. It was a warm day and neither of them had anything important to do. "Another cold one?" he called to Joel from the kitchen.

"No thanks," Joel answered. "This one's half full."

Jim came back out onto the deck, the screen door slammed behind him. He opened his beer and sat in the lawn chair. "What about you?" he asked, extending his legs and crossing his boots on the railing. "I mean, what would you do if you were drafted?"

Joel's eyes flashed. "My deferment is good for three more years while I'm getting my doctorate. If this asinine war is not over by then, we're in more trouble than we think."

A moment passed, and Jim continued, "Would you be in school now if there wasn't a war?"

Joel gazed out over the lake a long moment. "Yeah, but I might've taken a break and gone to Israel for a year. My old man being an MD, it was expected I'd get a doctorate in something. I sometimes feel guilty that it was too easy, too convenient. I mean, I'm against this damn war, believe it's immoral, and wish we could bring everyone home." Joel paused to drink from his beer. "And I also feel for the poor bastards that ran to Canada with the law after them." He paused and stared a moment at the deck.

"Then, sometimes, I feel bad that I didn't step up to serve my country. My family owes a lot to this nation. My great grandparents came here from the Ukraine to escape the czar's pogroms. In my head, I know this war is wrong, that we should leave people alone to solve their problems without our interference. But in my heart, I. . .so I took the easy way and tabled it for three years while I get my doctorate."

Another period of silence passed while they both gazed out over the lake.

"Don't make it so personal," Jim said. "We each have to make our own decisions. I got called. . .My father. . .Well any way, I and two million others went and served. Most of us were lucky and didn't get our asses blown off. Some did, but I didn't, and I'm not going to feel guilty about it." He paused a moment and watched a small sailboat raise its sail at the far end of the lake.

"Let's debate this some other time," Jim said. "I'm still thinking about it. But you didn't break any law nor are you are hiding here at UConn. You didn't run away from anything. I believe you would've gone to school to get a doctorate even if there wasn't a war going on."

Joel smiled. "You sound like the couch psychologist instead of me, and I admit your bedside manner is pretty effective. I'm already feeling less guilty. We descendants of Solomon need to reconcile our hearts with our heads for the world to be in balance. So, yeah, I think I'll go get another beer."

During the two weeks before the fall term started, Jim spent a half-hour doing sit-ups and pushups each morning in his room, then ran the five miles around the lake. He had left the army in good shape and intended to stay that way. Afternoons were sunning outside on the deck and swimming in the lake.

Ali never came out of his room before noon and immediately left the house. Jim was in bed when he heard him return at night. Like a mouse in a corncrib, Steve Jankowski was rarely seen outside of his room.

By Labor Day weekend, the evenings were cooler while the days remained sunny and warm. On Friday at noon, Joel stepped out on the deck. Jim was shirtless and reading an old magazine someone left at the house.

"Grab a towel and let's go babe watching," Joel said. "There's a natural pool with a great waterfall in the Housatonic River not far from here."

"What do you mean babe watching?" Jim put the magazine down.

"You'll see when we get there," Joel said. "It's not a family friendly place. You'll see what I mean."

Diana's Pool had been a summer gathering place for UConn students and faculty for generations. Jim parked his station wagon in a clearing next to a Volkswagen van sporting peace signs and protest stickers like a traveling salesman's suitcase. With towel in hand, he followed Joel along a worn trail. Before the river came into view, the roar of the falls could be heard, punctuated with shouts, splashing, and laughter.

They broke out of the woods and stood at the water's edge. Several people played under the falls while others sunned on rocks or waded in the river. At the far side of the pool, a naked couple waist deep in the water were making out. A nude girl, with flaming red hair and the biggest breasts Jim had ever seen on a real person, perched high on the bluff. She pinched her nose and jumped. "Goddamn!" she shouted after surfacing. "The water's fuckin' cold." Her freckled breasts floated in front of her like water wings.

"Nice mouth," Jim said, turning to Joel.

"Nice tits." Joel said.

Two naked guys on a ledge above the falls were calling to a group of giggling girls below them. An older couple Jim assumed to be faculty at the college, took off their clothes and sat naked in the sun, sharing a newspaper.

Joel claimed a flat rock for them near the falls. Jim pulled off his t-shirt and slipped out of his jeans but kept on his jockey briefs. Joel, like most others around the pool, doffed everything. Jim had never seen so much hair on one person. Noticing there wasn't an erection in sight except his own, he stayed on his stomach, catching it between his abs and the warm rock. Joel's penis looked sleepy in a nest of reddish-brown fur.

"How can you control that thing at a place like this?" Jim grinned.

"It's all in your state of mind." Joel stood over him. "If I had on briefs like you, I'd have a boner that would poke your eye out. When you take everything off and let it all hang like this, it just doesn't. . . Haven't you ever seen a nudist magazine?"

"Yeah," Jim said and ground his groin against the rock.

"What you usually don't see," Joel continued, "is the photographer taking those pictures. He's the only guy dressed, and he's sporting a hard-on. So, if you want to get rid of your stiffy, slip off your undies like the rest of us."

Jim watched the girl with big tits making her way back to the top of the falls. He flexed his flanks again and felt the pressure of the warm granite against him. "That's all right," he said. "I'll just enjoy it."

On Monday, Joel invited classmates from his graduate program out to the cottage for a Labor Day party. That afternoon, everyone lounged on the deck sharing pot as easily as his mother served iced tea back home. Jim declined when a joint came his way, and the casualness about it intrigued him. Here were children of judges, doctors, clergy, and PTA parents breaking the law; a felony in every state. At any moment the police could show up and arrest them all. He figured they'd be harder on him because he'd been an army officer and knew better.

After the sun went down, everyone went inside the house. Joel put his Beatles' "White Album" on the stereo and passed around a bowl of corn chips. Jim sat cross-legged on the floor between two thin frizzy-haired girls that looked almost like twins.

"What's a Texan doing here at UConn?" The one on his right with a leather headband asked. She slipped off her sandals and put her bare feet in Jim's lap to be rubbed.

"I was sent up here from Austin by the governor as a foreign exchange student." Jim massaged her unpainted toes. "We want to figure out how you Yankees beat us in the Civil War." She took a joint from her friend, inhaled deeply and held it a few moments before exhaling the smoke in little white puffs. "Funny."

The rest of the evening, girls giggled, and boys acted silly—much like they were a little drunk. Jim concluded that marijuana caused people to laugh at unfunny jokes more than they would otherwise. He still wasn't ready to try it. It was too soon. Only three weeks had passed since he had been required by law to comport himself as an officer and a gentleman. Four weeks ago, he could've fallen down drunk at the officers' club, and it would've been considered a rite of youthful passage. Smoking marijuana would have gotten him court martialed and five-to-ten at hard labor in a federal prison.

"Hey man." Joel came into the kitchen after everyone had left. Jim had started washing dishes piled up in the sink. The clock on the wall said it was three-thirty in the morning. "You've got to let your hair grow longer or something. Three people took me aside tonight to tell me they thought you were a Narc."

"Narc." Jim laughed. "Why a Narc?"

"You tell me." Joel sat at the table, eating the few corn chips left in the bowl. "By the way, what did you think of the two Moreno sisters? I saw you giving one of them a foot job. I'd like to give her a foot job. . .like my size thirteen."

Jim ignored the remark. "Who said I might be a Narc?"

"It was more than a few people. You had them all worried. I went to piss, and the toilet was stopped up. Someone had flushed a bag of stash down the crapper. It took me ten minutes to unclog it. What a waste.

CHAPTER 24

Ali Jabar was as much a mystery to him as Steve Jankowski. Ali claimed to be from Boston and said he was majoring in Sociology. He quoted Malcolm X and once argued late into the night with Jim and Joel that a race war was inevitable and necessary for black people to gain their rights. "Organize and fight!" he'd said with a big toothy grin. "Don't take it personally, brothers. Your skinny white asses are safe. Everyone knows you live with Ali Jabar."

The Sunday before the fall term started, it clouded up in the afternoon out at the lake and looked like rain. Jim and Ali sat at the kitchen table sharing a pot of coffee. "So why does the president of the Black Political Union live with a bunch of white guys?" Jim asked.

"Why not?" Ali shrugged his big shoulders. "I'm not intimidated by the man. It shows my bros I'm an equal. . .can sleep in the same house and eat at the same table." He paused for a moment. "Besides, I gotta live somewhere. This is a nice place."

School started the next morning, and the following days seemed disjointed as Jim reengaged the college routine after being away for so long. He signed up for six courses, which was the maximum; three classes on Monday, Wednesday, and Friday, and three on Tuesday and Thursday. The campus teemed with activity as twelve thousand students returned to Storrs for the fall term.

His transfer credits from Texas Tech classified him as a junior, but his change of majors from Agriculture to Economics, required him to take several leveling courses in social studies. Being the old guy in most of his classes bothered him. Freshmen smelled of milk and arrived on campus in the same uniform: dungarees, sandals or hiking boots called waffle stompers, and everyone had an olive-green G.I. utility jacket. The girls dressed like the boys and many had shorter hair. The boys that could, sported peach-fuzz efforts for facial hair. The girls ironed their tresses or permed Medusa-like curls—with beaded headbands for individuality.

They had little in common with the students at Texas Tech. The cowboys at Tech sported tailored Levi's over Tony Lama boots, and starched pearl-button shirts. Steam-molded beaver felt hats projected western vanity and a cocky self-assuredness. The girls liked cotton sundresses in warm months, and skirts and sweaters when the weather turned cool. On Saturdays, they had appointments to have their hair coifed by artisans in Lubbock salons.

Also, most girls in Lubbock would've been shocked at the profanity spewed by the comely coeds in Connecticut. It never failed to surprise him when an attractive girl, a future mother of sweet babies, the sugarplum princess of a proud father, shaped her rosebud lips and easily expelled words such as "shit" and "fuck" and "cocksucker."

He did find one similarity between Texas Tech and UConn. Classes were no different. With all the social changes occurring on the nation's campuses, the process of learning remained the same. Lectures, pop quizzes, term papers, reading assignments, and final exams still made up his schoolwork.

Jim rose early each morning at the lake, exercised, showered, and joined Joel and his friends for coffee at the Student Center snack bar. He attended class from ten till three with an hour break for lunch. Afternoons were spent at the library, and he was home by six. He and Joel usually ate dinner together, studied some in their rooms, watched Johnny Carson on television and were in bed by midnight.

He hadn't dated yet but had noticed several interesting prospects on campus. He'd detected some interest in the morning coffee group; a hooded glance and a coy flick of the tongue across the lips. He thought often about calling Sis Potter, had considered driving to Ridgefield for Labor Day, but then stayed at the cottage for the party with Joel's friends. There was no rush.

During the morning sessions before class at the snack bar, current events were discussed and argued. Everyone was against the war. A few praised the Viet Cong as if they were the Green Mountain Boys. Jim mostly listened. The collective cynicism about America saddened him.

"It's true," a girl was saying morning. "The fucking oil companies conspired with the corporate rice lobby. When Ho is defeated, they'll divide up the country. The oil companies will drill in the Gulf of Tonkin, and the rice companies plan to take over the peasants' farms in the Mekong Delta. It's a goddamn economic war. Our guys are fucking dying for the oil companies and Uncle Ben, the goddamn colonial cocksuckers."

"Where did you learn that crap?" Jim set his cup down and pushed back from the table. Every head at the table turned in his direction.

"Well," the girl hesitated a moment. "Everyone was talking about it last night in the dorm. I also heard it in a rap session at the Friends' Meeting House. Everyone knows it. Right?" She looked around for support.

"Why is it too hard for you to believe that we Americans are the good guys over there?" Weeks of frustration poured forth.

"Oh, a commie baiter," someone said, at the far end of the table.

"Wait," another responded. "I want to hear this."

"I've been sitting here for two weeks hearing how we're raping the country and oppressing the Vietnamese people." Jim picked up his coffee cup and stared at it a moment gathering his thoughts. "Have you ever considered that maybe our purpose is honorable?" He looked at the embarrassed girl across from him. "We're there not for any rice or oil but because we were asked by the democratically elected government to assist in preserving their freedom. . .to honor a commitment made by several presidents, even John Kennedy. Most South Vietnamese don't want to live under a tyrannical government. Over two million Catholics fled to the South in the fifties when Ho returned from his education in Russia and pro-claimed a communist state in the North.

He paused a moment. "When I was at the Pentagon, I saw tough sergeants weep while telling stories of their teams entering hamlets in the countryside and finding the village chief crucified upside down with his severed prick in his mouth. His pregnant wife was staked out on the ground in front of him with her belly opened. Her intestines and dead baby lay in a bloody pile beside her. That's how Ho's patriots treat their fellow countrymen with different po-litical opinions. And you say we should leave and surrender them to those sadistic monsters? Sorry, but I get angry when I hear people say we're fighting and dying over there to get their fucking rice."

No one at the table spoke. Jim looked at his watch. He had ten minutes to get to class. The girl glared at him.

"I apologize for my outburst." He smiled at her.

He was crossing the quadrangle for his ten o'clock class when one of the girls in the group caught up and walked beside him.

"You were pretty sure of yourself this morning," she said. "Your sincerity impressed me, even though I think it a bit naive."

He looked at the olive-skinned girl beside him. She had long black hair, dark eyes and full sensuous lips. "Thanks, I guess," he responded. "I'm Jim Davis."

"I know," she said, watching him out of the corner of her eye. "My name is Ariella. It's 'Lioness" in Hebrew. I'm from Tel Aviv."

"I'm from Morrison," he said.

"Morrison? Where's that?"

"Texas," he said, turning at the duck pond by the English Building. "See you tomorrow at the snack bar." He glanced over his shoulder and saw her watching him.

CHAPTER 25

As the days passed, Jim realized more and more how much things had changed during his time in the army. Groups on campus protested something every day. Mind-altering drugs were all around him as was experimentation with other lifestyles including nudity, communal living, group sex, and other activities that could get one arrested in several states. Radicals burned the Stars and Stripes while cheering for Ho Chi Minh. Anarchists denied the legitimacy of government and based their code on the goodness inherent in man. Every time Jim heard that, he thought about the goodness of man behind the creation and operation of Dachau.

While many of his peers immersed themselves in a hedonistic movement of great proportion, he watched and observed. The theme was love. Love solved all problems. Love could feed the hungry, cure the sick, and clothe the naked. *Make love not war. Everything is beautiful. I'm beautiful. You're beautiful. Were you at Woodstock?*

By the first of October, the voices with bullhorns at campus rallies had become louder and the language uglier. "Fuck authority. We don't need rules. Everything is beautiful. Fuck the rules. And fuck you if you don't agree with me."

One night after a particularly rough argument with Joel at the snack bar that had carried over to the cottage, he lay in bed waiting for sleep. Suddenly, he ached for home. It'd been weeks since he'd called his family. Home was over two thousand miles away. So far away and so long ago, it seemed like he'd once dreamed it.

CHAPTER 26

The cold nights of October ignited the wooded hills around the cottage. Bright yellows, reds, and oranges flamed through the trees around Andover Lake. With anti-war emotions at the college growing more intense, Jim felt even more like an intruder at the morning discussions at the snack bar.

"Don't worry about it," Joel said, pushing open the door to the deck on a crisp fall Sunday morning. He carried two cups of steaming coffee while Jim followed with doughnuts and the Sunday newspaper. "New Englanders are more careful with their friendships than you Texans."

"They look at me like I've got four heads." Jim wore a sweatshirt to keep away the morning chill.

"You've put them in a quandary," Joel said, setting his coffee mug on the deck rail. "They've never met anyone who argues for this crappy war other than you. I find it an interesting psychological study. Most students here believe only fat racist senators from dumb southern states want America to win this war. You? They haven't figured out." Joel brushed doughnut sugar out of his beard and picked up the sports section. "You're good looking in that curly-haired cowboy kind of way, and you're also a nice guy. It'd be easier for them if you were fat and ugly, had bad teeth, and maybe wore one of those spooky Klan hoods."

On Monday afternoon, the English professor closed the book he'd just read from to the class and stood beside his desk. The clock over the door showed three-thirty. "While you read *Othello*, think about the differences between comedy and tragedy. We'll talk about that on Wednesday."

Students gathered up their books and headed for the exit. Jim stood to put on his windbreaker.

"So, what's a Texan doing up here in Connecticut?"

She was tall; he guessed five-feet nine in her penny loafers.

Jim shrugged. "My horse turned north near Amarillo and got lost. I stayed over the winter here to attend college."

"Oh really, how. . .how not fascinating." She laughed, squinching up her cute nose.

He'd noticed her before. Brown hair flipped just above the shoulders, gold barrettes, plaid skirt, white blouse, and a navy cardigan contrasted sharply with the wardrobe worn by most girls on campus. He rested his hip against his desk. "How'd you know?"

"Not difficult," she said. "Your accent, and I'd recognize a Texan's butt in blue jeans anywhere."

His neck flushed. "What?" He coughed out a laugh. "It must be from a lifetime of wearing Mexican heeled boots like these." He lifted his foot showing a black calfskin. "And, how do you know so much about guys' butts?"

"I'm an expert." She smiled. "Daddy was the commanding general at Kelly Air Force Base in San Antonio before he retired. When I was home from boarding school I watched thousands of cute little buns marching on the parade field every Saturday. I learned to tell where most every boy in uniform was from just by watching him strut his stuff."

They both laughed. An awkward moment passed while he collected his things from under the desk.

"I'm Cheryl Hollis," she said when he turned back to her.

"Jim Davis." He shifted his books and shook her extended hand. She had a strong grip.

She nodded towards the door. ""I'll walk out with you. It's my last class, and I don't want to go back to the dorm. Do you like movies?"

"Sure," he said. "Most of them."

"Have you seen the new one over at the Storrs Theater?"

"Which one is that?" He watched her manicured fingers twirl a silver heart on a chain around her neck.

"*Easy Rider*, with Peter Fonda and that crazy Dennis Hopper. They say it has great music. This is the last weekend. Hope you don't mind me being so forward." She glanced at him as they walked through the English building. "I mean, you're not married, or going with someone, or anything?"

He looked at her. "No. No, I'm not."

"I don't go to movies alone." She shrugged. "Guys see a girl out alone and think she's fair game. Besides, a person shouldn't go alone to a movie. Sharing it is half the fun."

"We could go this Saturday if you'd like." His palms felt damp. "We could get a pizza first and—"

"That sounds great." She smiled at him.

"Good. What time should we—"

"Come by my resident hall at six-thirty," she said. "I'll meet you in the lobby of North."

They stopped in the corridor of the English building. A river of students flowed around them. "Okay, six-thirty," he said. "At North?"

"It'll be fun," she said, squeezing his arm.

He watched her disappear into the current of students. There was something familiar about her.

After dinner that evening, Jim and Joel were watching television in the living room. Jim had his stocking feet on the coffee table while Joel sat in the stuffed chair across from him. The evening news had just concluded.

Jim shook his head. "It's either feast or famine. I haven't had a date in eight weeks, and today I get asked out by two girls. A classmate in my English class asked me to take her to the movies on Saturday. Then, I saw Ariella on the way to my car in the parking lot, and she offered to cook me dinner at her place on Friday night. Hell would freeze over back home before a girl did that."

"Yeah, well don't get too cocky." Joel winked at him. "I don't know about the other girl, but I know what Ariella wants. I've seen the way she looks at you at the snack bar. Those almond eyes of hers strip you naked and slaps your bare ass. Ask the others if you don't believe me."

"Bullshit." Jim uncrossed his feet at the ankle. "I never noticed it, and I've got pretty good radar for stuff like that. She doesn't treat me any different than she does any of the other guys."

"You're blind, Cowboy," Joel laughed. "You may know when a steer's in heat—"

"Cow," Jim corrected. "Cows go into heat. Steers are castrated."

"Whatever. But you've a lot to learn about Jewish princesses like Ariella. They're better at it than most, ever since Esther saved our people with her feminine wiles. You don't have a chance once her legs are around your neck. It's the sniff of death, my grandfather, the Rabbi, used to say."

"And how do you know so much about it?" Jim laughed. "You haven't been out with a chick since I've been here."

"Don't forget I'm the one in this house studying human behavior." Joel picked up a textbook and waved it in the air. "I'll have a PhD in perversion and deviancy. It's all right here in black and white. You can look it up."

"I know, I know!" Jim laughed. "And most of those textbooks are written by old men with atrophied genitalia. The dictionary defines a psychologist as a guy who knows a thousand and one ways to make love but doesn't know any girls."

"See." Joel roared. "Even that Gentile, Webster, agrees with me."

Friday evening was a brilliant, clear October night. The air felt almost cold, and the sweater he wore over his collared shirt warmed him. He parked in front of Ariella's apartment building and walked up the steps. The crease in his jeans was knife sharp, and his boots were polished to a high gloss. He heard the bell ring somewhere inside. The door opened, and warm scented air washed over him.

"Hello, Jim Davis from Morrison, Texas." She floated before him in a gauzy white sheath, the hem brushed the top of her brown bare feet. With the apartment light behind her, he saw she wore nothing underneath.

"Hi." He smiled.

"Come in," she said in a husky whisper.

Stepping inside, he took in the tidy studio apartment, a stack of art books and lit candles on the coffee table. His gaze settled on Ariella.

She shut the door and snaked bare arms around his neck. Hard nipples pressed into him. "Hello, Cowboy," she breathed in his ear. "Let's ride." She rose on bare painted toes and put her lips on his. Her tongue penetrated his mouth, and he heard the tinkle of ankle bracelets. Her fingers trailed down his back, feeling his muscles. Her tongue traced down his throat. She slid to her knees and unbuckled his belt. "Oh." She looked up at him, her nostrils flared.

The rest of the night blurred into raw-nerve jangling pleasure. Ariella took the reins and drove the chariot. During one feverish moment, he regained control, but she checked, and he let the lioness take what she desired. When morning dawned, he lay next to her in the mussed bed, staring up at white ceiling tiles.

She slept while he dressed, her dark tresses spread across the pillows. Her breathing sounded steady—almost purring. He closed the front door behind him and stepped out into a rainy Saturday morning. His clawed back felt raw.

After parking at the cottage, he noticed his housemates weren't around. He dropped his clothes on the floor and crawled into bed. He had a lot to think about, but his mind, as his body, was still numb. His stomach rumbled, reminding him that Ariella didn't make good on her promise of dinner.

It was late afternoon when he woke and went into the kitchen to find a doughnut. It had stopped raining. After knocking out a set of pushups on the floor, he sat on the bed to put on sneakers. A run around the lake should shake the cobwebs. He checked his watch. Cheryl expected him at her dorm in two hours. As he stepped outside on the deck, the sun broke through the clouds. There was no traffic, and the lake road stretched out wet and flat ahead of him.

With his feet pounding blacktop, his mind glided freely. Events had been occurring so fast he hadn't had time to digest them. At a recent meeting on campus he'd heard a professor advocate disobedience of the law, even violence. A kid in the morning group announced he was renouncing his citizenship and leaving the country. He'd observed students and faculty smoking pot and hashish, unconcerned about the law. And he lived with a black revolutionary who considered white people as the enemy. All very different from anything he had known just two months before. *Is the world going nuts?*

After the first half-mile he upped the pace. He rounded the curve at the far end of the lake and headed into the wind. The pounding of his feet matched the blood pulsing in his temples. Passing the next curve, the wind pushed him along in ground-eating strides. His thoughts turned to the previous night. When he left Ariella's apartment that morning, he'd felt empty, numb, void of feeling; maybe because the conquest had been hers and not his. He smiled to himself. Being prey instead of predator hadn't diminished his ardor. He checked his watch. He had an hour to get ready for his next date. Turning up the drive to the cottage, he wondered what Cheryl's game would be.

At six-thirty on the dot, she met him at her dorm dressed for the evening in navy slacks with a matching sweater. The lobby buzzed with activity as the student receptionist behind the desk tried to keep up with the sign-ins and sign-outs.

Over a pizza at the Meatball Barn across the street from campus, Jim told her about his housemates. "Joel's like an obsessive English professor and people are verbs that have to be conjugated." He motioned for the waitress to bring another soda. "He's not aware he does it. Every time he meets someone, you can just see the wheels turning. He even gets me doing it sometimes."

"I'm majoring in special education, so I can work with the handicapped. Daddy, the general, says I'll be a great teacher because I like kids so much." She removed her gold clip earrings and smiled. I volunteer at the base hospital as a Candy Striper. It's so rewarding." She reached across the table and squeezed his hand.

Another general's daughter. What are the odds?

At the movie theater, she held his hand in her lap. Several times he felt her studying him. Afterward, they stopped for coffee at a diner. It was late when he walked her back across campus to her dorm.

"This looks like a nice place to sit." She gestured to a bench by the duck pond.

They sat in silence for a few minutes before Jim put his arm around her. She rested her head on his shoulder. Glancing at his watch, he saw it was one-thirty in the morning. He inhaled the scent of her hair and wondered what she wanted to happen next. He felt her sigh. For some reason he lacked inspiration. He felt no excitement, not the lust of the evening before with Ariella, nor the heart racing, hold-on-forever tingling he remembered with Anita Beth.

At this moment, he saw how it would develop. They'd make out on the bench; she'd remove his hands from forbidden places, and finally there would be the goodnight kiss with a body grind that said, "Wait till next time, big boy."

Phase two would include at least two more dinner and movie dates. They might wind up at his place where they'd grope around on the bed, but he'd still take her home and sleep alone with blue balls. Then subtly, almost imperceptibly, the two of them would become "*we*," and by Christmas she'd start positioning her mom and *Daddy, the general*, for a visit. By Easter, they'd all be planning his future. Oh, she'd let him think he was making the decisions along the way, but it would be her game. Any success would be *their* success. Any failure would be *his*. Michelle had set the same trap.

At her dorm, He kissed Cheryl goodnight and left her standing by the door. He considered calling Ariella but decided it was too late. At least with Ariella there were no hidden agendas. They each knew what they wanted and took it with no bill due. That thought caused an aching erection.

On Sunday morning, he rose late and went out to run. He sprinted around the last curve at the end of the lake, and past his driveway, slowed to a fast walk. His chest heaved and sweat ran into his eyes. He raised his arms up over his head to expand his diaphragm. He felt dizzy and bent forward, hands on his knees.

"You sure run a lot."

He didn't recognize the voice.

"Do you run around the lake every day? You must like to run. Everyone calls me Suzie. What's your name?"

He remained bent over. His stomach had crawled up into his throat and was attempting escape through his mouth. He raised his head. Blood pulsed, extending capillaries behind his cornea. His eyes focused and he saw a young girl perched cross-legged atop the stone wall in front of him. She couldn't have been over twelve. Her hair was tied back with a ribbon and she wore corduroy pants and a denim shirt.

"I'm sorry." He tried to slow his breathing. "What'd you say?"

"I said my name is Suzie and you must really like to run."

"Yeah, right," he said, straightening up. "Gotta keep in shape." He patted his abs.

She giggled. "But it looks like no fun."

"You're right," he said. "Now, that you mention it." He turned and started walking back toward the cottage. The girl jumped off the wall and caught up beside him.

"Are you at UConn? I'm in the seventh grade. I think I'll go to UConn. I really want to attend college in Rhode Island, but my father said I'd probably go to UConn and live at home. Doesn't that sound awful? Excuse me but," she almost stumbled as she hurried to stay up with him, "you didn't tell me your name."

"Jim. Jim Davis." He walked faster. "You always friendly with strangers?"

"Not always," she said.

"So, you're in the seventh grade," he said. "I bet your daddy keeps a gun by the door to keep the boys away."

"He doesn't like guns, and I don't have a boyfriend. Oh, there's boys at school that like me, but I find them so, well. . .immature."

Jim saw her glance at him.

"This is where you live, isn't it?" She pointed toward the cottage. They were at the entrance to his driveway. "Is it true you live with a Negro? The whole neighborhood talked about it when he moved in this summer. My father spoke to the police chief in town, but there was nothing they could do about it."

"Yeah, one of my housemates is black," he said. *Thought things were different here.* "But he's not what you call, 'a Negro.'"

"He isn't?" She looked confused. "But he's—"

Jim shook his head. "His father was President Kennedy's roommate at Harvard and is now the king of the richest gold-producing country in Africa."

"Really?" Her eyes widened.

"We don't talk about it. He wants to be treated like everyone else while he's in America. His name is Prince Ali Bama. He's the Crown Prince of Pisson. This is his last year at UConn. He's going back to Africa next spring for his coronation. I think President Nixon is going to be there. . .even Queen Elizabeth."

"Wow." She craned her neck to look up at the cottage. "A real prince right here at Andover Lake."

"Listen, Suzie." He leaned toward her. "Do me a favor and keep this a secret. His Majesty, the prince, doesn't want any special attention or anything. He enjoys his privacy, if you know what I mean." Jim winked at her.

"Oh, no. . . .I mean, I won't tell anyone." She backed away, looking up at the house. "I've got to go." She stepped forward and shook his hand in awkward formality, then turned and sprinted down the street.

CHAPTER 27

"**H**ey bros, you'll never guess what happened." Ali thundered into the kitchen where Jim and Joel were making tacos for dinner.

"I know, I know," Jim said, without looking up from dicing onions at the table. "Doctors determined that being black is a treatable skin condition?"

Joel choked back laughter and dropped a tortilla he was lifting from a pan of hot grease.

"Up your bony asses," Ali said. "I'm not kidding. I was in the village this afternoon and everyone, including wrinkly old white ladies treated me like a big shot movie star or something. Usually, I get looks that say 'get out of town, nigger.' Even the fat Police Chief crossed the street to ask if there was anything he could do to help me while I was here. I figured he was looking for some reason to bust me, so I just stared at him."

"Oh no." Jim laughed so hard he fell from his chair. Tears ran down his cheeks.

Joel and Ali stared at him on the kitchen floor. The room filled with the odor of burning grease and charred tortillas.

"What's so funny?" Joel said as he grabbed for the smoking pan before it burst into flames. Ali started opening doors and windows to air out the house.

"Okay. Okay." Jim gasped. "Let me catch my breath." He held on to the table and hoisted himself back into his chair. After several deep breaths and intermittent giggles, he regained his composure. "I don't believe this," Jim said, shaking his head. "I was jogging the other day and met this little girl from the neighborhood. She said people in town were nervous about a Negro living here at Andover Lake." He stifled another laugh. "I'm sorry, but I couldn't help myself." He looked at Ali. "I told her you were the crown prince of the richest country in Africa and were returning home next summer to be crowned king. I said your name was Prince Ali Bama." He paused a minute to wipe his eyes. Another giggle slipped out as his two friends began to understand. All three dissolved into howling laughter.

Ali pounded the kitchen wall with his hand, "Now, you gotta tell 'em that when I leave, I'm gonna give a ton of gold to the folks of every little virgin I screw. Tell 'em it's in my country's constitution and the U.S. State Department is keeping records and taking applications."

"Yeah, we'll say it's an act of high national service," Joel added, causing them all to shriek and fall apart again.

"But I told her it was a secret and she promised not to tell anyone," Jim said.

"The whole town knows." Ali shook his big afro. "Everyone was treating me like a rich white man. 'Yes, sir. No, sir. Please come again, sir.' Shit, I was one suspicious dude. I thought I was being set up for something. A black prince, huh?" Ali grinned, his white teeth dazzling. "That does it. This honky town just got itself one royal nigger. What country did you say I was from?"

"Pisson," Jim said, before he and Joel lost it again.

"Like, piss on ya?" Ali chuckled.

Jim nodded. He was laughing so hard he had no breath left to answer.

⊰⊱⬩⊰⊱

On Sunday night, Jim sat at the desk in his room trying to make sense of his notes in preparation for an upcoming Chemistry exam. His lab instructor was a Korean graduate student who had trouble with the English language. Jim's notes reflected it.

"What's the matter? You look like someone took away your pony." Joel stood at the bedroom door.

"Screw it." He put down his papers. "I'm trying to learn this stuff before midterms, but it's not sticking. I've read it three times."

Joel plopped down on Jim's bed. "That's not what I meant."

Jim frowned. "Then say what you mean. Don't practice your voodoo psych crap on me."

"Stay cool, man. I thought something might be bugging you the way you've been moping around the house, lately. Want to talk about it?"

"Sorry," Jim said. "I think now it was a mistake to come up here. Everyone advised against it, but I knew better. I had so many expectations. School's been going on weeks now, and I'm stuck in a rut. I go to class, come home and study. The next day I go to class, come home and study. I've been on two dates, one with a soul-eating siren, and the other with a master schemer. I could've done that in the army.

Pushing away from his desk, he went to stand in front of the window. He could see the neighbor's television in the cottage next door. "I also forgot how boring school can be. It's getting harder to get up in the mornings and go to class."

Joel stroked his beard and watched him. After a moment he spoke. "Hopefully this doesn't sound like a presumptuous psychologist in training but let me try something here. When you got out of the army, you left behind your identity developed over the last four years. The problem now is you haven't found a new one that's acceptable. You haven't found the square hole for your square peg. Forgive the pun." He grinned. "But the truth is, you've started the quest and that's the most fun. Most people don't realize that until it's too late. I mean, you knew who Lieutenant Jim Davis was, and tonight you're not sure about this new civilian in New England. And that's okay. You needn't worry until you stop trying to find out."

Jim looked out at the night. Everything Joel said made some sense. The anticipation of the journey, the discovery, is what inspired him to come to UConn in the first place. Perhaps the routine had dulled that vision. It was too soon to be second-guessing. He'd been here barely sixty days.

"Listen," Joel said. "You ever hear of an encounter group?"

He turned around and shook his head.

"It's been popular on the West Coast for a while at places like Big Sur and Sandstone, and now it's included in college curriculums. My graduate program this fall has one. There's twice as many girls as guys. We meet three times a week."

"Good odds," he said. "So, what happens in an encounter group?"

"It's hard to explain," Joel shrugged, "but we try to learn about ourselves and each other on a deeper level. The professor guides us through a few exercises. We interact one-on-one a lot and then come back together in the group and talk about the experience, our feelings."

He wrinkled his nose.

Joel tried again, "After the exercise we ask each other questions, like how we felt about the person we interacted with, and how we feel about what just happened. But the important thing is, each person has to tell the truth about their thoughts and feelings. Sometimes it can be a real downer learning that other people see through the defenses we put up, and the masks we hide behind."

"You mean," Jim said, "if you think someone's a liar, or has bad breath, or is ugly or unfair or something, you have to tell that person in front of the others?"

"Oh, that's easy," Joel said, leaning back on the bed. "The hard part is listening to someone say those things about you."

"I don't know." he shook his head. "Sounds weird. Would you take the class if it wasn't required?"

"Yeah," Joel said. "It's a fun course, but there are a lot of issues I need to work on that I've ignored for a long time. Also, there are some good things I have going for me that boost my self-esteem. See, the other side of the story also has to be told. You've got to be truthful about the positive stuff as well as the negative. It's easy to be critical, but personal growth comes when you see the good and the bad reflected back to you through people you trust."

Joel laughed. "I know it sounds like touchy feely, but all of us in the group have become good friends in a short time as we've learned about ourselves and each other on a deeper level. I'm telling you this because there's a guy in the department who's organizing a group off campus. He's looking for interesting people to join. I thought you might find it fun. It could also help you through this funk you're in. They'll meet once a week. If you're interested, I'll tell him tomorrow."

"Why haven't you said something about this before? You've been in this group for two months."

"It was risky." Joel shrugged. "You think I'm odd as it is."

"I'm game," Jim said. "Especially, if it's a good way to meet girls. You said something about finding a hole for my peg."

Joel laughed. "I hope my friend hasn't filled his group. I'll see him tomorrow in class." Joel turned and left him alone in his room, staring at his chemistry notes.

On the way to class the next morning, Jim thought about the encounter group. It could be an interesting break from routine. Sounded a little like Officer Candidate School where one learned about himself and others. The strong graduated with honors. Those with self-doubts gained confidence, and the weak perished. The army learned long ago that it couldn't take an asshole and produce a leader. Potts liked to say that assholes could sneak through ROTC but not OCS.

"You're in luck," Joel said when Jim sat down in the snack bar after class. "My friend has got an opening for one more guy. He wants to interview you at the Psych building this afternoon."

Jim frowned. "What do you mean 'interview?' Sounds like an audition. What does he do, award the spot to the weirdest guy?"

"Come on," Joel groaned. "You getting cold feet? It's to make sure the chemistry is right for everyone in the group. It can kill a group if the chemistry is wrong. How much fun would it be if everyone were just like you?"

"Okay, okay." he laughed. "Don't be so defensive. I'm being

honest about my feelings. I'll go see him." He looked at his watch and rose from the table. "What's his name?"

"Bernard," Joel shouted over the din as Jim made his way through the snack bar, "Bernard Lieberstein."

He found Bernard Lieberstein alone in a far corner of an empty classroom, his bushy eyebrows intertwined in serious contemplation of the open textbook in front of him. He could've passed for Joel's double. Chino pants, collapsed Hush Puppy shoes, wrinkled shirt, and short curly beard tagged him as a graduate student.

Bernard peered up at him through wire rim glasses. "You must be Joel's friend." He stood to shake hands. "Thanks for coming over. I like to have these little meetings before we decide whether the group will be a good experience for both you and me." He motioned to an empty chair. "This shouldn't take long."

Bernard sat back down and crossed his legs. His socks didn't match.

"To start," he continued, "I'd like to know more about you. Joel said you're from Texas, of all places."

Jim couldn't put his finger on it, but there was something unsettling about Bernard. Midway through their discussion, he caught it. Bernard avoided eye contact. His gaze was either directed to the floor when he spoke or fixed on some spot on the opposite wall. Jim remembered his high school coach's advice about not trusting anyone that wouldn't look you in the eye.

Jim asked Bernard about himself and how the group operated. Bernard's answers were vague on both subjects. Jim was surprised to learn Bernard received no payment or college credit for leading the group.

"I have personal growth needs that I'm able to meet by participating in these groups," Bernard said. "I enjoy the relationships that such dynamics create. I led two groups last semester, and I'm doing it again this year."

The interview went on for another hour. Several times Jim

shifted in his seat to put himself in Bernard's line of sight. Each time, Bernard looked away.

"Well, now," Bernard said in a let's-wrap-this-up tone. I do think we will enjoy your participation in our group. But there's one thing you should know before you make your decision. You will probably be. . .shall we say. . .the straightest person in the group? I'd like to know if you can handle that."

"What do you mean?"

"Joel may not have told you," Bernard said, "but my groups are a diverse mix of students and non-students, lifestyles and alternative lifestyles. There will be some so-called hippies who may experiment with drugs such as LSD and marijuana, some free spirits, a draft resister or two, people into different things. A person of your conventional background, small southern town, military officer, WASP, I think will bring an interesting element to our group. But I want to be sure that you can coexist with the others without, shall I say. . .freaking out."

Jim stared at Bernard. "I don't see a problem," he said after a moment. "I expected different kinds of people. Otherwise, I wouldn't join."

"Good, good." Bernard smiled, showing white teeth behind his trim beard. "We're starting with a weekend long session this Saturday. We'll meet on campus near the Home Economics Building at nine o'clock in the morning. I'm keeping the meeting location secret to avoid disruptive intrusions."

"What should I bring?" Jim stood.

"An open mind and perhaps a toothbrush." Bernard rose with him and extended his hand. "I look forward to knowing you better."

"I've got a question," Jim said, looking at Joel in his bedroom doorway. It was Wednesday night and Jim sat cross legged on his bed in his Jockey briefs. "What exactly are the rules for an encounter group? Bernard didn't cover them."

Joel shrugged. "That's just it, there are no standard rules. Just follow his direction. If he's good, and I hear he's not bad, he'll guide the group but not control it. The best advice I can give is get involved, don't hold back. This is one of those situations where you get as much out of it as you put in. It's kind of like sex in that way." He stroked his beard and grinned. "No one will make you participate, but it's not a spectator sport."

After Joel went off to his room, he lay staring at the ceiling. He wondered what the others in the group were like. How many girls? He hadn't asked, and Bernard didn't say. The sheets felt cool against his bare skin. He hadn't run in several days and promised himself he'd get up early to run the next morning. He set the alarm, turned off his desk lamp, and lay in darkness. He dreamed of Anita Beth. They were in her pink Impala. Her favorite song, *Teen Angel*, played on the radio and hot tears streaked her face.

On Thursday afternoon after classes, he spotted Ali in the lobby of the student center. Ali wore an army field jacket and combat boots and was handing out pamphlets in front of a makeshift booth. A red beret added to the paramilitary look.

"Hey," Jim called to him. "What're you selling?"

Several young black men in military fatigues stood around the booth. Their fliers announced an upcoming rally for the Black Panthers. A poster of a handsome young black man wearing a beret and sitting in a fan chair with a machine gun on his lap, provided the centerpiece of the booth.

"Hey, yourself." Ali glowered. "Donate some money here for a good cause. Everyone knows you southerners beat everything you got out of the backs of your field slaves." A glint of humor flickered in his eyes.

"I never hit anyone in the back." Jim said.

"Mother fucking, smart-ass whitey," someone said.

Jim swallowed a heated response, found a wrinkled dollar bill in his pocket and dropped it in the Colonel Sanders bucket on the table. "Anything to help a friend."

Ali turned to meet the glare of a thin boy with thick glasses. "Easy. His dollar is a hundred cents more than we had, brother."

"Fuck his dollar." The kid spat. "We need more than dollars to win this fucking war." The boy's defiance drained under Ali's gaze, and he returned to stacking pamphlets on the table.

Later that night, Jim lay in bed after the television went off the air, thinking about the events at the Student Center with Ali. He'd never encountered the anger and hate he saw that afternoon. A car door slammed, and he recognized the sound of Ali's boots in the hallway.

The next morning, Ali's snoring could be heard throughout the house. "How does he stay in school?" He and Joel were walking to their cars on the driveway. A cold nip was in the air, but the sky was a brilliant blue. "I've never seen him study. This Black Political League thing seems to be all consuming."

Joel tossed his books into his car. "There's lots of people like him on campus. They don't attend class but stay around to pursue their political agendas. Most leaders in the peace movement are doing it. All the protest rallies on campuses are not organized by students carrying eighteen-credit workloads.

"You know," Joel continued, "I fear we're headed toward a real revolution, and I don't mean flower power. If all the oppressed minorities get together, the blacks, the Native Americans, the poor, and if the anti-war organizations and all the anarchists join in, then I'm afraid this country will face one violent conflagration."

"And where do you come out on that?" Jim raised an eyebrow.

Joel gazed out over the lake. "Don't know. I'd like to think we can change without killing each other. Violence is foreign to my people's nature." He paused again and then grinned. "Right now, I'm just trying to finish a term paper titled 'The Significance of Number Dreams.'"

"Sounds pertinent." Jim laughed and opened his car door. "See you after class." As he steered his station wagon around the lake, a heavy sadness settled on him. Even the gorgeous fall day unfolding over the Connecticut countryside couldn't alleviate it.

He left his car in the parking lot and headed across campus

to his class in the chemistry building. He saw Cheryl Hollis tossing breadcrumbs to the ducks at the pond. She was pleasant enough to him in their English class, but his lack of interest had been recognized and accepted.

Later in the day, he and Joel sat on the deck at the cottage enjoying the last vestiges of Indian summer. He lay on a mat doing sit-ups while Joel lounged in a chair with a text book in his lap. "You know," Jim said, pausing in mid-sit, "I've asked Ariella out three times and she keeps turning me down. I'm not interested in a long-term relationship, but—"

"You don't know her," Joel said, closing his book. "As far as she's concerned, your hide is drying on the smokehouse door, as LBJ used to say. Anyway, you're not Jewish."

"What's that got to do with it?" Jim stopped his repetitions and looked at his housemate.

"Ariella grew up on a kibbutz in the desert. She's had a lover there since she was fourteen. They shared a crib in the nursery. She wouldn't risk a relationship with another guy when she knows she'll return to Israel and her Sabra boyfriend after finishing her graduate program."

"How do you know?" He leaned back on his elbows to catch his breath.

"I had a personal experience with Ariella last spring," Joel said. "My hairy hide is hanging beside yours on that smokehouse door."

He lay back, watching clouds drift across the sky. This was new territory for him. So was the first meeting the next morning of his new encounter group. It was to last through the weekend and involved people and a process he knew nothing about.

CHAPTER 28

"Call me when it's over and I'll pick you up," Joel said as Jim stepped out of his housemate's Volkswagen in front of the Home Economics building on Saturday morning. "I want to hear about everything that happens."

"I'll take notes." Jim shut the car door. "Thanks for the ride. I'll see you late tomorrow." He turned up the sidewalk and spotted Bernard with a group of people down by the pond. They all turned to look at him.

Bernard waved and started up the hill. "Glad you made it. Worried I might've scared you off. Come and meet everyone. We're waiting on a few more to arrive."

Bernard introduced him around. After shaking hands with some and nodding to others, he found a spot to sit on the dewy grass to wait. It was a cool morning and his sheepskin coat warmed him. His jeans were freshly laundered, and he wore his favorite blue button-down collared shirt. He reached for a twig and scraped mud off the sole of his boots.

Two more people showed up, and everyone greeted them like old friends. The new arrivals introduced themselves to Jim and joined the growing group. He saw he was the only guy who didn't have long hair. One boy had gathered his ponytail together with a tie that matched his Mexican serape. Jim had tried growing his hair longer but found it irritating on his neck and had visited the barbershop the day before the meeting. Looking around, he thought he stood out like a pig in a litter of puppies.

Bernard checked his watch. "Where's Trish? It's nine-thirty already."

"There." The kid with the ponytail pointed. Jim saw a petite blonde in belle-bottom jeans and a red sweater, coming down the hill from the parking lot. She waved.

"Good, good, good." Bernard rechecked his clipboard.

The cute girl moved about the group, hugging those she knew in twos and threes, with everyone squealing and chattering. Jim figured most of them had been in one of Bernard's groups before. *Encounter-group junkies.*

"Hi, I'm Trish Wallace." The new girl stood over him.

Jim pushed himself up off the grass. "Jim Davis." He took her extended hand. He stood a head taller and liked everything he saw. Long blonde hair framed sparkling blue eyes and a pert upturned nose. He thought of Tinker Bell in blue jeans.

"Welcome to the group. It'll be fun," she said, removing her hand but leaving the spell intact.

"Thanks, I'm sure it will." He hooked his thumbs in his jean pockets. Wanting something else to say, something smart and witty, he drew a blank. By the time his mouth had reengaged with his brain, she had gone to greet someone else.

"Okay everyone." Bernard stood atop a bench waving his clipboard. "Divide up and get in the first five cars in the parking lot. Those driving should follow me. Most of you know my van. Let's go, folks. We're running late."

Jim kept Trish in sight as he followed the crowd up the hill. He watched her walking with a tall kid wearing a red bandanna around his neck and butterfly patches on his Oshkosh B'Gosh overalls. The boy took an envelope from his pocket and put it into her hand. She cried out with delight and tiptoed up to kiss him on the cheek. At the parking lot, the group began filling cars.

Just ahead of him, Trish said something to a buxom girl in jeans and a white t-shirt. They locked arms and headed toward a blue Mustang. Jim followed, reaching the car just as Trish started the engine. She looked surprised to see him.

"Oh, Hi. We've got plenty of room," she said, bouncing out of the car and pulling the driver's seat forward.

"Thanks," he said, squeezing into the back seat. He nodded at the girl in the front seat. "Jim Davis."

"Janice Dansk," she said and turned to look out the window.

The line of cars followed Bernard's van through campus and past the football stadium. From the back seat, Jim watched another line of cars with blue and white ribbons fluttering from their radio antennas, pulling into the stadium parking lot. The scoreboard over the end zone read, "WELCOME UCONN ALUMNI -- 1969 HOMECOMING."

"Who are we playing? I didn't know it was homecoming. Bernard could've scheduled this next weekend."

"What?" Janice said without looking at him. "You mean the stupid football game? No one gives a damn. I haven't been to a football game since I've been here. Have you, Trish?"

Trish shook her head and was about to say something when the caravan accelerated through an intersection.

Janice turned toward Trish. "I had this incredible trip last weekend with this cute song writer from Hartford. I met him at a craft festival in Southbury. He was selling mimeographed copies of his songs. He invited me back to his apartment and promised to write a song about me.

"I don't know where he got his shit," she went on, "but it was the cleanest acid I've ever had. I mean no sick, shitty feeling that you get when they cut the stuff with speed or god-knows-what. This stuff was so mellow it made me feel through every pore in my skin. When we fucked, I completely lost control. I just melted into nothingness. You know what I mean?"

Trish wrinkled her nose and kept her eyes focused on the rear of Bernard's van. "I had an experience like that last summer in Boston," she said. "It was mushrooms a friend brought from Mexico. We didn't have sex, but we went to a Buster Keaton film festival in Cambridge. God, it was the grooviest."

Jim listened in the backseat, not saying anything. He caught Trish looking at him in the rearview mirror.

Janice pulled a joint out of her bag and struck a match. She took two deep drags, held it a moment, and exhaled a cloud of smoke. She turned around holding the joint up.

Jim smiled. "Maybe later."

"Good," she said. "More for Trish and me."

Jim gazed out the window. The acrid smoke in the car reminded him of the time he accidently set fire to an alfalfa field at the ranch with hot exhaust from a tractor. He didn't think they'd be interested in that story. Janice took two more deep drags and passed the joint to Trish.

"Speaking of good acid," Trish giggled, "Do you know where Coley Clark is this semester?" She and Janice were off again, exchanging stories about old friends from past encounter groups.

The caravan headed out of Storrs, and Jim settled back to watch the scenery. He felt a little bad about missing his first homecoming at UConn. It was the biggest weekend of the year at Texas Tech. Hotels sold out, and the big game was usually with SMU, Baylor, or Texas A&M. Everyone smuggled booze into the stadium in silver flasks to mix with Coca-Cola or Seven-Up. The student body stood to cheer throughout the entire game, which always left Jim hoarse for the rest of the weekend.

He thought of the Going Band from Raiderland storming into Jones Stadium before the game, high stepping to the pounding thunder of the drum corps positioned in the center of the football field. The band exploded into its own rendition of "Grandiose" and marched in stereophonic waves up and down the field. The masked rider on a spirited black stallion, raced into the stadium ahead of the fired-up football team. Homecomings are supposed to be like that, Jim thought as trees and houses and shopping strips flashed past his backseat window.

Other than the cute girl driving the car, his first impression of the group had been neutral at best. It was early to be making judgments, but Joel said to be honest. He wasn't sure he could be totally open about his inner most thoughts with a bunch of freaky strangers.

Jim watched Trish's face in the rearview mirror. She and Janice were carrying on an animated conversation. Her eyes sparkled, and her little nose crinkled up when she laughed. She moved a strand of blonde hair from her face and tucked it behind an ear. Cute girl, he thought. He glanced around the interior of her Mustang. *Cute girl and cute car*.

The caravan turned off the highway to continue on a gravel road into the woods. Bernard's van stopped in front of a two-story log cabin surrounded by tall pine trees.

"What a neat place." Janice said. "Whose pad?"

Trish shrugged. "I don't think it belongs to anybody we know."

Everyone unloaded from the cars and entered the cabin. The living room had been cleared of furniture, and pillows lay scattered about the brown shag carpet. Bernard signaled for all talking to cease and everyone removed their shoes and sat on the floor facing each other in a large circle. Jim placed his fleece lined coat on the carpet and sat on it. Morning sunlight streamed in through the windows. A quick count revealed seven girls and five guys. Everyone looked at Bernard.

Jim checked his watch and saw ten minutes had passed. They had been sitting in silence. He thought about addressing Bernard to request a review of the rules but didn't. He shifted his gaze from Bernard and travelled clockwise around the room, pausing to study each person. He sensed one other power center in the room besides him and Bernard. Janice Dansk sat four positions to his right. The three of them were positioned in the circle like a three-legged stool. Ten more minutes dragged by and nothing happened.

He looked at his watch and wondered if Joel's group had started, or rather. . . not started, this way. A few nervous giggles added to the tension. Everyone in the circle looked at each other then back at Bernard. More giggles broke out from a couple of girls sitting on the far side. They covered their faces with their hands. He looked at Bernard who grinned at their silliness.

"Okay, Bernard, what are we doing?" His voice cracked the silence in the room like a fart at vespers. "Let's get this thing started."

Everyone turned to him. He saw smug looks as each person in

the circle smiled knowingly. Bernard's bearded mouth blossomed into a grin, and Jim realized what everyone already knew. Bernard had his stooge.

"Okay, Jim. Please tell the group why you spoke first." Bernard's voice sounded unusually loud. "Why are you uncomfortable with silence?"

For the next hour, Jim spun himself into a cocoon while everyone took turns, led by Bernard, attempting to uncover the personality fault that caused him to be tormented by periods of silence.

"I think you are very uncomfortable with yourself." A girl he hadn't paid much attention to offered up her thoughts. "You don't like yourself, and that's sad. I mean, I used to be that way if you can believe it. I mean, you know. . .if you could just come to grips with the garbage inside yourself, and just say, 'It's me and I'm okay,' then you would feel a lot better." She glanced at Bernard for approval. "I mean, I think you're a beautiful person. Everybody has their own individual beauty, so you shouldn't punish yourself with this guilt trip. Am I right? Does everyone agree with me?" She looked around. Before Jim could respond, someone else started in with their own bullshit.

At one point he looked at Trish for help. She sat with her back against the wall across the circle from him, looking amused. When their eyes met, they momentarily held. She stifled a laugh and looked at Janice. He realized she wouldn't help him, but neither did she pile on. Lying back on the carpet, he gave up trying to defend himself.

When no one had anything additional to say, Bernard turned to him. "As you just saw, Jim, the only rules are to be honest with yourself and with the others in the group. Everyone should think of me as a participant and a guide, not the leader. I'll exercise authority only if I think a situation is getting out of hand, or if there's an important conflict to be resolved. Otherwise the group leads the group."

Jim closed his eyes. He had nothing to say. *At least things are moving, now.*

Bernard, the group's *non-leader*, introduced two activities. The first involved pairing up with the person next to you and communicating without speaking. In this exercise, in this encounter group with no rules, the *rule* was not to talk. The second activity was the same, except everyone chose the person they wanted to interact with.

Jim finished exchanging touches and exaggerated facial expressions with a guy named Franklin and turned to look for Trish. She was paired with Bernard. They sat on the floor in a corner of the room, facing each other. Their eyes were closed as they caressed each other's faces. Trish trailed her fingers over Bernard's hair and eyes. She paused a moment while Bernard's fingers caressed her lips. They look too comfortable together, then he saw the pale circle of skin on Bernard's ring finger.

He was wondering about Bernard's missing wedding ring when Janice pulled him to another corner in the room where they sat communicating non-verbally. He would have called it groping.

The session continued without breaks till mid-afternoon. At three o'clock, Bernard sent for sandwiches while everyone escaped outdoors to enjoy the autumn day. Jim stepped out on the porch and caught a glimpse of Bernard towing a girl named Renee up the stairs. Half an hour later, Bernard was back on the porch finishing off a sandwich. His feet were bare, and his shirt unbuttoned, exposing a thin chest covered with dark curly hair. Renee sat alone at the kitchen table, sipping a glass of water and staring out the window.

After the break, Bernard herded everyone back to the circle in the living room. Shrieks of delight followed his announcement that the rest of the session would be conducted without the distraction of clothing.

"You mean naked?" Franklin giggled.

Bernard ignored him. "No one should feel bad if you choose not to participate. Everything we do is voluntary. It's an individual decision, but I think this nude exercise will provide a new depth for our activities that we'll not be able to attain in our weekly sessions."

Jim looked across at Trish and raised an eyebrow. She whispered something to Janice, and they both laughed.

Bernard stood up. "You can leave your clothes upstairs in the front bedroom. Be back down in ten minutes. I've ordered pizzas to be delivered at nine-thirty. We won't be taking another break until then."

At first no one moved. Everyone scanned the circle to see who would be first. Joel hadn't prepared him for this.

Janice and Trish met him at the steps, grabbed his hands and ran up the stairs, pulling him behind them. The bedroom filled with nervous chatter while everyone stripped. A pile of clothes covered the bed as Jim made his way back down to the living room.

Two people had chosen not to participate in the nudity and sat on the floor watching everyone descend the stairs. He thought about covering himself with his hands but didn't. At the bottom step, he paused a moment and felt someone press against his back. Something bristly rubbed across his bare butt. Turning around, he found Janice laughing at his skittishness. Trish followed, her long blond hair covering her perky breasts. Nothing hid the dark curls below.

Bernard came down next, displaying a thin frame covered in fine body hair. It spread upward from his legs, over his soft belly and chest, across his shoulders and down his back. "Okay, let's get started," he said. "Everyone, return to your place in the circle."

Jim rested on his elbows, his long legs extending into the center of the circle. His circumcised penis lay heavy on his abs in a state of semi-erection. He smiled as several in the group shifted into more modest positions.

"Anyone want to share how they're feeling?" Bernard looked around the circle. "Renee, how about going first?"

"She's already been first." Franklin whispered to Jim.

Bernard frowned. "How about you, Janice?"

"I love this," Janice said, rising to her knees on the carpet. She sat back on her callused heels, her breasts swinging in front of her like two softballs inside a pair of gym socks. "I feel so free, so uninhibited being naked in front of people I love and trust. We should conduct all our meetings this way. What really surprises me though," she looked at Jim, "is how quickly our cowboy here got out of his duds. I mean, I thought you were this tight-ass, establishment kind of guy, but guess I was wrong. Look, you're, just letting it all hang out in front of everyone. I think it's beautiful."

Jim smiled at her and crossed his legs at the ankle. He remembered Joel's theory about it being more difficult to get an erection in public when naked. *He should see this.*

He had already learned something new about himself, and it was just their first meeting.

When another girl in the circle praised his lack of modesty, a surge of blood powered his penis, causing it to rise and slap against his stomach. He looked at Janice.

"That's so cool," she said, nodding her head. "This is what I like most about groups. You know, just being yourself with no masks to hide behind. Look at Jim." She gestured to him. "He's got a hard-on and doesn't care if the whole goddamn world sees it. It's all so natural, and I think you're all beautiful. You're my best friends and I feel like giving everyone a hug."

"Well," Bernard said, looking around the circle, "If that's how you feel, why not?"

Janice paused a moment to wipe her eyes. At the group's urging, she minced around the room, bending to hug every girl and guy to her ample breasts, with nipples like sundials. When she came to Jim, she knelt, straddling his legs, and enveloped him in her arms, pressing her breasts into his bare chest.

Over her shoulder, he saw Trish watching. She sat against the far wall, her knees drawn up to her chin. He smiled at her. The hint of a grin touched the corners of her mouth before she looked away.

The rest of the afternoon, he felt Trish watching him. The few times he caught her eye, she feigned interest in something else. When Bernard asked everyone to pair up for another exercise, Jim found her already matched. Once, she saw him approaching and turned away. He kept his distance after that, intrigued by her disinterest.

He guessed her to be five-foot two. Her fading tan revealed a preference for bikinis. She wore no cosmetics, and her breasts, neither large nor small, rode high on her ribcage. Naked as a wood nymph, she radiated the essence of female. He was stung.

By early evening, only one person in the circle had not joined the group's nudity. Nan, a dowdy housewife and mother of two, had joined the group to be with her friend, Elizabeth, a recent divorcee and single mother. Throughout the day, Nan sat away from the circle while Elizabeth participated in all the activities and sat naked among others young enough to be her children.

The pizza arrived as scheduled and Bernard announced a break. Empty boxes were soon strewn about the center of the circle. Bottles of beer and cans of soda were consumed. People conversed in muted tones. Renee sat beside Jim on the floor. He noticed she was a true red head. He remembered her going upstairs with Bernard during the afternoon break.

She was playfully tugging the hair on his lower leg with her toes when she stopped and stared past him. He followed her gaze and saw Bernard leading Elizabeth up the stairs. "Isn't he married?" he asked.

"Yeah. His wife and I are best friends," Renee answered. "We were all in high school together." She looked at Jim. "That surprise you?"

He shrugged.

She bit her lip and looked back at the stairs.

"It doesn't bother me if that's what you mean," he said. "I guess we're all trying to experience everything we can, doing, trying whatever we want as long as it doesn't hurt anyone else. That's what we're all searching for isn't it? True freedom."

"It doesn't hurt his wife," Renee said. "It's just between Bernard and me."

A moment of silence passed, and he flicked pizza crumbs from his pubic hair. He heard Renee giggle and saw her watching him. He grinned self-consciously and brushed himself clean. "If Bernard has needs that his wife can't fulfill," he said, "and you can, sounds logical." He leaned back, wriggled his toes and recrossed his bare feet at the ankles. He wasn't sure he believed it.

"Yeah, probably," Renee responded, her voice just above a whisper. She gazed back toward the stairs.

After the empty pizza boxes were removed to the garbage can, Jim found Trish napping in a corner with her head in Janice's lap. The others were clustered in twos and threes about the room talking quietly while waiting on Bernard and Elizabeth to return. When they finally came back downstairs, Jim checked his watch. It was eleven o'clock.

"What'd you guys do up there," Janice made no effort to conceal her annoyance. "read 'War and Peace' to each other?"

"Time passes slow for the rest of us when you two are having fun," another added.

Bernard smirked. "We were working some things out."

"More like working your thingy in and out," Janice said.

Elizabeth stood naked beside him caressing his arm. She threw her head back and laughed at Janice's joke. Her friend, Nan, winced.

At midnight, blankets were taken from a closet and distributed. The living room looked like a slumber party. The lights were turned out, and Jim had just gotten comfortable when his blanket lifted, and a warm body slipped under the covers. The intruder spooned backwards into him. He lifted his head and could make out only shapeless lumps around the room.

The identity of the person sharing his blankets was a mystery, but it was female. Her bare bottom pressed firmly against his stomach. He wondered if she were awake, if she had something particular in mind. Minutes passed, and steady breathing sounds came from his bedmate. She must be asleep, he thought.

He wished the same were true for his penis. It wanted to get up and go visiting. Bare skin touching him there didn't help. His raging hard-on pressed against his bed partner. She shifted, relieving the pressure. Jim turned away to face the wall. Her bare buttocks pressed back against his own, and he held his breath. Her steady breathing went on uninterrupted. More minutes passed, and his hand moved down to squeeze blood back into the rest of his body. His mystery bedmate turned and spooned against him, her breasts pressing into his bare back. Her hand snaked under his arm and lay across his chest.

Time passed without further movement. Interesting day so far, he thought, especially the little blonde and getting naked. He didn't like it when the group focused attention on him. He didn't like their speculating about secrets hidden in his psyche. It was none of their business.

Bernard's leadership reinforced something he had learned a long time ago. It's better to be the inquisitor than the subject, the hunter instead of prey, the officer instead of a private. The safest place to be was controlling the spotlight.

While his mysterious bed mate breathed on his shoulder Jim catalogued the other people in the group. Bernard had good reason to hide behind the spotlight. His encounter groups provided him a convenient way to get laid. Another surge of blood caused Jim to shift his position on the pallet.

The youngest in the group looked to be a couple, David and Cathy. They were hippies living on a farm commune somewhere near Storrs. He called her "my old lady" and she referred to him as "my old man" which Jim found funny since neither of them looked old enough to vote. They wore ragged jeans that exposed the knees, hiking boots, beaded headbands and matching gold loops in their pierced ears. After disrobing for the nude segment in the afternoon, they had clung to each other like two young chimpanzees. Janice told him that they were from Greenwich, Connecticut, and each had trust funds.

Rob, the boy who favored Oshkosh B'Gosh overalls, was the drugged-out son of a Princeton professor. When the session started that morning, he was operating at forty-five RPM's while the rest of the world ran at thirty-three and a third. Throughout the morning he had been funny and articulate. Bernard's rules forbade drugs to be brought into the group, so the rest of the afternoon, without an herbal or chemical boost, Rob's personality regressed to that of a sullen prison guard.

Kimberly, a skinny, sad-looking girl, never finished a sentence.

Whenever the group's attention turned to her, she wilted like salad in a hot oven. She was from New Hampshire and for most of the day had sat in the circle, braiding and unbraiding her hair.

Franklin was a classic mama's boy. His comments throughout the day had for the most part been embarrassingly inappropriate. Jim felt sorry for him because of the way he held his pudgy hand over his Cub Scout genitals during the nude session. Jim also sensed he had a crush on Bernard.

Elizabeth intrigued him almost as much as Trish. Her mature sexuality captured his and everyone else's attention. Being older and a mother, she was dangerous territory. It surprised him when she went upstairs with Bernard. This attractive sexy mother had fucked skinny, transparent Bernard and didn't care that everyone knew. Jim reached beneath the blanket to reposition a new hard-on.

Nan left right after the pizza, saying her family expected her home for the night. He felt sure they wouldn't see her again. He smiled to himself as he envisioned Nan's unsuspecting hubby getting an inspired romp in the sack that night from his needle-pointing wife.

He then wondered if Bernard's wife knew her friend, Renee, was screwing her husband. Renee was an aspiring singer. She played guitar and sung Judy Collins folk songs after dinner while everyone waited for Bernard and Elizabeth. Her voice sounded like crystal bells.

More than any others, big Janice, the Viking Warrior Queen, enjoyed the group's attention. She sought it, was nourished by it. She dominated most of the open discussion and volunteered first for every activity. Jim smiled to himself when he remembered her assault on David, the trust fund kid. "I can't believe you're not circumcised! I've never seen a dick wearing a sweater before. Can I touch it? It's so European."

Trish Wallace displayed a trusting friendly manner with everyone. The easy way she wore nudity during the day had a childlike innocence to it, but also a sexy vulnerability that in ancient times had launched armadas. Several times he'd caught her watching him but was still confused that she purposely avoided him. The warm body beside him sighed and turned. *Too tall for Trish and too slight for Janice.* Ruling out skinny Kimberly and clinging Cathy, left Elizabeth and Renee, both of whom had fucked Bernard that day. More reasons to not like Bernard. But which one?

CHAPTER 29

Across the room Trish lay under a blanket, eyes open, staring into the dark. An hour had passed since Elizabeth slipped under the covers with the cute Texan. No sound came from their blankets. *Why should I care if old Elizabeth screws the cowboy?* She closed her eyes. Warm air from a floor vent blew over her. Besides, there's Alec, she thought. Alec, her boyfriend in Boston, played saxophone in clubs around Cambridge and supported himself by selling ten-dollar bags of pot to students at Northeastern University. She thought he was a genius and that explained, like Mozart, his periodic fits of moody depression. His flare-ups were sometimes violent, but she was used to that from the men in her life.

Her father, an invalid and angry alcoholic, kept her family in a constant state of fear. After he lost his leg at the foundry, Trish had watched her mother grow old working day and night in South Boston to provide for the family. That'll never happen to me, Trish thought. *Never, never, never!*

With the blanket pulled up to her chin, she fell asleep and dreamed of cowboys and Jim Davis. They rode side-by-side on matching horses across a grassy plain with snow-capped mountains in the distance. He looked across at her and laughed, his blue eyes sparkling. He raced ahead, beckoning her to follow, but she reined up when two masked men blocked her way. She screamed in her sleep when their bandanas slipped, revealing the smirking faces of Alec and her father.

CHAPTER 30

Jim woke on Sunday morning to find most of the group up and already dressed. The aroma of perked coffee came from the kitchen where people had gathered around the gas stove for warmth. Whoever shared his bed was already gone. Remembering his clothes were still upstairs, he flung the blanket away and took the steps three at a time. "God damn, it's cold!"

When the coffee and doughnuts were gone, morning sun had warmed the cabin. Everyone returned to the living room to start the Sunday session. All seemed more relaxed than the day before, more comfortable with each other. Strangers no more. Perhaps being naked had helped. They found their places and sat on the carpet. His Levis hugged his legs and the warmth of his sheepskin coat felt good. He saw Trish's face still swollen with sleep. He smiled and winked at her.

"So how does everyone feel this morning?" Bernard looked around the circle. "I mean, after yesterday?"

"I'm empty, completely exhausted." Janice led off as usual. "The whole experience was draining. I mean, we all got to know each other on a whole different level and as we really are. The energy just flowed. Groups like that always do this to me. I can't wait till we start our Monday night sessions, so we can have experiences like that every week."

"And how do you feel about it?" Bernard shifted the spotlight around the circle to Jim.

"Uh. . .Okay, I guess." Jim looked at Trish. "It was okay." He held her gaze a moment, before turning back to Bernard.

Others spoke of their good feelings about the session, and

many claimed it changed their lives. Jim concluded all this was contrived for Bernard's benefit. When no one had anything else to say, Bernard introduced the weekend's final activity.

"It's what I call a Blind Walk," he said, his voice rising with enthusiasm. "This one will take a while, so we'll end the weekend with this exercise." The noise level in the room increased as everyone started chatting with their neighbors.

"Please listen-up," Bernard continued. "Each of you pair up with someone you haven't gotten to know yet and go outside to the woods. One of you close your eyes, and whatever happens, don't open them. It will spoil the experience. I repeat, keep your eyes closed. Your partner will take your hand and lead you on an adventure of senses like you've never experienced before. Guides, when you're finished, bring your partner back here to the cabin and switch roles. It's up to each of you to make it a special experience for the other. I leave you with two pieces of advice. Trust your guide when you're being led and take extra care of your partner when you're the leader. If there are no questions, take off and be back here in an hour."

Jim crossed the room toward Trish, arriving a second behind Bernard who had already taken her hand. She looked at him, then back at Bernard who was tugging her toward the front door. She turned back to Jim again. He held out his hand and spoke almost inaudibly, "Please?"

"Come on, Trish!" Bernard whined. "This one is mine. You said. . . ."

Fire flashed in Jim's eyes as he glared at the group leader. Trish pulled free from Bernard and reached for Jim's hand. Bernard stomped across the room, grabbed Renee away from Franklin, and disappeared through the front door.

Jim led Trish outside into the bright morning sunshine. Several pairs, holding hands like first graders at recess, moved into the woods in different directions. "Close your eyes and I'll lead first," he said. "I promise to take good care of you."

With a nervous laugh she closed her eyes and squeezed his hand. At first, she held back as he tugged her along. That soon changed, and she fell in step behind him. He took her down a gravel road and turned onto a trail threading through the woods. He guided her along a forest path strewn with pine needles, carried her across a rushing stream, and paused to let her fingers feel the bark pattern on an ancient tree trunk. He placed smooth river stones in her cupped hands and let her crumble dry leaves to confetti. They laughed. The only other sound in the forest was the wind high in the trees.

When time was up, he told her to open her eyes.

Trish hesitated, then did so and smiled. "Your turn now," she whispered. "Close your eyes."

They were deep in the woods when she stopped in a clearing where the carpet of fallen leaves had been made warm by the sun. She had him sit on the ground, Indian-style, and sat facing him. Grasping his wrists in her small hands she guided his fingers up to touch her hair and then slowly trace the contours of her face.

He smiled as his fingertips moved over her eyes, her nose and cheekbones, and came to rest on her moist lips. She kissed and licked each of his fingers and they both laughed. She guided his hands down her long slender neck and over her chest, finally bringing them together in her lap. He felt her studying him. Only the sounds of birds broke the silence. She lifted his hands to her breasts and moved his palms against her sweater. He grinned.

Trish rose to her knees and pulled him to his feet, balancing them both until he steadied. She let go of his hands and stepped away, leaving him alone in the middle of the clearing, standing tall and silent. She stepped forward and pressed her body into him. His arms gathered her to him. His hands cupped her little butt. Her hands went up behind his neck and pulled his open mouth down to her own.

Her presence in his arms was unexpected and her breath against his face made him blink. The first kiss was long and sweet, followed by another, hungry and biting, and then another. He felt her break away and then her cold face nuzzling into the warmth of his neck. For a long moment they held onto each other in the middle of the forest, each wondering how this moment would change their lives.

CHAPTER 31

Trish's blue Mustang slowed before turning off the highway onto the road that wound around Andover Lake. Late afternoon sun slanted through the trees.

"I appreciate the ride home." Jim held his hand out the passenger window catching the wind. "My housemate will be pissed I didn't call him. He wanted to pick me up and hear how it went."

Trish glanced at him from behind the wheel. "Then, why didn't he join us if he likes encounter groups?"

"He's already in one in his graduate program," Jim said. "After this weekend, I don't see how anyone could handle more than one at a time."

Neither spoke as the car followed the shoreline. The lake's placid surface reflected fall's colors on the surrounding hills. He grinned and shook his head.

"What's so funny?"

"I was just thinking about how weird this is."

"And what's that supposed to mean?"

"Well, here we are, both of us feeling a little awkward as we navigate our way through the boy meets girl stuff after we just spent a day and night with each other naked. I'm confused about what the next step should be."

"Me too," she said, laughing. "I keep thinking about you sleeping with Elizabeth last night and how I'm supposed to handle that little fact with everyone in the group knowing it."

"That was Elizabeth?"

Trish gave him an "as if you didn't know" look.

"I really didn't know," he said. "It was dark and. . . .It sure screwed up my night. I kept waiting for something to happen and it didn't. It was after three in the morning before I finally went to sleep."

"Well, she implied you two got it on," Trish said, keeping her eyes on the road. "Every time someone asked about it this morning, she rolled her eyes and said, 'It's as good as it looks.'"

"You're kidding." He clapped his hands together and laughed. "I swear I didn't know it was her till just now. I also swear on my mother's grave that nothing happened. We just slept."

"Your mother's dead?"

"No, that's just something we say in Texas that doesn't mean anything but—"

"Well, everyone saw her crawl under your blanket. Janice was so angry this morning, she wanted to pull Elizabeth's hair out."

"That would've made for a memorable weekend," he said. "But what about you?"

"What about me?"

"How did you feel?"

She shrugged. The car rounded a curve and they sped on in silence.

"Okay. Let's start over," he said. "Let's start from the beginning, like normal people. Pretend we just met. Okay, so how 'bout going to a movie with me tonight?"

"Thanks, but no." she responded, not taking her eyes off the road. "Perhaps, another time."

"No?" He looked at her. "What do you mean, no?"

"I'm not easy." She winked. "I make it a rule to turn down every guy the first time he asks me out.

"Even if he's seen you naked?"

"Especially if he's seen me naked."

"Does that happen often?"

She stuck her tongue out at him.

"Okay, okay, I can handle rejection as well as the next guy." He gazed out his window. Neither spoke for a moment. He turned back to her. "Would you go to a movie with me this evening?"

She glanced at him out of the corner of her eye.

"You didn't say how much time had to pass between asking."

"Oh. . .Oh, all right," she said after a long pause. "You Texans are so persistent. "I'll meet you at the theater in Storrs at seven o'clock." She grasped his wrist and looked at his watch. "That's in three hours."

"Why can't I come by your place and pick you up?"

The car swerved around a tight curve, and she grasped the wheel with both hands. "I'll meet you there. It's easier." She slowed for another sharp bend. "Maybe, next time."

"Whatever you say," he said, looking back at the road. "Turn in the next driveway on the left. It's that white cottage up the hill."

He stood on the grass watching flashes of blue through the trees until her car disappeared around the lake.

"Well?"

He turned to see Joel behind him. "Well, what?"

"First, who was the cute little blonde in the Mustang? And second, how did it go? I want to know everything; every exercise, every word, who said what to whom. How did Bernard do as a leader? I've been waiting around all day to hear how it went."

"She's just a girl in the group," Jim said, looking back across the lake to see if he could spot her car. "And not much happened. At least nothing worth talking about." He turned and took the steps up to the cottage with Joel hot on his trail.

"Nude? The whole group?" Joel's eyes widened as they stood in the kitchen. "You're kidding."

Jim took a beer from the fridge and went outside to the deck. He plopped down in a chair and opened the bottle.

Joel pulled up a chair. "You mean naked? Everyone?"

"Almost. One person held out for some reason. It was no big thing." Jim tried to sound nonchalant about it but in retrospect, the whole weekend seemed unreal. He'd have to tell Potts about it.

"Damn, my group hasn't done that." Joel's voice brought him back to the moment. "We probably can't since we're part of the university curriculum. I can see the dean giving the Trustees a tour of the psych clinic: 'And in this lab full of circumcised hard-ons and copulating coeds, our clinical psych students are studying prurient perversity. Mr. Joel Zippen, the hairy Jew giving it to Miss Wetsler there on the desk, is one of our top students, and his father is a very important man in Albany.'"

Jim blew beer spray across the deck as both he and Joel laughed.

"So, who's the good-looking bird in the Mustang?" Joel wiped his eyes with the tail of his t-shirt.

"Don't really know yet," Jim said, settling back in his chair and resting his boots on the deck rail. "But I'm going to find out starting tonight." His voice trailed off as he looked out over the lake. "This one's different."

"The Sterile Cuckoo" at the Storrs Theater proved to be a tear jerker. Liza Minnelli starred as an awkward teenager trying to hold onto her boyfriend after he went away to college. Jim held Trish's hand in the dark. Out of the corner of his eye, he saw tears streaking her face. He felt helpless and wanted to take her in his arms and hold her. When the movie ended, and the credits rolled, she buried her face in his chest and sobbed. Afterwards, they walked in the cold night air across campus talking about everything and sometimes about nothing. It was late when they arrived back at her car in an empty parking lot. He put his arms around her and pulled her against him.

She nuzzled his neck with her cold nose. "I really had fun tonight. I'm glad you don't take no for an answer."

He lifted her chin and kissed her warm lips. Her tongue explored his mouth.

She moved her fingers up his chest and pecked kisses over his face and neck. "What time do you finish class tomorrow?" she whispered.

"Three o'clock." He arched his neck when her lips found a sensitive spot.

"Meet me by the duck pond at three." Her tongue started a

slow journey from his ear down his tensed jaw. She stepped away, blew him a kiss, got in her car and drove off.

On Monday, they spent the afternoon browsing through the bookstore across the street from the college. Afterward, she followed him in her car out to the lake where Joel joined them for dinner at an Italian restaurant. Around midnight, she left to return to the house near Coventry that she said she shared with two girl friends from Boston.

The rest of the week, he met her every afternoon and they ended each day at his place for coffee and more conversation. On Thursday evening, midnight came and went, and she didn't leave.

"Do I need to use a. . . ." he started to ask. They were on his bed in his room.

"Shhh," she pressed a finger to his lips. "It's okay, I'm on the pill."

He took his time exploring her body with his hands and his lips. After placing a kiss on the inside of her leg, he felt her shiver. His mouth moved higher.

"Oh. . . ." She shuddered, her back arching off the bed.

He held her against him until her breathing slowed. Afterward, she pushed him onto his back, and he watched in the dark as she explored his muscular frame. For hours they moved together, both hungry for each other. He went slow at first, choreographing her petite body on his bed. When dawn lightened the sky outside his bedroom window, she dozed on top of him.

He felt her breath on his chest and wondered who this Trish Wallace was, and who else she had loved. He pushed a strand of blonde hair away from her face and cradled her closer. If the world ended at this moment, his life would be complete. She was the missing piece of his puzzle and he was lucky to have found her. No other girl had ever affected him this way. Not even Anita Beth. Is this for real, he wondered. Is this how it's supposed to be?

CHAPTER 32

Sunlight on her pillow woke her. She felt his presence in the bed and turned to look at him. He lay on his side facing away from her. She smelled his musk, his cologne, his essence. She scooted closer, and he reached behind him to pull her nakedness up against him. His hand brushed between her legs where she was swollen and tender. She leaned in and kissed his bare shoulder, wishing they could stay in bed forever. She started to say just that then remembered today was Friday.

CHAPTER 33

In the snack bar that afternoon, Jim carried two cups of coffee back to their table. He had finished his last class of the day and had found her waiting for him. "So, what should we do this weekend?" he asked after she kissed him. "I thought we might stay out at the lake and—"

"I can't.." She glanced away. "I'm driving to Boston. I haven't told you, but I go home every Friday and come back on Sunday."

"Oh," he said, sticking his bottom lip out like a petulant child. "What about our group meeting last weekend? You didn't go home then."

"I know." She touched his arm. "That was a special situation."

He took a sip of coffee and stared into his cup.

"I'm sorry if I'm ruining your weekend," she said, grasping his hand in hers and entwining their fingers. "But I've got to go. I always go home." She patted the back of his hand and stood up.

He watched her rise and swallowed hard. "But, I thought we could—"

"Please don't make me apologize again." She came around the table and kissed him on his forehead. "You'll have to find someone else to play with on weekends. I have to take off. If you're around Sunday when I get back, maybe we can see each other."

"Yeah, call me." He forced a smile. "I have to write a paper this weekend, anyway," he lied.

"I didn't mean that about finding someone else," she said softly. "I'll try not to be too late on Sunday." She pulled his face down and gave him a long kiss. "See you then, cowboy." She turned and left.

He moped around the house all weekend. Ali had gone to New

Haven for a meeting, and Joel accompanied his parents to a health conference in New York where his father was the featured speaker. On Saturday morning, Jim did some sit-ups on the living room floor and read a few chapters for his economics class. He had trouble concentrating and kept going to the window to watch rain pepper the glass. He ate cereal for lunch and took a nap till four in the afternoon. Nothing on television interested him. He thought about calling Elizabeth in their group, to see if she wanted to meet for dinner but decided against it. He found a Leon Uris book, "Mila 18," Joel left in the bathroom and read until two in the morning. It was still raining when he fell asleep.

On Sunday, he stayed in bed till noon to finish the novel. He put on a pair of sweats and made a breakfast of toast and a can of creamed corn he found in the pantry. Around five o'clock, the Philadelphia Eagles were losing by two points to the New York Giants on television with a minute to go when the phone rang.

"Jim, is that you?"

"Trish?" His spirits soared. "Where are you?"

"At my house in Coventry. The drive back in this storm took forever. Did you miss me?"

"God, yes. I read a book and got some work done." He noticed it had quit raining.

"Do you have plans for dinner? I could come over."

"I want you for dinner," he growled into the receiver. "Hurry up and get your cute little butt over here."

'Oh, you did miss me." She laughed. "I'll be over after I say hello to my housemates. I passed Jennifer and Anne Marie on the highway coming back from Boston. They should be here any minute."

He was showered and shaved when her Mustang turned into the driveway.

She stood on tiptoes in his living room with her arms around his neck. Her leather headband, denim mini-skirt, and knee-length moccasins made her look like a hippie Indian princess. "I've got a big surprise for you." She giggled.

"Oh, I've got one for you, too." He rubbed against her.

"That's no surprise," she said. "But I brought us back some hashish a friend laid on me." She held up a small leather bag with fringe on it, like an Indian medicine bag. "We did some at a party in Cambridge last night, and it blew me away. I think I'm still a little high."

He released her and went to stand at the living room window. It was dark, and the lights were on in the houses around the lake. "I don't know," he said. "I've got more reading to do for class tomorrow."

"You've never done hashish, have you?" She stood beside him and ran her hand over his back.

"I've never done anything like that. Not that I haven't wanted to, but—"

"I'm sorry," she said softly. "This is a very personal thing. No one should ever force it. Maybe we could—"

"No!" He turned to look at her. "This is as good a time as any. But you've got to help me. I don't even know how to smoke a cigarette."

"Don't worry about that." She put the bag on the mantle. "We'll use my water pipe."

After splitting a can of chili for dinner, they sat facing each other on the floor of his bedroom while he watched her prepare the pipe. He still wore the jeans and white socks he'd had on all afternoon. Trish had showered and put on one of his t-shirts. The only light came from the lamp on his desk. Trish struck a match and held the flame to a tiny green ball of hashish till it smoldered. She then sucked the water-cooled smoke through a rubber tube into her lungs and held it. Passing the end of the tube to him, she indicated for him to do the same.

His first few draws on the pipe did nothing. Then a sudden rush took his breath away. A few more long draws and he settled back against the bed frame. A mellow feeling smothered any lingering anxiety. The dim light from the desk lamp brightened into a carousel of vivid colors. He felt giddy, much like after drinking a few beers but without the bloated feeling. "So, this is what everyone's talking about," he said, grinning so wide he felt like his face would split. The sound of his voice boomed in the small bedroom. He laughed and rolled on the floor toward Trish.

She fell against him, giggling, and they wrestled around on the carpet next to his bed. She paused on top of him and looked down into his eyes. "What do you think?"

"It's dynamite," he said, gazing up into her dilated pupils. A serious look crossed his face. "Did anyone ever tell you your eyes are like cameras for your brain?"

"Uh oh," she said. "You really are stoned. You're getting heavy on me. Promise you won't."

His gaze had already focused on a water-stained ceiling tile and he didn't answer. The shape of the stain looked something like the state of Texas with Oklahoma attached at the top. There was even a darker spot on the tile near the Panhandle where Morrison should be. He wondered why he had never noticed the stain before since it was directly above his bed.

He watched Trish get up and pad barefoot into the living room to put a record on the stereo. While she was away, his thoughts turned inward. Why was he so worried about this? "The Smothers Brothers Comedy Hour" and "Laugh-In" made dope jokes in prime time on television. It was fun and funny, but it was also illegal, and that still worried him. Trish turned out the lamp on his desk and rejoined him on the floor. He lay next to her in the dark, listening to the Moody Blues on the stereo and tried not to think of those poor bastards in Texas who had traded years of their lives in state prison for the same experience.

They undressed each other. The sensations, heightened by the hashish, cascaded through his body like rushing water. He came first, then slowed and timed his second to the shudder that wracked her body. On Monday morning, they awoke in his bed wrapped in each other's arms. He was surprised to feel as good as he did. There was no hangover, nothing like what usually followed a bout of alcohol.

Sun streamed through the bedroom window and warmed the top quilt. She encircled his growing organ with her little hand and tormented his ear with her tongue. Morning classes were forgotten when she sat astride him. Afternoon classes were fleetingly considered.

That night they attended the encounter group's first Monday meeting. Jim sat next to Trish and wondered if the group suspected. The meeting was short, mostly Bernard doing a monologue on the importance of truth in relationships before he adjourned the session and led Renee to his van. Jim shook his head. *What a hypocrite.*

For the rest of the week, he met Trish after class at the student center, or by the duck pond if the weather was good. Most nights she stayed over and drove back to her place in the morning to change clothes before class. She had become a window to a new world for him. She spoke reverently about her time in August at the Woodstock music festival in upstate New York. She read him poetry, gave him hot oil massages, and helped him look inside himself, to be sensitive to his feelings. When she made love to him, it was as if they were the only two people on the planet.

He hadn't said much about his life growing up on the ranch and knew nothing about her life in Boston. It was a subject she skillfully avoided. "I wish you didn't have to go again this weekend," he said on Friday afternoon as they walked across campus to her car. "I mean I thought you might stay and we could—"

"James, please stop it," she said, reaching for his hand. "You're smothering me when you do that. I go to Boston every weekend. You know that. If you can't deal with it, maybe we need to think about this before it goes any further."

As she drove away, he stood alone in the parking lot, like Prince Charming, watching Cinderella run from the ball.

The weekend dragged by as he awaited her return. On Saturday, he called Potts in Virginia and found that he was away. The voice on the phone at the house in Arlington sounded unfamiliar. Must be a new housemate Jim thought as he hung up. He spent the rest of the weekend watching football games on television and worrying Trish might still be upset with him when she returned. He also couldn't help but think about the possible reasons why she went to Boston every Friday. Could there be someone else? When she showed up on Sunday evening, he apologized for his selfish behavior.

"I missed you, too." She nuzzled his ear and kissed him.

After the first couple of weeks, their group meetings on Monday nights became a distraction. He had no interest in developing meaningful relationships with anyone other than Trish and counted the minutes until the session ended, usually by eleven.

Janice had turned into a real grump with nothing positive to say about anyone or anything, and he didn't fail to notice Elizabeth's flirting glances and not-so-subtle come-ons. He knew Trish saw it, but she didn't say anything. After a while, Bernard seemed to lose interest in the group and failed to show up two Mondays in a row. In his absence, Janice took over as moderator. At the last meeting, she screamed so loud at Franklin that he peed in his pants. There were other things Jim would rather do on Monday nights, but Trish still wanted them to participate.

Autumn's colors faded, as did his enthusiasm for school and class work. On the second Friday in November, he waited for Trish in the student center, picking at a sandwich.

"Oh, chicken salad with walnuts," she said, sitting down in the chair across from him. "My favorite."

"I'll get you one." He started to get up.

"No, no. Stay." She grasped his arm. "I'll wait a few more hours and let you buy me a real dinner."

"But today's Friday?"

"I know," she said. Her eyes sparkled. "Surprise! I'm staying here with you this weekend, so we can play. I'm not going to Boston."

He grabbed her hand and kissed it all over while she giggled. She hadn't said why this weekend was different. He was just thankful he didn't have to spend it alone.

That night they went out for pizza and a movie and came home and went to bed. He took his time and tried to make it extra special.

Her soft moans inspired him. In the early morning hours, he lay beside her, feeling her heart beating fast. He got up to get her one of his t-shirts and found her asleep when he returned. He slipped into bed and pulled her close against him. *What made her stay this time? Why is it different? Why can't it be this way every weekend?*

On Saturday morning he rousted her for a walk in the mist-shrouded woods behind the cottage. Dead leaves covered the forest floor. He helped her climb over stone walls and stopped to point out blue eggshells cracked and dried to the bottom of an abandoned bird's nest. In a small clearing they sat cross-legged facing each other. They closed their eyes, clasped hands and attempted transmitting thoughts to each other. Moments passed and neither moved. He heard the whine of an eighteen-wheeler somewhere on a distant highway. The sound evaporated on the wind. He felt her stand up.

In his mind's eye, he saw her standing a short distance away, watching him. The crack of a twig alerted him a moment before a load of leaves and laughter rained down on him. Jim reached behind and pulled a foot out from under her. In a flash, he covered her in a leafy crypt while she wriggled and squealed and begged him to stop. He dropped down on one knee and cupped her face in his hands. "I love you, Trish Wallace."

She studied his face framed in brown leaves. "What?"

"I said, I love you."

She closed her eyes and raised her lips up to meet his.

When they returned to the cottage, the aroma of fresh perked coffee met them at the door. The kitchen table was set for three. Glasses of orange juice had been placed beside chipped china plates. Joel stood at the stove tending a pan of sizzling bacon. "Hope you guys are hungry."

"I'm famished," Jim said, grabbing Trish and lifting her up in a bear hug of coats, hats and mittens.

"Me, too." She placed a quick peck on Jim's lips and pushed away. She hung their wraps on hooks near the door and watched Joel lay out crisp strips of bacon on a paper towel. "Can I help?"

"Put out cereal and milk," Joel said, carrying a platter of scrambled eggs to the table. "Nothing fancy, here, but lots of it."

"Are the other guys around?" Jim asked, sitting down at the table. "I haven't seen either of 'em in a week."

"Jankowski went home for the weekend, and Ali hasn't been here in three days." Joel shoveled a spoonful of corn flakes into his mouth. White speckles of milk dotted his beard. "At least his bed doesn't look like it's been slept in. I heard he's in New Haven preparing street protests for the Bobby Seale trial scheduled this winter at the Federal Courthouse. The Feds claim Seale gave orders to the Black Panthers to knock off an informer. Ali clammed up when I asked him about it. It's supposed to be bigger than the Chicago Seven trial. A lot of rich people in New York are raising money for Seale's defense."

"I think the government's railroading him," Trish said, sipping her coffee. "Black people just want to be treated like human beings. I wouldn't've had their patience. I would've gotten a gun a long time ago."

"Hey," Jim broke in. "Don't spoil a beautiful Saturday morning discussing—"

"You have a twin sister, Trish?" Joel winked at her.

Jim laughed. "What would your folks say if you brought home a Catholic girl?"

"Mother would cry and claim I didn't love her. Then she'd make me feel guilty and get my father to take her to Florida. But my old man would slip me a hundred bucks and whisper, 'The blondes, son, the blondes are the best.'"

"He's right." Jim smiled at Trish across the table. "They're pretty amazing."

After breakfast, the three of them tossed Joel's guitar into Jim's station wagon and drove to nearby Coventry to visit Nathan Hale's monument, a granite tower in the town cemetery honoring the Revolutionary War hero. Jim parked on a side street, and they strolled through the tidy graveyard looking at interesting markers. Jim paused in front of a small granite head stone.

ETHAN MYLES NORRIS
Feb 4, 1762
Died At Birth In Christ's Arms

"Come look at this one," Trish called from two rows over. When they reached her side, she stood in front of a gray sandstone marker worn nearly unreadable by the passing of time.

PORTIA MALLORY
1726 - 1786
Repent ye sinner
Standing there reading this
For one day ye too
Will be rotting in this cold cold ground

Joel rubbed his beard. "A jolly soul, wasn't she?"

"Life of the party in Coventry," Jim said. "Danced at parties with a lamp shade on her head."

They stood for a few minutes pondering Portia's admonition from the grave until Trish pulled them in the direction of the car. "Come on," she said, "Let's get some wine and cheese and crank this party up."

They found a spot on the stone wall across from a convenience store in the village and finished off a bottle of Sangria. Trish fed each of them bites of cheese as they watched two couples, one carrying a sleeping toddler, come out of the antique store next door to the service station and get into a sedan with New York plates. A damp wind made the day feel chilly even though the sun had broken out of the clouds.

"Ol' Portia probably never felt whiskers against her cheek much less touched a man's pecker." Joel twisted the cap off their second bottle of wine and passed it to Jim.

"Reminds me of a widow back home," Jim said. "She wrote letters to the newspaper complaining the youth in town were going to hell because we listened to Satan's music on the radio while driving our cars up and down Main Street. She claimed it would lead to dancing and sex."

"Did it?" Trish raised an eyebrow.

"Sure did." Jim winked and took another bite of Brie. "She was a virtual oracle."

At the cottage that evening, the three shared the last of Trish's hashish on the floor in front of a fire while James Taylor's "Sweet Baby James" played on the stereo. Jim gazed into the flames. They'd had fun today. So much fun he hoped she'd want to stay in Storrs from now on instead of going to Boston on weekends. This wasn't the time to bring it up. *It's still too early. Perhaps tomorrow.*

James Taylor's acoustic guitar, the wine, and the contents of Trish's water pipe made everyone drowsy. By nine o'clock, she had fallen asleep with her head on his lap. He bade Joel good night and carried her to bed.

They both laughed as he struggled to pull her tight jeans off over her hips, and she unbuttoned his shirt. Their lovemaking was sweet and languorous and afterward they slept naked in each other's arms.

Someone's banging on my bedroom door. Jim's muddled mind careened around the cold room. He looked at his watch. It was nine-thirty, *and it's Sunday.* "Yeah? What?"

Joel stepped into the room and closed the door behind him. Trish lifted her head a moment and lay back on her pillow. Joel wore the same clothes he had on the night before. The imprint on his swollen face indicated he had slept on the carpet in front of the fire.

"There's a guy on the deck asking to see Trish," Joel said in a hushed voice. "I've never seen him before. Says his name is Alec. Says he's here from Boston to see Trish."

She opened her eyes and raised her head to look at Joel.

"Someone at your place told him you were over here."

"Oh, God!" She buried her face in her pillow.

Jim didn't have to ask.

Joel looked at him. "What do you want me to do? What should I tell him?"

Jim threw back the blanket and sat on the edge of the bed with his bare feet on the floor. "Say she's getting dressed. Have him wait in the living room. We'll be out in a minute."

While Joel tended to their guest, Jim slipped on a pair of briefs and snapped the elastic around his waist. Trish sat up in bed covering herself with the sheet. "I'm so sorry. I should've told you."

"Why didn't you?" He pulled on his jeans and buttoned them.

"I was afraid."

"Afraid of what?" He brought the ends of his belt together and cinched it tight around his hips.

"I'm not sure. I guess of losing you both."

"Get dressed," Jim said.

"There may be a fight," she said almost in a whisper. "Alec is like that. He can be—"

"Sounds like a neat guy. Must be fun." He wanted the barb to sting.

Deep down, he had known all along, but like a mouse in the house, thought he could live with it if it just stayed out of sight. This morning, the rat was in the living room.

Jim felt like an adulterer caught red-handed in his paramour's bedroom, but he became angry remembering this was his house and his bedroom. He brushed a hand through his hair. *The son-of-a-bitch asked for it, showing up here with no warning.* "Get dressed and come out after me."

When he opened the bedroom door, he saw her bury her face in her pillow.

"I'm Alec Reed." A thin boy with long dark hair extended a hand toward him. "You must be the Texan."

"Right." Jim grasped the hand firmly. "Jim Davis."

"Yeah, Trish told me about everyone in your encounter group," Alec continued. "Is that bastard, Bernard, still sticking his hands in every girl's pants? One day I'm gonna. . . ." He made a fist.

"Great place here," Alec continued, stepping to the living room window and looking out at the lake. "I'm glad she has good friends here at Storrs. It makes it easier when she's alone during the week." His skinny jeans hugged his narrow hips and his too small t-shirt exposed a soft belly.

Jim said nothing.

"I understand you guys have a tough exam coming up." Alec glanced back over his shoulder. "I felt sorry for her studying all weekend and drove out to surprise her. What's a guy from Texas doing here at UConn?"

Jim shrugged. Alec's chatter sounded strained.

"Sorry to take you all by surprise this early in the morning."

"How about some corn flakes or juice?" Jim went into the kitchen. Alec followed and sat at the table. "I knocked on her door and told her you were here," Jim said. "It'll be a bit before she's ready." *This asshole thinks this is some kind of sleepover.*

In the kitchen, he caught Joel's attention, and Joel began playing his part in the charade. He filled three mugs with coffee and brought them to the table. "There's more," he said, sliding a mug in front of Alec. "Jim here kept the coffee pot percolating all weekend with the exam he and Trish have been, uh. . .studying for."

Alec put sugar into his cup and stirred it with the spoon from the sugar bowl. "Say, I copped a batch of great hash in New York last week. I can lay a gram on each of you for just my cost. This stuff's the best." His eyes darted back and forth between them.

"Great," Joel nodded. "I'd like some." He raised his eyebrows at Jim.

"None for me," Jim said, rising from his chair to get milk. He shut the fridge door and returned to the table. Alec was cutting a glob of paste from a green ball. He rolled it in foil and had just pocketed Joel's ten spot when Trish appeared in the living room.

"Good morning," Joel said before she gave away their game. "Alec here says he drove over to surprise you."

"Yeah," Jim joined in, "And thanks for staying last night and helping us through those math problems." He looked at Alec. "She's an Einstein when it comes to calculus. Our exam tomorrow is going to be tough."

Trish looked back and forth from Jim to Joel like a spectator at a table tennis match before Jim saw she got it. She sat on Alec's lap, put her arms around his neck and kissed him on the cheek. "Hi, Baby."

"Hi, yourself." Alec pushed her away and blew on his coffee.

Jim clinched his fists. He wanted to drag Alec out of his chair by his long hair, but this was not his matter. Whatever happened had to be her decision. If he forced it, he might lose her. She'd chosen to stay with him for the weekend and had lied to Alec. I can wait, he thought to himself. *I can wait.*

Trish moved to a chair. "Isn't this a far-out cottage with the lake and all?"

"I already said that before you came in," Alec replied. "Took you long enough to get dressed. Guess you missed that."

Jim stood at the door and watched the two of them walk down the driveway to Alec's car. Trish looked deep in explanation. He turned and saw Joel looking at him.

"You okay?"

"I'm going to get dressed."

In his room, he put on a shirt and thumbed the buttons into place. He felt somewhat relieved there hadn't been a fight. Not that he was afraid of Alec or any other man when he knew he was in the right. But this time he wasn't so sure. This time he was the trespasser. He sat on the edge of the bed and pulled on his boots. The bed creaked as he stood to check himself in the mirror. He felt less vulnerable fully dressed. His eye caught something on the floor between the bed and wall and he reached to pick up a pair of panties. He imagined Trish looking for them that morning and abandoning her search in desperation. He tossed them on his bed and left the room.

Joel was wiping the table when he entered the kitchen. Jim poured another cup of coffee and sat at the table. He started to say something when an angry knock blistered the front door. Joel opened the door and a hand shot forward, palm up.

"My hash." Alec looked wild-eyed. "I want my fucking hash back."

Joel reached into his pocket and handed Alec the ball of aluminum foil.

Jim rose from the table. "What's the matter?"

"What do you mean, 'what's the fuckin' matter?'" Alec sputtered. "I come here as a friend and find you've been fucking my girl. If I had a gun I'd—"

Jim glared at him. Alec diverted his eyes.

"Let's take this outside," Jim said.

The cold air braced him as Alec followed him out. They stopped at the stone wall edging the woods behind the cottage and faced each other.

"Where's Trish?" He clinched and unclenched his fists. "I didn't see her in your car."

"I don't know where she is." Alec looked down at the ground and pushed his hands into his jean pockets.

"What do you mean you don't know?" he said. "I saw her leave with you."

"I said I don't know!" Alec's eyes darted about. "She jumped out of the car by the highway and ran into the woods."

"And why'd she do that?" Jim's voice rose. "Why'd she jump out?"

"I. . .I don't know. Just leave us alone? We were fine till you stuck your big—"

"Why did she jump out of your car?" Jim took a step forward. "You've got to the count of three."

"I don't know," Alec's voice dropped to a whisper. "Maybe she was afraid." He looked away, licked his lips and shivered. He looked like he hurt all over.

Jim took another step toward him. "Why would she be afraid?"

"Uh. . . ."

"Why? Dammit!" He grabbed Alec's arm and shoved him to the ground. He drew back his fist. "Answer me, you little asshole, or—"

"I only slapped her." Alec's eyes were wide. "I. . .I asked if she screwed you, and she said she did. I saw red. I stopped the car and then I. . .not hard. . .just a, you know, just a slap."

Anger blurred Jim's vision. His nostrils flared.

"Just a little slap," Alec went on. "It scared her more than hurt. She jumped out and took off into the woods. I was so angry. I came back here to get my hash, and. . . ."

"And what?" Jim said through gritted teeth.

"And punch you out." The last part of the sentence was almost a whisper.

Jim took a deep breath and pulled Alec to his feet. Alec brushed dirt from his jeans.

"Okay," His voice was steady, "for some reason she doesn't want to make the hard decision, but she has to choose. I learned about you just this morning. I suspected, but—"

"That's why I drove to Storrs," Alec sputtered. "She started talking about this new guy in her group. She quit calling during the week and was never at her place when I phoned. When she said she wasn't coming to Boston this weekend, I came to see for myself."

They studied each other for a moment. Alec looked away. He folded his thin arms across his chest and looked out toward the lake.

Jim picked up a stick and threw it into the woods. "You should know," he said in a strong voice, "I love her."

Alec spun about. "Yeah, but you don't know her. Man, I mean, I know everything about her. You'd drop her like a hot rock if you knew."

"I'm finding out more every day," Jim said, "At least she's not afraid of me."

Alec turned back to the lake. After a few moments he spoke, "So what do we do?"

Jim picked up another stick and looked at Alec. "You drive back to her house and wait. She probably hitched a ride home. If she shows up here, I'll bring her over. After y'all talk, I want to speak with her. As far as I'm concerned, she's got to make a decision, a clean break from one of us. I'll take that chance, because I won't go on like this. I promise you and I'll promise her, that I'll abide by whatever decision she makes. And Alec," he narrowed his eyes. "I expect you to do the same."

"That's what we should do." Alec uncrossed his arms and looked at him. "I'll be as happy as you to get this over. She's got to choose."

Jim saw Alec's spirits had elevated. *Maybe he thinks he has a better chance with her, or, he's relieved I'm not going to beat the crap out of him.* "Alec," he said through gritted teeth, "if you ever hit her again, I'll kick your ass so hard you'll have to blow your nose to shit!"

The phone rang once before Jim answered it. He glanced at his watch and saw it was past five o'clock. There was a pause, and then he heard her voice come over the line.

"Are you mad at me?"

He swallowed the lump in his throat. "You okay? Did he hurt you?"

"I'm fine. I caught a ride home. I'm just embarrassed."

"When can I see you?"

"I know we need to talk, but I can't right now. Alec told me what you want me to do. I'll tell you my decision tomorrow. I've promised him that, too. Meet me at the student center when you get out of class."

"I love you," Jim said.

"I know."

CHAPTER 34

The night seemed like it would never end. Jim stared into the dark, his thoughts careening around, bumping into people and events past and present. He closed his eyes and saw the strained look on his mother's face when he left home for the army; his father's scowl. A parade of people passed in slow motion: Coach Dowling at the football field. John Henry behind the wheel of the ranch pickup, Linda Sue next to him, eyes brimming with tears.

Like a spinning carousel, the faces of Anita Beth and Frank Brown, Michelle and General Redding, Sis Potts, Ariella, and Billy Thompson all twirled faster and faster, blending into a stream of color. The spinning disk slowed, slow... slower. When it stopped, he saw Trish. Tears streaking her face. She tried to smile. The sound of his voice calling her name pierced the dark. He opened his eyes.

A glance at the alarm clock by his bed revealed only minutes had passed. He turned toward the wall, the bedding bunched at his feet. Like the accused in a prison cell, he waited through the night for the jury to determine his fate.

Dammit! I know better. Once again, his happiness lay in someone else's control. Years had passed after Anita Beth moved away when he was a freshman in high school, but the memory of that loss still pained, like an old football injury that never healed. A reminder of the time he zigged when he should have zagged.

He thought of what Linda Sue told him the day she married his brother. There were only scant references to her in his mother's letters. "Everyone's doing fine," she began each note, followed by news about church, the football team, and recent funerals. He wondered if Linda Sue had told John Henry about them. *Does she ever think about me?* He hoped not. . .sort of.

He'd been careful about letting another girl capture his heart after losing Anita. *At least until now. Until Trish.* But like a backsliding alcoholic staring at an empty booze bottle, he'd done it again. *Maybe I should get out of bed and phone Potts. I could use his no-bullshit advice.* How long had it been? A card had arrived at the cottage during the first week of class addressed to:

The former Lieutenant James Baxter Davis."

Your departure from the army caused Hanoi to sense our weakness and increase military pressure on Saigon. The President has called a National Security Council Meeting to determine how to fill the void. All Lieutenants with little peters have been ordered to standby.

Looking forward to seeing you at Thanksgiving. Be sure to get a haircut, you hippie commie.

Miss ya, Cowboy,
Potts

It was hard to believe three months had passed since he left Washington. Several times he'd started to write Potts only to abandon the effort when words failed to adequately explain the new things happening to him. Also, in the back of his mind lingered the probability that Potts wouldn't approve.

Potts often boasted about the Potter family's generations of tradition, while Jim knew little of his family history. He once saw an early photograph of Baines at his Aunt Sassy's home in Waco. He'd been looking through a box of family photos and came across a black and white of a young man wearing a wide-brim hat angled to one side. Baggy trousers were tucked into cowboy boots and a pistol hung holstered on his hip. He was leaning against a porch post, his arms crossed.

"Why, that's your daddy." Aunt Sassy had said. "Every girl in Bosque County swished her skirts in front of him, and I know a few hearts he broke, too. Your daddy'd scold me if he knew I was telling on him."

There were a million questions he would someday like to ask Baines but knew he never would. Tonight, he wanted to know if his father had ever known love *and lost it.*

Another glance at the clock removed any doubt the night was refusing to let go. Jim turned on the bed once more, pounded the pillow with his fist, rotated it, pounded it again, and flopped over on his back. *Come on. . .Don't look at that damn clock.*

Settling noises from the cottage cracked through the darkness like faraway rifle fire. He wondered what Trish was doing this very moment. He thought of Alec. He pounded his pillow again and stared at the glowing dial beside his bed.

Jim closed his eyes and attempted to clear his mind, but synapses kept firing. He saw Trish sitting on the grass by the duck pond; her laughter rang across campus like a clear bell. Students and ducks paused to watch her. She stood up on her toes like a ballerina and twirled around and around, her long blonde hair swirling about her face.

The picture changed, and he saw her across a table from him, her eyes downcast. She said she decided to return to Boston with Alec and couldn't see him anymore. She spoke so softly. He blinked hard, again, again, again, until the scene erased. Just before dawn broke, his mind found refuge in fitful sleep.

On Monday morning he woke late and jogged twice around the lake, blowing off his classes. At two o'clock the snack bar buzzed with students having a late lunch. After negotiating his way through the noisy room, he sat at a corner table littered with the remains of the previous occupants. David and Cathy from the encounter group stopped to say hello but moved on when it was obvious his thoughts were elsewhere.

At three o'clock, he searched the crowd for Trish. At four o'clock, he left the table to call her house. The phone rang and rang but no one answered. He returned to the snack bar, reclaimed his table and scanned the flow of students. His heart jumped several times when he thought he spotted her.

At six o'clock, he looked at his watch. It was time to give up. Her absence screamed her answer loud and clear. *Dammit!* He leaned forward on the table and rubbed his face in his hands. It's probably better this way, he rationalized, trying to dull the pain that drilled into his core.

He pushed through the glass doors out into the cold evening air and headed across the quadrangle toward the parking lot. He could only think about putting one foot in front of the other. Faceless people passed him on the sidewalk. *Maybe this is another dream. Maybe it's the middle of last night, and I'll wake up and go to campus tomorrow and she'll be there waiting for me.*

At the edge of the parking lot, he paused. Had someone called his name? There it was again. Behind him. He spun around and peered into the dusky evening. A figure ran toward him. In the dim light, he could make out blond hair. He caught her in mid-leap and swung her high into the air.

"Oh god," Trish hissed, planting kisses all over his face. "I was so worried I'd missed you. You weren't in the student center, and I was afraid." Tears spilled down her cheeks.

He held her against his chest, buried his face in her hair and inhaled her scent. "Where were you? I'd given up."

"I went to Boston this morning to collect my things from Alec's place. I'm so sorry. I didn't think I'd be this late, but he wouldn't let go."

Jim stiffened. "Did that son-of-a-bitch…."

"No, no." She shook her head. "I'm okay. It was difficult for a time, but after a lot of discussion and tears, he finally understood it was over. I needed to be clear about that with him. Did you think I wasn't coming?" She pushed back from his embrace and looked up at him, her eyes red and puffy. "Oh, my poor baby, I'm sorry if I worried you. I always make you worry."

CHAPTER 35

Within the week, he had moved his things from the cottage at Andover Lake into Trish's room at her house in Coventry. "Better me here with three girls than you the only girl in a house with four guys. Besides, it hurts my heart when we're apart."

"And you're a poet and don't know it." She wrinkled her nose and laughed.

Her other two housemates were not unhappy to have him living there.

"He's cute," Jennifer McCabe said his first day there as she rolled a fat joint at the kitchen table. He had gone to their room to put his things away. "This must be serious stuff between you two now that Alec is out of the picture." Jennifer raised the white torpedo to her lips and licked it to seal the edge.

"Not that serious," Trish said, taking the lit joint from Jennifer and dragging smoke deep into her lungs. "There's no exclusive commitment or anything." She passed it on to Ann Marie Farelli who had just joined them. "He and I've talked about how to define our relationship, and we're in agreement. He's special to me as I am to him, but we need to be prepared for the unexpected. Things never stay the same forever, in life or in relationships. Change is the constant. We're going to enjoy it as it is and not make it something it isn't. That's how I got in trouble with Alec."

"And he agrees with that crap?" Ann Marie coughed out a lung full of smoke. "Where does that cowboy hide his angel wings?"

"He's very cool." Trish stifled a giggle. "And very mature and doesn't require more from me. It gets rid of the artificial stuff that screws up relationships. He's going to keep his room at Andover Lake, so we won't feel like we have to be together. I'm so proud he can repress the male instinct to dominate."

"Hope that's the only male instinct he represses." Ann Marie raised an eyebrow. "Is it true what they say about tall Texans?"

Jennifer laughed. "Trish told me he's a large caliber, and I don't think she was describing a pistol in his pocket. The three friends laughed until their sides ached.

The girls' house on Fox Trail in the village of Coventry was only a few miles from campus. The beauty parlor scent of powders, perfumes, and soap, most of it Ann Marie's, permeated the three-bedroom summer cottage that sat on a hill overlooking Coventry Lake. The single bathroom was cluttered with drying undergarments and lots of glass bottles containing compounds, creams and conditioners that fell from the crowded shelves, window sill, and the back of the bathtub whenever Jim opened and closed the door.

As the outsider, he tried extra hard to be helpful by keeping the place picked up, washing the dishes each night after dinner, and waking the girls every morning with a fresh pot of coffee. Before retiring to their rooms at night, they all gathered around the television in the living room and watched Dick Cavett wrestle wits with a literary giant or tease some busty Hollywood bimbo.

During their first weeks together, Trish didn't say much about her family. The subject remained off limits for some reason. She didn't like the war in Vietnam but mostly was apolitical. He learned that she loved poetry, art and music, and introduced him to Ralph Waldo Emerson and Rod McKuen. It intrigued him that she toyed with drugs as casually as she did, the mind-altering kind, as opposed to hard addictive stuff. Sex was also something that she seemed casual about. She had gone on the pill as a college freshman. Each morning he watched her select the day's allocation from a circular plastic dispenser; a routine like brushing teeth.

"Man, you need to come by the house and meet the girls," Jim said. He and Joel were having coffee before morning classes. "Especially, Ann Marie. She's one sexy chick with the biggest rack." Jim held his hands out in front to demonstrate. "Trish said her father is the dry cleaner king of Boston. Big bucks there. I'd fix you up, but she's dating some speed freak from New York. Anthony comes up from the city every Friday, and they disappear into her room. On Saturday afternoon, he crawls out looking like a dog's chew toy, and she bounces out all glowing and chatty. It breaks my heart." Jim shook his head. "I don't know what she sees in the skinny punk. Her daddy'd kill the little junkie if he knew. He'd slam dunk him through one of his wash and rinse cycles."

"But she's not Jewish." Joel shrugged. "Mother would disinherit me and use the money to plant a new forest in Israel if she thought I was going out with a Catholic girl."

Jim laughed. "You'd convert tomorrow if you saw the way she hangs out at the house without any clothes on."

Joel's eyes widened. "You're kidding."

"Nope." Jim shook his head. "Buck naked except for jewelry. No one's modest when it's just us girls around. Ann Marie keeps the heat up in the house to be comfortable, and I sweat through my clothes."

Joel took a pen out and wrote something in a notebook.

"Come over one night and we'll fix tacos," Jim watched his friend return the pen to his bag. "I can't wait for you to meet them. If Ann Marie doesn't float your boat, there's always Jennifer. She's a drama major. She plays Led Zeppelin at full volume in her room which drives her poor dog, nuts. He's an Irish Setter." He paused a moment to sip coffee.

"Oh, Trish said you should come over this weekend. They're throwing a party on Saturday to introduce me to their friends. A crowd is coming out from Boston."

"Is Jennifer Jewish?" Joel set his cup on the table.

He shrugged. "Jennifer McCabe? Probably Irish."

"Definitely Catholic." Joel shook his head. "My mother would shit."

Cars began arriving at Fox Trail early Saturday morning. Most were students at colleges in and around Boston, and some were dropouts living communally around Cambridge. The uniform was bell-bottoms, beads, headbands, and ponytails for both males and females. Trish introduced Jim to each as they arrived and then ran off to ensure everyone was having a good time. Jennifer's record player was moved out into the living room, and Led Zeppelin blasted at full volume.

By late afternoon, smoke in the house blurred all vision, and drugs had modulated everything except the ever-pounding rock music. People sat in clusters around the living room, while a few stared into space as psychedelic compounds slowed the world on its axis.

Bottles of cheap wine were passed around to soothe raw throats. He drank two bottles of Boones Farm through the afternoon and got a serious buzz. Feeling like he might throw up, he twice went to the bathroom and stood at the sink looking in the mirror while nothing happened. After dark, someone changed the albums on the stereo, and Ravi Shankar and his sitar set the mood for the rest of the night.

Trish joined him in the corner behind the floor speakers where he had attempted escape from the loud music. Ringo, Jennifer's Irish Setter, lay with his shaggy head in Jim's lap, eyes closed while Jim scratched behind his ears.

"Having fun, baby?" She kissed him. "Sorry I haven't spent much time with you, but I was making sure our friends were taken care of. I haven't seen some of these freaks in years."

"What about Ann Marie and Jennifer? Can't they. . . ."

She rolled her eyes. "Ann Marie went to her bedroom with Anthony over an hour ago. He popped some speed, so they're gone until tomorrow morning. Jennifer did mescaline with her cousin, and they're grooving on carpet patterns on her bedroom floor. That leaves me."

"Well, what about us?"

Trish reached into the pocket of her denim bell-bottoms and

withdrew a tin aspirin box. She opened it, selected a curious white pill and held it up to his mouth. "Open wide."

"What?" He pulled away from her hand. "What? What is that?"

"Be a big boy and open your mouth," she said, laughing. "Come on, trust me. There." She dropped the pill on the back of his tongue.

He pulled a swig from a bottle of wine. Trish picked out another pill and put it on her tongue. She drank from the bottle and handed it back to him.

"What was it?" he asked, taking another swig.

"Just a tab of acid," she said with a mischievous grin. "It'll take half an hour before you start to feel anything, so relax. I'll be back by then to share the trip."

He watched her go into the kitchen and get into conversation with a tall girl in a peasant dress and long blonde braids. His heart started to beat faster. He felt angry and anxious. But there was nothing he could do about it.

An odor of burning pine needles filled the room. Jim pushed himself up off the floor fearing the house was on fire. He saw the incense stick a guy was lighting in a brass burner on the coffee table and settled back.

The smoke spiraled up from the burner and formed identifiable shapes. At the same time, the interior walls of the cottage began undulating like the belly of a harem dancer. The drab colors in the carpet and furniture pulsed. His gaze jerked about the room, seeing everything for a second. . .a minute. . .an eternity.

"Beautiful, isn't it?" said a sexy voice beside him.

He wondered how long Trish had been there. But time seemed irrelevant; a difficult concept to think about. Seeds of thought came and went, too elusive to hold. Looking deep into her eyes, he saw a stranger. *She's probably seeing into me, too.* He blinked and looked away. *Had she noticed? Did she see?* He felt adrift, unfastened, exposed—vulnerable.

As he held onto her hand in the corner of the dark living room, his thoughts careened through space and time. Every now and then, he focused on something familiar which gave him bearings, a sense of place, a feeling of security. He knew the drug distorted everything, but like riding a raging roller coaster, he had no alternative but to stay on it to the end.

A boom of laughter made him jump. The sound stopped as soon as it started. His eyes darted about searching for the source. His mind locked onto the identity of the laugher. It was him.

Five hours had passed since he'd swallowed the pill. During that time, poetic truths were revealed to him by Led Zeppelin, the Doors, Mountain, and other rock groups. A million eureka experiences, one right after the other, synapses popping and crackling....

On the back side of the trip, he and Trish clung to each other. *Where does she get her little bag of psychedelic surprises she never seems to be without? And how much does she have left?*

Activity in the house was like watching a movie on a close-up screen. Strangers chatted in groups and intimate whispering pairs. He didn't feel part of it. He had difficulty understanding anything being said because he heard everything. Nothing was filtered. Sounds poured into his receivers at full volume. One person laughed and from twelve feet away—like a camera with a zoom lens, he saw into the open mouth and down the throat. He noted the cavities, counted the silvery fillings, and gagged on the foul breath.

When he thought sad thoughts, he fell into a terrible depression. Funny thoughts entered his head, and everyone turned to look when his belly laugh boomed out into the room. A guy with dirty bare feet strode through the room licking the inside of an Oreo cookie and Jim felt his stomach rumble. *Oreos, peanut butter and jelly, brownies, cheesy pizza! Oh god. . . .*

Standing on unsure legs, he made his way to the kitchen. He stopped in the doorway, his dilated eyes adjusting to the overhead light. A boy with a ponytail and bloodshot eyes, sat at the kitchen table. He had his sleeve rolled up and a piece of rubber tubing tied around his bicep. A fat vein glowed blue on his forearm. The kid picked up a syringe and raised the cross-shaped apparatus to the light, like offering up a prayer. A clear droplet appeared on the tip of the needle, sparkling like cut crystal. The spike punctured the arm and pumped in its contents. The needle popped free, and Jim winced. A thin line of blood trickled from the fresh hole.

The young man placed the empty vessel on the table and closed his eyes. After a moment, he opened them; an embarrassed grin revealed a row of broken teeth. Jim made his way back to Trish in the corner, forgetting why he had gone to the kitchen in the first place. His mother would fear for his soul if she saw him now. Baines's admonition rang in his ears, *"Be sure your actions bring honor on yourself and your family."*

He closed his eyes and saw his father sitting in the empty bleachers of a football stadium. He saw himself in the middle of the field explaining to Baines that the rest of the world was different. That people held disparate values and what one considered wrong, wasn't necessarily wrong for another, and he believed everyone should experiment, see for themselves, taste forbidden fruit. *Why is it wrong if it hurts no one? Who set you up to judge?*

Baines cupped his hands around his mouth and called down to him. The words sounded faint - like they were carried on the wind. *"When in Abraham's house, ye will do as Abraham says.'"*

Jim felt a weight on his arm and opened his eyes. Trish had fallen asleep against him. Lingering traces of acid were causing sporadic rushes through his nervous system. An incense stick smoldered in the darkness. The room smelled like a dying campfire. He pushed Ringo away and stretched out on the floor beside Trish.

Sometime later, he woke in the dark to grunts punctuated with moans coming from the sofa. He lifted his head and recognized the junkie from the kitchen and the girl with braids like Heidi. Her dress lay on the floor and her braids dangled over the arm of the sofa. The couple moved together, her bare legs scissoring his rising and falling flanks.

A short time later, a cold misty dawn had broken over the New England countryside when a muted whimper woke him. In the gray light, he saw the pair on the sofa still going at it. The boy standing behind now, holding both her braids in his fist like bridle reins. Their pale bodies glistened. He remembered the boy injecting liquid lightning into his veins. She can thank the pharmacist for her Priapus, he thought to himself.

Morning sun had burned away the fog on the hills when he felt Trish move beside him. He rubbed sleep from his eyes. An afghan covered the couple on the couch. The room smelled of sex and sandal wood. When he sat up, Ringo raised his head, and Trish turned toward him. He leaned down and whispered in her ear, "Good morning." He brushed blonde strands away from her puffy face and kissed her cheek. "Your little nose is cold."

"I'm freezing all over." She squeaked and pulled her blanket closer around her neck.

"Goddamn it! Who shit on the floor?" A voice growled from down the hall. "Fuck, yes, I stepped in it."

"Way to go, Ringo!" Jim scratched the big dog behind his ears.

After a shower, shave, and a clean shirt from his closet, Jim returned to the living room to discover the house filled with mouth-watering aromas. He entered the kitchen, expecting to see an army of people putting the morning repast together. The all-night lover, sat bare-chested and alone at the table, surrounded by good things to eat. Cinnamon rolls rose brown and sugary in the oven, a pitcher of orange juice crowned the counter, and platters heaped with bacon and eggs were on the stove. Amphetamines had provided the girl a memorable night on the couch and would also feed everyone in the house a morning feast.

Trish perched on Jim's lap at the kitchen table feeding him the last cinnamon bun. He swallowed and frowned, "Why didn't you tell me it was acid?"

"I wasn't sure you would take it."

"Maybe I wouldn't have," he said with mock concern. "But I would've appreciated being given the choice."

"Are you mad at me?" She batted her eyelashes at him.

"Where'd you get it?"

"Why? Are you a narc?" She held up another bite of the sticky bun.

"Nope." He grinned. "I just hope there's more where that came from. I don't want last night to be my first and only ride on a magic carpet."

"You liked it didn't you?" She smacked a kiss on his cheek. "You really did like it. Far out! I think that's so groovy. Don't worry your cute head," she said, mussing his hair and making him laugh. "I can get all we want."

She slipped off his lap to go chat with Jennifer and Anne Marie in the hallway. He smiled as he watched her go, but behind his eyes, on the battleground of his conscience, something lay wounded.

CHAPTER 36

November's days slipped away like brown leaves from the big maple tree in the front yard. Weekends were parties at Fox Trail or friends' apartments. Monday night group meetings turned into gabfests—the war, good grass, who was doing who, where, and when, and good rock music. The Beatles were still mourned after their break-up that summer, but groups like Poco, Buffalo Springfield, James Taylor, and a thousand others created enough good music to make it a short wake.

On mornings at the snack bar, he no longer let himself be drawn into debates about the war. Often in the past, he'd realized too late he'd been baited, and his arguments fell on closed minds. Besides, it wasn't his fight anymore.

The drugs Trish kept in the house no longer worried him. Her stash didn't include hard stuff like smack or cocaine. "Tried it once," was all she'd said. "No fun."

Jim considered himself an experimenter. Grass only made his throat sore. Hashish intoxicated for a few hours like a six-pack, but LSD provided a twelve-hour ride on a ballistic missile. He asked Joel about it one morning at the snack bar.

"There can be consequences beyond just what you do to yourself." Joel wrinkled his brow. "The Connecticut State Police wouldn't think twice about tossing both your asses into jail for illegal possession. Just be careful and keep my phone number in your wallet."

His class attendance had dropped from regular to rarely, and he was living more and more in the moment. Sometimes, usually in the middle of the night, pangs of guilt needled him. Two days before Thanksgiving, he called Potts in Washington. The crisp efficiency of the Pentagon operator made him sit up. "Mr. Davis, Lieutenant Potter will take your call, now."

"God damn it, Cowboy." Potts' voice came over the line. "Why haven't I heard from you? Thought you fell in a hole up there. But all's forgiven if you—"

"Sorry, Potts, I can't make it to Ridgefield for Thanksgiving. My girlfriend and I are staying up here to take care of some neglected schoolwork. Our housemates are going home, so we'll have the place to ourselves. It's a good chance to catch up."

Long silence.

"Uh, okay. . .too bad, Jimbo." Potts said. "We do what we have to do. Mother will be disappointed. She'd planned pecan pie for you instead of our traditional pumpkin. I also hoped we could have a fling of sorts before I turn in my combat boots next month."

"Hey, I almost forgot that. Trust me, it will feel a lot different being plain old Potts Potter out in the world instead of Lieutenant Potter."

"Can't wait," Potts said. "My room has been packed for weeks. The new housemate is coming by tomorrow. Looks like our old place in Arlington will carry on with another round of warriors."

"Have you seen the general?" Jim asked. He started to say *and Michelle*.

"Not lately," Potts said. "I hear Michelle is attached to the hip of Captain Kip Hagrid. Remember that brown noser? He's an aide-de-camp over at the Joint Chiefs."

Jim didn't reply, and Potts continued. "We'll miss you at the turkey table, Cowboy. Let's get together soon. You say there's a girlfriend? Good work. I want to hear everything that's happened these past four months. God, it seems like a year."

"We'll do that soon, okay? I hope y'all have a great Thanksgiving."

Jim placed the phone in its cradle and crawled back into bed. Potts had sounded disappointed. He hoped he wouldn't stay pissed for cancelling on him. He hadn't said anything to Trish about Potts' invitation to Oak Lawn for Thanksgiving thinking she'd go home to

Boston to her parents. Last night she surprised him when she said she wanted to stay at the cottage with him over the break.

It was already mid-morning, and the girls had left for campus. The paper due today in his English class lay unfinished on his desk. He pulled the covers over his head and tried to sleep. Someday he would tell Potts everything. He flipped over on his back and stared at the ceiling. *And why do I think I need his approval?*

Thanksgiving Day was gray and rainy outside and dark and chilly inside the cottage. He and Trish clung to each other in bed until two in the afternoon when the acid they had taken finally surrendered its grip. A roaring fire in the fireplace warmed the cottage. He slipped on a pair of jeans and shirt and went barefoot into the living room to watch the University of Texas and Texas A&M football game on television. Trish labored in the kitchen, preparing a dinner of baked chicken and other good things. Mouthwatering aromas from the oven, together with marching band music, lifted his spirits. Whenever the camera panned over the crowd at the game he looked for John Henry and his parents.

Trish flitted in and out of the kitchen, asking him to taste things. She wore one of his bulky wool sweaters over a long skirt that brushed the top of her yellow socks. Her blonde hair was shiny from her shower and smelled of apple blossoms. She looked adorable.

After dinner he pushed away from the table. "Everything was delicious," he said, smiling. "But I want to save room for your tasty dessert."

"What dessert? I told you yesterday that I don't have anything sweet to eat."

"Oh yeah, you do," he said in a husky voice. He leaned forward in his chair and slipped his hand up her bare leg. "I've been thinking about it all afternoon."

Trish laughed and squeezed her knees together, capturing his hand. "Don't be naughty at the dinner table. Your parents taught you better manners. Have you called them yet?"

He withdrew his hand. "Nah, they're somewhere on the road

headed back to Morrison after the game. They won't be home till tomorrow. I'll call on the weekend. What about your folks?"

Trish shrugged and rose to take her plate to the sink. "Help me clean up and I'll think about letting you have that dessert."

After drying and putting away the last plate, he joined her on the carpeted floor in the living room where she prepared a water pipe. After they finished the bowl, he began unbuttoning his shirt. With their eyes locked on each other, neither spoke while his Levis dropped on the floor. Kneeling, he pushed her on her back in front of the fire. After cushioning her head with his sweater, he made long languorous love to her while flames flickered and died in the hearth.

CHAPTER 37

Potts turned his Corvette into the Texaco station in Coventry and rolled down the window. New England's first snow of the year had just started to glaze his windshield. The attendant stood in the station's open doorway, wiping his hands on a rag and looking up at the snow coming down. He stuffed the rag into his back pocket and approached the car. "What'll it be?" A large snowflake landed on his nose. He brushed it off with a thick finger.

"Fill it up," Potts said, stepping out of the car. The drive upstate from Ridgefield had taken just over two hours. The sky, pewter gray during the afternoon, was fast losing light. He tugged off his driving gloves. "How does one get to a street around here called Fox Trail?"

The attendant wiped the rag across his face as fuel coursed into the tank. "Don't sound like no street," he said. "Sounds like a trail."

"Yes, well." Potts started to say something clever but didn't.

"Bet you don't know that's Nathan Hale's monument over there." The attendant nodded toward a granite monolith at the town cemetery. "But, he ain't buried there. The Red Coats never intended us to find his body. Also, see that little church there." He pointed to a white steepled building. "That'n seen both mine and Nathan's christenings." He let that fact soak in a bit before leaning against Potts' car and detailing laborious instructions on how Potts could find his way to Fox Trail. Gestures of right and left with grease-encrusted hands, and long pauses to remember street names, were interspersed with anecdotes of Coventry's people and history.

Potts paid for the gas, thanked the attendant for his help and drove through the village. A curtain of snowflakes descended on his windshield, making the narrow roads even more of an adventure.

Warm air from the vents and The Fifth Dimension on the radio made it womb-like inside the sports car while it slipped and slid up the steep inclines.

"There," he said out loud. The street sign in his headlights was almost blotted out with an accumulation of snow. The fellow at the gas station had been right. The road, now almost lost in the blizzard, looked more like a hidden trail.

At the top of the hill Potts recognized Jim's station wagon parked in the drive. *He'll probably think I came up to check on him. He had sounded somewhat evasive when he backed out of Thanksgiving at Oak Lawn.*

After a non-functioning doorbell alerted no one of his arrival, Potts broke the silence with a gloved fist on the doorframe. Somewhere in the house, a dog barked. He stepped off the porch and looked up at the sky. The snowflakes were larger now. Watching his breath form vapor clouds in the icy air, he heard the door behind him first refuse, then burst open.

"My God, Potts!" Jim stepped out onto the porch. "Where did you come from?" Jim's shirttail hung out over his jeans, and he wore white socks on his feet. "Get inside before you freeze your ass off." He clasped Potts' hand and then grabbed him in a hard embrace.

"Hope I'm not inconveniencing you, old boy." Potts said, pulling off his gloves and sticking them in his coat pocket. "I should've called but—"

"No, no, you're welcome anytime," Jim said, holding the door open. "There's no one I'd rather see more right now than you. God, you look good."

Ringo, lying in front of the hearth, raised his head to look at Potts, then went back to sleep.

"Stand over by the fire and warm up. You look like a cashmere Popsicle," Jim said. "I'm the only one home right now." He hung Potts' scarf on a hook by the door. "The girls will be back soon. It's getting damn cold out there."

Potts rubbed his hands together in front of the blaze. "Had to be in Ridgefield on family business, so decided to come up and see my favorite Texan. Truthfully, I was concerned about you surviving the onset of winter."

Jim sat in the stuffed chair, slinging a leg over the frayed arm. "So far my surviving has been huddling here in front of the fire. By the looks of the woodpile out back, I've got maybe two more days before I'm flushed out. How's your family?"

"Disappointed you missed Mum's turkey and dressing at Thanksgiving," Potts said. "She never cooks except on special occasions, and this year she outdid herself. She switched on the oven for the turkey and retired to the library to address Christmas cards, leaving everything else for poor Eliza, the cook. The meal turned out splendid. She was quite proud of herself. Dad says he can't wait till the next holiday to see what culinary creations she surprises us with." They both laughed.

"By the way," Potts turned to face him, "Sis missed you. She said you were too fun at the party last August. She insists you call her at Smith. I didn't say anything about your girlfriend. Maybe I didn't do you any favor there."

Jim shrugged. "It's early in the game. It could last a week, a month—who knows? We're taking it day-by-day. Tell Sis I'll catch up with her one day soon. I've often thought about that great party last summer. What a hoot."

If asked, he would have said that so far, their reunion felt stiff, like they were both trying too hard.

"Hey, old buddy," He stood and started tucking his shirttail into his jeans, "Let's drive down to the village pub and share some brews. There's nothing in the house here except some Tang and a carton of questionable milk."

"I could go for a brewski." Potts nodded.

"I'll get my boots." Jim stepped over Ringo on his way to the bedroom. "Maybe Trish'll join us later for dinner."

Potts and Ringo eyed each other a moment before the red setter laid his head back on the floor and sighed deeply.

Inside the Nathan Hale Pub, the jukebox played a Dionne

Warwick song. A mixture of students from the university and workers from a nearby mill comprised the noisy crowd.

"Are you kidding?" Potts said. "Three girls and you're the only guy? What are you trying to do? Get your share and everyone else's, too?"

Jim reached for the bowl of peanuts. "Told you, all my attention is on Trish. The other two were her roommates when I moved in. You'll meet them tonight. They're both cuties."

"Tell me more about this dish, I mean Trish," Potts said, and ordered another beer. "Sounds more serious than you let on. You never kept house with Michelle and you two were engaged." Outside the tavern, snowplows could be heard scraping the streets.

"What's to say?" Jim shrugged. "You'll meet her tonight and can see for yourself. She graduates this coming May with an Education degree. I don't know much about her folks. She's pretty quiet about them, and she's a real sweetheart—a little naive sometimes and too trusting for her own good. You'll see." He considered telling Potts about Alec but didn't.

The second beer washed away any awkwardness and brought back feelings of good times. The third beer accompanied their passage through stories that were personal and funny only to them. Everyone in the bar turned to watch while they guffawed and slapped each other on the back, their eyes filled with watery hilarity. The fourth beer and the warmth of the pub quieted their mood. "So," Potts' said, looking serious. "I start back at Dartmouth in January. What's it like being the old man on campus?"

Jim thought a moment before answering. A Joe Cocker song started on the jukebox and two couples got up to dance. Jim leaned forward, both hands clutching his beer, "You know, I'm experiencing things I never dreamed about." He rotated the bottle with his fingers. "And my father would shit if he knew I lived with three chicks." They both laughed, and Jim drank from his beer. He thought about stopping there but felt a need to tell Potts more. "It's different now than when we were in college before. I've had the chance to try some new things—things that would've shocked me a few months ago. For the first time I've questioned some of the old rules I grew up with, and I've made up my own mind based on actual experience. I've surprised myself with some of my conclusions."

"Like what?" Potts furrowed his brow.

"Oh, like setting up house with a girl I'm not married to. I probably could get arrested for that in Texas. Like participating in my encounter group where everyone gets naked, guys and girls. I admit it was hard not to think about humping the bones of every girl there." Jim laughed. "Maybe that should be illegal.

"Also, living in the same house with a black man," he continued. "A black man hell bent on revolution. Not that I agree," he said, seeing concern in Potts' eyes. "But we lived in the same house and peacefully existed together. If I'd walked in his shoes all my life, who knows, I might've taken up a gun a long time ago." Jim took a deep breath. "And probably the most surprising to you and to me, I've played around with stuff like pot, LSD, and hashish. The mind-expanding experience, the physical sensations, the psychedelic stuff."

"Shit!" Potts looked away.

"It's not like you think," Jim said. "The bad experiences some people have. . .the tripping out, doing crazy things. Nothing like that has happened to me or anyone I know. And everyone around here plays with the stuff."

More moments passed while neither of them spoke. Jim scraped at the paper label on his bottle.

Potts stared at his own beer. "Have you been using a lot of drugs?"

"I haven't been *using* anything!" Jim sat up stiff. "You know me better than that. There are assholes out there who are real junkies, but that's not me, nor anyone I know. Nowhere near it!" He piled up pieces of label on the table. "It's kind of like when you jacked off as a kid even though you were told it would make you go blind and stuff. Well, you did it anyway, and you were surprised and pleased with the results. Not enough to lock yourself in the bathroom all day, every day. Well, maybe that first week." He grinned. Someone bumped into his chair. The bar had filled up with folks waiting out the storm. The noise in the pub had increased in direct proportion to the cigarette smoke.

"I haven't actually done that much," Jim continued, "and when I did, I was careful. Usually home with Trish. In fact, it's probably better for me than the times you and I got blottoed on Friday nights at the officers' club. Remember?"

Jim pushed his chair back from the table. "I don't want to blow this out of proportion. Just know I'm careful about it and not stupid. I wouldn't touch the addictive stuff, the narcotics. But the mind-expanding acid, mescaline, hashish. . .you get this rush of energy, of clear vision. It's a temporary sensation, a real high, and then it's gone. Dr. Leary, a Harvard Psychiatrist, advocates the benefits of mind-expanding chemicals."

"Timothy Leary is a fucking lunatic!" Potts exploded. "He's a wild-eyed, burnt-out Ivy League professor who can't keep himself under control long enough to stay out of jail. That's the main thing I'm concerned about, Cowboy. The damn stuff is illegal. I don't care if it cures cancer or the heartbreak of psoriasis. Right now, it's damn illegal, and people are rotting in fucking prison for years because of the *great rush* and *learning experience* they had with that psychedelic shit. I'll tell you what they learned. They figured out what stupid asses they were to go for a shitty short-term high and risk everything really important to them, like family, friends, their future, and their fucking freedom."

"That's because of the hypocrisy of our laws," Jim snapped back. "And those can be changed. I had two uncles who died of cirrhosis of the liver because they were alcoholics. Yet booze is served on Capitol Hill and in cathedrals all over this country."

"What would you have them do?" Potts said. "Pass around plates of rolled-up marijuana cigarettes and set out little silver bowls of LSD pills for everyone to munch on like popcorn?" The absurdity of his suggestion caused them both to laugh. The laughter died, and silence grew in its place. Jim didn't want to fight.

"I'm not sure what I really think about all of it," he spoke softly. "It's still too new. Ninety days ago, I said the same things you just did. I'm still studying the question and everything's on the table. You're right about one thing. My biggest concern is the law. I think sometimes that I agree with the hippies when they say nothing should be illegal unless it hurts someone else."

"That's bullshit." Potts said, and took a quick swig of his beer.

"All my life," Jim continued, "I've judged my actions and everyone else's through a prism of absolute right and wrong. Here at UConn, I've learned there's many different *right* ways. I've learned its okay to be Jew or Christian, Hindu or Buddhist, agnostic or atheist. That it's okay to be black, white, red, yellow, and brown, or even plaid. I've met a lot of smart, sincere people lately who hate and protest the war in Vietnam, and before I moved up here, I knew just as many smart, sincere people who believe America's engaged in an honorable effort. It's confusing, Potts. And one thing's for sure, there are no easy answers. There's no absolutes of right and wrong like I think it was for our parents."

The jukebox went silent, and the two couples left the dance floor. The waitress followed them to take their drink order. On her way back to the bar, she pointed at Potts' half empty beer bottle and raised an eyebrow. He smiled at her and shook his head.

"Everyone's perception is different," he said after the waitress went on her way. "Each of us sees through lenses reflecting our own self-interest. I hadn't really thought about it until a couple of weeks ago. I was on an acid trip and thinking about the differences between my older brother and me, between me and my folks. Heavy duty acid stuff," he said, grinning.

Potts looked away.

"Anyway, I realized that for twenty years the Bible and my parents' interpretation of it, was my rule book. I don't have any regrets about that. I never questioned. Never addressed the validity of the concept. Oh, deep down, I wondered like every other kid, but I never really questioned or doubted.

"Now that I'm older, hopefully wiser, more experienced, I see there are many different interpretations, and they each support valid, but different, even opposing lifestyles. My folks back home and your family in Ridgefield probably rank hippies with godless communists. But then the Bible says we should tend the poor and share our possessions and use our talents for the benefit of others instead of just enriching ourselves. Legislated in government, good people would cry socialism, accuse it of being un-American and anti-God, and use the Bible like a club to hit some long-haired hippie in the head and then lock him away in prison for fifteen years-to-life for just smoking a marijuana cigarette."

The two friends sat in silence. Jim's throat felt dry. He lifted his beer and drank till the bottle was empty.

"I don't know," Potts said. He ran a hand through his dark hair. "It sounds like you're saying there are no absolute truths; there's no right and wrong for society as a whole, and there shouldn't be any rules. That one shouldn't judge another." He shook his head. "Sorry, I can't buy that. We humans have made a lot of mistakes since we've been on the planet, and our rules evolved to keep us from making them again. I agree that there are people who have different values and beliefs than we two WASPS do, but it doesn't make ours invalid."

Jim put his feet up on the wood chair next to him. "But it also doesn't make what we believe right for everybody else," he responded. "That's my point. I'm not sure where I am on all this. I don't have a firm position. Trish says the most important thing I've learned these past months is tolerance. To give space to people with different beliefs and ideas. The cost, however, has been high. It's turned my tidy little world upside down. Decisions that were easy before, so absolute, aren't that simple. It's like I've lost my yard stick, so now I don't even measure."

"And that's fucking anarchy," Potts blurted out. "There needs to be rules, and they need to be enforced or there's chaos."

"But, whose rules?" Jim shot back. "And whose rules are going to be right next week? Those with the most guns or with the largest voting majority? And if I choose as a free man with certain inalienable rights not to go along with them and no one else is hurt, or suffers in any way because of my decision, why should I be punished or persecuted?

"It's like the child whose parents said he should never go out the back door because there was a vicious dog there that would bite him. As long as the inside of the house keeps his interest and he can't reach the door handle anyway, he doesn't care about that rule. Then one day he hears laughter in the backyard. He stands on a chair to reach the handle and opens the door. Seeing nothing, he steps out into the backyard fearful of being devoured. Instead, he discovers a cocker spaniel and children playing. From then on, the kid will defy every rule and open every door to see what's beyond."

There was a long pause and Jim saw concern shadowing Potts' face. "Hey, don't worry about it, buddy." He smiled. "This will work itself out. You know me. I'm not going to do anything too stupid. Since I left being an officer and a gentleman behind, I'm simply trying out this free will stuff. At the same time, I don't need to tell you that it's fun experiencing forbidden things. I'm just hoping I don't get caught."

"Cowboy," Potts looked troubled. "I'll trust you won't get in over your head but be damn careful. The Potter family can't abide friends in the penitentiary." The smile on his face was not reflected in his eyes.

"I'll drink to that," Jim said, raising his empty beer bottle.

"I almost forgot," Potts said, shifting subjects, "The hockey coach at Dartmouth called me every week since September to make sure I'm getting into shape. I'll take some leave to be at home in Connecticut for Christmas then go back to Washington to process out. Why don't we meet at Oak Lawn for Christmas, and you ride to Washington with me? I'll drop you back here after the New Year on my way up to school. That'll give us a week to celebrate my return to civilian life. What do you say?"

"I'd like that," Jim said, relieved their conversation was back on solid ground. Why had he engaged Potts in a no-win debate of values? "Let's go back to the house and see what the girls want to do for dinner?" He stood and pulled on his coat.

Exiting the pub, they braced themselves against the icy wind blowing across the piles of snow bordering the parking lot. In the car on the way back, neither of them said much while the headlights carved a path up the icy hill. Jim saw Jennifer's car parked in the driveway next to Trish's Mustang.

CHAPTER 38

The fire in the living room had burned down to glowing embers, and the loud music coming from Jennifer's bedroom sounded like Led Zeppelin hammering on the roof. Jim found Trish on their bed thumbing through a book.

"Look what I got at the book store this afternoon," she said when he stretched out beside her. "It's Rod McKuen's new book. He's so groovy."

He leaned over and kissed her on her nose. "I think you're pretty groovy. I have a surprise for you. Come see who is in the living room."

"Someone's here? I wondered why your car was outside, and you weren't around." She bounded off the bed and towed him by his hand into the living room.

Potts rose from the chair by the fireplace. "Hi, I'm Jack Potter."

"Potts?" Trish looked back and forth between them. "James, you should have told me Potts was here!" She released his hand and went to hug his friend. "It's so cool to finally meet. Jim talks about you all the time." She broke their embrace but continued holding onto his arm. "Sometimes I feel like I lived with you crazy guys in that house in Virginia."

"Jim told me much about you, and I wrongly accused him of exaggerating," Potts teased. "Congratulations, Cowboy." He winked at Jim. "She's all that you said and certainly more than you deserve."

Jim nodded. It was important that Potts like his girl, even if he didn't approve of anything else he was doing.

Jennifer made it a foursome for dinner at the little Italian place in town. They planned a movie afterward if there was time. It started to snow again as they entered the smoky restaurant. Jennifer sat across from Potts and stared quietly at him when he carried the conversation. Potts watched wide-eyed as she devoured her lasagna, finishing her plate long before the others. Jim and Trish smiled knowingly at each other. They had seen her light up a water pipe in her room before they went out.

"Trish is really something," Potts said as he and Jim stood together at the urinal in the men's room. Ice chips covered the bottom of the porcelain trough. They both targeted the same piece.

"I'll give you a 9.5 on her," Potts said, "which is more than you ever got from me before. Even the Russian and East German judges gave you a higher score for Michelle than I did."

Jim looked up from the diminishing ice chunk. "Well, thanks for telling me that now. You would've let me walk in front of that oncoming truck and never said anything about it?"

"You were over twenty-one and knew what you were doing." Potts zipped his trousers. "It didn't seem right to you either, or today you would be known around the officers' club at Fort Myer as the general's son-in-law. You could've been the youngest major in the army. Of course, only you and I would know your meteoric rise was because of your hard work and stellar military record, and not just because your father-in-law will probably be the next Army Chief of Staff."

"Didn't think you were supposed to talk with your mouth full," Jim said, buttoning his jeans.

"What do you mean?" Potts washed his hands at the sink.

"That Potter silver spoon must get in your way a lot." Jim dodged the wadded-up paper towel thrown at him.

"Only when attempting intelligent conversation with the peasants." Potts pulled another hand towel from the dispenser.

The girls were waiting at the table with their coats on.

"We need to hurry if we're going to make the nine-thirty show," Trish said, hustling them into their jackets. "Jim knows I hate going into a movie after it's started."

Outside in the parking lot, new snow gave a crystalline sparkle to the world. He started the engine to let his car warm up while he cleaned the windshield with an ice scraper. Tires crunched over packed snow as he turned out onto the freshly plowed highway. Ten minutes later, he parked in front of the Huskie Cinema in Storrs across from campus.

All through the movie, he and Trish huddled together in the balcony and giggled at his tawdry jokes about the terrible film. Next to them, Jennifer maneuvered Potts' arm around her and had her head on his chest. Jim saw her hand find its way to Potts' leg and her fingers traversed up and down his gabardines. Any question about her intentions was answered when her tongue went into his ear. Potts hesitated a moment, then countered with a hand on her breast. She nearly climbed into his lap.

The four friends left the movie before it was over and drove home through more falling snow. Jim gripped the steering wheel with both hands and peered beyond the icy glaze on the windshield. Trish rested her head on his shoulder while heavy breathing in the back seat fogged up the windows. Jim wanted to look back and see what Potts was doing but didn't dare take his eyes off the disappearing road.

Ann Marie met them at the front door wearing only loop earrings and a gold ankle bracelet that Jim called her "chase me, catch me, fuck me chain." She'd just finished a bath and was painting her toenails. Potts stood mute at the front door, watching her walk naked back to her chair. She put a high-arched, chain-enslaved foot on the ottoman and dabbed a tissue at an errant spot of polish. Jennifer grabbed Potts' hand and pulled him to her room.

It was nearly noon the next day when Led Zeppelin announced at full volume that Potts and Jennifer were awake. They emerged together from her bedroom and found Jim in briefs and t-shirt sitting cross-legged on the living room floor with the day's newspaper spread around him. Jennifer pirouetted barefoot into the kitchen and left Potts behind looking pale and limp. He scooted Ringo off the sofa and lay down. He watched Jim turn through the morning paper. Every now and then he glanced at Ann Marie's closed door.

"Really socked it to her last night, huh, old buddy?" Jim swallowed a laugh as Potts stared unblinking from the couch. "Gave her a real Potter workout and no one else will ever satisfy her again, right?"

Potts raised his hand and flipped Jim the middle-digit. Jim fell back on the carpet and howled. Led Zeppelin's electric guitars boomed through the Sheet Rock drowning out his laughter. Ringo waited at the front door to be let outside and watched Jim pound the floor with his fists.

Jennifer came back into the living room carrying a glass of orange juice and a plate heaped with scrambled eggs. She knelt on the floor beside the sofa and fed bites to Potts while humming along with the loud music. Trish followed, in flannel gown and braids, carrying two full plates and sat beside Jim. He ate and continued perusing the paper. Every now and then Trish leaned over to kiss him. The stereo in Jennifer's room kept dropping Led Zeppelin albums onto the turntable. Ringo, still waiting at the front door, glared at him as if he were to blame.

After breakfast, Potts helped Jennifer wash dishes in the kitchen while he and Trish got dressed. Potts dried the last glass and announced it was time to leave for Washington. "I apologize for eating and running." He smiled at Jennifer. "But I'm still being paid to defend the country for the next two weeks. Plus, I've got to stop in Ridgefield on the way to sign some papers. My grandfather's attorney is expecting me at three-thirty."

After Potts donned his leather jacket, Trish hugged him goodbye. Jennifer whispered something in his ear and gave him a passionate open mouth kiss. Looking sad, she led Ringo back to her bedroom and shut the door. Jim grabbed his coat and followed Potts outside. The day was clear and bitingly cold. A shell of hard snow and ice crystals encased the Corvette.

"It was great of you to come all the way up here to check on me," Jim said, putting his hand on Potts' shoulder. "And the girls enjoyed meeting you. I talk about you all the time. Trish said this morning that I was lucky to have you for a friend. And you know what? She's damn right!" He clasped Potts in a bear hug. "I promise to try and get to Oak Lawn at Christmas. Be sure and tell your parents that I said so."

"Jim, I. . . ." Potts looked down at the snow-covered ground. "Jimbo. . ." He tried again, "I understand you think you know what you're doing here, but honestly, I don't feel good about it. It isn't Trish, I think she's great and all, but I'm afraid you might be getting in over your head. Blame my puritan ancestors if you want, but I think a man should take a stand on what he believes is right. I didn't like it when the country went crazy these last few years and now, seeing my best friend. . .like a brother even—" Potts kicked the front tire of his car. A chunk of dirty snow fell under the wheel. "Look, let's keep the Christmas thing on hold right now. I'm not sure if the family is going to our place in Colorado for the holidays or not. Mum said something about it when I was home. I'll call you."

Jim was stunned.

"Take care, Cowboy."

Potts' retreat left him mute.

"And I hope you find whatever it is you're looking for. Just be careful." Potts attempted a smile.

Jim started to say something but couldn't.

With a wave to Trish at the door, Potts tossed his scarf around his neck and slid into the driver's seat. The Corvette rumbled to life, and the reverberation of the pipes played against the quiet winter afternoon. Jim stood with his hands stuffed into the pockets of his sheepskin coat and watched the car disappear down the hill. The loud roar of the engine coming up through the woods indicated Potts had turned onto the highway. The whine of changing gears faded in the distance until the only sound left was the wind blowing through the trees.

Jim didn't return to the warmth of the living room but went up the hill to sit alone on the stone wall bordering the woods behind the house. The afternoon light had started to wane when he saw Trish come outside. He watched her trod through the snow around the cottage looking like an Eskimo in the Yukon. Her hood turned this way and that as she called his name. She went back inside, leaving him alone on the wall.

When he returned to the house, he said nothing of where he had been, or explained his absence. Trish made him a cup of hot chocolate capped with little white marshmallows. He sat at the kitchen table and teased Jennifer about her seduction of Potts and spoon feeding him back to health. Jennifer forced a smile. She was busy memorizing her lines for a class assignment.

"My professor is the sexiest drama teacher in the department," she said when Trish asked about it, "He thinks I have a hidden talent that's just perfect for this scene we're doing in Monday's workshop."

"He's right about her talent being hidden," Jim whispered to Trish when Jennifer went to get a nail file from her room. "It's probably buried somewhere with the Ark of the Covenant."

"Why?" Trish furrowed her brow, "Who is Art?"

"Never mind," Jim said, "it's—"

Ann Marie entered the kitchen, nude except for her ever-present jewelry, and sleepily asked if there was anything to eat. Ringo followed her and buried his cold nose in the dark triangle at the juncture of her legs.

"Eeek! Goddamn queer dog, get away from me!" She pushed the setter away with one hand while covering herself with the other. "Somebody, help me! Jennifer, your stupid dog is trying to have sex with me."

"Way to go, Ringo." Jim laughed as the two girls pulled the dog away. "You did what I and every other guy who's ever visited this house only dreamed about doing." Ann Marie stuck her tongue out at him then sashayed her bare ass back to her room.

It was almost dark when he drove Trish down the hill to the A&P to buy groceries. A car passed going in the opposite direction and flashed its headlights. He turned on his lights and dialed the radio to a Johnny Mathis song. "I'm glad you finally met Potts," he said, glancing at her on the seat beside him. "My mother always said you can tell a lot about a fellow by his friends."

"Then, you must be quite a guy," Trish said, scooting closer. She looped her arm through his.

"Yeah, he's one of a kind." He nodded, still troubled about how the visit ended.

CHAPTER 39

The encounter group's Hanukkah and Christmas party the first week of December celebrated the holidays as well as the conclusion of their weekly meetings. Everyone was there. After the chips and Cheese-Whiz were gone, Rob, the Princeton professor's son, lit up a couple of pipes and passed them around. Bernard said nothing about this violation of his "no dope" rules and took his turn when the pipe came his way. Toward the end of the evening, he called everyone together in a circle on the floor and stood in the center to address them. "All of you who've been in my other groups know I end each semester with what's called a love roundtable. It's a final chance for you to say something to that special person or persons in the group. Franklin, let's start with you and go clockwise around the room."

The mood in the room turned somber. Franklin stared at the floor and started to perspire as he singled out a few people for what he said was their "friendship and understanding." He then shifted his gaze and comments to Bernard in almost worshipful reverence. After the third person did the same thing, Jim smiled to himself. He now understood Bernard's little ritual. Bernard was locked in on a big fix. At their turn, each person went on about how much the group had meant to them and how they loved Bernard for tapping that unique something that made them a better person. They all said it differently, but the message was the same. In some weird way they attempted to outdo each other. All the while Bernard sat with head bowed, a beatific expression on his face, as declarations of love and appreciation were draped on his hairy, narrow shoulders.

Trish surprised him by adding her own shovel-full and finished without saying anything about meeting him.

"The most important thing that happened to me in this group was finding Trish." Jim spoke in a loud voice when it was his turn. "She's opened doors to new worlds and given me innocence, and love. . .and great adventure." He put his arm around her and felt her body tense.

"Is that all?" Bernard asked after several seconds of uncomfortable silence had passed. "I mean do you have anything else to say?"

Jim recognized Bernard's question for what it was, a demand for his wages. They exchanged looks across the circle. *Damn if I'm going to give the little cheat any satisfaction.* "That's it," he said. "I have nothing else to say."

The party soon broke up. Trish talked with Janice on the sofa while he went into the kitchen to pick at the remains of the snack tray. He found an olive and tossed it into his mouth. He opened the sliding glass door and stepped out onto the balcony overlooking the apartment building's lighted, snow-banked, parking lot.

"Thought I saw you come out here." The sultry voice behind him sounded familiar.

"Just getting some air." He heard the door slide shut. Arms encircled his waist. The high cushiony breasts told him it wasn't Trish. He turned around.

"Hello, Cowboy." Elizabeth smiled up at him. She pressed her breasts into the front of his shirt. "I confess I wasn't totally honest tonight," she said. "The most important thing I got out of this group is something that I lost. . .and that was my fear of rejection. I've decided that since I'm well past thirty, I should reach out for the things I want. I can't depend on someone to read my mind."

"And, what do you want?" Jim cleared his throat.

"This. . . ." She slipped her hand down into the front of his jeans. "God, your fingers are cold!"

"Your big cock will warm them up." She breathed in his ear. "I've wanted this since the first weekend at the cabin in the woods. Remember? I couldn't keep my eyes off you. When Bernard turned out the lights, I thought if I got under your quilt, you would wake up and screw my brains out. At the time, it was such a big risk. When you didn't do anything, I laid there most of the night wondering what was wrong with me. I touched you here." She fondled him. "While you were sleeping. It felt heavy, so hot." She sighed. "Just like now. So, I decided to try again before it's too late." Her voice dropped to a whisper. "I've always wanted to be had by a real cowboy." She brushed her lips across his and squeezed him again.

"Look, Elizabeth." He pulled her hand out of his pants and encircled her in his arms. "I think you're one damn sexy woman, and given another place and other circumstances, this cowboy would show you how we really rodeo."

"I'd like that. . .sometime." She lowered her eyes.

"I'm flattered." Jim grinned. "The hard evidence was just in your hand. But my heart and my head are right now on someone else's pillow." He pushed a lock of hair away from her eyes and kissed her forehead. "Pretty lady, you're my second-favorite person in this loony group, and I hope you have a very merry Christmas."

She patted him on his chest with both hands. "Okay, but remember—if you change your mind, call me."

"Yes, ma'am, I sure will," He said. They locked arms and rejoined the dying party.

In the early morning hours, he woke Trish and made love to her.

"I don't remember raw oysters at the party." Her voice sounded husky as they lay together after two sweaty trysts.

He grew hard again.

"Oh no," she whimpered as he rolled her up onto his chest. "I'm going to be bowlegged for a week."

"It was the Cheese-Whiz." He mouthed her ear.

Whatever she was about to say drifted into a long low moan.

Dawn broke just as Jim rolled over and looked at her. He brushed strands of hair away from her face, and she opened her eyes.

"I love you," he whispered.

CHAPTER 40

F inal exams at UConn for the fall semester began in mid-December. Everyone at the house scrambled to salvage their grades. Jim knew it was too late to make the term a success, too many missed classes, but a last-minute effort combined with some luck could prevent a total disaster. The week went by in a blur. He rose early each morning to get in additional hours of study and went to bed late and exhausted. After his last test on Friday, he drove back to the cottage, crawled under the covers and fell asleep. Sometime during the night, he felt the mattress sag followed by Trish's warmth as she curled against him. In the morning he felt the bed move again when she got up, leaving him to sleep undisturbed. Jennifer cooperated by silencing her stereo.

He heard the bedroom door open, but no one entered, nor did he hear the door close again. After a bit of silence, he felt warm breath on his cheek and opened one eye. A black nose rested on the bed inches from his own and two brown eyes peered at him. "Mornin', Ringo." He swung his feet out from under the quilts and sat on the edge of the bed. The Irish Setter wagged his tail. "Glad to see me up, huh boy?" He rubbed the dog's head. "What time is it anyway?"

Checking his watch on the night stand, he saw it was already noon. He padded naked down the hallway to the bathroom. On the return trip he heard Trish on the phone in the kitchen.

"I'll be home next week for Christmas. I'm sorry about Thanksgiving, but I had to stay here and study. I'll spend as much time with you this holiday as I can. Yes, I promise. I will. You too, Mom. I miss you, too."

Jim went back to the bedroom and shut the door. She had told him she was going home for the holidays. He wasn't invited as she hadn't told her parents about him. He'd spoken with Joel about it. "What do I say to Trish's father when I first meet him, and he knows we're shacking up?"

"You say you love her," Joel had said.

He stepped into his jeans and began to think about his own plans for the holidays. Potts hadn't called, which didn't surprise him. He pulled on a wool sweater and checked the mirror above the dresser to brush his hair. It was way past time for a haircut.

The girls were all leaving for their parents' homes in Boston over the break. If he didn't plan something fast, he would be left alone at the house. Spending Christmas alone was a depressing thought. He sat on the bed and pulled on a pair of socks, followed by his boots. After ruling out flying home to Texas because of the expense, he was out of ideas.

"James, are you up?" He heard Trish calling from the kitchen. A peppery aroma filled the house. His stomach rumbled. It had been over twenty-four hours since his last meal.

"I'm getting dressed. Whatever you're making in the kitchen sure smells good."

The living room drapes were open, letting in the Winter afternoon's grey light. He found her over a steaming pot, stirring with a big wooden spoon. Two empty Campbell Soup cans were on the counter.

"Hungry?" She angled her cheek for a kiss.

"I could eat you." He wrapped his arms around her and nipped at an ear lobe.

"Don't." She pushed him away. "I'm making you soup and you're going to ruin it. It has to be stirred while it heats on the stove for ten minutes."

"Who was on the phone?" He rummaged in the cabinets for a cookie.

"My mother wanted to make sure I was coming home," she said, turning the fire down under the pot.

He sat at the table and opened a package of Oreos. Trish came up behind him and put her arms around his neck, "Have you decided what you're going to do while I'm away?"

"I thought Ringo and I would go down to the SPCA and, you know, put on a Bob Hope type show for all the poor mutts that can't make it home for the holiday. Don't worry about me," he said, seeing she wasn't laughing. "I'll be okay."

"I know you will," she sighed. "Ringo is going home with Jennifer. Even he has plans for Christmas." She kissed him on the top of his head and went back to stirring the soup.

Jim took a handful of Oreos, walked into the living room and stood at the window separating the chocolate wafers and licking out the cream filling. A basketball game between two college teams he didn't care about was on television. Searching through the catch-all bucket by the sofa for magazines and newspapers, he picked out a recent copy of Jennifer's *Village Voice*. She subscribed to the New York weekly to keep up with the latest plays that were always opening and closing off Broadway. He enjoyed reading the personals section.

Moon Flower, my stamen longs for your pistol. Call me and let's make honey.... Norman.

Another one read:

I am woman, looking for major domo. Seeking peak experiences on life's short journey. No marrieds.... Earth Mother.

He laughed out loud. Ringo, sleeping nearby on the floor, lifted his head and looked at him. "I think Earth Mother and horny Norman need to get together. What do you think, Ringo?"

The dog banged his feathery tail on the floor.

Reading on through the ads, he paused to check one out a second time.

NYU student going home for the holidays, has Village apartment to sublet for the month of December. Michael......(212) 555-6436

Reading on, he spotted more ads offering apartments to sublet. He put the paper down, and an idea began to take root. Rising from the chair, he collected sticks from the kindling box to build the first fire of the day. As he watched flames ignite the wood, the idea continued to grow.

"Hey, I think I know what I'm going to do over the holidays." He sat down at the kitchen table and unfolded the newspaper as Trish set out two bowls for their lunch. "I think I'll spend Christmas in New York, in the city. You know. . .chestnuts roasting on an open fire, Jack Frost nipping at your whatever, ice skating at Rockefeller Center and everything. I spent a couple of weekends in the city with some friends when I was in the army. God, what an adventure that could be. Christmas in the city.

"That sounds groovy. Where will you stay?" She put the pot of soup on the table and sat in the chair next to him. "Going with friends is one thing, but all alone in the city. I dunno."

"Look." He pushed the newspaper in front of her. "I can sublet an apartment, or even share one, maybe down in the Village. My folks would croak if they knew I was living in Greenwich Village. Maybe I can get a job at one of the big department stores during the Christmas rush. I have enough money to stay up here till my next G.I. check comes, but if I went into the city I'd have to at least earn my expenses. Can you see me wearing a suit and helping well-dressed gentlemen select Italian leather gloves and expensive colognes? I could do it." He laughed. "I know I could."

"You would have way too much fun," Trish said. "Maybe I'll even train down from Boston to spend some time with you."

Monday afternoon, he stood on the front porch of the cottage with his arms around her saying goodbye. Ann Marie and Jennifer had already left with Ringo in Ann Marie's car.

"I'm already missing you."

She nuzzled his face. "Don't let those big city hucksters take advantage of my cowboy."

"Just hurry and meet me in New York. I'll call you as soon as I have us a place to stay."

"I hope you can get us a private bedroom," she said, looking serious.

He bent down and kissed her.

The next morning, eight days before Christmas, he packed a bag and headed for New York. After parking his station wagon between snow drifts in the lot at the bus station in Hartford, he bought a round-trip ticket. He counted eighty dollars remaining in his wallet.

It was a four-hour bus ride into the city with stops in New Haven, Bridgeport, and White Plains. The window by his seat was too dirty to see out, and the bus stank of cigarette smoke. He tried to sleep, but the best he could do was rest with his eyes closed and think about all he had to do when he arrived in New York. Eighty dollars was not much to live on for two weeks, but the return ticket in his pocket was his safety net.

The crowd at the bus terminal in Manhattan went about its business paying him no attention. His darting eyes missed nothing; the lines of people at the ticket counters, the newsstands on every corner, uniformed custodians sweeping up cigarette butts and candy wrappers. The crowds hurrying about the terminal made him feel like he should speed it up. It was two-thirty in the afternoon when he passed through the glass doors of Port Authority onto busy, brash, Forty-Second Street.

With limited resources, he decided to first try and secure a job before paying for a place to stay. He consulted a tattered directory chained to an abused pay phone on the sidewalk and copied down the addresses of the major department stores. After walking up and down Fifth Avenue and through midtown slush for two hours, his boots were crusted white with street salt, and his arms were tired from carrying his bag. The story at each place had been the same. Macys, Gimbels, Bergdorf, had already hired all they needed for the holidays. Just as it looked like he'd have to take a late bus back to Hartford, his luck changed.

"We have an opening for a box boy, but you're way too qualified for that." The woman behind the office desk scanned his application. Her hands were manicured and accented with tasteful jewelry. Not a hair out of place and her woolen suit and matching leather pumps looked expensive. The frosted glass door to her office was adorned with the words PERSONNEL MANAGER in raised gold letters.

She crossed her legs, dangled one pump on the toe of her foot and peered over the top of her eyeglasses. "The position pays three dollars an hour and involves manual labor, no thinking required." She smiled. "It's carrying gift boxes from the basement to different departments as they request them. If you require a sales position, you might try another store. I wish we had something better."

Jim leaned forward in his chair, "If that's an offer, I'll take it. I promise this Christmas will be remembered as the time Jim Davis worked as a box boy at Lord & Taylor."

"I'm sure it will," she said, arching an eyebrow. "I'm sure it will." She picked up the phone on her desk, "Benny, take Mr. Davis down to meet Mrs. Rodriguez before she goes home. He's the new boy she requested. He'll start tomorrow." She walked him to the door. "Don't let Mrs. Rodriguez get to you. She's been here way too long and thinks everyone we employ is lazy or a fugitive." She shook his hand. "Good luck, James, I hope your stay in the city is an enjoyable one."

If Mrs. Rodriguez was pleased, she didn't show it. "Be heer nine o'clock sharp an don ware no durty clodes," she said, skipping the courtesies. "Ju will be in de store where customers weel see ju. Now get atta heer, I wanna go home."

"Yes, Ma'am," Jim said. "I'll be here at nine o'clock."

I've done it, he thought as he walked out through the busy store. A job at Lord & Taylor on my first day in New York. Hell, my first four hours in the city. *This is my town. I own it!*

On the sidewalk, he found a pay phone and called the list of numbers he had about apartments to sublet. In each case, he was too late. His next option was a rooming house he had seen advertised in the *"Village Voice."* No one answered when he called so he decided to go downtown and check it out.

The subway doors slammed shut and the train jerked forward. The car was packed with commuters headed home. Holding on to the overhead strap, he clutched his bag under his arm. When he exited the subway station at Seventh Avenue and 14th Street, darkness had settled over the city. Light from store fronts spilled through grimy windows onto the littered sidewalk. He walked the streets until he found the Alden House Hotel, which turned out to be a rooming house near Washington Square. The ad said it catered to New York University staff and students.

The entrance was on the side of a red brick building which also housed a deli on the ground floor. The aroma of sausages and cooked cabbage filled the foyer. The walls of the hallway were covered with iridescent murals painted by some psychedelic Michelangelo. Grand landscapes populated with stick figures alternated with abstracts of colorful geometric patterns. He passed a few doors with stenciled numbers on them and stopped in front of one marked Manager's Office. After two knocks, the door opened a crack. A pair of heavy-lidded eyes looked him over. "Waddya want?"

"A room, if you have one," he responded. The door swung open, exposing a skinny guy wearing a stained undershirt and ratty dungarees. His thinning hair hadn't seen shampoo recently, and the wild look in his eyes told Jim he had been smoking or shooting something.

"Five bucks a day, a week in advance," the fellow dared. Jim pulled thirty-five dollars out of his jeans and handed it to the jittery character. The man grinned. "For a while there, I thought you might be a fuckin' narc. We don't want no fuckin' trouble here. Everyone likes their privacy. Your room's up the stairs and down the hall. Towels and bedding are on the dresser. The bathroom's off the hall and don't leave the fuckin' water running." He pressed a key into Jim's hand and slammed the door.

Jim climbed the stairway that leaned at an angle away from the wall. Passing the bathroom, he stopped and flipped on the light, revealing a decaying room of chipped porcelain, peeling paint and broken tiles. He cut the switch and walked on down the hall. He opened the door to his room and a musty smell greeted him. He found the switch, and a bare bulb dangling on a wire in the middle of the room glowed like a flare. An iron bed, a dresser, and a ladder-back chair were the only furniture. A door next to the bed opened to a small closet. *Not that bad. I've seen worse.*

He set about unpacking his belongings. *Trish will like it. At least it's private.*

A dollar bought him a sandwich and coke at the deli downstairs. After eating at a table in the corner by the window, he found a pay phone and placed a call to Boston. "You've got to come down as soon as you can," he said when Trish came on the line. "It's right in the middle of the Village just off Bleecker Street. You'll love it. You can visit the shops and cafes during the day, and we can go out at night after I get off work."

"It'll take me a couple of days to arrange it," she said, lowering her voice. "Maybe I can come Friday and stay the weekend. Besides, I need to bring your Christmas present. You haven't forgotten mine, have you?"

"Bought you a diamond tiara at Tiffany's but decided it just wasn't you so I returned it. Got any ideas?"

"You better not forget, that's the only advice I have." She giggled. "Unless you'd like sleeping alone on the sofa next semester."

"I'll go back and get the tiara," he said, laughing. "Listen, work on arranging things for Friday, and I'll call you on Thursday to confirm. God, I hope you can come. I miss you so much, my heart hurts."

"You're sweet. I can't wait to see you, too."

The next morning, he was up early and walked to the store in midtown to save the subway fare. He was glad the job didn't require him to wear a suit. Jeans and a wool sweater over an oxford shirt were more comfortable. It was freezing outside, and the distance was greater than he realized. By the time he reached the store, his ears and face were numb. He decided it was better to take the subway regardless of the fare.

The job was no brain buster. He traveled back and forth between the basement and the merchandise departments delivering boxes, big ones to electronics and toys, medium size boxes to lingerie, and tiny ones for jewelry. All had the Lord & Taylor script across the top. He liked watching the holiday shoppers and looked for celebrities during his trips up and down and around the store.

While the rest of the world enjoyed the mechanicals in the windows and the Christmas music flowing through the store to lighten the spirit and the pocketbook, Mrs. Rodriguez kept the basement boiling with activity. Shoppers were unaware of the army of people bustling about ensuring a full complement of products in every size and color in each department. As he learned the layout, the large store became less intimidating. Sales clerks called him by name when he delivered their boxes. On Thursday, he phoned Trish during his lunch break.

"It's all arranged." She sounded excited. "I'll be there tomorrow morning at eleven-thirty. I promised my mom that I'd be home Christmas Eve, so I can only stay a few days."

"That's great!" He yelled into the phone. "But you know I work every day till five."

"Don't worry about me," she said. "I'll find things to do until you get off. Then we'll have fun."

"Well, let me warn you about our room. . . ." The roar of a city bus drowned him out as it stopped at the curb.

"I'm sure it's fine," she responded. "Take lunch early tomorrow and meet me at the train. I'm bringing your presents with me. You'll love them."

On the way back to the store, he passed a Salvation Army band playing "Joy To The World." "Have a great day," he said to a man dressed in a Santa suit and ringing a brass bell. He spent the remainder of his lunch break walking the streets of midtown inhaling the aroma of street vendors' charcoal and roasting wares.

On Friday, a far-off light in the tunnel signaled the arrival of her train. In a few moments, the roar of mechanical engines throttling back and metal grinding against metal confirmed it. Jim stood near the stairs, looking like Paul Bunyan in jeans and flannel shirt. He saw Trish step onto the platform looking for him in the crowd. She wore a green army fatigue jacket, and her blonde hair tucked under a knit cap. "Hey little girl," he said when their eyes met. "Want a piece of candy and go for a ride in my car?"

She cocked her head. "My mother warned me about men like you."

"Come here." He laughed; his arms open and inviting. Trish dropped her bag at his feet and went up on tiptoes to kiss him. He clasped his hands together in the small of her back and squeezed her to him. Her leather loafers left the ground and found support on the tops of his boots. He broke the kiss and pressed his face against her hair. Her familiar scent filled his senses. "God, I'm glad you're here."

"Me too." She breathed into the curve of his neck. "I was worried you wouldn't find me."

They stopped at TAD'S for a quick inexpensive steak and salad served on orange plastic trays. He had only a half hour left of his lunch break, so Trish listened attentively as he talked nonstop about his work at Lord & Taylor. Back at the store, he handed her the key to his room. "I should be there no later than six," he said. "I hope you don't get too bored."

"I might go up to Central Park before I go down to the village," she said, kissing him. "New York is such a magical place this time of year. Don't worry about me. I'll have a good time."

"Just be careful." He kissed her cold nose. "A lot of sex maniacs are loose in this town, and it's difficult to pick them out from us regular folks. He took her hand and put it on the front of his jeans.

"Jim!" She jerked her hand away. "Someone could see us."

"Who cares?" He put his arms around her again. "No one does. We could boff in the middle of Forty-Second Street, and traffic would just go around us. Some city workers would put out those orange plastic cones and maybe a sign that says, 'Man at Work,' but that's it."

"Well, I would care!" She responded with mock indignation and kissed him. She rubbed her nose against his own. "Don't be late."

After the store closed, he bought a token and hurried onto the subway at Thirty-Fourth Street. Several stops later, he exited the station at Christopher Street and walked toward the rooming house. Kids on Bleecker Street with no place to go, huddled over steam grates on the sidewalk to keep warm. Strings of colored lights blinking in shop windows reflected off new snow. Opening the door to his room, he found Trish putting the finishing touches on the decor.

"You're home early," she said, helping him remove his coat. "I didn't get a chance to finish."

On the dresser, flowers in a glass vase sat adjacent to a brass incense burner and a framed photograph of her he had taken at Thanksgiving. Christmas lights were strung around the door frame, and a short straggly tree stood in the corner decorated with only one blue glass ball. Gaily wrapped packages were on the floor underneath its sparse branches.

"This place needed a woman's touch." She giggled, watching him survey the room.

"You've ruined my room!" he howled in fake anger. "I worked hard all week to get it just right for you." He lunged and grabbed her by the waist. She squealed and tried to get away. "I'll teach you," he said, picking her up in the air and dumping her onto the bed. She rolled away, but he caught her and pinned her on her back.

"Get off me, you ape. You're crushing me!" She struggled some more, then gave up. "Do you like it? I thought I'd surprise you."

"I love it, and I love you," he said, rolling over and pulling her on top of him. She kissed him passionately while he removed their clothes. She sat astride and rode him to conclusion while the colored lights on the door twinkled, splashing patterns of holiday cheer about the room.

An hour later, he lay on his back, tracing swirls on her bare shoulder with his fingers. Her warm cheek rested on his chest and one knee was drawn up across his bare leg. They each remained silent, thinking private thoughts and listening to each other's breathing. The sounds of the city floated up from the street below.

"Wake up, sleepy head." Her voice sounded far away. "Time to open our Christmas presents."

He saw her sitting on the bed next to him wearing one of his over-size t-shirts. The room was dark except for the twinkling lights on the door.

"What time is it?" He sat up. "I must've dozed."

"It's only eight-thirty. Come on, it's still early. Let's open presents and then go get something to eat. Are you hungry? I'm starving."

She moved to the floor by their little Charlie Brown Christmas tree and started gathering wrapped boxes. He finished dressing and joined her. "Open this one first," she said, handing him a package wrapped in green foil and tied with a yellow ribbon."

The box contained small brushes and glass jars of Day-Glo Body Paints. "Those are for later," she explained. "I always wanted to be a great artist but instead of the Sistine Chapel, I'll have to settle for your sexy body."

He leaned forward and looked at her. "Why wait? Let's do it now."

"No, no!" She laughed and pushed him away. "I want to finish opening presents. Don't you have one for me?" Her bottom lip stuck out in a pout.

He reached for his coat draped across the chair and withdrew a small package from the pocket. It was wrapped in Lord & Taylor's best. His twenty-five percent employee discount made the little watch he bought her affordable.

She lifted the top of the box. "Oh, Jim," she whispered, seeing the new Timex nestled in red satin. Tears began to flow. "This is a real Christmas present, not stupid stuff like I got you."

He put his arm around her. "I hoped you'd like it," he said. "Now you don't have any more excuses for being late. And I wanted body paints more than anything this Christmas."

"Oh, you did not." She managed a smile while tears glistened on her cheeks. "Here, you have more presents to open." She placed two packages in his lap. She put on her new watch and admired the alligator strap and thin gold casing while he finished unwrapping his gifts; a box of incense sticks for the brass burner on the dresser and a black velvet box containing twelve little white pills.

"Twelve tabs of acid," she said when he looked at her. "You know, like for the twelve days of Christmas. A friend got them for me. I tried one, and they're fantastic. We have all next semester to use them."

He studied the pills in the velvet box while she watched him. A look of concern darkened her face.

"They're terrific," he said, closing the box and setting it on the floor among the other opened presents. "Six trips to Fantasyland for each of us." He pushed her back on the floor.

She put her arms around his neck and looked up at him. "I love my watch. It's the first one I've ever owned. You shouldn't have spent so much money, but I'm glad you did."

"Someday I want to be able to give you everything you ever dreamed about," he said, and kissed her.

CHAPTER 41

Dinner was burgers at a tavern on Seventh Avenue. Afterward, they walked, hand-in-hand, enjoying the night and each other. In the heart of the Village, loud rock & roll music blared from the open door of a club called the Bitter End. They stood across the street and watched the crowd lined up at the door. Jim laughed. "I think I just saw Che Gueverra go inside."

Trish squeezed his hand.

She resembled a Russian Cossack with her jeans bloused into high leather boots and a white shawl over her army jacket for extra warmth. She wore no makeup, and the cold night air ruddied her cheeks and made her eyes sparkle. He saw her as child and old soul; worldly, yet waif-like and vulnerable. They continued walking up Bleecker Street, and he put his arm protectively around her.

They passed through Washington Square on the way back to the rooming house, and it surprised him to see the park bustling with so many people out on a cold night. Most seemed to be just hanging around on the street. Some looked vacant-eyed from either malnutrition or too many drugs or both, and all were underdressed for the bitter cold that iced the city. Two boys in their early teens approached them and asked for a dollar. Jim fished in his pocket and found two quarters. "It's all I got, guys," he said, dropping the coins into a grimy hand. "Merry Christmas."

"Yeah you, too." The tall skinny one put the change in his pocket and looked around for another mark.

Jim and Trish walked past the memorial arch smeared with antiwar slogans and out onto the street, leaving the park and its sad inhabitants behind.

"These poor kids must be runaways waiting for spring," he said, looking at her. Trish clasped his hand in both of hers and didn't respond.

At the rooming house, they found a painting party in progress. "Get a brush and join us," the manager in painter's cap and overalls called to them from top of a ladder.

Looking down the corridor, he saw the multi-colored murals disappearing under a coat of bright yellow paint. Someone had brought in buckets of reflective yellow highway paint and the hallway was acquiring the look of Fort Knox. He recognized several people as residents of the hotel whom he had seen come and go during the week. Most everyone wore as much paint as the wall. Marijuana smoke hung in the air and showed in the red eyes and giggles of the partying painters.

Two brushes were handed to them, and they selected a large unpainted section by the stairs. Trish made very careful strokes with her brush taking pains to ensure the thick yellow paint went on evenly. Jim's strokes were big and sweeping in an effort to cover more territory more quickly. After ten minutes, the freshly painted plaster in his area fell from the wall with a crash, leaving a cloud of dust, a pile of wet, yellow plaster crumbles, and a gaping wound in the wall.

"Just paint over it," the manager yelled down the hall through a chorus of laughter. "We've got lots of paint."

At midnight, Jim cleaned their brushes in a can of solvent and led a tired Trish up to bed. When he left for work the next morning, the party had ended, the job finished, and the hallway walls and ceiling glowed bright yellow.

After punching in on Saturday morning, Mrs. Rodriguez took him down to the mail room in the basement. His new job was to post and bag packages to be picked up on-site by the Post Office. The packages, all sizes and shapes and wrapped in brown paper, slid down a network of chutes from the upper floors to an enormous wooden bin. He was to pick a package, read the amount of postage marked in the corner, crank out the metered stamp from the postage machine, stick it to the package, and drop it in one of ten canvas mail bags suspended on a metal rack. When the bags were full, he was to lock them with the official U.S. Post Office seal and stack them in a corner to be picked up by the mail truck which came twice a day.

"Ju mus work fass or de bin weel speel out," Mrs. Rodriguez warned then left him alone to work. The brown boxes poured down the chutes like a waterfall piling higher and higher toward the ceiling. He grabbed a package off the stack and tried to catch up. At first it seemed like a losing battle till he learned that if he selected the largest packages first he could more quickly reduce the volume of the pile. During slow times he would work the smaller packages to reduce the quantity. By mid-afternoon, the work had become repetitive and boring. He preferred delivering boxes around the store, but Mrs. Rodriguez had said this was one of the more important jobs, and he would earn an additional fifty cents per hour. The repetition dulled his senses and caused his idle mind to wander.

The tight security measures the store used to prevent employee theft had interested him since his first day at work. Workers entered through the side door every morning. Bags and coats, which could conceal store merchandise, were checked at the security desk in an outer room. At quitting time, employees picked up their belongings in the outer room before exiting the store. Several times he saw them being frisked by security guards before leaving the building.

As the river of packages continued pouring into the basement, and the sealed mail bags piled up on the floor to await the trucks, his mind searched for the hole in the system. *How can it be beat?* His hands flew mechanically from bin, to postage machine, to mail bag, and back again while his mind traversed all the store's aisles and hallways. He mentally rode all the escalators and elevators. When it looked like he had run out of angles, it hit him. A slow grin creased his face as he realized it was right in front of his nose, literally. He, James Baxter Davis from Morrison, Texas, was the open door to the heart of the store.

He laughed out loud when he realized he was a big enough hole to drive a mail truck through. His hands were the last to touch every package before it went under supervision of the U.S. Government. There was nothing to stop him from changing the address on every uncertified package. There was no record, no one checked his work after the mail bag was sealed shut. The Post Office kept no record of what they picked up, nor maintained any information about where most packages were eventually delivered. All he had to do was pencil in his own address on any regular mail package going to Connecticut and wait for the Post Office to deliver his booty. He continued stamping and stacking and envisioned a parade of mail trucks driving up Fox Trail; a surprise in every package. It was an amusing thought, one of those mind games that helped pass the boring hours at the noisy, clacking, posting machine.

At four in the afternoon, just before the last mail pickup of the day, he decided to risk a test with one package. Finding a medium size box addressed to someone in Hartford, he scratched through the name and penciled in Trish Wallace, 112 Fox Trail, Coventry, Connecticut. He metered the proper postage onto the package and dropped it in the mail bag. After depositing several more packages, he sealed that bag and tossed it on the pile. At five o'clock, the mail truck backed down the ramp into the basement on schedule. After loading the final bag, Jim watched as the truck climbed out of the bowels of the store and onto the streets of New York City, on its way to the mail terminal.

"I hope it's a fur coat. . .or maybe a diamond necklace." Trish laughed as they shared a spaghetti dinner at a a small Italian restaurant in Little Italy.

"I don't think so," he said. "I picked a medium-size package. Too small for a coat, and too large for jewelry. I hope it's just an inexpensive item of clothing or maybe a man's tie. I don't want to deprive some kid of his Christmas toy or get stuck with a felony charge. In fact, I wish I could someday inform the store about how it happened, so they could fix it. Now, it's too risky."

After dinner, they walked over to NYU to a free Charlie Chaplin Film Festival. On the way home, they stopped for coffee at an all-night bistro.

Sunday was Trish's last day before she returned to Boston. Mrs. Rodriguez gave him the day off, so they had the whole day to themselves. They slept late, made love till the afternoon, and window shopped in midtown while sharing a big pretzel with mustard. People hurried about the streets, arms loaded with brightly wrapped packages and their faces full of holiday stress. At Rockefeller Center, he and Trish watched skaters glide about the ice and admired the decorated tree, standing tall and stately in the center of the world.

On Fifth Avenue across from Saint Patrick's Cathedral, Trish stopped to pet the horses slouching in the cold in front of their carriages. She pitied them for their harnessed slavery, while he sympathized with the drivers who waited on the carriage seats wearing threadbare Dickensian coats and top hats. He remembered working at the family ranch during icy winters. It was far different to be outside in the frigid air for fun rather than having to work in it like the carriage drivers.

Dinner was at a coffee shop over on Madison Avenue. Inside, warm air fogged the windows while the staff yelled orders and insults at each other in foreign languages. He was animated as he related another story about working at the store, and Trish laughed and hung on every word. When they were together she made him feel like the only other person in the world. Back at the rooming house, in their cozy cave in the city jungle, they sat on the bed and with a razor blade divided one of the little pills she had given him. Night moved slowly through lower Manhattan while in their room just off Bleecker Street, they made love until dawn. The acid coursing through their bodies accented the real. He woke at dawn to find the room cold, dank, and depressing.

It was Christmas Eve morning. He rode the subway with Trish to Penn Station for her train back to Boston. They sat close together on the seat oblivious to the crowd around them. On the platform at the station, neither spoke while he opened the front of his sheepskin coat and enclosed her inside it. She tilted her face up to him and they kissed. He held her against him, not wanting to let go.

"I had a great time," she whispered.

"Me, too. Just wish you wouldn't leave."

"I have to," she said. "My mom's expecting me home today."

The uniformed conductor looked at his watch. "Bo'oard!"

She went up on her toes to kiss him and backed away from him toward the train. "I can't wait to see my surprise gift from Lord & Taylor." She laughed. "Merry Christmas," she mouthed, standing beside the open car as hissing noises filled the tunnel. She said something else.

"What's that?" he yelled over the din. The train shunted with a loud clang, and she was ushered into the car by the conductor before the door closed. He thought she'd said she loved him. He thought it. He wished it.

The train pulled away from the platform, and he watched until it disappeared into the tunnel. *What's happening to me?* He felt a momentary panic. *What am I getting into?* When he exited the station, he was met by the full force of a new snowstorm in the city.

It was his last day at work. The store would be closed on Christmas Day and was packed with last-minute shoppers. Things were slow in the mail room as few packages were mailed out on Christmas Eve. At three o'clock in the afternoon Mrs. Rodriguez came down to see him. "Ju can go home now. Dere ees no more work and ju haf worked hard. Ju goot worker, Jeemy."

"Thanks, Mrs. Rodriguez," he said. "Thanks very much." He stopped by her desk to pick up his check and cashed it at the store bursar on his way out. A hundred and eighteen dollars, more money than he came into the city with just a week ago. He treated himself to a grand dinner at Mama Leone's, stuffing himself on pasta and garlic bread, and later window shopped around Times Square, enjoying the fantasy world of New York on Christmas Eve. Snow began to fall again. Santa bells clanged at kettles outside department stores as shoppers tossed in change and said "Merry Christmas" to strangers.

At the corner of Forty-Second Street and Sixth Avenue, a Salvation Army band made the air festive with brass and carols. That's Mom's favorite, he thought. *Hark the herald angels sing, glory to the newborn King.* He missed home. But mostly he missed Trish.

As colorful and exciting as the city was on Christmas Eve, it was just as deserted and depressing on Christmas Day. No one was out on the streets except those with no place to be, and no one to be with. Home and family occupied his thoughts along with Anita Beth, Linda Sue, Michelle, and what might have been. He stayed in his room most of the day, venturing out only once to eat and to call home.

They were all at the ranch. "Wish Merry Christmas to everyone for me from up here in New York."

"Now you be careful and write us more than you do. These telephone calls are a lot more expensive than a letter."

"I will, Mom. Tell everyone Merry Christmas."

"Good-bye," she said. "I love you and am real proud of you, Jimmy."

"I love you, too. Tell Dad I. . . .Well, bye, Mom." He walked back through empty streets to his room. He ached for Trish. The damn day seemed like it would never end.

That night he lay in darkness watching the string of lights twinkle around his door. He thought about what his mother said, "I'm real proud of you." He turned on his side and closed his eyes. After a while he opened them again and stared at the incense burner on the dresser. *If I'm going to be alone, then I'll be at my own place surrounded by my own things.*

Early the next morning he packed his bag, slipped his room key under the manager's door and boarded the first bus for Hartford. A pair of borrowed jumper cables and a friendly cop in the Hartford parking lot helped get his car started. Driving up Fox Trail, the cottage looked almost buried in snow. For the next several days he sat in front of the fire and wrote letters to old friends that he never mailed.

At two o'clock in the afternoon on December 29th, the mail arrived delivering the package from Lord & Taylor. He shook the box, felt movement and heard a soft rustle. He placed the package on the kitchen table to await the girls' return. Opening it crossed his mind, but it would be more fun with Trish. Every time he went into the kitchen, the package on the table beckoned.

Late that afternoon, he built a fire in the fireplace and cut a small piece of hashish from a greenish block he found in the top dresser drawer next to an empty packet of Trish's birth control pills. Turning on the television, he found an *"I Love Lucy"* rerun, and lit the hash in the water pipe Jennifer kept on the mantle. He held the smoke in his lungs as long as he could. After exhaling, he took four more deep tokes from the pipe.

A shiver passed through his body and he relaxed. After a few minutes a warm feeling settled over him and the world began to slow. The television was too loud, so he turned the sound off. Lucy was still on, but it didn't matter. Her mime told the whole story. He laughed. It was the funniest thing he'd ever seen. He rolled over and over on the floor laughing. He giggled. He howled, and snot flew out of his nose. He laughed harder.

Hunger was his next sensation. He hadn't eaten since breakfast, and that was only coffee and a peanut butter sandwich. Rummaging around in the kitchen, he found an open bag of potato chips and sat at the table. As he ate the stale salty chips one at a time, he stared at the package from Lord & Taylor. He picked it up and shook it. Something rustled. He broke the tape at one end of the package and peeked in. It was a gold metal tin with a decorative blue top. On the side, in blue script, it read, *A Product of England's Finest Bakery.*

"Food," he said out loud. *Pastries maybe. Something sweet. Anything's better than these leathery potato chips.* The brown shipping paper soon lay in shreds, and the tin sat before him. "Butter cookies," he said aloud. A treasure trove of round and oblong, golden, sugary, butter cookies. Each cookie provided a unique experience. He was keenly aware of the many different textures, shapes, and tastes. Some were broken; others were whole and complete; perfect cookies. As soon as he finished eating one, it was forgotten, and he started another. He dampened his finger with his tongue to pick up the last vestiges. The silvery bottom reflected his image. There were crumbs on his face and about his mouth. With a flick of the tongue they disappeared—the empty tin the only remaining evidence of his perfect crime.

On December 29th and 30th, an unexpected blizzard dumped thirty more inches of snow on Coventry. He was stranded at the cottage for three days before the snowplows could get in and free the houses up on Fox Trail. By New Year's Eve his boredom and loneliness felt terminal.

At seven o'clock in the evening he built a fire, stacked enough dry logs next to the hearth to last him through the night, and opened the little velvet box Trish had given him for Christmas. He licked a finger and touched one of the tiny pills. It stuck on the glue of his saliva. He placed it on the back of his tongue and swallowed. It was the first and last time he ever took acid alone.

CHAPTER 42

Sunday morning, Jim woke to find an ice storm had come through during the night making the streets glazed and dangerous. He worried about the girls driving back to school from Boston and watched for them at the window. Radio reports said the highways were crowded with students returning to college after the long holiday. It had turned dark outside when he heard Trish's and Ann Marie's cars pull into the driveway.

"I'll be out to help with those bags," he called from the front door and went back to the bedroom to don boots and a coat. When he went outside, he ran into Ann Marie and Jennifer carrying in a case of beer with a large red bow on it.

"Merry Christmas!" they shouted in unison.

"A case of Coors. I don't believe it," he said, taking the box from them. He held it out in the porch light. "Thanks. The perfect gift for a Texan."

"We thought so." Ann Marie giggled. "We had a friend bring it back from Colorado."

He saw Trish standing at the trunk of her car. "Hey babe, wait a minute. I'll give you a hand." He set the case of Coors down on the porch and crunched through snow. "How was the drive. . ."

"Just leave my stuff in the living room," she said, brushing past him. "I'll get it later."

He watched her go into the house.

Ann Marie was on the sofa filing her nails, and Jennifer stood in the kitchen looking in the open refrigerator when he set the last bag in the living room and nodded toward Trish's closed door.

Ann Marie shrugged. "I thought you guys had a fight or something."

He shook his head.

Ringo nudged his hand. "Hello there, boy." Jim knelt and rubbed the Irish Setter's ears. "Did you take good care of my girls?"

Ringo licked his face and went sniffing around the room before flopping down in his spot by the fireplace.

He went into the bedroom and sat on the bed next to Trish. She lay facing the wall with her back to him. "What's wrong?" He stroked her arm. "You okay?"

She turned and looked at him. Tears coursed down her cheeks. "I'm sorry. I feel sad about a million things right now. I just need some time alone."

He wanted to ask more but decided against it. Taking her hand in his, he squeezed it. On his way out, he switched off the light and closed the door.

CHAPTER 43

Trish buried her face in her pillow and the tears flowed. She wanted to tell him how she had planned to spend New Year's Eve with him at the cottage when her father's binge on Christmas Day ruined the family's holiday and almost killed him. The doctor insisted he remain abstinent during his recovery. A couple of days without alcohol and her father's abuse turned razor-sharp. Her mother had pleaded with her to stay and help until school started. Now, guilt ate at her insides as she thought of her mother alone facing her father's hateful tirades. *I couldn't take it anymore, I couldn't, I couldn't.* She wept into the pillow. *And I can never tell Jim.*

CHAPTER 44

J im entered the bedroom an hour later and found her asleep under the covers. He undressed and lay next to her in the dark. He had never seen her so upset. What happened to the sparkling happy Trish he put on the train in New York on Christmas Eve? What happened during the holidays and why wouldn't she tell him about it? After a long moment, the old green-eyed monster showed up. *Alec.*

The next morning, they walked together across campus checking their grades from the previous semester. She still hadn't said anything about the previous night. As they went from building-to-building, he kept up a running banter and was rewarded now and then with a wan smile. Grade lists were posted by the classroom doors. He had done better than expected: a couple of B's in some easy subjects but most were C's, and the expected F in Chemistry turned into a D. Trish's grades were much better; A's in her Education courses and B's in the rest. Her graduation was only a semester away.

When the second term started, everyone on campus settled in for a long hard winter. The crust of snow covering the ground grew thicker and dirtier with each passing day. January turned into a string of short grey days and long nights. It was dark when the house stirred in the morning, and it was dark when everyone returned home after classes. Much to his relief, Trish seemed to have gotten over whatever had bothered her after Christmas and was back to her perky self.

The electric radiators in the living room and in their bedroom did little to combat winter's icy chill. The two warmest places in the cottage were in front of the fire and under the down comforter on their bed. During long winter evenings, he told her stories of growing up in Morrison, of stubborn horses, obstinate football coaches, and brilliant sunsets over the canyon.

"And did you brand baby cows with red hot branding irons like in the movies?" She sat curled up on his lap in front of the fire, her head on his shoulder. "So cruel. Burning a baby cow on his bum."

"Nah." He laughed. "Some still do that, but we put metal tags in their ears. Tags are a lot easier than branding—for both the cowboy and the calf."

"You and your brother working with your dad on the ranch sounds like "Bonanza"—the Cartwright family on the Ponderosa. Your big brother is Hoss and you're the cute one, like Little Joe." She put her arms around his neck and kissed his cheek. "I always wanted a cowboy."

"Yeah," Jim said. "Just like the Cartwrights."

After returning home from class in the afternoons, he disliked the cold so much that he rarely left the cottage. It was so cold most mornings in the bedroom he could see his own breath. It was too easy to blow off class and roll over under the warm covers. What happened to the young lieutenant who could've been a general, he wondered one day after waking to find it past two in the afternoon.

Joel dropped by some days after class to visit and often stayed for dinner. The semester was going slow for him as well. He had dated a Jewish girl in his graduate program in December and even thought something might come of it, but she returned from the holidays married to a Presbyterian from Rhode Island. "He's a gynecologist," Joel said. "Think about it, a gentile gynecologist. Mother doesn't think it's natural. She said it's like a Jew being a country singer."

Just after Valentines' Day, Joel brought a new couple by the cottage. He had known Mike and Jerri Schwartz in Albany. Jim thought Jerri looked like a chunky Doris Day and Mike reminded him of

Bernard with his trimmed beard and Hush Puppy shoes. Over the next few weeks Mike and Jerri spent a lot of time at the cottage. They were pleasant enough but what interested Jim most was they had an open marriage.

Jerri, a doctoral candidate in philosophy, was regularly seeing an undergraduate student from Norwalk on Wednesday afternoons. "I go over to his place," she said one night as the two couples shared a water pipe in front of the living room fire. "He's only twenty but I can't get enough of him when he. . .you know?" She winked at Trish. " He's so creative and so intelligent. We talk about everything. His roommates sometimes get in the way. I've had to scoot naked out of the bathroom when one or the other has come in to pee. After a while, everyone gets used to it."

Jim watched Mike for any sign suggesting he wasn't so keen about it, while Jerri went on about her trysts, and how they benefited their marriage. Mike smiled under his beard but said nothing.

"I think she's got a stud and Mike just has a hard-on," Jim said to Trish one night when they dropped the couple off at their home after a movie.

"Don't make fun of them," Trish said. She slid away and sat with her back against the passenger door. "What they're doing is very courageous. I think it's possible to love more than one person at the same time. Jerri told me they've worked hard to eliminate jealousy, which is very destructive, like acid, to a relationship. They should be commended for having a modern marriage."

They drove a while in silence while alarm bells were going off in Jim's head. *Is this what happened in Boston at Christmas?*

"Well, if ol' Mikey makes a move on you," Jim said, "I'll bust his fuzzy head like an egg shell."

"Oh, and that's a real enlightened attitude. I'm glad you're so tolerant of—"

"Has he propositioned you?" he interrupted. There was a momentary pause.

"Has Jerri made a move on you?" she countered.

"No, but it's not the same thing." He faltered.

"Oh sure," she said. "Well, James, the world is changing."

Another long silence passed.

"As long as they are happy," he said. "I guess they should do whatever's right for them, whatever feels good. For some reason though, I sense Mike's not that happy about it. Either he's jealous or isn't getting his share. Probably, the latter."

"Oh, you boys have only one thing on your mind."

"And you love it," Jim said, reaching for her hand and pulling her over to him. She rested her head on his shoulder. He smelled the scent of soap in her blonde hair as they drove through the snow-covered countryside.

"Truthfully, has Jerri come on to you?" she asked.

"Never, if you don't count the hand job last Saturday in the kitchen." He grinned.

The last Friday in February, he met Trish after class at the Student Center. He helped her bundle up in coat, gloves, and woolen hat, and led her across packed snow to the parking lot. They were the first home. The cottage felt like an icebox. He carried in wood from the porch and readied a fire while she put on one of his flannel shirts and jumped under a quilt on the sofa. With the fire blazing, he peeled off his own layers of clothing. Standing naked at the foot of the couch, he pulled her cover away, baring Trish's goose pimpled legs to the cold air.

"No. Please don't!" She grabbed for the blanket, and they wrestled together on the sofa. She spooned herself back into him and they watched the fire. "Why're you always so warm and I'm so cold?"

"It's the jalapenos I ate as a kid." His hands moved under her flannel shirt touching all the right places. The fire crackled and popped as the flames consumed wet wood.

Dinner that evening included Joel and Ann Marie's Anthony, and Mike and Jerri. Conversation at the table was peppered with discussions of protest rallies on campus, and the activities of several radical student groups. Jennifer updated everyone on her pursuit of her sexy drama teacher, while Jerri reported on her afternoon with a new lover. After dinner, he and Trish shared a water pipe in their room and then devoured each other. Jerri's description of her new stud's ardor fueled their passion. Afterwards they lay in each other's arms, quite in their own thoughts, until sleep overtook them.

Jim stood in front of the sink looking in the bathroom mirror. Like most Saturday mornings, he and Trish had slept late. He turned on the tap and lathered up his face. After wetting his razor, he carved a clean path from cheek to jaw.

"Jennifer and I are going to do laundry." Trish called from outside the bathroom door. "I took the sheets off our bed."

"Okay!" he responded loud enough to be heard over the running water. "Bring me back a donut. A chocolate one." His breath fogged the glass.

The front door opened and closed. He rinsed the razor and looked in the mirror. In his mind's eye he saw her lugging pillowcases full of dirty clothes through the snow to her car. What had begun as an adventure with Trish last October had now grown beyond anything he ever imagined. She filled up his life. He savored each day with her, each moment. It felt too right. He pulled on a clean pair of jeans and a sweater and went to sit on the couch to watch cartoons while he waited for the girls to return.

CHAPTER 45

Trish parked in front of the Laundromat, and Jennifer went next door to a convenience store to get change for the machines. Waiting in the car, Trish caught the scent of Jim's cologne from the laundry in the back seat. She worried she had fallen in love with him. She had never experienced anything this intense—and it terrified her.

In the past, her relationships always ended the same way. The boy became too possessive, and that was her cue to bail. Over time she had developed a sixth sense that told her when to start crafting an escape. She had been at that point with Alec when she met Jim in the encounter group. His being from Texas had caused her to let down her guard. It had started out very loosey goosey, and she always thought he would someday leave her to go home. But as the semester dragged on, her sixth sense had begun firing off red flares. She watched Jennifer returning to the car with a fistful of quarters and felt a growing sense of panic. *What do I do now?*

CHAPTER 46

By late March, the sun warmed the winds, and the world outside the cottage on Fox Trail began to thaw. Mid-semester exams came and went.

"I've done as good as I can on my own," Jim said to Joel as they refilled their coffee cups at the snack bar on campus. "The only way I can improve my grades now is to attend class more often, and I will now that the thermometer outside our kitchen window is registering again."

The following Saturday, Jennifer and Ann Marie went to Boston for the weekend leaving him and Trish alone at the house. At noon they took the last two acid tablets in the black box she had given him for Christmas and made a pallet on the floor in front of a hissing fire. "The gift that keeps on giving," he said, as he closed the empty box. The Moody Blues' "Threshold of a Dream" played on the stereo. After a while he became acutely aware of the lingering aroma of their breakfast, the dirty plates still unwashed on the kitchen table. The smell of sausage and eggs permeated the walls and carpet and became the total scent of the universe.

In mid-afternoon, they lay naked and exhausted together under a blanket in front of the hearth's dying embers. He held her tight against him, afraid she would fall off the planet should he let go. It felt like they were the only two people in creation. *Adam and Eve hiding from God after eating the fruit of knowledge.*

She was child and playmate, friend and lover, and Mother Earth. He couldn't remember how many times they'd made love. Was it once? A hundred? Or not at all? Why count? Who's counting?

Jim moved his arm from under her head. Her blonde hair spilled over the floor. He pushed himself up on one elbow and looked down at her. Her mouth formed a smile. She reached for his free hand and kissed his open palm. Her eyes remained closed.

"You're beautiful," he whispered.

Her arm went up around him and pulled his face down to hers.

"I love you with all my heart," he said, nuzzling her bare shoulder.

"I know." She pushed his lips down to her breasts.

"I want you to be the mother of my children," he said. He drew back to observe her reaction.

She pulled his head back down. "That feels so good. Don't stop."

Panic raced through Trish's chest. Her mind sprinted away, leaving an empty shell as he began to make love to her. *What does he mean? I can't end up like that—like my mother. What have I done? Stupid! Stupid! Stupid! He as so much asked me to marry him. What else could he have meant? He wants me to be the mother of his children. Children! Oh, my god.*

She would never forget that day, that scary morning. She had been playing with dolls in her bedroom and whispering lullabies to them to not disturb her father sleeping in the adjacent room. She froze when he suddenly awoke and started bellowing for her mother. She held still, not daring to breathe. His barrages grew louder followed by the noise of breaking glass.

The sound of her mother's sobs seeped under the door. It wasn't a hurt cry, like when she scraped a knee. It was a sad, soulful sound that transfixed Trish. Somewhere, sometime during that part of her childhood, she had vowed never to become like her mother, a butterfly trapped by a horrid spider.

It must be the acid, Jim thought as Trish clung to him and sobbed.

CHAPTER 47

As April dragged on, Jim sensed things were changing. Trish found fault where she hadn't before. She snapped at him about nothing in front of Jennifer and Ann Marie and got angry over his jokes only meant to lighten the tense atmosphere. After their fights, instead of accepting his efforts to make up, she remained moody. Even the girls walked on eggshells around her at the cottage. When Easter and spring break arrived, he suggested a week apart might help. He hoped the problem was cabin fever caused by the long winter. They all could use some space.

"Trish is going home for the week," he was talking to Potts on the phone, "and I thought I'd visit you up at Dartmouth."

"Hey, that would be great," Potts responded. "We have lots to talk about."

"Yeah, it'll be fun," Jim said. He was glad that his old friend sounded happy to hear from him. They hadn't spoken since before Christmas when Potts withdrew his invitation to spend the holiday at Oak Lawn. "I'll be up Friday night," Jim continued. "I'll bring a sleeping bag. Your roommate will be okay with me staying there?"

"Think so." Potts laughed. "He's a Democrat but comes from a fine Chicago family."

Friday morning was an endurance test. He and Trish were alone at the cottage as the girls had departed the night before with Ringo. While packing in their room, Jim spoke as little as possible to prevent another argument. After moving their bags onto the porch, he waited for her to finish in the bathroom. Out in the yard, the sun felt warm on his face and brown rivulets trickled out from under crusty piles of snow.

He locked the front door to the cottage and helped load her bags into her Mustang. He shut the trunk and saw her standing beside the driver's door, her eyes full of sadness. "Hey, it's okay, it's only for a week," he said. "Some time apart will be good for both of us."

"I know, I know," she said and looked away.

He took a step toward her but stopped when she opened the car door.

"Have a good week with your folks, and I'll see you back here on Sunday," he said.

"Tell Potts 'hi' for me." Neither of them moved. "Good-bye, Jim," she said, and got in behind the wheel.

He thought he saw a tear on her cheek, and something twisted in his gut. The engine cranked, and she backed out of the driveway. He waved, but she didn't look back.

All the way to New Hampshire, he worried. It had been a hard winter and they had pretty much stayed inside the last three months. How could you not get on each other's nerves cooped up together like that? This week apart could be just what they needed. He already missed her.

Dartmouth's spring vacation wasn't for another week, so the campus teemed with activity. He found Potts' dorm, and his friend seemed pleased to see him. Potts crammed the week full of hockey games, hockey practice, and hockey team parties. They spent late-night hours at the Rongovian Embassy in Hanover sucking down beers and telling army stories. Potts told him he felt ancient around the young kids at school whose main concern was their number in the draft lottery.

On Saturday afternoon before going out to celebrate his last night in New Hampshire, Jim called the house in Coventry to see if anyone had returned.

"Hello?" Trish's voice surprised him.

"Hey, you're back early. Are the girls with you?"

"No, just me." She sounded distant. "You and Potts having a good time?"

251

"It's been fun, but I miss you and can't wait to get home. Did you have a good week in Boston? How are your parents?"

"Fine, everything. . .everyone is fine. When are you coming back?"

"I'm leaving here early tomorrow morning. I should be there around two o'clock if the weather stays clear."

"Good. We need to talk."

There it was. It didn't surprise him. Deep in his gut he had been expecting something like this. And now it lay there in the open, ugly and wriggling.

"What about?" He felt like she had just pulled the pin on a hand grenade.

"We'll talk when you get here. We just need to talk about some things."

"About us?"

"I don't want to do it over the phone. It can wait till you get here tomorrow. Just hurry back."

"You won't tell me now?"

"No. Just hurry up and come home."

"You know I'll worry about it all night and all the way home tomorrow. I can't stand the suspense."

"Don't worry about it. Have a good time tonight and drive back safely tomorrow. But just come home."

It was a quarter to two in the afternoon when his station wagon came to rest on the driveway. Her Mustang was parked by the side door. The familiar sight made him feel a little better. He beeped the horn and grabbed his bag from the back seat. When he opened the front door, he felt like he had been kicked in the stomach by a mule.

Three suitcases were lined up in the middle of the living room. Trish sat at the kitchen table writing on a piece of paper. He looked at the luggage and then at her.

"I was leaving you a note," she said. "It was killing me, waiting for you to get home."

He felt like an ice statue, a living being frozen in time.

"I'm dropping out of school and going back to Boston." She put the pen down. "Alec and I spent some time together while I was home this week. It felt really good. We concluded it didn't work out for us before because he was in Boston and I was here every week."

She sounded like she was chatting with a girlfriend about a new dress. He saw her lips moving, heard the words, but really didn't hear. Inside he screamed, *What about us? What about your graduation in May? Fuck Alec! What about us? What about me?*

"Well, anyway. . . ." She came into the living room. "I've decided I'm just tired of school, maybe it was the long winter or something, but I want more of a break than one week, so, what the heck, I dropped out. It was so easy. I can always return next fall and finish. I'll get a job in Boston for the next six months, and I'm going to play, enjoy my life for a change. And Alec is so different. He's not so angry all the time and so hung-up on himself and his problems. He's a lot happier and not doing so much dope. He's thinking about not dealing anymore."

"What about us?" Jim said, his voice sounded hoarse.

"Maybe this is the good part," she said.

Jim remained silent. *What does she mean good part? Good, like we're going to remove your testicles, but we'll use a very sharp knife?*

"Alec, understands that you and I have feelings for each other, and he thinks that's cool. He's much more secure than before."

Feelings? What the hell does she mean, feelings? I want her to be my mate for life, my wife, the mother of my children!

"So, we've agreed that I'll spend weekends with you in Storrs and go back to Boston to stay with him during the week. A reverse of how it was last fall, except this time, you will both know about each other. What do you think?"

His brain had jammed. He wanted to grab her shoulders and shake her. At the same time, he wanted to wrap her in his arms and never let her go. He wanted to ask. . .no, beg her not to leave. Instead, he said nothing. He stood frozen. A pillar of salt.

Trish floated across the room toward him. Like a small boat in a harbor, she docked, slipped her arms around his neck and kissed him. "It'll be okay. You'll see," she said softly. "It's hard for you to understand all this now, but the question is, do you still want to see me? Do you want me to come to Storrs to spend weekends with you?"

His arms hung useless at his side. He swallowed a hard lump in his throat. "Yes, I. . . .Yes."

"Okay, it's a deal." She unwound from him and stood beside her bags. "Then, I'll be back here next Friday afternoon. I'll be back before you realize I'm even gone. The phone number and address of where I'll be staying is on the table."

He saw the envelope on the dinette.

"I'm leaving most of my stuff here and will take it as needed. You can have my two drawers in our dresser. I've already emptied them."

She sounded too businesslike. She had already divided the property. The dresser drawers were his part of the settlement.

Trish picked up two of her bags and moved them to the door. She put on her coat and turned back to him. For a moment her mask slipped, and a look of sadness clouded her eyes. He saw her bite her lip and attempt a smile. "So, I'll see you next weekend. Wish me luck."

A look of hurt crossed her face when he didn't respond. There were a million things he wanted to say, to cry out in wounded rage, but he couldn't speak. His thoughts scurried about in his skull attempting emergency action as he watched her walk out the door. Her Mustang sprayed gravel when she drove away.

The late-night news was on the tube when Jennifer and Ann Marie arrived at the house. They found him on the sofa staring at the soundless screen, his legs stretched out in front of him with his boots resting on the coffee table. A half empty bottle of Jack Daniels on the floor beside him. His eyes were partially open, but there was no other sign of life. Jennifer and Ann Marie hovered over him.

"We think it's great for you guys to have an open relationship like this, so mature, and. . .and unselfish." Ann Marie stood behind the sofa massaging his neck muscles.

"Really groovy," Jennifer emoted enthusiasm, learned in acting class in which she earned a D. "Trish can now enjoy life twice as much, and you're free to do the same."

He didn't hear much more. The figures in the room blurred. Voices blended and became distant. The bottle of Jack Daniels had been left at the house by Potts when he visited before Christmas. He thought he heard Potts' voice, "It'll be okay, Cowboy. This will all work out tomorrow."

He had an eerie awareness of being out of his body. He was looking down on the girls struggling to undress him. The last thing he remembered was Ann Marie's round bottom in his face as she straddled his leg tugging at his boot. The boot loosened and slipped away the same moment as his consciousness.

CHAPTER 48

Jim opened his eyes. Sunlight filled the room. Trish's scent in the bedding reminded him of his loss. He moved his hand over the sheets and finding nothing, grasped her pillow and pulled it to him. His head pounded like a metronome, and he felt waves of nausea sweeping over him. The room spun, and he took deep breaths to keep from throwing up. Bile leaked into his mouth, the burning vapors vented through his nose. When the crisis passed, he looked at the clock next to the bed. It was ten-thirty. His stomach convulsed again, and he knew he had missed another day of classes. Cradling her pillow in his arms, his brain disengaged, and he fell back asleep. At one in the afternoon he made a trip to the bathroom. On the way back, he stopped by the kitchen and found a carton of orange juice in the fridge. He finished it off.

When Ann Marie arrived home, he was back in bed. He sensed a presence in the room but didn't open his eyes. When the covers lifted, he recognized her perfume. The mattress shifted. Her hand brushed across his chest. Rubbery nipples pressed into his bare back.

Her caresses, warm and soothing, feathered down his abdomen. He rolled onto his back and pulled her on top of him. She felt heavier than Trish, everything bigger and softer. Her tongue made love to his ear and her teeth nipped his shoulder. Hard nipples trailed down his tense body. She moved slowly. . .kissing, licking, and biting. Her sharp metal earrings scraped his legs and all feeling became warmth and wetness. Grief and anger poured from him as he took her again and again. He worried briefly that he might hurt her but sensed his fury fueled her own fires.

It was dark outside when he woke. Ann Marie slept beside him. He went into the bathroom to take a long hot shower. When he came out with a towel around his waist, he found her in the living room, in a sweatshirt and jeans, thumbing through a magazine.

She looked up at him. "You hungry?"

He studied her a moment, wondering if he should be the first to say something about what had happened.

"We could wait for Jennifer then go for pizza," she said, looking back at her magazine.

He leaned against the doorframe and ran a hand through his wet hair. "I can't remember the last time I ate. If Jenn's not here by the time I'm dressed, let's bring her something back."

"How're you feeling?" Ann Marie put the magazine on the coffee table.

"Better than I look but food will help. Give me a minute and I'll be ready."

They didn't talk much as they ate at a table in the crowded pizza shop across the street from campus. Heat from the ovens steamed up the front, and smoke hung in the air like a gauzy curtain.

"You guys will get back together again," Ann Marie said. "Why else would she spend weekends with you?" Ann Marie reached for the last slice on the battered metal tray.

He shrugged. "We'll see, I guess. But it can never be the same." He got up from the table and went to the cashier to order a calzone-to-go for Jennifer.

"You know," Ann Marie said in the car as they drove home. "I love Anthony, but I couldn't stand to see you hurting. After all, you are my housemate and my friend."

Jim glanced at her on the seat next to him, "I'm sorry if you feel bad about—"

"No, I don't have any regrets," she said, putting her bejeweled hand on his arm. "I just meant that it won't change anything between me and Anthony. We're lovers and you are my friend. Two different things. If I can't fuck a friend to make him feel better, then screw Anthony. I just mean. . . ."

"Thanks." He patted her hand on his arm. "You're pretty damn special, and I'm glad we're housemates. . .and friends."

"Me too," she said, scooting closer and kissing him on his cheek. "Besides, I've wanted to see what you were like in bed ever since you moved in."

"Oh?" He laughed. "And?"

"I missed the spurs." She giggled. "Everything else was what I expected. I can't believe Trish would. . . ."

"Me neither," he said.

When he parked in the driveway, loud rock music blared through the open front door. Ringo followed him into the house from the porch whining and grumbling. Ann Marie took the calzone into Jennifer's room while he picked up Trish's letter and settled into the chair by the fireplace. As he read it for the first time, the wound reopened.

My Dear Jim,

I waited at the house for two days to tell you about my decision to return to Boston, but I chickened out and decided to write you, instead. I know your logical mind will not understand nor accept my decision to change our relationship, but give me a chance to explain.

I have special feelings for you that I recognize as approaching love, if not love itself. And if you could accept that with no obligations or demands, then maybe I wouldn't have to make this difficult decision. But you are expecting more from me than I am prepared to give anyone at this time.

I recognized this week that I still have feelings for Alec. I've treated him terribly and he is forgiving. He wants only what I can give him and expects nothing more. He also accepts that you remain very important to me.

I'm leaving school for the rest of the semester and moving back to Boston to get a job. I'll probably return in the fall, but I'm not sure it will be UConn, perhaps Northeastern or Boston U. Alec has asked me to stay at his place in Cambridge so if you need to reach me, the address and phone number is on the envelope.

Jim, I love you but in a way you cannot understand or accept. It's impossible for me to give what you want. I'm not sure I even know how. I'd like to be in your life someway, to continue seeing you, that is if you don't hate me. I can come to Storrs on weekends, but it's okay if you don't want me to come. Alec supports this. Unfortunately, that's all I can give to those I love. I don't understand it any more than you do.

Please, please, please understand and don't hate me. Call if you want to see me in Storrs next weekend.

Trish

He reread the letter and gazed into the cold fireplace. The next thing he knew, he stood in the kitchen dialing the number on the envelope. *If she's going to ration herself, I want my share.* As he waited for the line to connect, he thought about Mike and Jerri Schwartz. He hadn't seen them in a couple of weeks. Had they heard about Trish moving out? What about Joel? Guess *I should call him.*

The phone clicked and digested his call. Anxiety gnawed at him. *Maybe she's changed her mind?*

"Hello?"

He paused a moment to calm the anger boiling in his guts. Six months before, things had been reversed.

"Hello, Alec? Jim Davis, here. I want to speak with Trish." No small talk. He had nothing to say to Alec.

"Uh. . .Just a minute." The tone of Alec's voice told him the feeling was mutual.

An unnerving silence passed before she came on the line. "Are you feeling better? Jennifer was afraid you'd overdosed on whiskey. I've never seen you drink anything but beer and wine."

"I'm okay," he said. Her cheerfulness lifted his spirits. "I just read the letter you left and thought I'd see how you're doing."

"Okay, I guess. Actually, I'm doing great."

He hoped she was lying.

"Are you sober now? You ought to stick to the water pipe and good Columbian grass. It's natural, nutritious and makes you funny, but doesn't make you sick."

"Sober enough to know I'd feel a lot better if you were here with me," he said. A long moment passed while he waited for her to respond. She didn't, and he picked up again before the silence became too awkward. "Anyway, I decided if Mike and Jerri can do it. . .see other people that is, and still keep a relationship together, then I'll give it a try." He didn't say it as convincing as he wished. "Will I see you this weekend?"

"I told you I'll come to Storrs every weekend if you want."

He paused a moment, "Yes, I definitely want. Besides, everyone here misses you." He tried to sound upbeat. "Any luck finding a job?"

"Today was my first day to look. There's something at the Medical School at Harvard that's promising. They need an assistant lab technician who's had some chemistry. I'm keeping my fingers crossed."

"Hope it works out," he said. "If that's what you want." There was only one more thing left to say. "Uh Trish. . ." he swallowed, moving the lump down into his chest.

"Yes?" she responded softly.

"I love you and miss you."

"Me too," she whispered, and hung up.

For the rest of the week he stayed in his room. Ann Marie twice entered his bed but failed to generate any hard interest. Each time, he fell asleep in her arms. Food was forgotten, as were basic requirements for hygiene. By Thursday night, his bedroom smelled like a locker room, and he had a wasted unshaven appearance.

His agreement to share Trish was only a staying action. Every moment his mind worked overtime devising, reviewing, discarding plans. The task was more difficult because he still didn't have a clear understanding of why she had left him. On Friday morning he showered and shaved, put fresh sheets on the bed and opened the windows to air out the place. A little after five Trish arrived in high spirits. In the excitement Ringo lost control on the living room carpet.

Before dinner, the girls sat in a circle on the living room floor catching up on Boston and old friends. Jim lay on the sofa watching them. *She's back. Even if just for the weekend.*

She didn't mention Alec, and no one asked. When they went to bed that night, the room scented with new candles, Jim was gentle and attentive. For the next two days, he couldn't keep his eyes or hands off her. Time flew past at supersonic speed and Sunday evening, she left him to drive back to Boston.

Monday morning, he attended a few classes before giving up and returning home to bed. Joel stopped by and sat in the darkened bedroom cajoling him to get on with his life.

Tuesday, it rained all day, and again on Wednesday. Thursday turned clear and sunny. He spent the day cleaning the bedroom, his car, and himself. At five o'clock on Friday, he heard her car door slam. Saturday evolved into one of those warm spring days in New England that makes one forget the harsh winter. The temperature inched up into the mid-seventies and the crocuses were blooming in yards all around Coventry. Trish packed a lunch and they carried it down to a picnic table at Coventry Lake. New buds dotted trees and bushes all around the shoreline. He spread a blanket under a tree. After finishing a bottle of wine and their sandwiches, they lay next to each other and talked, and laughed, and pointed out figures in the clouds scudding across the blue sky. The afternoon grew warmer, and he removed his shirt. Trish turned onto her stomach to look at him. Her finger traced the curve of his bicep.

"I haven't told you yet because I was waiting for the perfect time," she said. "But I got that job at Harvard. I start at the lab on Monday."

He closed his eyes. "Congratulations," he said without enthusiasm. "It's what you wanted."

"I think so," she said, turning over on her back. "The pay is ten dollars an hour, so I should save some money. It's also a professional job at Harvard, which will look good on my resume. Much better than waiting tables or working at the phone company."

That evening they drove to Mike and Jerri's apartment for dinner with several new couples. Afterwards everyone passed around water pipes in the living room. He saw Jerri washing dishes in the kitchen and grabbed a towel to dry.

"So, how is it going with you two?" Jerri asked, passing him a wet platter.

"The jury is still out," he said, putting the platter in the cabinet. "We're winging it. I wish there was an instruction book. Trish is making up the rules as we go, and I'm just going along. What about you guys? How're you and your Wednesday afternoon pal making out?"

"We're not." Jerri shrugged. Her arms were covered in soap bubbles. "He came back after spring break a changed person. He met some people in New York that turned him onto Krishna. He left school, shaved his head, and moved to their god damn commune in Oregon." She passed him two water tumblers to dry.

"Mike says I should take a break; that it was getting out of hand, but I miss him. He was a cute guy and a fabulous fuck."

On Sunday afternoon, Jim stood with Ringo at the top of the hill and watched Trish drive away. The day had seemed strained, but he chalked it up to anxiety about starting her new job. As he watched her Mustang turn onto the highway, he had a feeling that something was terribly wrong.

Monday, he attended a full day of classes and ran into Elizabeth from the encounter group on the steps at the Student Center. Her long hair glistened in the sunlight and her sleeveless sweater displayed the fullness of her breasts. He asked about her kids.

"They're living with their father this semester," she said. "I see them two weekends a month. And how are you doing?" She looked into his eyes as if reading his thoughts. She touched his arm, and he looked down at her hand. It was a woman's hand, long fingers with coral manicured nails. Blue veins traced the tendons. She smiled at him and squeezed. "I heard about Trish. You okay? Come to dinner one day this week and we can talk about that and other things."

"Thanks," he smiled. "I'd like that."

She squeezed him again, her dark eyes sparkled.

Driving home, he thought about Elizabeth's invitation. *Maybe another time, another place.* Right now, there was only room in his life for one girl, and he was scrambling hard to keep her.

When Friday came, he cleaned house in preparation for their third weekend together. A foreboding feeling dogged him all day, but he dismissed it as jealous paranoia. Mike and Jerri had invited them to their apartment for dinner that evening. He didn't particularly want to go, but Trish enjoyed their company.

By eight o'clock, she hadn't arrived, nor had she called.

Now that she's working, she probably didn't leave Boston until after six, Jim reasoned. He paced the living room and went to the window each time he heard a car on the road.

At nine, he phoned Jerri to say Trish had been delayed and go ahead and eat without them. "I'll call when she gets here, he said, "Maybe we'll come over for coffee if it's not too late."

Rain fell on the roof, and a fog lay over the valley below the house. The phone remained silent as if keeping secrets. Ringo slept next to the fire that sizzled and popped with wet wood. At ten, he turned on the television to check the news. After watching Star Trek episodes till midnight, he attempted to snooze.

Returning from the window after another false alarm, he flopped down in the chair and swore under his breath. Ringo raised his head and yawned. Jim stared into the dying fire and thought about all the things that might have happened. *Maybe a wreck and she's in a hospital. Her car could even be in a ditch off the highway.*

At one in the morning he put some grass in Jennifer's water

pipe hoping it would put him to sleep. Instead, his thoughts raced about New England looking for Trish. She could've been kidnapped by some maniac roaming the highway. He had warned her about picking up hitchhikers more than once. Maybe she decided to make their breakup complete. How would she tell him? Not showing up was a good way. He thought about calling Alec's house in Cambridge.

As the night wore on, his thoughts turned to home and working on the ranch in the hot sun till muscles ached, then cooling down with a drink of cold well water, the water pouring forth from a galvanized pipe, pumped up from a subterranean aquifer by the windmill standing spread-legged on the West Texas plains. He thought of John Henry and Linda Sue and wondered if his brother ever lay in bed at night worrying about his problems. Would his brother understand his pain? *Oh god, where's Potts when I need him?* "Trish! Trish! Trish!" He moaned into the sofa pillow. *Please call me!*

It was Saturday morning when Jennifer returned from her date and found him sleeping on the couch. Ringo had peed on the floor and sat by the door looking guilty. Jim was shaving when Ann Marie arrived home.

"You mean she didn't even call? Anthony brought me back today, so we could spend time together. You should call her to see if anything's wrong. This isn't like Trish, not to call or anything."

By four o'clock in the afternoon, he could no longer wait. Nor would he stand by and watch their relationship die unattended. Finding the crumpled envelope with her number, he went to the phone in the kitchen. Jennifer and Ann Marie were both napping. The house wore an eerie silence. Ringo followed and lay beside the kitchen table, licking Jim's bare feet.

He counted ten rings and pictured a black telephone on a small table in a hallway somewhere in Cambridge. "Eleven, twelve." He matched each ring to a red strawberry in the print wallpaper by the phone. No one's home, he thought. The phone's ringing away in an empty house. *Dammit, where are they?* He was about to hang up when the ringing stopped.

"Hello?" a voice answered. "Hello? Hello?"

"Alec?" He found his breath. "Is Trish there?" As soon as he said it, he regretted the too casual tone of his voice.

Silence thundered along the wire, but he knew Alec hadn't hung up on him. "This is Jim Davis. Let me talk to Trish." His voice sounded crisp with authority and tinged with anger. "I want to talk to her, now!"

More seconds of silence passed. "She doesn't want to talk to you." His words were almost slurred. "She doesn't want to talk to you or see you again."

"What was that?" Alarm filled his chest. "Let me talk to her. Dammit, give her the phone so she can tell me herself!"

No response.

He tried again. "If what you say is true, I have to hear it from Trish."

"I'm sorry," Alec said in a whisper, "She can't come to the phone." His voice sounded far away. "It'd be best if you didn't call here. Go back to Texas and live your life. Just leave us alone."

Jim lowered his voice. "I want to hear it from her. If that's what she wants, she's got to tell me herself. She'll have no trouble from me. But," this time he spiked his words, "I don't trust you. I don't like you. And you don't like me. That's okay, but listen carefully, asshole, I won't take this shit from you."

Another long moment passed before Alec spoke. He sounded sleepy, like he hadn't heard anything Jim had said. "I'm sorry, she can't talk to you."

The phone clicked.

"The son-of-a-bitch hung up on me!" Jim slammed down the receiver.

Ringo looked up from the floor with cocked ears.

"I ought to kill the bastard!" Jim kicked a chair into the kitchen table.

Ringo started barking.

"It's okay, boy, it's okay." Jim patted Ringo's head. "It's okay," he said again without believing it.

He went into the living room and stared out the window. He needed a plan and not the parade of half options that kept firing his emotions. If she really wanted to break things off, it would've been easier for everyone to have told him on the phone. All she had to say was "I don't want to see you." Six simple words. That's why he didn't believe Alec, and until he knew for sure, he wasn't going away so easily. Alec worried him. He sounded spaced out.

It was dark outside when the girls went into town to bring back pizza. Jim stayed behind in case Trish called. What if Alec had been high, he thought, and became crazed when she was leaving for Storrs? Maybe he should go to Boston to find out for himself. Maybe call the Cambridge police and ask them to check on it. That this possibly was her way of breaking up prevented him from doing just that.

The pizza was eaten at the kitchen table while he and the girls rehashed his phone conversation with Alec.

"I can't believe she wouldn't speak to you?" Jennifer glanced at Ann Marie. "Maybe she wasn't there."

Jim shook his head. "I don't know. Alec said she didn't want to talk to me ever again. The bastard advised me to forget her."

"You're right not to trust him." Ann Marie started clearing the table. "I never liked Alec. I don't trust anyone who sells dope to his friends for profit. You feel like everything's business, even if it's not."

She paused at the sink and turned to him, "My big brother, Vincent, is a friend of his. Friend isn't the right word, he buys all his stash from Alec. I could ask him to stop by and check on Trish? I'm out of grass anyway. He could use that as an excuse."

"Do you think he would?" Jim went over to her and leaned on the counter. "What bothers me most is not knowing anything. If everything's okay, I'll get over it. But if she's in trouble, I'd never forgive myself for doing nothing."

"I'll call him." Ann Marie dried her hands. "I'll use the phone in my room."

Jim moved to the sink and finished washing the dishes. For the first time in two days he felt hopeful. He put the plates away and Jennifer wiped off the dinette. Ann Marie came back brushing her hair. Her pink satin robe hung open.

"Vinnie is such a lug," she said, tilting her head to one side as she brushed. "He was leaving on a date but said he'd go by Alec's. He's such a sweetheart." Ann Marie tilted her head to let her long hair fall on the other side. She saw the question in Jim's eyes. "He said he'd call us tonight regardless how late it is."

"Thanks, I. . . ."

"What are friends for?" she said. "I've got to get ready. Anthony's coming over after the protest rally on campus. He said there's talk about burning down the ROTC building. I hope he doesn't get hurt."

Jim fell asleep on the sofa while awaiting word from Boston. While he slept, the image of a young boy appeared in his dream, naked and trussed on a stone alter. A figure emerged from a gray mist. The old man looked like Baines. He held up an obsidian blade and a look of sadness clouded his eyes as he offered the knife for approval.

CHAPTER 49

Jim's eyes flew open. Ann Marie was shaking his shoulder.
"Wake up. Vinnie wants to talk to you."

He checked his watch. It was three in the morning. "I didn't hear the phone ring."

"He's been to Alec's."

Jim went into the kitchen and picked up the phone. "This is Jim."

"Listen, pal," Vinnie cut him off. "You'd better get here and take care of your little girlfriend."

"What happened? What'd the bastard do?"

"The stupid fucks took some new shit his supplier laid on him. I think it's called Angel Shit or Angel Dust, something like that. Alec said they've been out of it since Wednesday. Your phone call scared the fuck out of him. He's paranoid, afraid you'll call the cops."

"What about Trish?"

"She needs help. Get your ass here, pronto. Alec's too fuckin' scared to do anything. I saw her for only a minute. She was in bed and conscious, you know, aware that I was there, but looked spaced out. I mean, like just staring. They haven't had any food since Wednesday. Alec's been puttin' her in the shower to keep her conscious. She's too weak to stand, can barely hold her head up." Vinnie lowered his voice, "Get your ass to Cambridge."

Jim didn't like Vinnie's tone. *Like, a real man wouldn't let his girl get in such a situation.*

"Call me at home if you need any help. Annie's got my number."

"Thanks," Jim said. "I'll take care of this." He put the receiver down and stood up. His body shook with rage.

Ann Marie grabbed his arm. "What about Trish?"

He related what Vinnie had said as he changed clothes.

"Alec oughta be hung on a meat hook." Her earrings jangled like wind chimes. "I've never heard of Angel Dust. Some creep at MIT probably made it in his dorm with his chemistry set."

Jim pulled on his boots and thought of the time he disarmed the mine in the freighter's cargo hold. Like then, he has a big problem to solve and needs to stay calm. While shaving, a plan took form. He went into the kitchen and found the girls at the table drawing a map to Alec's house in Cambridge. He picked up the phone and called Joel. The receiver clicked. "Joel, wake up, it's me. Sorry it's so late or maybe early, but I need your help."

"My what? What time is it? God, it's five in the morning. Who is this?"

"It's me, Jim. Trish is in trouble and we need to go get her. Can you be ready in an hour?"

"My god, man, tell her to call AAA." Joel sounded irritated.

Jim heard a female voice in the background.

"A tow truck could be there in a few minutes," Joel continued. "It'll take us two hours to get to Boston."

"Not that kind of trouble." Jim talked slowly, realizing his friend was just coming awake. "She's in real danger. She overdosed on something Alec gave her. She's been out of it for three days now."

There was a long pause. "I'll be ready in fifteen minutes," Joel said. "It'll take you that long to get here."

"Thanks, I'll owe you one. Save me a place on your psychologist's couch when this is over."

Joel was standing outside on his deck when Jim turned up the driveway at Andover Lake. Ariella's car sat parked behind Joel's Volkswagen.

They drove the eighty-five miles to Boston while the sun climbed into the clear Sunday-morning sky. Jim didn't feel like talking. *What if she's permanently damaged? Will I have the guts to stick around and care for her?* He wiped his cheeks with the back of his hand and glanced at Joel. He fished in his shirt pocket and handed Joel a piece of paper. "Can you make heads or tails out of this map the girls drew?"

"You bet," Joel said, sitting up. "I wasn't in the army like you, but I once tried to join the Girl Scouts at my parents' synagogue."

With Joel navigating, Jim turned off the highway and onto Cambridge's narrow streets. Several wrong turns later, they found the house and parked next to Trish's blue Mustang. Jim checked his watch. It was nine o'clock. Newspapers cluttered the yard. The Victorian house needed paint. The windows were heavily curtained and two overflowing trash cans sat in front of the stoop.

Jim's wiped his palms on his jeans and took a deep breath. "Okay," he said. "Let's go."

The two car doors slammed simultaneously, and they walked together like gunslingers up the front steps. Jim rapped on the doorframe. His eyes took in the overgrown forsythia at the railing, knobby with new buds, and two metal lawn chairs at the end of the porch.

The door creaked, and Alec stared out at them. His sunken eyes moved from Jim to Joel and then back to Jim. He stepped back, opening the front door wide like he had been expecting them. Wearing only gray underwear he led them through a dark foyer. Jim missed nothing as they passed through the house. In the parlor, a silk parachute hung from the ceiling giving it the look of a harem tent. Pillows on the floor encircled a low table. A brass water pipe stood like a sculpture in the center of the table.

Alec opened a door to a bedroom and stood aside for Jim to pass. As the pale light from the hallway spilled into the room, Jim recognized Trish lying motionless in a mussed four-poster. Joel crossed to the windows and pulled aside the heavy curtains. Sunlight flooded the room. Trish lay naked on top of a bare mattress surrounded by lumps of damp bedding. Her blonde hair was a medusa mess. Her eyes were open and staring up at the ceiling. As Jim approached, she turned her head ever so slightly. Then like a snail crossing a rock, her eyes moved from the ceiling to his face. They warmed in recognition.

His mind reeled as he looked down at her on the filthy bed. "Alec! Get your butt in here and tell me what happened. Don't leave a damned thing out." He wished he was wearing his army uniform.

"It's not my fault." Alec whimpered. "No one forced her. She's. . .It was supposed to be good stuff. I didn't expect. I, I didn't mean to hurt her. I took the shit myself. We relied on some friends and—"

"We're taking Trish to get help," Jim said. "You're lucky she's alive. If and when she gets better, and you better pray that she does, I'll let you know. Otherwise, stay away from her. You understand?" Jim stood in front of Alec with clenched fists.

Alec stared at the floor. "I, I didn't do a good job taking care of either one of us."

Bullshit! Jim thought. *He doesn't want me to bring in the cops. There's probably enough drugs in this place to open a pharmacy.*

Involving the police had crossed his mind. If she suffered real damage, then he would have no choice. His primary concern was getting her home—and well.

Joel took Alec out in the hall while Jim got Trish sitting on the edge of the bed. Her head lolled on her chest. Slight movement gave him encouragement, but she had yet to speak. He sat with his arm around her while Joel went for a glass of water. After a few sips, she held up her hand to stop. He knelt in front of her and clasped her hands.

"I know it's hard to talk, but it's important that we know what you want us to do. Please try and understand our questions. We only want to help. If you can understand me, just nod your head." He held his breath.

Slowly, her head bent forward.

"Good girl. Now listen carefully. Do you want to go to a hospital?"

Her eyes widened, and her head moved from side to side.

"Do you want to go home to your parents?"

Again, her head moved back and forth, and her gaze fell away. A moment passed while he and Joel looked at each other. Her bottom lip trembled, and tears streamed down her cheeks. Jim's heart pounded in his ears. In a tiny voice as sweet as a hummingbird's breath she finally spoke, "Take me home with you."

A surge of energy powered Jim to his feet. "She wants to go with us." He gave her more sips of water while Joel packed her suitcases he found in the closet. After putting a terry cloth robe on her and white socks over her bare feet, he lifted her up in his arms. She felt so light, like an empty box.

With Alec moving ahead opening doors, he carried her outside and laid her in the back seat of his car. Joel followed with two bags, tossed them into the rear of the station wagon and returned to the house for the last suitcase. Jim sat in the back seat cradling her head in his lap. "It's going to be okay," he whispered. He kissed her on the forehead. "You'll be all right. It's all under control."

Joel tossed in the last bag, slammed the tailgate and slid behind the wheel. He fired up the engine and handed the map back to Jim. "Read the directions to me, and I'll have us home before you know it." They drove through Cambridge to Storrow Drive and followed the Charles River to the Mass Turnpike. As the car glided through New England toward Storrs, Trish slept. Joel fiddled with the knobs on the radio until James Taylor's acoustic guitar and vocal harmony came through crystal clear.

Jim moved a stray strand of hair from Trish's face and watched her sleep. He had a thousand questions but right now it was enough that he was taking her home.

CHAPTER 50

When they arrived back at the cottage in Coventry, Jennifer and Ann Marie rushed out to meet them. Ringo barked in excitement as Jim carried Trish in and laid her down in the bedroom. "Get out, Ringo," he hissed. He sat on the edge of the bed and checked her pulse. It felt weak. Joel brought in her bags while Ann Marie wet a washcloth and poured a glass of juice for Trish. Jennifer ran crying to her room.

"Here, just sip it." Jim held the glass for her. "Good girl," he said after it was empty. He wiped her face with the damp cloth and laid it across her brow. In a few minutes she was asleep. Ann Marie offered to sit with her while he took Joel to Ariella's apartment.

A spring thunderstorm opened up as he drove.

"Listen," Joel said, "I've got friends at the psych clinic on campus. The Chief of Staff was a classmate of my father's. If you want, I'll call him and ask if he would see Trish. I know he'd be discreet. She's not a student here anymore, but he might do it as a favor."

"I'd appreciate that." Jim glanced over at him. "I've been trying to figure out the next step."

"I'll call Dr. Healey first thing in the morning," Joel said. Drops of rain splashed on the windshield.

Jim stopped in front of Ariella's building and shut off the engine. "So, how are things between you two?"

Joel paused before opening the car door. "About the same. Nothing long term. We've got a workable understanding. She only wants my Adonis body, and I've learned to expect nothing more."

"She's just using you." Jim grinned. "You realize that? She'll suck the life out of your shell and leave you a broken, fucked-out zombie. How can you live with yourself?"

"I know. It's sick. I feel so cheap, but it's so damn much fun."

They both laughed.

"Thanks for going with me, today," Jim said, his voice turning husky. "Couldn't have done it without you."

"My pleasure." Joel punched him on the arm. "Besides, it wasn't all unselfish. This could become a major case in my dissertation. Who knows, I might win a Nobel Prize for my thesis on the 'The Cowboy and The Flower Child.'"

"But really," Jim said, "thanks for your help."

Joel stepped out into the rain. "I'll call you in the morning about the clinic."

Trish was awake and propped up in bed when he returned. The girls had finished bathing her, and Jennifer was brushing tangles out of her hair. Ann Marie was feeding her bites of boiled egg in between sips of cranberry juice.

The ordeal of the bath and meal over, she went back to sleep. They woke her late in the afternoon and again in the evening to feed and give her more juice. They then let her sleep for the night.

She was breathing easily when Jim slipped into bed beside her. He planned to stay the night on the sofa but wanted to lie with her for a bit. Staring into the darkness, he worried about what lay ahead. *What if she's brain damaged? How will I tell her parents?* Pulling her close to him, he pushed away the bad thoughts.

What happens if she recovers? Will she leave me again? Closing his eyes, he considered praying. Something he hadn't done in a long time. He couldn't remember the last time.

Jesus, I don't deserve anything from you now, but, but for Trish's sake, please make her healthy and happy again. I love her so much, and I want to be with her forever. If it be your will. Amen. He wanted it even if it *wasn't* His will.

Sleep eluded him. He felt more out-of-control of things than ever before. Trish moved against him, and he listened to her steady breathing. A calm suddenly came over him. It was clear what he must do, what he wanted to do. *I'll go home* to Texas *and take her with me.* Home now seemed so safe. He'd strayed far, but no one back in Morrison knew anything about that.

He left the bed and made his way to the bathroom. On his return, Ringo met him at the door, and he knelt to rub his head. "You're a good boy, Ringo," he whispered. "Sorry I yelled at you this afternoon. You look after her when I'm not around, okay?" Ringo banged his tail on the floor.

After he slid back into bed beside Trish, he closed his eyes. It was settled. When the semester ended, he would return to the ranch, to his family, and take Trish with him. That piece completed the puzzle. His mind began to grow numb. The sound of a Joan Baez song seeped out from under Jennifer's door along with the scent of burning incense. Trish moved against him and emitted a sigh. Her freshly washed hair smelled of flowers.

In his dream he saw the ranch in the distance. As they approached the house, his mother came running out to meet them. Baines stood on the porch watching. Several times during the night he woke with a start, afraid the person beside him was only a dream.

The next morning, he turned to look at Trish. She was watching him, worry clouding her face. Pushing himself up, he encircled her in his arms. "It's okay, babe," he whispered. "It's going to be okay. Everything will be fine."

Noises in the house signaled the girls were up. He was struggling to pull a sweater over Trish's head when Jennifer came in to help. At the breakfast table there was very little talking. Trish picked at a pastry and drank two glasses of orange juice. He tried to lighten the mood by teasing Jennifer about the role of a nun she was to play in her drama workshop that afternoon. He thought he saw the beginning of a smile on Trish's lips.

After breakfast, he helped her back to bed while the girls cleaned the table. Everyone's spirits were lifted now that they had seen some light return to her eyes. At ten o'clock Joel called. "It's all set," he said. "Dr. Healy will see her at eleven-thirty this morning. How's she doing?"

"She ate a little something several times yesterday. We gave her liquids, and she had a light breakfast." Jim tried to sound optimistic. "She actually made it into the kitchen on her own this morning to eat with us."

"Sounds like she's improving. That's good."

"Every time I look at her, I think about how close we came to losing her."

"By the way," Joel said, "I told Dr. Healy everything. If we're going to ask him to be discreet, he should know what he's being discreet about. Besides, he needs the details to make a proper diagnosis. Hope you don't mind."

"I'm glad you told him," Jim said. "I'm not sure I could've."

"I'll be in lab till two-thirty," Joel said, "but I'll be thinking about you guys. Call me as soon as you know something."

"I will and thanks, buddy. I owe you another one. If I can ever. . .you know."

"Stay focused on getting our little girl well. I'll stop by this evening."

As he walked Trish out to his car for her appointment with Doctor Healy, he noticed flowering shrubs and sprouting bulbs in the yard had replaced brown slush. She had enough strength to move on her own, but progress was made in careful steps. The girls hadn't been able to brush out all the tangles in her hair and tied a silk scarf around her head to cover the worst.

At the campus clinic, he found a parking space near the door. Trish gripped his arm as they walked into the white tiled lobby. He eased her into a chair and noticed from the clock on the wall that they were early. The receptionist behind the counter nodded at them. He recognized her as a girl Joel once brought out to the lake. Her name eluded him.

"Hi, it's good to see you again," he said, approaching the counter. "How are you?"

"Good." She smiled. "Joel called this morning and said you were seeing Dr. Healy. I hope everything's all right."

"Thanks," Jim responded. "So do we."

"I'll tell the doctor you're here."

He looked across the room at Trish and gave her a thumbs-up.

An older man in a brown sport coat entered the reception room and stood behind the counter. The aroma of his pipe tobacco filled the air while he shuffled through a stack of papers. He put some folders in a file cabinet and crossed the room toward Trish. Jim followed him and stood beside her chair. The man paused to relight his pipe. As the smoke puffed out in little clouds, he looked at Jim and then at Trish. "Can you walk, Patricia?"

Trish slowly pushed herself out of the chair and stood. She wavered a bit before steadying herself on the doctor's outstretched hand.

"I'm Dr. Healy." He smiled, sending the skin around his eyes into deep wrinkles. "Joel said you'd be coming by. Let's go have a little talk and run some tests." He guided her toward his office. Jim followed. At the reception counter, Dr. Healy stopped and turned to him. "Young man, are you a relative?"

"No, sir. I'm—"

"Then you wait out here until we're done."

The doctor and Trish disappeared behind a frosted glass door while Jim stood with his hands jammed in his jeans pockets. He went back to the waiting room chairs and sat down. The doctor had made him feel like some juvenile delinquent. He took off his jacket, draped it over a chair and leaned forward with his hands on his knees.

He stared down at the dried mud on his boots and noticed his jeans fraying at the back of the cuff. Whenever he lost a few pounds, his jeans rode lower on his hips. He was thinking about that when a doctor in a white lab coat entered the clinic lobby, went over to the counter and carried on a whispered conversation with the receptionist. He disappeared through the same door that Trish and Dr. Healy had passed through earlier. Jim looked at the receptionist. He wished he could remember her name.

"Can I get you a cup of coffee?"

"I'm fine. Thanks, anyway." He looked back at the crusted mud on his boots.

Forty-five minutes later, he stood gazing out through the clinic's small-paned windows when Dr. Healy appeared beside him. The doctor motioned for them to sit. The other white-coated physician joined them, carrying a clipboard. Dr. Healy studied Jim across the top of his eyeglasses. "Young man, tell me what type of drug Patricia took when she became ill?"

Jim's back stiffened. "I wasn't there, Doctor, so I don't exactly know. I was told that it was some new stuff called Angel Powder or Star Dust, something like that."

The doctor paused a moment before continuing, "Are you Patricia's boyfriend?"

"Yes, sir. I am. I mean, I was and, well, now I am again."

The doctor's face softened. "She had a very close call. Too close I'm afraid, but she was very lucky. I believe Patricia's going to be all right."

Jim looked at Dr. Healy and then at the other physician. They were both smiling.

"She has no permanent damage, as far as we can tell," Dr. Healy continued. "It's a common problem among young people today who play with the drugs being sold on the street. Our tests indicate her symptoms are a reaction to what was mixed with the drug, more than the drug itself. Simply put, Patricia is suffering from strychnine poisoning. Strychnine is used to kill rodents, particularly rats. Mixed in very small quantities with mind-altering hallucinogens, it heightens the effect by increasing the sensitivity of the central nervous system.

"Someone made a mistake in proportions. I suggest if you know where this drug came from, or anyone else who may have it, you warn them immediately. They're in grave danger. Patricia is very, very lucky."

Dr. Healy stood and looked down at him. "I'll need a few more minutes with her, but she should completely recover after a couple weeks of rest."

The doctor went back into his office followed by his associate while Jim paced the room, stuffing his hands into his pockets and pulling them out, and shoving them back in again. He fought to keep from leaping into the air and shouting. The doctor's words kept reverberating in his ears. *She should completely recover.*

He closed his eyes and said a silent prayer of thanks. As he mouthed "Amen," the door to the doctor's office opened and Trish stepped out. She smiled, and he saw the relief in her face. Both their tears flowed as she stepped into his open arms.

Dr. Healy appeared, relighting his pipe. "Son, you get Patricia home now and take good care of her. Make sure she gets plenty of rest and fluids."

"Dr. Healy," Jim said, extending his hand. "We can't thank you enough."

"Yes, well, you look after her," the doctor said, releasing Jim's hand. "Also, tell Joel he should come to dinner. My wife has a new recipe for veal he'll like. His parents asked us to look after him."

CHAPTER 51

In May, the planet softened, and warm wind blew across New England. With Trish back at the cottage and getting stronger, Jim regained some semblance of order to his life. He also had a plan. Step one was getting her well. Step two was taking her home to Texas.

After class during the week, he returned to the cottage to care for her, and she showed improvement with each passing day. He cooked their meals and spoon fed her at the kitchen table, with steady conversation to keep her mind engaged. He left her alone only while at school, but his thoughts were occupied during lectures with what he could do to further her recovery. He was her coach and cheerleader, and his efforts were rewarded as her vitality returned.

Drugs and talk of drugs were banned from the house. "I've got too many other things to worry about right now," he said to the girls. Jennifer reduced the volume of her stereo without being asked, and Ringo resumed sleeping on her bed.

The warm days brought out more than just new leaves on the trees. Protest rallies were occurring daily on campus.

"It's like a war zone at the college," Jim said one evening at dinner.

Trish looked at him and took another bite of spaghetti.

"Things are getting crazy after those kids were killed at Kent State." He put down his fork. "The administration may cancel finals and give everyone a Pass or Fail grade. We'll get credit for the course, but for our grade point average, it'll be like the semester never happened. In my classes today, two profs were no shows."

He didn't tell her about yesterday when he and Joel argued for two hours about the war. Jim was even more convinced that it was the right decision to take Trish to Texas. They'd enroll at Texas Tech in September and both could finish next May. He had broached the subject a few times with her but hadn't pushed it.

In mid-May, the university closed for the semester, but Storrs remained a hotbed of protest activity. The town commons and campus teemed with students who didn't want to go home. Spontaneous rallies occurred on the lawn in front of the Admin Building with speakers bellowing curse-laden tirades against the government and the university through megaphones. There were also protests by black student organizations against the Bobby Seale and Angela Davis murder trials about to get underway in New Haven. Jim looked for Ali in the crowds but didn't see him. Joel said Ali moved out of the lake cottage the first of May.

Ann Marie and Jennifer packed up and left Coventry for summer jobs on Cape Cod. Before saying good-bye, Jennifer surprised Jim with a gift. "He doesn't really belong to me anymore," she said, handing him a bag containing Ringo's leash and rubber toys. "I think he'll enjoy a master more than a mistress. Besides, my parents wouldn't take him for the summer, and I can't keep him at the Cape."

"I'll take good care of him," Jim said. "Ringo and I are pals. Aren't we, boy?" He knelt and rubbed Ringo's back. The Irish Setter licked his face while wagging his feathery tail.

A half hour after the girls left for Boston, Potts drove up to the cottage in his Corvette. Dartmouth had also closed early, and he'd stopped by to see Jennifer on his way to Ridgefield.

"Too bad you just missed her," Jim said. He and Trish sat with Potts on the porch step in the early evening. "You should've called. I'm sure she would've stayed an extra day if she had known." The air was cool and sweet with the scent of lilac. He and Potts tossed pebbles at a rusty can half buried in the dirt next to the graveled driveway.

"Jenn's waiting tables at the Lobster Pot out on the Cape this summer," Trish said. "I've got the address if you go see her."

Potts rattled the can with his next throw. "I might do that. The summer's already off kilter. My plans for the next three months haven't jelled. I had just started thinking about final exams when all hell broke loose after Kent State." He threw another pebble and missed the can.

"I think I'll leave you two and go to bed," Trish said, standing and patting Jim on the back. "I get tired early in the evenings. It's good to see you, Potts." She smiled at Jim. "You two stay out here as long as you want. I'm sure you have a lot to talk about." She kissed him goodnight and went into the house.

Jim watched Potts in the glow of the porch light as his friend threw several more stones at the can. "Okay, so what do you think?" He asked, reaching down for a handful of gravel.

"About what?" Potts said, picking up more ammunition for himself.

"Oh, I don't know," He shrugged. "What's bothering you?"

Potts sat silent for a moment then flung a large pebble far into the darkness. "I think a bunch of poor National Guard lugs are never going to have another good night's sleep because a mob of longhaired, America-hating hippies thought they'd go out for an afternoon and play let's terrorize the army boys."

He threw his whole handful of gravel across the lawn. "Jimbo, that could've been you and me on that field with the Ohio National Guard. Unfortunately, the longhairs are now heroes and martyrs. Ten years from now, no one will remember the poor drafted grunts that had to sleep in leech infested jungles and returned home in body bags or without arms and legs after Jane Fonda's best friends ambushed them in some stinking rice paddy."

"The world's upside down," Jim said. "That's why I'm taking Trish and going home." He paused a moment before continuing. "Never thought I would, Potts." He slapped at an early mosquito. "But I came damn close to losing control. I thought everything was going great till Trish left, and then I couldn't find my ass with both hands. The scary thing is I didn't care about anything after that." He tossed a stone at the can and missed. "I have one big concern about going home and that's my old man. Baines and Trish will think each other are from another planet. She has this image of him being like Lorne Green on Bonanza. She's in for a surprise. I can just see my old man pounding that bible of his while I'm explaining to him that I came up here to find who I am and what I believe."

"Well, did you?" Potts' toss hit the center of the can with a punctuated rattle.

"Did I what?"

"Did you found out who you are and what you believe?" Potts' next throw clipped the can, flipping it out of the ground.

"When I left home for the army, My dad told me to be sure my actions brought honor on me and my family. I'm not proud of everything I've done, but there's not much I would change. I grew a lot. I tested things that I was taught at home and church. Many were validated, and I realized some weren't right for me. Doesn't mean they aren't right for my old man or someone else, but that's their business."

Jim looked at Potts for a response and received none. Potts continued tossing pebbles at the tin can.

"I've lived with people of different races and religions," Jim continued. "My old man would crap if he knew that. And I've learned there's room for more than one point of view, race, and religion." He chuckled. "In Morrison, I sometimes wasn't sure there was room in town for both the Methodists and the Baptists."

He paused a moment. "But you know what else I learned? It makes me laugh to think about it, but I learned we WASPs don't have a lock on intolerance and narrow-mindedness. I met more closed-minded, intolerant hippies and college professors this year than you can imagine. Attend a rally on campus and try to offer an opposing view or opinion. They don't want to hear what you have to say or give you the chance to say it. Hypocrisy and hate are not exclusive to either side."

Jim felt something wet on his neck and turned to find Ringo

behind him. He put his arm around the dog's neck and patted him while Ringo's tongue laved his face.

"So, when are you leaving?" Potts asked.

"In a couple of weeks," Jim replied. "We're paid up here at the cottage till then. We'll finish next year at Texas Tech. I think it'll be good for Trish to get away from here. If we can start the summer session in Lubbock next month, I bet we can both graduate in the spring. Trish needs her last thirty credits at Tech to graduate from there. It'll mean an extra semester for her but—"

"Back to the Lone Star State and high-octane barbeque." Potts petted Ringo. "What does she think about moving out to Indian territory and living on rancid bear grease and black-eyed peas?"

"We've discussed it. I wouldn't say she's terribly excited about it, but she's had a bad time of it here. She tells me she'll go, and that's good enough for me."

Potts hung around the rest of the week, and the three friends slept late, took walks in the woods, picnicked by the lake, and drank cold Sangria in the evenings. Trish got stronger each day. By the time Potts left on Sunday, she was her spirited self.

On Monday afternoon, Jim entered the snack bar and found Joel sitting alone at a table.

"Thanks for meeting on short notice." Joel looked shaken, "I thought it best not to talk on the phone."

Jim pulled up a chair and sat down.

"Two FBI guys were at the house this morning," Joel continued. "They asked me a lot of questions about Ali."

"What kind of questions?"

"Shit! You know. They wanted to know everything. When did I last see him? Did I know where they could find him?"

"What'd you tell them?"

"I said he moved out the first of May and I haven't seen him since. I thought they were going to arrest me or something. Damn, I'm glad they didn't have a search warrant. I'm not sure what drugs are around the house. I'd better clean the place out when I get back."

"Whoa, whoa," Jim said. "Why were they interested in Ali?"

"Don't know. They were asking the questions, not me. They wanted to know if I knew how to find him. They asked me that in one form or another a hundred times. They were damn persistent."

"Do you know where he is?"

"Shit no. Have you seen him around?"

"No." Jim shook his head. "Not in a while."

"Should we warn him? Is that illegal?"

"Probably," Jim said. " Did they tell you not to?"

"Not that I remember."

"Then that's what we'll do and nothing more. If he needs our help, he'll ask us."

"You're right." Joel said. "No reason to get crazy about this. How's Trish doing?"

"She's up and about. Has her strength back. Dr. Healy saw her for the last time a couple days ago. He said the poison had worked its way out of her system. She's going to Texas with me in a week. We'll finish college there. It'll be good for both of us."

"Whatever works for you guys," Joel said, standing up at the table. "Let's try to get together one last time before everyone takes off."

Jim watched his old housemate exit through the glass doors and disappear into a crowd. He sat at the table finishing his coffee and thought about Ali. He hoped he wasn't in any trouble.

CHAPTER 52

Trish knew he had been hurt when she returned to Alec, and she wanted to make it up to him, but going to Texas frightened her beyond words. She hadn't been truthful with him about her fears. Their departure date was two weeks away, and the world could change by then. At least she hoped it would. It had to.

As the days passed, she lay on a pallet in the yard and strung colorful bead necklaces for him to wear. Each night, she cooed in the safety of his arms and made love to him in their bed. She bought him an old guitar at an estate sale and taught him to play some simple chords. In the evenings they sat around a candle on the living room floor sharing their dreams for the future and singing easy folk songs. *You Are My Sunshine* was her favorite.

CHAPTER 53

Jim thought he couldn't be happier. The girl he loved with all his heart had fully recovered. She had spurned her former lover and returned to him. Now, he was taking her home to meet the family, to live in his world. He hadn't mentioned marriage. There was plenty of time. It was like pinning a calf. If you rushed it, the calf was prone to bolt.

A week before they were to leave for Texas, he detected a sadness shadowing her eyes. Figuring it natural for her to be apprehensive about leaving the familiar, he talked about the ranch, cowboy dances and rodeos, college football games, and how much fun they would have. Trish smiled and said she couldn't wait, but the look in her eyes told him different.

On Monday of their last week, they spent the day packing up the house and went to bed late. They didn't make love but instead held each other until they both fell asleep. In the early morning hours, he woke. Trish had moved away from him to the edge of the bed with her face buried in her pillow. He felt the bed shudder.

He put his hand on her shoulder to let her know he was there, and she sobbed harder. After a few moments her weeping subsided. With the spell passed, she spooned herself back into him and fell asleep. The next morning, she suggested they pack a picnic and go down to the lake. No mention was made of the previous night's crisis.

Two mornings before they were to leave, she was buttering toast at the kitchen table when he joined her. Ringo lay on the floor working the squeaky apparatus out of a rubber toy. Jim poured a cup of coffee at the stove, leaned over to kiss her, and sat at the table. She wore one of his t-shirts and a pair of cutoff shorts. She attempted a smile. Her eyes had a redness around the edges, evidence of last night's tears.

The day was to be spent packing housewares into boxes and sending some of Trish's things with a friend to Boston. He feared bringing up the subject of her nightly spells but something inside him would not let it lie. He drank his coffee and watched her over the rim of his cup. She stopped buttering toast and stared at the plate. He reached across the table for her hand. "What's the matter, babe?" he asked. "Why are you so unhappy?"

Her bottom lip quivered. "I don't know." She wiped her eyes with her fingers. "I keep telling myself this is stupid. I'm the luckiest girl to have survived what I came through and to have you love me. But for some reason, mostly at night in the dark, I just fill up with this overwhelming fear." New tears ran down her face.

"See, look at me." She choked back more sobs. "I don't know why I'm doing this. I must be crazy."

He pulled her to her feet and held her against him through more shuddering sobs.

"This is so stupid." She cried into his chest. "But I can't do anything about it, and I'm trying hard. Honest, Jim, I'm trying as hard as I can."

"I know. I know," he said. "It's okay." Alarms were going off in his head. A cold fear crept into his core.

The next morning things took a turn for the worse. The long night had passed with him awash in worry while Trish emptied a box of Kleenex, one tissue at a time. They were to leave the following day and they had a million things to do. After breakfast, Trish remained moody and withdrawn. He fought paralyzing worry. Several times she went into the bedroom and shut the door, only to emerge a half hour later with her eyes red and swollen, her face still hot with tears.

At three in the afternoon, they were packing boxes in the kitchen when she turned and saw him watching her. She studied the questioning look on his face, and what little control she had dissolved. "Oh God! Oh God!" She ran down the hall to the bedroom.

He heard the springs creak as she fell onto the bed. He followed and stood in the doorway. This was the confrontation he had hoped to avoid. He started into the room but paused for a moment, watching her stifle sobs into a pillow. Crossing the room, he sat next to her. She grew silent. He knew the problem. Had known it since that first time she cried herself to sleep.

"You don't want to go, do you?" He knew the answer.

She turned from the pillow and looked at him.

"You're going because you feel obligated. Because I went to Boston to save you. But, you don't owe me anything. I went to Boston to save both of us."

She sat up and studied his face.

"I think I knew all along you didn't want to go," he continued. "I'm not sure that it's Texas, or going with me, or what, but the result's the same."

A long silence passed before she responded. "You are the most important person in the world to me." She began to weep again. "I owe you my life, and the last thing I want to do is hurt you. I decided that if you believed this was for the best, then I'd go. God knows I can't trust my own decisions after what happened. But Jim, I'm scared to death. You're right, I don't want to go and. . . ." She covered her face with her hands.

"But, Trish, I have to go. It kills me to leave you here, and I'd give anything if you would come with me, but. . . ." He swallowed hard. "But not because you think you owe me." He felt drained. At the same time, he sensed her relief and knew he had lost her again. *Goddamn her*! *Goddamn her for not loving me as much as I love her!* He turned away, not wanting her to see his anguish.

"I'm leaving," he said, pushing up from the bed and walking to the door. "Can't stay. I've got to get my own life back in order. There's no reason to delay another day." He turned and faced her. "You sure you'll be all right?"

"I, I'll be okay," she stammered. "You don't need to worry about me anymore."

He looked at her for a long moment.

"Jim," she called as he started to turn away, "I won't blame you if you hate me. It would probably be easier for both of us if you did. I was just getting used to loving you when you tossed this Texas thing at me." Her voice dropped to a whisper. "It was too much. I couldn't tell you then, not after everything you've done. I couldn't hurt you again." They looked into each other's eyes, each waiting for the other to speak. He turned and left her alone in the room.

It didn't take him long to carry his things out to the station wagon. Trish sat on the front step, watching him load the car. Neither said anything until the last bag was in and the tailgate closed. Ringo found his place on the back seat.

Jim turned to Trish. "I'll call when I get there." His words sounded flat. . .empty.

"I'd like that," she said walking to the car. She reached for his hand as he opened the car door. "Is this how it felt when I left you?"

"Do you feel dead inside?"

"Kind of like that," she whispered.

"Yeah, that's how it felt," he said, swallowing the catch in his voice.

"Bye, Trish." He leaned down and kissed her cheek. "It was fun."

He slipped behind the wheel and slammed the car door. The afternoon sun hovered above Coventry Lake as he drove away from Fox Trail for the last time. He couldn't understand all that had just happened. Not right now. Three days of highway driving lay ahead of him. There would be plenty of time to think about it. Right now, it just hurt.

Trish stood in the front yard, watching his white station wagon round the curve and disappear in the trees. She wrapped her arms around herself. God, this feels strange, she thought continuing to stare at the place on the road where she last saw his car. Now *what do I do? Where do I go? Oh God, what have I done?*

CHAPTER 54

The roaring yellow backhoe raked its steel maw across virgin ground, leaving a fresh gash in the Texas landscape. In its wake, insects skittered about looking for new places to hide. The operator had the bucket poised for another bite when his eye caught a flash from something in the freshly exposed dirt. He squinted up at the sun and then checked his watch. Almost lunchtime, he thought. He had been out on the job since early that morning and had made good progress on the new County Road being cut through ranch land near Byrus Creek between Hillsboro and Waco. He set the bucket on the ground, killed the engine, and stepped down from the cab.

He grabbed his lunch bucket and looked around for a place to eat. Once again, he caught a flash of reflected sunlight from something in the ditch. Hoping to find an Indian artifact or some other treasure, he skidded down the embankment. There it is, he thought to himself seeing a piece of metal protruding from the loose dirt. Scraping away soil with his hand, he uncovered a belt buckle, bent and scratched by the shovel. He tugged at the buckle, but it was caught on something. Digging away more dirt, he saw it attached to a rotting leather belt—and the dry, brittle bones of its owner.

PART FOUR

CHAPTER 55

Jim stopped at a truck stop on the New Jersey Turnpike just outside of New York City, to call home. Standing at the phone booth, he listened to it ring while a parade of eighteen-wheelers pulled off the highway and lined up in the parking lot behind him. Five months had passed since he last spoke to anyone at the ranch.

"Hello?" A voice on the other end answered.

"Who's this?" He shouted to be heard. "John Henry! That you?"

"Hey, Jimmy. You little toad fart. Where the hell are you? Sounds like you're calling from inside Momma's old washing machine."

He smiled at the sound of his brother's voice. "I'm in New Jersey." He held the phone closer to his mouth. "I'm on my way home, to Morrison. Is Mom or Dad there?"

"Hell no, they're never here. They're out running around somewhere. They went to town for groceries and Mom had a hair appointment. They should be back soon. I stopped by the house here to pick up our mail. Hey, little buddy, so you're finally coming home? They'll be happy to hear that. Momma thought she had lost her baby boy for good."

Jim cupped the receiver with his hand. "It'll take me a couple of days if I don't have car trouble. Tell everyone I'm looking forward to seeing them."

"Well, hurry and get your butt back here where you belong. Linda Sue said just the other day that you'd probably marry some Yankee girl up there in Connecticut and bring her home like Rock Hudson did Elizabeth Taylor in *Giant*. You know that Linda Sue, she thinks we're all in some dumb Hollywood movie."

He paused a moment at the mention of his sister-in-law. So, she'd been talking about him. What if he had brought Trish home? "Nothing like that," he said. "Tell Mom I can't wait to taste her cornbread. I'll see you all in a couple of days."

As he steered back onto the turnpike, he tuned the car radio to WABC in New York and Cousin Brucie's afternoon rock and roll program. A Led Zeppelin song started playing and Ringo whimpered in the back seat. "Sorry," Jim said, and turned off the radio.

As the industrial wasteland of New Jersey passed by outside the car window, he adjusted the air conditioner and settled back. John Henry sounded great, he thought. Things didn't seem much different between them. His big brother still made him feel like he was ten years old. He thought about Linda Sue. They had been married a long time, now. *Does my brother know about us?*

Nearly five years had passed since he left the ranch, and so much in his life had changed. He felt anxious about seeing his dad again. He wondered if the old man ever worried about him being killed after drafting him into the army? *Would he've felt any responsibility?*

As the interstates took him south and west, his thoughts turned back to Trish. He wasn't sure he had done the right thing leaving her alone in Connecticut. He could've stayed with her or tried to cajole her into coming with him. Neither alternative seemed any better.

It was late in the afternoon on the second day when he saw the black metal mailbox where the ranch road intersected the asphalt. Warm wind blew in through his open window bringing the smell of fresh plowed soil and a touch of ragweed. He turned off the pavement onto the dirt road and stopped to check the mail. When he opened the car door Ringo bolted from the back seat and began sniffing the ground. Jim gazed up the road and waited for Ringo to finish his business. Cattle grazing in the pasture looked like a picture from a favorite book. At the house, two pickups were parked in front of the picket fence that encircled the yard. He remembered his mother had insisted that Baines put up that fence to keep livestock out of her flowers. A late model Oldsmobile sat alongside the two pickups. *Mom's got a new car.*

After herding Ringo back into the car, he crossed the cattle guard and drove up the road. The two pickups were identical except one looked cleaner than the other and sported a C.B. antenna. *Must be John Henry's truck.* A busted hay bale littered the bed of the other pickup. Jim parked in front of the house and sat back. Butterflies filled his stomach. Ringo paced back and forth on the back seat, looking out one window and then the other. The flowers around the house were in full palette, and the porch furniture looked freshly painted.

No one seemed to be around. *Surely, they heard me drive up. My car made a racket like a Sherman tank when it passed over the cattle guard.* The front door opened, and his mother came down the steps and out into the yard at a half walk, half run.

"Oh, my Lord. Looky who's here." She wiped her hands on her apron. "Baines, y'all come see who just drove up."

He opened the car door and stepped out. Ringo followed. Other than a thickening around the middle, his mother looked the same. They met at the fence where he grabbed her in a bear hug. Ringo barked and ran circles around them.

"Dear Lord, Jimmy, be careful before I break something. It's so good to see you." She kissed him, patted his arm and hugged him again. "I've missed you," she said, kissing him on the side of his face. "My goodness, it's so good to have you home."

"I missed you too, Mom."

The screen door slammed, and Baines and John Henry stepped out onto the porch. "Hey there, bud." His brother waved his hat at him and put it on his head at a cocky angle. He bent forward at the waist and spit tobacco juice over the porch into the flower bed.

His father nodded. Helen led him up the steps to the porch still holding onto his arm. She blinked back tears. "My, my, my, isn't he a sight for sore eyes?"

"You can say that again." John Henry grabbed him in a hug. "Welcome home, little brother."

"Thanks," he said, grinning and feeling all warm inside. "Good to be back, to be home." He didn't know what else to say. This reception was unexpected. Why had he doubted? Tears blurred his vision. He pushed away from John Henry and faced his father. "Hi, Dad." For a split second, he thought Baines flinched. "Been a long time."

"You decided to come home?" His father's voice sounded crusted with age. "Told your momma you'd come back, but she didn't believe me."

Jim smiled. "You haven't changed much in five years."

"Son—" Baines put on his Stetson. "I ain't changed much in seventy years."

Jim noticed his father's thinning gray hair, the deep creases at the eyes and the waist grown puffy. "I don't know," he winked at his big brother, "Hope I look as good as you do when I'm thirty."

"The Lord looks after those that sees after Him," Baines said, his voice rising.

"Well, my goodness," Helen sighed. "I bet you're tired from all that driving. Let's go inside where it's cool and have a glass of iced tea. I made some fresh." She steered Jim toward the front door. "John Henry, get the ice tray out of the refrigerator. Now you all come in the house where it's cool. That sun's hot enough to bake bread."

"Not as hot as it is down in hell for those that don't follow His word," Baines said, standing aside as Helen ushered her two sons into the house.

"Thanks for the rescue, Mom." John Henry dropped his hat on the coffee table in the living room and followed Jim and his mother into the kitchen. "The old man's gettin' more preachy every day."

"Your daddy means well," Helen said, pouring iced tea into four goblets. "He's raised you boys the best way he knows. I've seen him awake at night worrying about both of you. You are grown men now, but we can't just stop being your momma and daddy. You'll know when you have your own little ones."

Jim took a long swig of sweet tea. Same old Baines, he thought, still spouting scripture.

His mother's kitchen glowed with a warmth that matched his

feelings. He leaned against the counter and watched his family. It felt good being home. Maybe it was the right thing to do after all. His mother took her goblet and sat at the kitchen table. She looked at him and smiled. Her eyes sparkled. She reminded him of Trish.

Outside, Baines sat on the porch step, studying the big red dog lying beside Jim's station wagon. After a long moment, Baines extended a calloused hand toward him. "Come here, boy, I ain't gonna hurt ya."

Ringo watched him a moment, stood, shook himself and ambled toward the old man with lowered head. Baines patted him and scratched his ears. The big dog dropped down on the step and put his nose in Baines' lap.

"Come on, boy." Baines said, standing up. "Let's go for a ride before dinner. I'll show you around the place." Ringo looked over his shoulder at the screen door and then back at Baines beside his pickup, holding the door open. "Let's go, boy," Baines said. Ringo looked back at the screen door, bolted from the porch and vaulted up into the pickup seat.

"But Mom, I can graduate next spring if I complete this summer term." Jim was explaining why he could stay only a few days before leaving to find an apartment in Lubbock and register for summer school. John Henry had gone into the hallway to phone Linda Sue. "As long as the G.I. Bill provides me a monthly check to go to college, I consider it a full-time job. Besides, I want to finish and get on with my life. Most of my buddies in the army already graduated. And I'm already twenty-five."

His mother rose from the table and put a hand on his shoulder. "You've changed." She brushed her hand through his hair. "You're not the same Jimmy who left here. More serious, more man." She kissed him on the cheek. "I also can see something's troubling you. Did you leave some unfinished business up there in Connecticut?"

He looked down at the table. "It's finished." He took a long drink of his tea. Helen patted his shoulder and went to refill the ice tray.

At five o'clock, she made John Henry go get Linda Sue and bring her back for dinner. While his brother was gone, Jim paced the kitchen. His mother peeled potatoes at the sink and watched the news on the small color television at the end of the counter. He heard car doors slam, took a few deep breaths and went out on the porch.

"Oh, my gosh." Linda Sue ran up the steps. "Just look at you." She threw her arms around his neck and hugged him. "I can't believe it. We thought you'd forgotten about us back here in sleepy ol' Morrison."

His brother followed her up the steps, shaking his head in mock exasperation. "I thought she was gonna jump outta the pickup on the way over here she was so excited." John Henry pulled Linda Sue away from Jim and threw his squealing wife over his shoulder like a sack of feed. Her boots kicked the air and her laughter filled the house as he carried her into the kitchen and dropped her into a chair. Jim followed and sat at the table with them, answering a million questions about life in the army and college in New England until their mother made them clear out so she could set the table for supper.

Seeing Linda Sue again had been nothing like he'd expected. He hadn't really known what to expect, but she made it easy. Throughout the meal, she and John Henry were attentive to each other and acted like old married folks. She's prettier than ever, he thought as he watched her clear dishes from the table. Her white sleeveless western shirt showed off a summer tan, and the print scarf holding back her ponytail, made her eyes look cobalt blue.

After dinner, Helen went into the living room to read her daily devotional, and Baines and John Henry left together for a deacon's meeting at the church. Ringo followed them outside and lay down on the porch.

"Let's walk out to the barn," Linda Sue said, drying her hands on a towel at the sink.

Uh oh, Jim thought. *Here it comes.*

"I want to show you John's new cutting horse," she continued.

"I bought Phaedra for him on his last birthday, but he hasn't ridden her much." She laughed. "He just goes out there and spends hours grooming her and cooing to her like she was a baby." Linda Sue took Jim's hand and pulled him to his feet. "Come on, it won't kill you. Momma," she called out to Helen, "we'll be back in a bit."

Fireflies flashed in the dusky evening as they followed the path out to the horse barn. The moon had come up and bathed everything in a cool light.

"I'm really glad you're home," she said, taking his hand and squeezing it. "I want you to know that."

He stopped and looked at her, "Linda Sue, I—"

"But," she interrupted him. "I love John Henry with all my heart. I really do. And I had to tell you before we both got miserable about something stupid that happened a long time ago when we were kids." She glanced back toward the house. "I was sick with fear when you left for the army. Afraid you would get killed or never come back. I hated Baines for making you go. I thought he knew about us and was sending you away from me.

"Then, as time passed, I learned how caring and loving John Henry really is, and I became sick with guilt at how unfair I had been to him. I was in such a depressed state." She nervously laughed and shrugged her shoulders. "I cried all the time. I wasn't fit to live with. Several times I even thought of running away or, or worse."

"Linda, I. . . ."

She shushed him with a finger on his lips.

"Poor John was really worried. He looked after me like an anxious mare over her newborn. He was so good and sweet, but it just made me feel even more guilty and depressed. Things were getting worse when, finally, your mother came to me and offered her friendship and her help. Helen, dear, dear Helen, saved my life."

Jim saw tears welling up in her eyes. They trailed down her cheeks, glistening in the moonlight.

"We prayed together, and we talked," Linda Sue continued. "I told her how I set out to win your love, to become the kind of person you'd love. I confessed to dating John Henry just to make you jealous, and how I lost control of everything and wound up marrying him to pay you back for hurting me."

She paused a moment to wipe her eyes. "And I also told her that I had fallen in love with John and now feared losing him if he ever found out. Your mother was so sweet. She held me and told me it was okay. That I should forget all that in the past and just count my lucky stars to be married to the man I love and who loves me."

Linda Sue started to cry. "Since then, I've lived this moment a thousand times. I've thought about what I'd say to you, and what you'd say to me and everything, but nothing ever sounded right. Anyway, you should know that I love my man, my John Henry, who never remembers my birthday or our anniversary, but would slay dragons for me and probably even drink poison if I asked him."

Jim reached for both of her hands. "You weren't the only one worried about this moment." He swallowed hard. "Like you said, we were just kids back then. Water under the bridge. I'm happy for you and John Henry. There isn't another girl I'd rather have as a sister-in-law."

"And I wouldn't want anyone else for a brother-in-law," she said, a faint smile on her lips. In the moonlight, on the path between the house and barns, they embraced and laughed, and laughed some more.

CHAPTER 56

Still tired from the long drive, Jim slept the next morning until the last possible minute before joining the family in the kitchen for breakfast.

"I already worked half a day," Baines grumped when he pulled out a chair and sat down. "Papa always said it's a sin to stay in bed after the sun's risen."

John Henry winked at Jim and spread Helen's peach jam on a warm biscuit.

Jim drank his coffee and listened while his brother and father discussed the projects underway at the ranch. His mother told him about a friend of the family who had just passed away, and another who wasn't going to last much longer. "Oh, Jimmy," she said, her brow wrinkling. "Surely you remember Earl Jones. He always asks about you."

"Sure, Mom." He took another sip of coffee. "How's he doing?" He didn't remember Earl, or most of the other people his mother referenced. The names sounded familiar, but he had difficulty connecting them with a face.

At that moment he felt an aching emptiness. His mother's voice faded, and Trish filled his thoughts. *Where is she and what is she doing?*

The night before when alone in bed, his worry had wandered into dark territory. After finally falling asleep, he saw her thrashing naked and helpless in the four-poster in the dank, musty bedroom in Boston. Waking in a cold sweat, he had stared into the darkness until dawn broke. This was how he felt, what he was thinking—but he couldn't share it with his family.

After breakfast, he took Ringo and accompanied his brother on a drive around the ranch. "I thought it would be hard for the old man to turn it over to me," John Henry said as the pickup tires kicked up dust on the dirt road. "You know how he controls everything. But Dad made it clear it was now my job to manage the hired hands and oversee the cattle operation."

He listened as John Henry went on about a new bull he had bought in South Texas to improve the herd and the new feed formulas he was experimenting with to add more pounds of meat at less cost. His brother's ideas, and the growth the ranch had experienced was impressive, but he also knew the old man hadn't turned over complete control. He still wrote all the checks. Jim smiled to himself. As-long-as Baines controlled the checkbook, his brother couldn't get in serious trouble before being found out. Jim put his hand out the passenger window to catch warm air. *Baines controls the ranch and John Henry and will until the day he dies.*

CHAPTER 57

"Jimmy, I wish you'd go by and see Mrs. Stanley when you're in town," his mother said, while clearing the table. The family had just finished lunch. "She'd get a kick out of that. Her sister, Ethel, before she died, asked about you at church all the time."

"I will, Mom," he said, handing her his plate. "I'll drop by one day this week." He went into the living room and stood looking out the window at Ringo asleep in the sun on the front porch. Just now, he didn't feel like seeing anyone. He missed Trish so much that he hurt inside. Sometimes it nearly immobilized him.

"She must be pretty special, huh?" John Henry asked as they drove to town to buy a roll of barbed wire at the lumber yard.

Jim watched his brother remove his hat and set it on the seat between them. The question had caught him off guard. "Who?"

"The girl that's got you all tied up in knots."

He turned and gazed out the window at the rolling grassland. "Yep," he finally said. "She's pretty special."

Several minutes passed and neither of them spoke.

"Looks like those thunderheads on the horizon over there might dump some good rain on us this afternoon," John Henry said.

"Jimmy!" His mother's voice came down the hallway. "Someone wants to speak with you on the phone. It's long distance."

"Just a minute," he hollered back. Leaving his suitcase open on the bed, he pulled on a freshly laundered shirt. It still felt warm from the clothes line. He had spent the afternoon packing his things. Summer school at Tech started in a week, and he was driving to

Lubbock the next day to find an apartment. On his way to the kitchen to take the phone call, he tucked the shirt into his jeans.

"Hey, Cowboy." The familiar voice made him smile. "Guess where I am?"

"Potts, is that really you?"

"Yeah, I'm here in Dallas visiting a girl, a family friend who goes to Wellesley. I plan to be in your fine state for two weeks and thought I'd come out West to see you for a couple of days. That is, if I can find Lubbock. Must I take a covered wagon, and can you get the cavalry to escort me through indian territory?"

"Smart-ass," Jim said, laughing. "I can't believe it. Must be the spirits at work. You couldn't have shown up at a better time."

"Not spirits, old friend. Just American Airlines. I called Jennifer at the Cape last weekend after discovering your phone in Coventry had been disconnected. She told me what happened with you and Trish. Why didn't you call me?" He didn't wait for an answer. "Jenn said Trish moved back home with her parents, and you left for Texas. I thought you two were a long-term item. Anyway, I'd promised Sandra that I'd visit her in Dallas. Our dads were frat brothers at Dartmouth. My family's not going to the summer house in Maine until mid-July. Well, long story. Here I am."

"Potts, you old sod." Jim laughed. "Can you find your way out here?"

"Does Lubbock have an airport?"

"Hell, yes."

"Then I'll be there day after tomorrow."

"Look for me in the baggage area," Jim said.

"I'll sniff for your eau de cow shit cologne." Potts laughed.

"Hell, everyone out here smells like that. Just don't let some rough looking cowboy show you how to play Round-up and Pen the Pony. Those guys can smell a sissy as soon as one crosses the Red River."

"Just be at the airport. I'll come out to the frontier to visit you, but all my body parts will be your responsibility."

"It's a deal." Jim laughed again. "Consider your ass in my good hands. Ugh, that didn't sound right. Anyway, I can't wait, Potts. See you Friday." As he set the receiver back in its cradle, he smiled. Now he had two reasons to feel good. Potts was coming to visit, and he just learned that Trish hadn't gone back to live with Alec.

CHAPTER 58

Baines left the house after breakfast to tend morning chores. This was his favorite time of day when he could survey everything, fresh. The ranch had been a scrubby piece of ground when he brought Helen and the boys out here after the war. With his own hands and few resources, he had turned a thousand acres into a good living for his family.

At the barn he pulled on work gloves and leaned on the fence to watch a group of cows clustered at the feed trough. Everything he could see was a product of his hard work. Grass covered the pastures like a lush carpet, the result of a seed experiment with Texas A&M. The new barn complex had been his design, but the new corral was John Henry's idea. He'd resisted replacing board rails with galvanized iron pipe. Now he appreciated its durability and clean look. "Those iron pipes will be here a hundred years after I'm gone," he had said to Helen.

"I hope you told that to John Henry," she'd countered.

He hadn't but knew that she did. What troubled him most about his first born was that John Henry didn't work as hard as he had, didn't seem as committed. "He and Linda Sue are always going somewhere," he often complained to Helen. "Every free minute he gets, he's in that pickup and gone to town. Golf in the summer, football in the fall, skiing in Red River in winter. If I'd spent as little time on this place as he does, we'd all be in the poor house."

But what galled him most was that the ranch was doing just fine under John Henry's stewardship. The grass had never been higher, the cattle fatter, and the bank accounts fuller.

Baines pushed open the gate to let a pen of feeder calves out to graze. As he watched them romp into the pasture, he thought about his second son. Jimmy had been more troublesome growing up, always asking "why" when told to do something. *Like there was supposed to be a good reason.* Still, he'd always done what was right.

Baines saw a lot of himself in his youngest son. There was a time he'd planned to leave Byrus Creek, to experience life and he would have too, but for. . .well. Baines shooed the last calf out of the pen and closed the gate. *Hope I did right with those boys. Nothin' in this life is easy. If it is, it usually ain't worth diddly.*

"Baines? Baines!" Helen's voice interrupted his thoughts. Looking across the fence, he saw her hustling toward him from the house. Nearing sixty, she was still an attractive woman and wore the hard life of a rancher's wife better than most. The expression on her face indicated she had something important to tell him.

"Your sister just called," she said as she approached, breathing rapidly. "Sassy sounded agitated. I said you'd already left the house, but she insisted you call her right away. You know how she can get." Helen pushed a strand of hair away from her face. "I asked what it was about, and she just said you'd better call her."

A dull pain pounded in Baines' chest as he walked toward his office in the barn. The ache subsided, but he felt drained. He and his little brother, Bobby, were the only ones left. The others had been dead for years. He'd stayed home at Byrus Creek, the bachelor son, until Momma and Papa both passed just before the second war in Europe. Thomas had been killed in a freak hunting accident, and Carter Allen was buried at the bottom of Pearl Harbor inside the *USS Arizona*. Still to this day, he and Bobby had never talked about the events of that long-ago night. Bobby had been so young. He and his second wife, Ruthie, lived on the home place at Byrus Creek.

The nightmares had finally stopped some years before, about the time John Henry got married and Jimmy left for the army. He figured Josh Culver's spirit had settled into Hell by now. They'd probably meet there soon. Every day of the last fifty years he'd asked the Lord for forgiveness. He hoped Papa and his brothers repented before they died.

His sister, Sassy, lived alone after her third husband passed and owned a ranch near Corpus. He hadn't spoken to her in years. At the cluttered desk in his office on the barn's second floor, he held the phone to his ear and listened to it ring three times.

"Baines, is that you?" Sassy's shrill voice caught him by surprise.

"What is it, Sassy? Why'd you call?" He stood to pace as far as the phone cord would allow.

"Did you see that article in the paper about that old skeleton they found near Byrus Creek?" Her question struck him like a lightning bolt. "I phoned Bobby to see if he knew anything about it. His wife told me it was dug up only a few miles from their house and said no one 'round town had any idea who it might be. But you know, don't you, Baines? You and Bobby know!"

He closed his eyes and tried to blot out the vision of Josh Culver's bloody corpse, its open mouth spitting dirt and accusation.

"It's Josh, ain't it? I knew y'all'd killed him. My God, Baines, tell the truth for once. Did Papa kill Josh? Did y'all let me think he ran off and left me alone to raise my baby girl?"

The phone felt heavy in his hand. The question had been asked and for the first time in fifty years, he could exorcise the demon. "Yeah, Cassandra," Baines said hoarsely. "We killed him. Papa and Thomas shot him. I helped bury him." Baines felt a thousand years old. He put the phone back in it cradle and stared out the office window. "Sorry, Papa." He spoke in a whisper. "Always been sorry."

CHAPTER 59

Thursday morning, Jim drove the sixty-five miles to Lubbock and signed a lease on a furnished one-bedroom at the La Casa Apartments on University Avenue near the college. He remembered the complex, having attended some SAE keg parties there. They had been the most popular apartments in Lubbock. Today, they were a little worn but fresh paint and carpet had given his second-floor unit new life. The furniture was standard apartment Danish Modern, which meant teak tables and thin cushions on the sofa and chair. The bedroom held a double bed, night stand, and a dresser.

He spent the afternoon unloading his car and visited the supermarket to stock the kitchen with groceries. The evening found him at the swimming pool in the courtyard where he met a few of his neighbors. Most were Tech students remaining in town for summer school.

On Friday at noon he left for the airport to meet Potts' flight from Dallas. Lubbock wasn't green and horsey like Ridgefield, nor the ranch groomed like Oak Lawn, but he would show his old housemate a good time.

When Potts deplaned onto the tarmac, they both braced and saluted one another.

"God it's good to see you." Jim grabbed Pott's extended hand.

"So," Potts stood back with his fists on his hips and surveyed the flat landscape. "This is Texas? Where's the harp music and streets paved with gold? Oh yeah, I'm confusing it with another place." He laughed. "A lesser one, I'm sure, according to you Texans."

"You're damn right." Jim put his arm around Potts' shoulder.

"Let's get out of here before some wild cowboy discovers you're in town."

They retrieved Potts' suitcase from baggage claim, tossed it in the back of his station wagon and drove to the apartment. "Put on swim trunks," Jim said, showing him where to stow his stuff. " On Fridays, the apartment management springs for a keg down by the pool to celebrate the weekend."

"That's pretty close to heaven in my book," Potts said, unbuttoning his shirt. "My antenna tracked a couple of comely co-eds dangling their tawny legs in the water when we came up the stairs. If their bikinis were any smaller, they'd be arrested in some countries."

"Yeah, and did you see the two bruisers on lounge chairs behind them?" Jim laughed. "They're linebackers for the football team. I saw them watching you all the way up the stairs. Don't think they appreciated you admiring their honeys."

"Fuck 'em if they can't take a joke—or some competition." Potts winked and pulled on a pair of denim cutoffs.

"Here's to sun, fun, brew, broads, and teeny bikinis that don't cover shit." Potts said, lifting his beer cup to Jim as they sat on their towels by the pool. He cocked his head toward a cute blonde giving the giant beside her a back rub. The guy had his eyes closed and grunted as she squeezed and pounded his thick neck and shoulder muscles.

"Especially to teeny bikinis," Jim said. The icy beer cleansed his throat. "God, that's good." He took another long swig. They stayed on their towels the rest of the afternoon, polishing off beers and catching up. When he returned from refilling his beer cup a fifth time, he felt lightheaded.

Potts had stepped up on the diving board at the far end of the pool. Several girls watched him bounce on the end of the board before he knifed into the water and swam a lap. When he emerged from the pool, he stopped at the keg to get another beer.

"Miss Trish much?" Potts asked, wiping water from his face.

Jim hesitated a moment before answering, "Yeah, I do. I don't understand it yet, but she's afraid of making a commitment. It was okay in the beginning, when we both wanted our space, but then I fell in love and it all went to hell."

He ran his beer cup over his sun-flushed face. "One snowy night last winter at the cottage in Connecticut, we dropped some acid and were playing around on the sofa waiting for it to kick in. I put on a Donovan record. We were alone in the house. She straddled my legs, just looking at my face and tracing my lips with her finger. Every so often she'd lean forward and kiss me." He paused a moment. "And then I blew it. I told her I loved her."

Potts rolled over on his side and looked at him.

"She sat on my lap staring into my eyes," Jim continued. "I thought maybe she didn't hear me. But then she said something like, 'You will love me until you stop loving me.'" He shook his head. "I thought about that a lot driving back to Texas last week. Somewhere between Nashville and Little Rock, I came to understand it's not that she doesn't love me, but she's afraid to love me. She's scared of being hurt."

Potts swirled the beer in his cup and said nothing.

"The dilemma is," Jim went on, "I may understand the problem, but have no idea what to do about it."

Potts took a long swig from his beer cup. There were no wisecracks or funny sarcasm. His presence was the salve Jim needed. As the sun went down, they left the pool to dress for dinner. Jim drove them to a hole-in-the-wall Tex-Mex cantina in East Lubbock and introduced Potts to enchiladas, tamales, refried beans, and nachos. Afterwards, they decided to go honky tonking and stopped by the apartment to get Potts a pair of Jim's boots to replace his white canvas sneakers.

"Those sissy shoes of yours would guarantee a fight where we're going," Jim said. "And I don't want to have to pull you out from under a bunch of drunk cowboys."

The VFW Hall in the farming community of Slaton was twenty miles from Lubbock. As a college freshman at Tech, Jim had often gone to Slaton on Friday nights with friends from the dorm to see the Hoyle Nix Band tear it up with their song "Big Balls in Cowtown."

After parking in the VFW's gravel lot, he and Potts navigated through clusters of cowboys loitering by pickups and drinking beer. Inside the smoky dance hall, he found a table and ordered setups. They drank Jack Daniel's with water and laughed at everything the other said. Couples circled the dance floor with a sliding two-step, and Jim spotted a table of pretty girls sitting alone. He went over and asked one to dance. Potts said he needed a couple more drinks before trying it.

After Jim returned to the table, Potts pointed out two older women with big hair who had played grab-ass with him when he passed their table on a trip to the bathroom. Three bourbon and waters later, Potts asked a pretty little redhead to dance and looked as loose and proficient on the floor as any of the bull riders gliding around in their stovepipe jeans and Mexican-heeled boots.

"Hey, Cowboy, this is fun!" Potts yelled over the loud music as they passed each other on the dance floor. "Let's do this at Oak Lawn next time you're in Connecticut." The two girls with them glanced at one another and smiled. The prepubescent daughter of the bandleader was doing a nasally job with Patsy Cline's "Blue Moon Over Kentucky." Jim laughed out loud as he imagined shit kickers parking pickups in the circular drive at Oak Lawn and grinding out cigarettes on the parquet floors.

During the band's break, he and Potts introduced themselves to a group of cowgirls from Tech who had driven together to the dance. The girls' fancy outfits, hand-tooled boots, and large diamonds provided by rich doting daddies, intrigued Potts. At midnight, they asked two of them back to the apartment for *whatever*. During the drive to Lubbock, they stopped for coffee at an all-night truck stop and discovered the girls were sisters from San Angelo whose daddy owned "thousands and thousands of Angora goats."

The next morning, he padded into the living room and nudged Potts and the sister under the blanket with him on the sofa bed.

The four of them finished off a box of Cheerios and a quart of milk for breakfast and went to lie by the swimming pool. The morning sun felt good to Jim as it baked out last night's debauchery. In the light of day, his date seemed bigger and more angular, more mannish than she had the night before. The two sisters sat fully clothed under an umbrella at a patio table, filling an ashtray with lipstick smeared cigarette butts. Potts dozed on a towel, leaving it to him to entertain them. Early in the afternoon, the two "goat sisters" were picked up by a friend, and Jim drove a sunburned Potts to Morrison for dinner at the ranch with his folks.

His mother's T-bone steaks, biscuits, and corn on the cob, topped off with her homemade peach ice cream, celebrated Potts' visit. His dad seemed more reserved than usual. He worried that his father disapproved of Potts. After dinner Baines excused himself and went to bed. Jim watched Ringo follow him to the bedroom and lie by the door. *Is the old man ill?* John Henry and Linda Sue were away water skiing with friends for the weekend. Maybe that's what's bothering him, Jim thought. Baines had grumped about it several times during dinner.

After helping his mother clear the table, he drove Potts around the ranch in Baines' pickup. They parked near the canyon and stepped out to take in the view. Standing on the canyon rim, Jim unzipped his fly and relieved himself out into open space. Following his lead, Potts looked over and grinned. "Think it's true what they say about friends that piss together?"

"My brother and I had pissing contests when we were kids," Jim said, as they sat on a rock ledge watching the sun drop behind a mesa. "We pissed everywhere—on campfires, in insect holes. There isn't much around this ranch we haven't peed on."

"Nice thought." Potts laughed and heaved a stone high into the air. They watched it arc and fall to the canyon floor. When the sun winked out on the far horizon, they loaded up and headed back to the house.

"You know, Potts, er, Jack," Helen said, while pouring him a glass of iced tea in the living room after they returned, "I never thought I'd like a *damn* Yankee." She smiled at her little curse word. "But it's easy to make an exception for you. I'm sorry you can't stay for a longer visit."

"Thanks, Mrs. Davis." Potts put sugar in his tea and stirred. "This has been a great trip, and I must say you are the model of southern beauty and grace." Jim recognized his friend was piling it on, and his mother was eating it up. "And Jim," Potts continued, "I admit that everything you told me about your mother is absolutely true. I thought you were exaggerating."

Helen blushed and put a plate of cookies in front of him. "Our front door is always open for you, young man. Be sure to use it. You're always welcome in this house and at my table."

"No wonder you lying bastards won the War of Northern Aggression," Jim said in his room as they undressed for bed.

"You mean the War of Rebellion?" Potts laughed. "Besides, I meant everything I said to your mother. I'd never lie to her, especially while a guest in her home." A well-aimed pillow knocked him backwards onto John Henry's old bed.

Jim knew everyone in the house heard their laughter. Ringo stuck his head in to check on all the commotion before returning to Baines' room. The two friends continued talking and laughing late into the night. Before falling asleep, he thought about Trish again and wondered where she was and what she was doing at that moment. . . and if she missed him like he missed her.

Potts' visit ended too soon. On Sunday morning, they attended church with his parents in Morrison, so Helen could show off "her boys." All through the service, Jim watched his father. Baines sat slumped in the pew, pale and dewy eyed. His large hands showed a slight tremor. After church the family stood on the sidewalk in front of the sanctuary while friends stopped to meet Potts. Again, his old housemate charmed everyone.

As they drove to the airport that afternoon, heat rose from the pavement in shimmering waves. Potts gazed out the window as they passed the Tech campus and the football stadium. "You know," he said, "There's a whole different world out here west of the Hudson River. Not once did I hear someone say anything negative about America. No scruffy long-haired hippies, no hate graffiti on buildings. The worst thing I saw was a sign on a construction fence on campus that said *Beat the Hell out of the Aggies*. It's as if Lubbock is a different country. Either that, or the two coasts are more separated from the heartland than even they know."

"Probably," Jim said, parking in front of the terminal. "But if you went all over this nation, I think you'd find a great deal of sameness. Take you and me. We're from different backgrounds, different states, different educational and economic environments. Yet we're a lot alike and pretty much believe in the same things, share the same basic values." He nodded hello to a cowboy carrying a beat-up valise into the terminal.

"I think people have a distorted perspective because newspapers and television focus mostly on the extremes, the violence and the controversy. It's the squeaky wheel theory. When I was in school in Connecticut, I thought a revolution was coming, and I wasn't the only one. It was promoted on campus and in underground newspapers. Meanwhile the places like Lubbock, Morrison, and Peoria were anchors that kept the country from sliding into the abyss."

"Maybe," Potts said. "I hope so."

Jim stood on the terminal's observation deck and watched Potts' plane disappear into clouds boiling up over the plains of West Texas. *Looks like a big thunderstorm coming. Hope there's no hail in it. Sure could use the moisture.*

CHAPTER 60

The first week of summer school on the Texas Tech campus passed in a blur. After his last period on Friday, he headed out to the ranch where he spent the weekend bringing in the new hay crop. He rode the flat-bed in the field and stacked hay bales while John Henry and a hired hand tossed them up on the trailer. By the end of the weekend his muscles ached, and his hands sported several painful raw spots.

On Saturday and Sunday, Baines rocked on the porch for a couple of hours in the afternoon and was already in bed when he and his brother came in from the field for supper.

"What's with Dad? Is he sick or something?" Jim asked at dinner on Sunday as his mother passed a bowl of beans. "I've never seen him like this."

Helen cut the cornbread and passed it to him. "Your daddy has worked hard his whole life. He deserves to take it easy now that he's got two big strapping boys home to look after things." His mother ladled beans into her plate, and her furrowed brow showed more worry than she let on.

"Dad said he picked up a flu bug over at the auction barn in Matador," John Henry added. "I think it's that, or he's got a cold or something."

"I don't know," Jim said. "Have you ever seen him go to bed this early before? Never, not while I lived here." He looked down the hall towards Baines' bedroom. Ringo lay in front of the closed door.

"Maybe, he's just getting old," John Henry said.

"He'll be back to his old self pretty quick," Helen replied. "He just needs some rest. That man is the hardest working human I know."

Summer classes ended at noon and the courtyard at the apartments became a bee hive of activity every afternoon. When the sun went down, keg parties rotated among apartments like musical chairs. Jim concluded he was one of the few who cared about studying. His classes for the semester included Corporate Finance and Statistics, two subjects he couldn't skate. Studying was not an option.

There were always more girls than boys at the pool, in keeping with the summer enrollment at the college. He found himself the object of interest of a few nubile neighbors, but with Trish still fresh on his mind, he didn't respond. Each afternoon he picked a spot at the pool away from the crowd. Polite when approached, he remained neutral to coy smiles and hooded glances.

His last conversation with Trish in Connecticut played over and over in his head. It had happened so fast and was so final. Dissecting those days a hundred different ways didn't help him understand. He needed to get it behind him and get on with his life.

The last Sunday in June, his mother followed him out to his car as he was leaving to go back to Lubbock. The look on her face told him she wanted to discuss something important. She glanced back over her shoulder and said in a hushed whisper, "Jimmy, I'm worried sick about your daddy. We've got to do something."

"Why won't he see a doctor?"

"That stubborn old mule won't go to any doctor." Helen fingered her apron. "He says most people who go to the hospital leave straight from there for the funeral home. It makes me crazy how he sits in that bedroom all day just staring out the window." Her gaze went down to the ground and she shook her head. Tears streaked her face. Jim put his arms around her.

"He won't even speak to me anymore," she whispered. "It's as if he's given up and is slipping away from me."

"I'll talk with John Henry," Jim said. "Don't worry, Mom. We'll beat it, whatever it is."

As he drove to Lubbock, he thought about what his mother had said. He had never known his old man to give up on anything. "Mule-stubborn" was how others described him. Baines had married late, and Jim often wondered about his early life, but it was never discussed. His father never talked about it. Jim had met his Uncle Bobby and Aunt Ruthie a couple of times, but they provided no clue. Baines had spoken of life at Byrus Creek, but it was mostly about how hard the family worked to survive off the land.

Jim fiddled with the radio to find a better station and wondered if his dad had been a virgin when he married. He hoped not. He smiled. *So then, who? Where? When?*

Passing through the outskirts of Lubbock, He tried to think of Baines' favorite color, his favorite anything, but came up empty. When he turned out the lights in his apartment and crawled under the covers, he lay awake, attempting to meld himself into his father's mind, to see him as a person with history rather than a stone-cold institution. It didn't work. Before drifting off to sleep, his thoughts wandered away to find Trish. He missed her. He ached for her.

The next morning, it was difficult to concentrate in his finance class. He gazed out the window while the professor droned on about income statements and balance sheets. In his mind's eye, he saw Trish at an outdoor cafe in Boston and then strolling down a tree-shaded sidewalk. Like a guardian angel, he floated above her. He put his elbows on his desk and pressed his fingers to his temple, trying to send her a message: to prick her thoughts. A silly game he knew, but it made him feel better.

Back at his apartment after lunch, he thought about calling her. He stared at the wall phone in the kitchen and wondered what he would say if she answered. What would *she* say? *What hadn't been said?* The jangling of the telephone startled him. The sound of Potts' voice made him smile.

"Hey, Cowboy. Just wanted to say what a great time I had down in Texas. I tried getting our cook to make enchiladas and refried beans, but he put up stiff resistance. Said he doesn't do third-world food."

Jim laughed. "Go buy canned tamales and enchiladas at the grocery store. Old El Paso, I think. I'll send you a whole case of—"

"Hold off on that," Potts said. "Phase Two of my plan is to work on Mother. The cook would prepare creamed auto parts if she asked him. Anyway, I'm up here in Maine for the rest of the month. Spoke to Jennifer on the phone yesterday. She said Trish is returning to UConn this fall to do her student teaching gig and graduate in December. I thought you'd be interested."

"Uh. . .Thanks," Jim said. "Not that it makes much difference, now."

"I'll call you before leaving Maine to check in. You ever see those girls we met at the dance, those goat sisters from San someplace?"

"San Angelo," Jim said. "Nope, haven't been back to Slaton, and I haven't seen them around campus. Any message you want me to pass on?"

"Just curious." Potts laughed. "I've had some weird dreams involving goats in high heels and smoking cigarettes. You have a great summer and I'll keep track of Trish through Jennifer."

"Thanks, Potts. I—"

"Hey, we're mates. All for one and one for all. The motto of the Green Berets, or is it the Marines?"

"The Three Musketeers," Jim said, laughing.

"It's still a good motto," Potts said.

"Works for me," Jim replied. "Let me know if you hear anything from Boston."

After hanging up, he couldn't dislodge the empty feeling in his chest. *Her life goes on as if I never existed.* He pumped out two sets of pushups on the carpet to get rid of the tension, donned swim trunks and went outside. It had been cloudy all morning, and only three other people were at the pool. He slathered on baby oil, lay on his back with his eyes closed, and tried to nap. *So, Potts is talking to Jennifer. How serious can that be? Crazy Jennifer is Potts' mother's worst nightmare.*

The first week of August, his mother called to tell him Baines had taken a turn for the worse. "Now, he refuses to leave his room, not even to sit on the porch, and he doesn't say anything—just a bunch of unintelligible grunts. Jimmy, I'm afraid."

"I'll be home on Friday. We'll see what we can do." It killed him to see his mother worry so.

On Thursday, John Henry phoned. "Momma said he tosses and turns all night in bed like he's wrestling with the devil. She moved into our old room to get some sleep. Lord knows she needs the rest. It's wore her out."

"I heard," Jim said. "Let's talk about this when I get there tomorrow. I'll be at the ranch all weekend. Let's take him to see a doctor. If he won't go, maybe have one come out to the house."

"Yeah, I'm afraid not," John Henry said. "You know he doesn't care for doctors. Linda Sue and I won't be here tomorrow, but I'll see you Saturday at Momma's."

On Saturday morning, Jim opened the door to his parents' bedroom and saw his father sitting on the edge of the bed in his underwear. His pasty skin hung loose on his large frame. The room's curtains were drawn, blocking out all sunlight.

"How do you feel?" Jim said when their eyes met. "Want something to eat? Mom fixed a great breakfast with biscuits and gravy."

Baines looked away.

He stepped into the room, and left the door open for some light. "Can I help you to the bathroom? You want something to eat?"

The old man grunted.

He hung in the doorway a few more moments. When he started to back out of the room, his father turned to him. Jim paused. *He wants to say something.* He could see it in his eyes. Jim waited a moment. Baines turned away.

"I'll tell Mom you're awake," he said, and closed the door.

Later that morning, the sun was at its zenith and the temperature was soaring as Jim and his brother walked a fence line that ran through a dry stream bed. They were looking for loose boards and nailing them back into cedar posts. John Henry worked the inside of the fence while he handled the outside. It was too hot to rain, and the few clouds overhead provided little protection. They worked bare-chested, having left their shirts in the pickup. His brother's milk-white torso was accented by the deep brown of his neck and forearms.

"I give up," John Henry said, pushing his hat back on his head. "I've talked to that old man till I'm blue in the face. If Momma can't get him to see the doctor, how can we?"

"You know it's bad when she calls me long distance," Jim responded. "I don't know how much longer she can hold up."

They stopped at a fence post while John Henry checked the bottom rail. "Linda Sue goes over there every day to help out as much as she can. It lets Momma get away from the house to buy groceries or have her hair done." He took a nail from his pocket and banged it into a loose board. "She came home yesterday and said Baines got all upset when she went into his room to straighten things up. She picked up a newspaper article off his dresser about a highway crew finding some old skeleton, and he nearly had a fit." John Henry checked another board and banged a nail into it. "I told her to leave him alone and not go back there, but she refuses to let him buffalo her. Especially since Momma needs her help."

Jim shook his head. "If anyone can handle him, it's Linda Sue." He held a splintered rail in place with his hip while hammering it into the post. He pulled a bandanna from his pocket, wiped sweat from his face and noticed his brother's bare shoulders had reddened in the sun. Horned toads and spring-loaded grasshoppers moved out of their way as they continued along the fence line.

"And you know how stubborn she can be," John Henry said, pulling his hat low on his brow. He chuckled. "I remember you two used to know each other pretty damn well."

Jim kept his eyes focused on the ground in front of him.

___

"Yep, that gal's a real firecracker," John Henry went on. "The best thing that ever happened to me was when y'all split up back in high school. I never dated much. Didn't feel comfortable around girls. Not like you did. Just didn't know how to act without looking like some idiot. Then Linda Sue. . . ."

They stopped to hammer another board. Jim's neck prickled. He wasn't sure where his brother was headed, but he feared they were already in quicksand. It also occurred to him that John Henry had been planning this conversation for a long time.

"You know, little brother," John Henry said, "when we got married, she still carried a torch for you." He looked at Jim across the fence.

"I don't know about that," Jim said, feeling heat from his brother's eyes.

"After we got married," John Henry continued. "I'd come home from class when we were at A&M and I could tell she'd been crying. We never talked about it. Tried a few times but couldn't." His voice softened. "I knew what was bothering her and about died inside every time it happened." He looked up. "I could only hope that she'd someday, somehow, get over it. I decided the only thing to do was just love her as hard as I could while she weathered it. To this day, she probably thinks she handled it all alone, all by herself, but she'd be wrong. I was right there beside her the whole way."

They continued in embarrassed silence along the fence. At the end of the line, they stopped and faced each other.

John Henry hooked the claw hammer in his belt. "About a year after you went into the army, Linda Sue finally quit those crying fits. For the first time in a long time she started to laugh. It took a while, but in her own way she showed me that she really loved me."

Jim waited a moment to see if his brother had more to say. He put his hand on John Henry's shoulder. "She's got to be thanking her lucky stars now that she picked the right Davis boy. Yep, no doubt about it."

His brother's eyes searched his face for a moment then pulled him into a bear hug. "God damn it, little bro, I know she did, too," he said hoarsely. "Things seem to work out like that, don't they?" John Henry stepped back and slapped dust from his jeans. "I almost forgot. We want you to come over for dinner tonight at our house. She's fixing fried chicken, mashed potatoes, and gravy." He playfully punched Jim on his arm. "She made me promise to invite you before I left the house this morning."

Jim rubbed the red spot on his bicep as they headed back across the pasture toward the pickup. His big brother said nothing, and he interpreted his silence as relief that this conversation was now history.

He stood beside the open door of the pickup, buttoning his shirt. "If it's okay, I'll come over for supper after I help Momma put dad to bed."

"Bring a big appetite," John Henry said, stuffing his shirttail into his jeans. "That chicken has got four breasts, at least four pulley bones, and no legs or thighs. Did you ever hear of such a damn thing?"

Jim chuckled. At the Sunday dinner table, their mother had always reserved the white-meat chicken breast for Baines while she took the pulley bone. He and John Henry were left with the legs and thighs.

After dinner, Linda Sue served coffee outside on the redwood deck John Henry had built onto the front of their trailer home. The setting sun sprayed vermillion streaks across the dark gray sky. Fireflies began their pyrotechnic dance in the yard while under the deck, crickets tuned up their instruments. Little had been said at dinner about his father's illness. Linda Sue told him about the newspaper article she saw in Baines' room. She had no idea why he had been so upset. The three of them drank their coffee and watched the sun slip below the horizon.

"You heard about Billy Thompson since you been home?" John Henry winked at Linda Sue.

"Is he back here?" Jim asked. "Mom wrote me that he'd become a missionary and gone to Africa or someplace."

"Yeah, well, Billy didn't stay a missionary for long." Linda Sue rolled her eyes. "He and Jake Tannihill took Mr. Thompson's money after he died in that car wreck over near Ralls and bought an airplane."

John Henry shook his head. "The dumb asses were ferrying bales of marijuana in from Mexico when they got caught by the feds at some dirt strip near San Saba. It's a good thing Billy's dad didn't have to see his pride and joy carried off to prison for twenty-five years." John Henry brushed an insect away from his ear. "I thought Billy was smarter'n that."

"Didn't know Mr. Thompson died in a car wreck," Jim said. "And how'd Billy get involved with—?"

"Same story for all them criminals down at the state prison in Huntsville if you ask me," John Henry said. "Women and booze. Booze and women."

"More like a thirst for quick money," Linda Sue added. "He came back after a year in Africa and was a different person. His hair was long and dirty, and his teeth were bad because of some narcotic he had become addicted to while there. He tried to get a loan from the bank to invest in some scheme back in Nigeria or someplace, but they turned him down. That's when he and Jake bought the plane."

"By the way," John Henry changed the subject. "You remember Ronnie Jinkins? He played football with us."

"Yeah," Jim grinned, "Ol' horse dick. . . ."

Linda Sue started putting empty coffee cups on a tray. "I won't listen to you two potty mouths act like freshmen in high school."

"Oh, hon." John Henry got up and put his arms around her. "I was just goin' to tell him that Jinkins is now sales manager for a sports equipment company out of Fort Worth, and Coach Dowling works for him." He looked at Jim and laughed out a big belly laugh. "Ol' Fat Butt Dowling works for Ronnie. Who would've ever thought it when he ran our asses off with those bull-in-the-ring drills?"

He watched Linda Sue carry the tray into the house. When the door closed he turned to his brother. "What do you hear about Anita Beth?"

"Not much." John Henry sat down in his chair. "Don't think she ever came back here after her mother sold the ranch. One of the Stalcup brothers saw her a year or so ago at some fancy night club in Houston. At least he thought it was her. She wore a lot of makeup and was with some older guy in a suit who looked like an insurance salesman. He said he went over to say hi, but she ignored him. She was smoking cigarettes and drinking whiskey out of a paper cup. Stalcup thought she might be embarrassed that someone from home had caught her."

"It's not her home anymore," Jim said. "Sounds like she was just rude."

"Maybe." John Henry slapped at a mosquito. "Let's go see if Linda Sue has any more of that chocolate cake. I could eat a mountain of that."

Jim looked at John Henry's expanding middle and laughed. "Big brother, you look like you already ate a mountain."

That was a fun evening, Jim thought as he drove back to his parents' house. The place was dark when he parked by the picket fence and doused his headlights. The news about Jake Tannihill and Billy Thompson had saddened him. Maybe he should go to Huntsville and visit them in prison.

He wondered if John Henry said anything to Linda Sue about their conversation out on the fence line that afternoon. He had already gotten straight with her and, today, he and his brother had cleared the air. Tonight, was the first time he didn't feel like he was walking through a minefield when he was around the two of them. He gave John Henry credit for that. His big brother had handled the problem the same way he took out linebackers when he played football—head on.

CHAPTER 61

On Monday afternoon, he lay on a lounge chair at the apartment pool, reading an assignment for the next day's class. His thoughts kept returning to what John Henry had said. *"The only thing I could do was love her as hard as I could while she weathered it."*

He put down the textbook and watched a young couple lay towels out on the deck by the pool. The girl wore a sorority tee shirt and an engagement ring on her left hand. The girl poured lotion into her hand and rubbed it on her boyfriend's back. Watching them made him ache for Trish's touch. Maybe I should've stayed with her in Connecticut. Things might've worked out. Maybe I should have stayed.

After his last class on Wednesday, he crossed the campus and paused to drink at an outdoor water fountain. The noonday temperature was nearing a hundred. The dean's office had called to say they received his transcript from UConn and asked him to drop by to discuss it with a Mrs. Talbott. The person on the phone explained that his records had taken longer to arrive because the files had been destroyed when UConn's administration building was occupied by protestors.

The matron on the other side of the desk held his file in her lap and peered at him over reading glasses. "Mr. Davis, we can accept all of these credits from UConn. You can graduate in December if you complete a full load during the fall term."

He leaned forward in his chair. "That's good news. In fact, it's terrific news."

Mrs. Talbot removed her glasses and let them dangle from the chain around her neck. "If you satisfactorily complete your courses this fall, you can wear the cap and gown at our December commencement. Of course, you'll have to finish this summer term as well, but your grades indicate you have that well in hand."

When he pushed through the glass door to the outside, a blast of hot air hit him in the face. He headed toward the Student Union to grab a sandwich while the mid-day sun glared off the concrete sidewalk. The lawn sprinklers were working overtime.

Mrs. Talbot's news had come as a welcome surprise. He had resigned himself to finishing next spring, but this gave him a five-month head start on his future. *It also means Trish and I'll graduate at the same time.*

On Thursday morning, he put his book bag in the back seat of his station wagon and got in behind the wheel to drive to campus. The summer term would end in two weeks followed by a five-day break before the start of fall classes. He had spent the previous night reviewing a list of companies that came to campus to recruit December graduates. Several banks in Dallas and Houston had already scheduled interviews in September. He planned to stop by the placement office between classes and sign up before all the slots were taken. He wasn't sure he wanted a career as a banker but with a business degree in economics, it was a good option.

After his last class of the morning, he stood at the bus stop by the Student Union building, waiting for the shuttle to the parking lot. It was a good thing he'd gone by the placement center. First National Bank in Dallas had one interview slot left open and other firms' schedules were filling up. He'd signed up for all of them.

A crowd of students had gathered at the corner. He stepped off the curb and looked both ways. The shuttle bus stopped three blocks away. He thought he'd call Potts and tell him about graduating in December. As he got in line with the students for the shuttle , something caught his eye. He turned around.

She sat alone at the end of the bench. A pink cotton sundress and leather strapped sandals showed off a summer tan. Her long blonde hair glistened in the sunlight. She smiled. "Hi, Cowboy."

"But. . . ." His voice caught.

"What took you so long? I've been waiting here for over an hour." Trish teased.

God, she's so beautiful.

She rose from the bench and stepped into his outstretched arms.

He buried his face in her hair. Her familiar fragrance made his senses reel.

She went up on her toes and whispered in his ear. "I love you, Jim Davis. I came here to tell you. I love you and there will never be anybody else but you."

"Oh God," he said hoarsely. "I've missed you so much. Why did I ever leave you up there? I was so stupid. I. . .I love you more than you'll ever know."

"Oh, I know." She nuzzled her face into his neck. "I was the one that acted the fool, but I always knew I loved you. I knew. I knew. I knew. But I was afraid."

The shuttle bus came and went, leaving them alone on the corner. "

"How'd you know where to find me?"

"I took a taxi from the airport to your apartment. Potts gave me the address. One of your nice neighbors let me leave my bags in his place, and I caught a ride here. After walking around campus with no luck, I decided to sit on that bench there until you found me."

"You are so damn lucky." He laughed and kissed her perky little nose. "You could've been on that bench for weeks. I can see the headline now: 'MUMMIFIED BARBIE IN PINK SUNDRESS FOUND ON CAMPUS.'" They both laughed as he took her arm and guided her across the street. "Let's not wait for another bus. It's a good distance out to where my car is parked, but I feel like walking. I'll carry you if you get tired."

She squeezed his hand and smiled up at him. Her teeth flashed white in the sunshine. "Jim Davis, you're good but not that good," she said, laughing. "I wouldn't have waited for you on that bench for longer than two weeks. That's when fall classes begin at UConn, and I promised my mother that I'd graduate in December."

They waited for a car to pass, then crossed another street and walked along the tree shaded sidewalk past the Ag Sciences building. "I shouldn't have dropped out last spring," she went on, lowering her voice. "After my father died this summer, my mother decided to go back to school to get her degree. We can only afford one of us in college at a time, so I've got to hurry and finish."

He stopped and turned to her. "What? Your father died? When? I mean, you should've called me." He gathered her in his arms. "I would've come to Boston to be with you. I didn't know."

"It's okay." She kissed his cheek. "You are sweet. It was hard, but life seems less crazy now. I still have a lot to work through. I mean about my father and all. You and I never talked about him or even my mom for that matter. Maybe we can do that during the next two weeks before I go back. It's important to me."

They linked arms and walked across sun-drenched lawns toward the parking lot. Sprinkler systems chugga-chugged, throwing ropes of water over fresh mown grass. Jim told her about Potts' visit and about having learned he could graduate in December. He told her about his father's puzzling illness and the toll it had taken on his mother. She asked him about his brother and Linda Sue.

"They're doing great," he said. "They had problems like all new-lyweds, but they love each other, and it shows. You'll see."

Trish held onto him while they passed the business school building. He told her about his apartment and the job interviews he had signed up for that morning. He put his arm around her shoulder and felt a slight shiver. *Maybe I'm going too fast.* They had two weeks to rediscover each other and figure out their future.

"Which one do you like?" Trish asked, holding up two bikinis. "They're both new."

"Neither. I like you best in nothing." Jim growled and pulled her down onto the bed. He nipped her ear with his teeth, making her moan and pulled her panties down and over her feet.

She rolled on top of him and kissed his eyes and nose, and his open mouth. "You haven't changed," she said, rolling her hips.

"God, you feel good." His voice husky. He trailed his fingers down her bare back and up again. "I've dreamed all summer about this moment and here we are. You feel so smooth, so sexy, so. . . ." He didn't finish the sentence as she moved down his chest, her tongue tracing his tense muscles.

Six hours later they were ordering a late dinner at the Aztec Palace on 19th Street. "You'll love the tacos," He said after the waitress left the table with their order. "I could eat a horse."

"You always were hungry after an afternoon like today." Trish dipped a chip in the salsa.

"Oh, I remember a large pizza was never safe around you after—"

"Oh, stop it." Trish slapped his hand. "It's not nice to tease a girl about how much she eats."

"Like I was saying." He grinned. "You'll enjoy both the taco and enchilada platters you ordered."

After dinner, they drove back to his apartment and sat outside by the pool. Music could be heard coming from a nearby unit. Every now and then someone passed going to or from a party.

He looked at her after a long silence. "Tell me about your father. Was his death expected?"

Trish pushed her hair behind her ears and looked at him a moment before answering. "He'd been ill a long time," she said. "After losing his leg in an accident at the factory where he worked just before I was born, he turned angry and bitter. Alcohol became his crutch and our nightmare. His rages terrorized me, and I watched my mother suffer over the years. When I got older, I stayed away from home as much as possible, but that didn't make it better because I knew I was leaving her alone to deal with his abuse."

"I didn't know," Jim said.

"I didn't want you to know. I didn't want anyone to know."

A door opened, and loud music spilled out into the courtyard. The door closed, and it grew quite again.

"Jennifer and Ann Marie knew my father was a drunk," she continued, "but even they didn't know everything. Not how bad it really was. Alec knew. I think that's why it was so hard for me to leave him. He knew and still said he loved me. I realized only later that he used that knowledge to control me."

Jim put his boots up in an empty chair. "How'd you keep it a secret all those months we were together? I thought I knew everything there was to know."

"When he died in June, my mother and I discussed that a lot," she said. "We realized we had both carried this secret in our own way. None of her friends knew how bad things were for her. Not even Father Hennessy at church, and he stopped by often to check on us. She said it was her cross and her choice to carry it. But it was also my cross, and I had no part in the decision."

Trish put her hand on his arm. "That's why the idea of marriage or any permanent relationship scared me to death. It sucked the life out of my mother, and I swore I'd never get trapped like that."

A long moment passed before either of them spoke. He felt her watching him in the dark. "How is that different, now?" he asked.

"I'm not exactly sure," she said in a soft voice. "But I came here to see you without knowing how you felt or would react. I took a risk that I would've never taken before. You could've been back with an old sweetheart or still be angry and told me to get lost."

"I wasn't, and I didn't," he said, reaching for her hand. "And I couldn't."

"I know, and that's another reason I love you." Tears welled up in her eyes. "My father was a sweet person when my mother fell in love with him. After the alcohol took control, she still saw the same funny boy with the dark curly hair that she loved those many years before. Unfortunately, that was a conversation she and I never had until after he died. I only knew him as a loud drunken monster that scared me and made my mother cry."

After a long silence, Jim stood and held out his hand. "Let's go to bed. I wish there was something I could say or do to help make all that pain go away."

"Oh, there is," she said. "Just say you love me every time you think it." She pulled his arm around her shoulder as they walked to the apartment. "And you can never say it too much."

"I love you. I love you. I love you," he said and took a deep breath. "I love you. I love you. I love you."

"Okay. Okay." She laughed. "Maybe you can say it too much."

CHAPTER 62

"I got a surprise for you all when I get there this afternoon." Jim was speaking to John Henry who'd answered the phone at the ranch. "I'll be there around three, and I'm bringing a present for everyone. Tell Mom to cook something special for dinner and make a freezer of her peach ice cream. We'll leave Lubbock after my last class and stop for lunch on the way. What? What do you mean I said '*We*?'" Jim laughed. "No, no, no, I mean, *I'll* be there at three."

After hanging up the phone, He stood at the bedroom door watching Trish don one of her bikinis to go to the pool. "John Henry's too smart for his britches," he said. "He knows something's up. Wish there was some way to throw him off."

"Call him back and say Potts is in town," Trish said, adjusting her top.

"Nah, he knows Potts is in Maine. Anyway, everyone will know the truth this afternoon."

"And what is that?" she asked, looking in the mirror and brushing her hair.

"That I'm bringing my girl home to meet the family," Jim said, pulling her onto the bed with him. "Hmmm, maybe I should forget about class this morning and—"

"Oh no, you don't." She pushed away. "You did enough of that last winter in Connecticut. Now get your cute butt off to school and make us some A's."

While his Economics professor droned on in class about supply and demand curves, he thought about what Trish had told him the night before. He knew now why she had run away, but there were still risks. Their future remained unsettled. They hadn't discussed it. Maybe that would change this weekend at the ranch.

At three o'clock he pulled up and parked in front of the house. Ringo bounded off the porch and ran to the car.

"Hey there, Ringo" Trish knelt to greet him. "Remember me?" Ringo waggled towards her, licked her out-stretched hand and bounded over to Jim.

"Yeah, boy." He petted the dog's head and laughed. "It's our Trish, alright. Doesn't she smell great? Anybody home?" He took Trish's hand and led her up the porch steps. Her blonde hair was in a ponytail, and she wore a yellow sundress and sandals. The front door opened, and John Henry stepped out, followed by Helen and Linda Sue.

"Told ya he was bringing her home." John Henry stuck his thumbs in his belt loops and grinned.

"Everyone," Jim said, nodding toward Trish. "I want you to meet Patricia Wallace. She's visiting from Boston. We were at UConn together."

His mother stepped forward to take both Trish's hands. "I'm so glad to meet you. Jimmy has told us so much about you." She gave him a sidelong glance. "Now, Patricia, come inside where it's cool and have some iced tea. This is John Henry, and this here is his wife, Linda Sue."

John Henry nodded, a self-satisfied grin still in place.

Linda Sue leaned forward and hugged her. "I'm so glad to meet you," she said. "I want to hear all about Boston. I've always wanted to go up there and see where this nation was born. All that history. . . .

"Everyone inside." Helen shooed them through the front door and into the parlor. "Now Patricia, do you like your tea sweetened or unsweetened? I also have some lemon."

Trish looked at Jim.

"Sweetened with lemon," he said. "She likes it just the way you always fix it, Mom."

As he followed the girls into the house, his brother's hand clamped down onto his shoulder. "Why you little toad fart, you should've told me you were bringing the *missus* home."

"Didn't know until yesterday," he said. "She surprised me."

"She looks just like Sandra Dee in that Hawaiian movie we saw out at the drive-in." John Henry winked his approval and followed them all into the house.

Dinner that evening was mostly fried: round steak, potatoes, and okra accompanied by Helen's cornbread squares.

"I apologize for my husband's absence from the dinner table," Helen said to Trish as she refilled everyone's tea goblets. "I'm sure Jimmy told you he's ill right now. I know he's sorry he's missing this. Hopefully he'll be feeling better on Sunday before y'all leave."

Jim looked at his brother; John Henry looked at Linda Sue, who got up and started clearing the table.

"So, who doesn't want homemade peach ice cream?" Helen burbled as she carried a tray loaded with bowls into the dining room. "Jimmy ordered it special for this evening. Now, we all know why." She beamed as she set a bowl in front of each of them. "Linda Sue, would you please get that box of wafer cookies in the pantry? They're so good with ice cream."

Jim finished his second bowl and pushed back from the table. He looked at Trish. Everything had gone well. She'd mixed it up with his brother and kept a running discussion with Linda Sue about Lexington and Concord and Paul Revere's ride to warn of the approaching British. His mother hadn't said much during the meal, but more than once he'd caught her looking at him and smiling.

"I want to take Trish out to the barns before it gets dark and show her what a real cattle operation looks like," he said, looking at his mother for permission to leave the table. "Tomorrow, I'll take the pickup and show her around the ranch."

"Y'all plan to have supper tomorrow at our house," Linda Sue said. It'll give Momma a break from fixing a meal."

"Now, that's no break for me," Helen said, gathering up the empty dessert bowls. "But y'all go ahead and eat over there. I'll make a nice pineapple upside down cake to have with your coffee." She smiled at Trish. "My boys enjoy a good pineapple upside down cake."

"It's a deal." Jim stood. "What time?"

"Six o'clock," John Henry said. "And come hungry. I'm gonna show this Yankee girl how we grill a steak here in Texas where they was invented."

"Be careful where you step," Jim said as he and Trish approached the barn in the dusky light. "Remind me to borrow a pair of Linda Sue's boots for you. In fact, we'll go into town and I'll buy you your own cowgirl boots. He helped her to sit on the top rail of the corral. The calves in the pen stared at them. Every now and then one swished its tail and stirred a cloud of flies.

"Ugh, it stinks." Trish wrinkled her nose.

"Some say it's the smell of money." Jim laughed. "But it's just cow shit."

"Your family is very nice." She smiled down at him. "Your mother is so sweet, but it makes me feel a little self-conscious the way she fawns over me."

"That's her way," he said. "We Davis men learned a long time ago to let Momma have her way."

"I'm sorry about your father. I hope I get to meet him."

Jim shrugged. "We'll see. You weren't the only one with father issues."

A long silence passed. A horse neighed in one of the stalls. "So, what's next for us?" He asked. "I mean, where do we go from here?"

Trish stared at him a moment without answering, then looked away.

"Look at me," he said, rubbing her legs. "I need you to look at me."

She turned back to him. "What do you mean?"

"There's too much cow shit on the ground for me to get on my knees, but. . . ." He held both her hands and looked up into her eyes. "Patricia Wallace, I love you with all my heart. So, I'm asking—will you marry me?"

She smiled. "You once asked me to be the mother of your children." She leaned forward and kissed him.

"That's probably the smartest thing I ever did," he whispered, "but I recall we were both stoned at the time." He pulled her mouth down to his for a longer kiss. "So, will you marry me? Will you be Mrs. James Davis, or maybe Ms. Patricia Wallace-Davis? It's your choice. Come on, dammit. Say *yes*. I'm dying here."

"This is so establishment." She giggled. "But, yes, James. Yes, yes, yes, I'll marry you. And yes, I'll also be the mother of your children. You'll make a wonderful handsome father."

She slid off the rail into his arms. After a long kiss he held her close against him and felt her warm breath on his neck.

"What will your family say?" she asked, as they turned and walked arm-in-arm toward the house.

"They know," he said.

"How?

"They just know." He put his arm around her.

"I do hope I get to meet your father before we leave on Sunday," she said.

"Me too, but don't count on it. If this goes on much longer, John Henry and I are going to tie him up and haul him to a doctor in a horse trailer."

As they approached the back porch, they saw one lamp on in the living room. "What are the sleeping arrangements," she asked in a low whisper. "I don't want your mother to think I'm a Yankee slut."

"You get John Henry's old bed across from mine," he said. "And no peeking at my pee pee when I'm naked or sneaking into my bed to take advantage of me."

"Ow!" He yelped when Trish pinched him.

"I thought you'd stay with John Henry and Linda Sue," he said, opening the screen door to the back porch, "but Mom wouldn't hear it. So, it'll be a sleepover like when we were kids."

"Did you have lots of sex at sleepovers when you were a kid?" She turned toward him on the step and gave him another long kiss.

"I didn't go to sleepovers," he said, kissing each of her eyelids. "I had chores and football."

At the Jeans and Things western wear store in town, he watched Trish struggle to tug off a red boot that was too tight. "Those reds are for rodeo queens and require matching outfits. You need a pair of tough all-round boots that you can slop through mud, stomp rattlesnakes, and kick me when I get outta line." He grinned. "Try on that pair of Tony Lamas." He pointed to a box on the floor.

They had driven into Morrison after breakfast, and the clerk at the store had brought out every pair they had in her size.

"So, its new boots instead of an engagement ring?" She looked at him with a raised eyebrow.

"Oh, you noticed?" he said. "Don't worry about that. I'll do it right."

What if I get both the red and the black?" She winked at him. "Then we can shop for outfits to match the red ones. I always wanted to be a rodeo queen."

"Anything your little heart desires." He smiled. "Just make sure they feel good. A bad pair of boots can ruin a person's feet. And I love your little cuties just the way they are."

"Should I get some jeans while we're here and maybe a shirt or two? These bell-bottoms I'm wearing are the only jeans I brought with me."

"As I said, anything your little heart desires. But don't throw away those old hippie hip huggers. I like 'em."

"You like them because they show my butt crack," she said in a loud whisper.

"Oh, hello there, Mrs. Anderson," he mocked, nodding to a lady in the store too far away hear him. "Yes, this is my fiancée, the future mother of my children, and yep, that's her cute butt crack."

After loading packages into the pickup, they stopped at the Dixie Dog Stand on Main Street for a burger. Afterwards, he drove them back to the ranch and parked at the rim of the canyon. They hiked the narrow trail down to the canyon floor to a tree shaded natural spring. The surface of the water was covered with lily pads. Trish sat at the pond's edge and jumped when something made a loud splash.

"Just an old bull frog," he said, noting the alarm in her eyes. He reached down for a stone and tossed it where the frog had gone in. "You scared him."

"This is a beautiful place," Trish said, looking around. "So peaceful, so. . .so. . . ."

"Like the Ponderosa?"

"But this is real. And you do look cute like Little Joe when you wear your cowboy hat. I don't remember you having one in Connecticut."

"I didn't." He removed his hat and held it in one hand. "Cowboys wear these for function, not just for style. Wasn't a reason to wear one at UConn. Besides, I stood out enough as it was."

He brushed a spot on the ground beside her and sat down. "Yep, it's beautiful here, but this place was never meant to be mine," he said. "This land is in Baines' and John Henry's blood. You could say it was my launch pad, my beginning, but not my end. One day we'll bury them both here."

"Where do you want to be buried?" Trish squinted her eyes and looked up at the canyon rim.

After a reflective silence, he answered, "Somewhere next to you in a butter cookie tin from Lord & Taylor in New York."

She turned to look at him and they both dissolved in laughter. Trish fell on top of him and they rolled together in the grass. "Wasn't that funny? We have so many neat memories."

"Yep," he responded. The bad memories were fading fast.

On Sunday evening at dinner, they announced their engagement to his family. Helen had just returned to the table from delivering Baines' meal to his room when Jim stood to share the news. "We don't have all the details worked out yet, but we hope to have most things finalized before Trish goes back to Boston."

"I'm sure Patricia's mother will have some ideas of her own," his mother said. "You can't just leave out the mother of the bride. Not when Patricia is her only child."

"You're right, as usual, Mom." He looked at Trish. We know the first thing to do is graduate and get our degrees. Trish is returning to UConn for the fall semester, and I'll finish here at Tech in December. The wedding will be sometime next January."

"But you'll be apart so long," Linda Sue said, a look of concern on her face. Won't that be hard?"

"Yeah, real hard." He stared down at his boots.

"We'll see each other at the breaks," Trish said, putting her hand on his shoulder. "At Thanksgiving and Christmas, and we'll write every day and call on weekends. Right?"

He smiled at her. "I knew guys in the army that were separated from their wives and children for a year or more while they were in Vietnam. They made it work and so will we."

"It's a good plan," his mother said. "I for one don't want to miss that wedding up there in Boston.

As Jim turned his station wagon onto the highway to Lubbock, Trish watched him with her back against the passenger door. "How many finals do you have this week? I want to let you study, but we have less than two weeks left. My flight leaves in nine days."

"I have two finals and they're both this Thursday." He looked down at her foot on the seat between them and smiled. "Like your new boots?"

"I do." She rubbed her hand over the brown supple calfskin. "They're kind of hot in summer compared to sandals, but they make me feel, I don't know, more confident, more powerful, like I could kick someone's ass."

"Oh, no." He laughed. "I've created a monster. Let's see, Jesus wore sandals, and the kick-ass Romans wore hobnail boots. Wow, who knew? All along it was just the footwear."

The conversation became muted as they drove through the warm summer night. Much had been crammed into the weekend, and they still had a lot to think about. "What're you doing this week while I'm studying at the library?" he asked as they passed a truck on the highway.

"Don't worry about me. I think I'll laze around by the pool and wait for you," she said, reaching over to caress the back of his neck. "You waited for me lots last year."

The next Saturday morning, Jim turned off the highway, clanked across the cattle guard, and drove toward the ranch house. It had rained all night, and a steady drizzle continued to fall. Trish woke from a nap and sat up. The smell of wet dirt came through the car's air vent as they slipped and slid along the muddy road, the windshield wipers working double-time.

"Looks like we'll have to change our plans for today," he said. Lightning flashed across the sky followed by a thundering rumble. "Maybe it'll clear up this afternoon, so we can ride horses tomorrow. The arroyos in the canyon will be full of water, and there'll be some pretty nice waterfalls after a rain like this."

"You could use a rest day," she said sleepily. "Now that finals are over, maybe we can go hide in a movie theater this afternoon and watch something uncomplicated."

"John Henry will love this rain. We call it a soaker." He felt the heavy station wagon sliding through the mud. He patted Trish's leg and wondered about the fresh ruts he was following in the road. Someone had preceded them out this morning. As they neared the house he saw John Henry's pickup. "My brother's here."

"I like him." Trish pushed her hair behind an ear. "I really do, but you two are so different. Your mother said she doesn't see it."

He leaned forward to peer through the rain, and the muscles tensed in his neck. Two cars were parked just beyond his mother's Oldsmobile. The flashers on the roof of one identified it as the sheriff's car. The gray sedan next to it also looked like an official vehicle.

He stopped at the picket fence and switched off the motor. Low clouds opened up and another downpour blurred the landscape. He studied the two cars. *Why is the sheriff out here?*

"Get ready to make a break for it," he said. The sound of rain pelting the car began to slacken. "Let's go." He jumped out pulling Trish with him. As they raced up the walkway to the porch, a flash of lightning caught the corner of his eye and a clap of thunder rolled over the plains. He shook the water from his hair and wiped his boots on the mat before opening the front door. When they stepped into the lighted parlor, his brother and two men rose to greet them. Each held a china cup of his mother's coffee.

"Well, look who's here," John Henry said, setting his cup down on a side table. "Jimmy, this here is Emmett Block." John Henry nodded toward a bear of a man wearing khaki pants tucked into cowboy boots. "Emmett's our sheriff here in the county. And this is Ranger McMann." He indicated a tall slender fellow wearing a long-sleeve white shirt and a skinny tie.

"The name's Jeb. Call me Jeb," the ranger said. He bent to set his cup down on an end table and shook Jim's hand.

Jim looked at his brother. "Where's Mom? What's this about? Is dad alright?"

"He's okay, I guess." John Henry shrugged. "I mean, there's been no change that I've seen since y'all were here last weekend. Sheriff here says Baines called his office yesterday afternoon and asked him to come out this morning and bring a ranger with him. He phoned me late last night and said to be here at ten this morning and tell you to come. I spoke to Mom earlier this morning and she didn't know anything about it. I called your apartment, and no one answered, so figured you were on your way. You now know as much about this as I do. We're all wondering what he. . . ."

Movement in the room made everyone turn. Baines stood beside Helen. His khakis looked freshly ironed and his hair had been oiled and combed, his face nicked from shaving. Helen held his arm to help balance him. Jim saw the worried look on her face. Ringo leaned protectively against Baines' leg, his brown eyes locked onto the two strange men in the room. Baines motioned everyone to sit, and assisted by Helen, moved slowly into the parlor. Jim stepped forward to assist but was waved aside.

"Sit down, all of you, please," Baines said in a gravelly voice.

The two lawmen glanced at each other and took seats on the couch, hats resting on their laps. Jim remained standing near the front door. Trish slipped behind him and put her hand on his back. Another thunderclap rattled the windows. Everyone watched Helen guide Baines by his arm until he dropped heavily into the stuffed chair in front of the picture window. She stood next to him rubbing his shoulder. Ringo lay on the floor at Baines' feet, his head on his paws, his eyes never leaving the two men on the sofa. An anxious silence permeated the room. Sheriff Block and Ranger McMann shifted in their seats.

"I want to thank you men for coming." Baines' voice sounded steady, but his hands trembled as they grasped the chair's padded arms. "I asked y'all to come out here today to hear. . .I guess to hear my confession." He stopped talking and a long silence followed.

"It happened a long time ago, and I know Papa didn't intend to." He paused a moment and bowed his head. "Papa should've done this years ago, but he didn't. I guess it's not for me to judge. The Bible says we should honor our father and our mother. I did the best I could."

Jim looked at John Henry. His brother shook his head, indicating he had no idea what their father was talking about.

"A terrible crime has been committed but an even greater sin." Baines' voice took on the cadence of a tent preacher. "Papa taught us there's nothing' worse under the laws of God than murdering another man. . .to snuff out that precious spark of life, even if they deserved it. Many years ago, we, my brothers and I, broke God's law and the law of Caesar. Most everyone's gone now but me, and I'm ready to give myself up to Caesar's justice. I've already surrendered my soul to the Lord."

Jim took a step backward and Trish entwined her fingers in his. John Henry leaned forward in his seat and covered his face with his hands. The two lawmen remained still as statues while Baines recalled the events of that night more than fifty years ago, the night of his sixteenth birthday.

"I'd never seen Papa so angry," Baines said, dropping his gaze to the floor. "Everyone knew Sassy was his favorite. Folks in Byrus Creek knew it. Papa never expected that any man would make Sassy pregnant and then not marry her. But Josh Culver wasn't blameless. Was no reason to talk like that about Sassy, saying she was a whore and all right there to Papa's face. Josh shouldn't've done that. He'd be alive today if. . . ." Baines paused a moment, then coughed. No one in the room spoke. Helen leaned over his chair stroking his hair.

"Papa and Thomas shotgunned him, and we boys buried him out there in that field," Baines continued. "Papa and Thomas waited for us in the truck. I guess they didn't want to see it again, the corpse and all. When we got home that night, no one talked about it. None of us ever spoke about it after that. We boys just did what we were told and never talked about it. Back then, no one challenged Papa about anything."

Jim closed his eyes a moment. For all these years that buried truth had lain heavy as an anvil on his dad's heart. All the questions, all that he had wondered about his father's life began to fall into place. As his dad related the events of that night, Jim noticed his father's voice growing stronger, his hands more animated. His palsied limbs steadied, and every now and then his dry lips cracked into a wry smile. He spoke about his brothers and sisters, and the good times they had at the swimming hole down on the Brazos River—the place that reminded them of the Bible's Garden of Eden. No one interrupted. No one asked questions. John Henry stared at the floor.

"I'm sorry for what Papa and us boys did," Baines said, his voice dropping. "I'm sorry for that. I'm sorry that I'm not the man. . .the father. . .my boys here thought I was, that I should've been. And I'm sorry I'm not the man, the husband, my wife, this good woman here, deserves." He patted Helen's hand on his shoulder. "For years I lied and deceived. God knows I'd breathe my own life into Josh Culver's body if it'd change things."

A long silence followed as Jim watched Baines fumble in his shirt pocket, pull out a folded newspaper clipping and hand it to Helen. She read it, paused a moment to wipe her eyes and passed the clipping to the ranger. He studied it a moment before passing it on. When the article reached Jim, he recognized it as the one Linda Sue had seen in Baines' room. It told of a skeleton uncovered by a highway crew in Bosque County not far from Byrus Creek. No one had any idea who it might've been. A search of county records showed no one in the area had been reported missing in the years around 1920. There was evidence of foul play.

Ranger McMann rose from the couch, holding his hat at his side. Jim saw dried mud on his boots. "Mr. Davis, this is interesting information you've given us this morning." The ranger turned and nodded at Emmett Block. "If you'll excuse us a moment we need to talk."

The sheriff pushed up off the sofa and followed the ranger out on the front porch. Jim heard rain pelting the roof when the front door opened and closed.

Baines looked at John Henry and then over at him. For the first time, he saw his father as a frightened, fallible man. His dad had lived his adult life fearing his sons would find him out to be a phony.

He moved forward and knelt beside Baines' chair, bringing himself eye level with his father. Baines reached for his hand, his grasp tentative. Jim felt John Henry settle beside him. Tears streaked his brother's face.

"I'm sorry, Daddy," John Henry said in a hoarse whisper. He took Baines' free hand. "We didn't know. I didn't know. I would've. . . ." He swallowed hard and left the rest of the sentence unsaid.

Baines blinked back tears.

"Excuse me, gentlemen." Ranger McMann stood beside the sofa. He had his hat on like he was about to leave. Emmett Block stood behind him. The two brothers rose together, flanking their father. A low growl rumbled in Ringo's throat.

"Mr. Davis," the ranger began, casting a quick glance at Ringo. "We're not real clear on what our authority is in this matter. Sheriff Block will send the information you gave us to Bosque County. I'm sure the sheriff down there will be grateful for your help in uncovering the mystery of that old skeleton they dug up. Someone may want to come up here and speak with you to get more details, possibly take a deposition, but I don't see how any district attorney is gonna trouble a grand jury with this. It was just too long ago."

He paused a moment before going on. "You know, Mr. Davis, fifty years in anyone's book is a mighty long time. Your father and brother, the ones who actually shot that man, have gone on to their maker's judgment. During the last fifty years, this country fought three major wars. Fifty years before that was the War Between the States, and fifty years before that, ol' Andy Jackson whipped the British at New Orleans. Another fifty years before that, we were bowing to the King of England. Like I said, Mr. Davis, fifty years is a long time."

The ranger paused a moment like he wanted to say something more. He tipped his hat toward Helen. "Mrs. Davis, we thank you kindly for a fine cup of coffee this rainy morning." He looked at Jim and nodded. "The sheriff and me'll be gettin' along now. You folks have a good weekend."

Jim accompanied the two lawmen outside. "My family's in debt to you both," he said, shaking their hands. "I hope the authorities down there don't—"

"Wouldn't worry too much about that," Ranger McMann said. "It all happened so long ago, and he was only a boy. Anyhow, look at him. They can't do nothing to him he ain't already done to himself a hundred times over." The ranger hooked his thumbs behind his belt and gazed up at the roiling sky. "Looks like it'll rain all weekend. We sure do need it."

"Yes, sir, we do," Jim said. "Y'all drive carefully now." The two lawmen dashed across the flooded yard to their cars as another clap of thunder drowned out his words. After the two vehicles reached the highway and disappeared in the distance, he turned and reentered the house.

CHAPTER 63

O n Tuesday, Jim spent most of the afternoon at the library gathering information on the Dallas banks he had scheduled interviews with in the fall. On his way back to the apartment, he stopped by the administration building to check his summer grades. He had earned an A in each of his classes. A good grade point average would help in getting a better job offer.

Trish had made friends at the apartment swimming pool with a young couple from Dallas, and the four of them went for burgers that evening at the Char Grill on College Avenue. Their new friends announced they were getting married in two weeks and begged them to come to the wedding. They were disappointed when she said she was leaving in three days for Connecticut. At the apartment afterwards, he and Trish were getting ready for bed when the phone rang.

"Hello." He covered the receiver and looked at Trish. "It's my brother." He sat on the sofa in just a t-shirt and put his bare feet on the coffee table. So, how's Mom and Dad after the excitement of this past weekend?"

"Momma can't get him to slow down," John Henry said. "He got up and worked cattle all day on his old mare. That damn Ringo kept racing ahead of the horses, barking at everything and everybody. The old man just sat back in his saddle and laughed. Not long ago he would've plugged a bullet in any ol' dog that did that."

"Any word from the Sheriff down at Byrus Creek?"

"Nothing, yet. I take the ranger at his word. We'll deal with it when it happens, but I sure do like what it's done for the old man. I think we'll get some more years out of him—good years at that. It's got to be a relief."

"You're right about that," Jim agreed. "I'm glad he's up and out of that bedroom. It's gotta be a load of worry off Mom."

"The preacher says, 'Judge not lest you be judged,'" John Henry said. "I agree with that. I feel bad that he carried that cross all those years by himself. That had to be hard."

"Yep," Jim said. "We all have our skeletons in our closets—metaphorically that is."

"Meta. . .what? Don't go using those big Connecticut words on me. I want to hear all about your skeletons, little brother."

"Fat chance of that." Jim laughed.

"But I got more news." John Henry's voice went up a few decibels. "Linda Sue's pregnant as a penguin. You're going to be an uncle in January. We found out yesterday but didn't tell anyone till this evening when we surprised the folks at dinner. Can you believe it?"

He laughed at his brother's excitement. "That's wonderful. They must really be happy. Mom might have another Davis boy at Morrison High School to watch play football."

"Know what she's doing first thing?" John Henry said. "She's making him a maroon football jersey with Texas A&M on it. And he's not even born yet."

"That's fine," Jim said, "but I'll make sure my nephew, or maybe my niece, gets a red and black one from Texas Tech. We're excited for you guys. Give Linda Sue a hug for us and tell her we'll be happy with either a halfback or a cutie pie cheerleader."

"She's already come up with something you could do to help out," John Henry lowered his voice. "She said you could get one of them free-loving, hippie college girls to be nice to me when she gets too big and fat."

"That doesn't sound like Linda Sue." Jim laughed. "Sounds more like your own wishful thinking. Tell my sister-in-law that I only know good wholesome girls like her."

John Henry laughed. "I'll tell her. She's handling this just great, so confident and damn sure of herself. She's going to be a great little mother."

"You damn right, she will," Jim said. "That baby's going to get one hell of a start in life with you guys for parents and Mom and Baines for grandparents."

"Listen, I got to call my Aggie buddies. They've been accusing me of firing blanks ever since Linda Sue and I got married."

"Well, thanks for letting us know. And congratulations. This is terrific news."

"Oh, and tell Trish that we really enjoyed her," John Henry said. "Linda Sue says they'll be best friends. We'll miss her when she goes back to Boston. You coming to the ranch this weekend?"

"Maybe." He looked over at Trish brushing her hair. Three days from now, I put her on a plane to Boston, so we want to spend every moment we can together. I haven't thought about much after that. I'll call on Friday and let you know what I'm doing."

"I understand," John Henry said. "If my Linda Sue were to go away for a long time, I don't—"

"Me, too," Jim said, finishing his brother's thought. "Me, too."

Jim checked his watch and saw it was after midnight. They had been in bed for over an hour, and he was still wide awake. A country song played somewhere in the apartments. He heard a splash down at the swimming pool followed by loud cursing. All went silent while Trish lay with her head on his chest.

"What are you thinking about?" She teased her palm over his bare abdomen. "Better be about me."

"About you and me," he said. "About us, and about our future together." After a long silence, he rolled her over and nuzzled his nose into her neck. "About my brother and Linda Sue being parents. About me being an uncle and my folks being grandparents. And about you and me one day having our own little Tinker Bell. . .or maybe a little rowdy cowboy."

She pulled his mouth down to her own and they kissed—deep

and soulful. After breaking for air, she looked up into his eyes, "Just keep talking," she said softly, "I like the way you cowboys think. . .and I like the way you move, and. . . ." She raised her lips back up to his. "Oh, I like everything about you, Cowboy."

The End